L.W. JACOBS

APOSTATE'S PILGRIMAGE

www.aethonbooks.com

APOSTATE'S PILGRAMAGE

©2019-2021 LEVI JACOBS

This book is protected under the copyright laws of the United States of America. No part of this publication may be reproduced, stored in a retrieval system, or transmitted, in any form or by any means, without the prior permission in writing of the publisher, nor be otherwise circulated in any form of binding or cover other than that in which it is published and without a similar condition including this condition being imposed on the subsequent purchaser. Any reproduction or unauthorized use of the material or artwork contained herein is prohibited without the express written permission of the authors.

Aethon Books supports the right to free expression and the value of copyright. The purpose of copyright is to encourage writers and artists to produce the creative works that enrich our culture.

The scanning, uploading, and distribution of this book without permission is a theft of the author's intellectual property. If you would like to use material from the book (other than for review purposes), please contact editor@aethonbooks.com. Thank you for your support of the author's rights.

www.aethonbooks.com

Print and eBook formatting, and cover design by Steve Beaulieu. Artwork provided by Mateusz Michalski. Cartography provided by Francois Beauregard.

Published by Aethon Books LLC. 2020

Aethon Books is not responsible for websites (or their content) that are not owned by the publisher.

This book is a work of fiction. Names, characters, places, and incidents are the product of the author's imagination or are used fictitiously. Any resemblance to actual events, locales, or persons, living or dead is coincidental.

All rights reserved.

ALSO IN SERIES

BEGGAR'S REBELLION
PAUPER'S EMPIRE
APOSTATE'S PILGRAMAGE
ACOLYTE'S UNDERWORLD

Hightown
to Prison Camp
New Ayugea
Bluffhouses
Bluffhouses
Riverbottom
Ayugea
Genga River

*To my unborn daughter,
in celebration of the struggles and joy that wait for you.*

1

What I do, I do not for personal gain, though there is that too. I do it for the world. Enough of wars and political successions. Let us have a thousand years of Councilate reign, rather than a hundred years of revolution. Let us have a peace of blood, if that's what it takes.
 —Journeyman Ydilwen, *final address to Yatiport Cell*

Tai and Ella's boots crunched in the stillness, snowflakes falling thick from a winter-grey sky. Hightown was a forest of burned-out buildings around them, scorched bricks and toppled walls reaching from the city like umber branches, crowned in pale snow. Winter lay heavy on the air, a feeling Tai associated with long months huddled around smoky fires in one hideout or another, chilled to the bone and living on thin broth. This would be his first cold season as something more than an orphan or a street tough. Something *much* more—he was the leader of the city now, with his own bed in a well-heated bluffhouse and people who looked up to him.

Some days it was hard to believe.

Ella shivered next to him, her olive face framed in a wolf's-fur cloak. "You seriously do this every year?"

"Which part, the freezing? Or the strolling with beautiful Councilate ladies?" That part was even harder to believe. It had been a month since Semeca's attack, since they finally acknowledged what was between them, and having Ella close was still intoxicating. He hardly felt the cold.

"The freezing, you oaf."

He smiled. "You get used to it." Even so he tugged her hand closer into his pocket, glad for the warmth of their fingers twined together.

"You should stop doing this," she said as they passed through the frozen remains of Mummer's Square. They were heading out to gather wintergrass, part of their strategy to feed the city. "You're a leader now. You have people to do this for you."

He shook his head. "That's the kind of leader Semeca was, or Sablo. Not me. Besides," he took a deep breath and exhaled white, "it's nice to get out and get some fresh air."

"You're insane," she said, snuggling in closer. "And wonderful, of course."

"Insanely wonderful?" They stepped out onto the surface of the Sanga, the narrow river frozen solid at this time of year. Ahead the open field of bittermelon vines was lumpy under a fresh coat of snow, and Ella's face went still.

"Hey," he said. "We don't have to go this way, if you don't want." This was where she and her students had fought their way from the mines to Newgen under heavy attack. They'd cleared the bodies before the snow came, but the ground was still churned and discolored under the snow.

"No," she said, "it's okay. We won, and they died fighting for what is right. It just—" She took a breath. "That was a hard time."

He nodded. Most of the survivors felt this way, their relief in the days after Semeca's attack colored by grief. Even with people returning who had fled in the final weeks, the city had maybe four hundred people now. A month ago it had been twice that.

He'd taken charge of a city in mourning, and the people needed something more than warm walls and food. He'd arranged for traditional vigils to be held every day, wishing the ancestors safe passage and inviting them to come into the youth still in need of spirit guides.

It was hard to know what to think of the old ways, now that he'd learned that the voices were more like leeches than ancestral guides. So much had changed, but he still felt there was value in tradition. To complicate things further, the Cult of the Blood was going strong, claiming his latest battle as another victory for "Lord Tai." The followers still hung on his words as though he knew the secrets to the universe. It was another reason he liked to get out every day, despite the cold.

"Hey," Ella broke the silence, "Sorry, I didn't mean to be so dour. I know that time was hard for you, too."

"It's okay," he said, not wanting to remember his days in the woods while his friends fought and died. While a revenant led him around on a broken leg pretending to be Fisher. "Dour? What does that mean?"

She smiled. "It's another fancy Yersh word. It means heavy and unhappy. What would you say in Achuri?"

He thought for a minute and came up with a word, and talk turned to the differences between the two languages as they crossed the long field and got deep enough into the trees to find fresh wintergrass.

They worked mostly in silence, clipping the purplish grass above the snowline to give the roots a chance to regrow. Wintergrass smelled like it tasted, sour and bitter, but it was better than starving, and the meager grain reserves they'd started the winter with were gone. With the fields burned and passage into Gendrys snowed over, they had no other options for food. It would be a long winter, but he was used to those. All Achuri were.

Soft footsteps crunched behind him. "You can't sneak up on me that easy," he said without turning. "And if you even try to—"

Pain hit him, like an axe strike to the spine. Tai gasped, losing the grip on his shears and falling into the snow. What—

"I'm sorry," a man said, stepping out from behind a leatherleaf in the corner of his vision. Ella screamed to his right, and Tai's head snapped up, pain forgotten. He struck resonance.

Nothing happened.

"You won't be able to use that against me," the man said, looking distracted. He had Yati features, wiry red hair and a stout build, and was dressed for the deep winter.

"Who are you?" Ella gasped behind him.

"My name is Ydilwen," the man said, "but that's not important. What matters is who you are. Tai Kulga god slayer, yes? And his Worldsmouth scholar?"

How did he know that? The man had to be a mindseye. Or had word spread beyond Ayugen? It didn't matter. He was threatening Ella. He needed to die.

Tai pushed himself up, reaching for the long dagger he kept at his side.

"Please don't make this harder than it needs to be," Ydilwen said quickly. "I can—"

Tai lunged, sprinting the short gap between them. He stumbled halfway there, like the snow had turned to mud, but kept running. The ground grew stickier the closer he got, until his sprint slowed to a walk, then to a stall as he struggled to even lift his feet. "What—resonance is this?"

The Yatiman still frowned in concentration. "This is no resonance. But don't worry. I don't intend to kill you."

It clicked then—Sablo's strange attack outside Gendrys. That had stolen his *uai* too. Ydilwen was a ninespear.

On the far side of Ydilwen, Ella got to her feet. The thick man turned to her, as if Tai was no longer a threat. Tai, who'd killed an *immortal being* just last month. Defeated an entire army the month before that. Tai wrenched at his foot—stuck solid. He struck resonance again—nothing.

"You," Ydilwen said. "Ellumia, isn't it? I am told you've discovered interesting things with the resonances. I hope you'll be open to discussing them with me once we are through here."

"Discuss this," Ella spat, flinging a knife at him.

Ydilwen started but the knife went wide. Still, he hadn't stopped it with whatever powers he was using. That meant there was a chance.

"I really am sorry," the man said, "but I can't risk you taking Semeca's power."

Tai kept his dagger low, pulling his arm back. His arms were still free, and he was just barely in the Yatiman's vision. If he could throw it just right—

Ella's eyes flicked to him, then back to Ydilwen. Spirits send she understood to distract him.

"Her power?" Ella said. "We already took her power once. That power is nothing compared to what I know. What *we* know. And if you think you'll be able to walk out of here—"

Tai slung the dagger at the Yatiman's side. It struck true, sliding through the cloak and deep into the man's flesh.

Ydilwen gasped, and like that Tai's feet were free. He shot forward, slamming his hand into the hilt of the dagger, driving it toward the lungs and heart. Ydilwen's gasp slurred to a scream and Tai pulled the dagger out, preparing to the cut the man's throat.

"Tai, no!" Ella yelled. "Your sight!"

He paused for a moment, caught in the rush, in his need to protect her. His sight—mindsight. Right. They could learn something. Tai struck resonance, his *uai* weak but back, and pushed into the ninespear's mind.

Shock. Pain. He still wasn't good at reading thoughts deeper than immediate ones—mindsight was like reading scraps of paper caught in a rushing stream—but he looked anyway, squinting. He saw flashes—endless days in snowy forests, desperate moments stealing from villagers, and hunting—but not animals. Hunting what? He tried to focus. Hunting dead people?

"What were you hoping to do here?" Ella cut in, cold rage on her face.

"Stop—a war," Ydilwen gasped, sliding to the ground as Tai released him. Blood pumped hot and heavy from his side, melting a red stain in the snow.

Ella shook her head, but Tai read the answer as she asked the question, rising to the front of Ydilwen's mind. "He wanted to thrall us," Tai said. "To trap our *uai* somehow. He thought—" He squinted, scraps of thought in the ninespear's mind swirling slower and muddier. "He thought we would use it to get Semeca's power back."

"Not just her power," Ydilwen said, his voice weak. "Her ambition."

Tai glanced at Ella, rush of battle seeping from his blood. She looked as confused as he felt.

Ella turned back to the dying man. "How did you do this?"

His eyes fluttered closed. "Healworker," he murmured. "Get —a healworker. Explain everything."

Tai needed no healworker to see the man was too far gone to get back to the city, even if they wafted. "Who sent you?" he asked. "An archrevenant? Sablo?"

"No one," Ydilwen muttered, a strange grin on his face as he slumped into the snow. "My mother. Just wanted—"

Tai pushed the snow back, trying to read his mind, but the

current was dark, the thoughts indistinct. "He's dying," he said. "Ella?"

Ella bit her lip. "Ydilwen. We can still help you. How did you do this?"

There was no response, blood pumping slow from the hole in his side.

"Ydilwen!"

He gave a shuddering sigh and lay still. Tai pushed a moment further in his mind, seeking anything, but the scraps of thought sank from sight. He was dead.

Tai stood and moved to Ella. "Are you okay?"

"I'm fine," she frowned. "We're alive. But what—what *was* that?"

"It was a ninespears thing, I think. Remember what Sablo did, before we got to Gendrys?"

"Yes," she said, "but that was just our *uai*. This was like—like I was frozen to the ground."

Tai nodded. "Me, too. That's why I couldn't get to him. That's why I couldn't get to *you*. I—" He shook his head, only realizing now how afraid he'd been. More afraid than he'd ever been for himself.

Ella smiled, leaning in to him. "Thank you. But I can take care of myself, most of the time."

"Not if you don't know what we're up against. If I hadn't had that dagger--" He shook his head, shoulder muscles knotting.

She released a ragged breath, looking at the corpse. "Can all the ninespears do this?"

"I don't know," Tai said, pulling her close. "But I know someone who does."

2

Tai flew low over the snow-covered trees, face wrapped in furs and body covered in three layers of coats. He was still freezing, and starting to doubt the wisdom of coming out here. The note had said he would know the clearing, which could only mean one place in the southern forests. The clearing where he'd spent three days with a broken leg, while his friends fought and died. The clearing where he'd fought a wildly powerful revenant.

The clearing where Nauro had left him to die.

He had no defenses. No idea what Nauro was capable of. Tai had barely defeated the revenant Naveinya, and if Nauro attacked anything like Sablo or Ydilwen had, he would be as good as dead. Ella had been against him going—everyone had been against him going, but that was one of the good things about them choosing him as a leader. He knew it needed to be done, and he was the only one who could do it, so he went anyway. They needed answers. And now that Ydilwen was dead, Nauro was the only one he knew that could give them.

Even if the man had been willing to let all of Ayugen die to prove a point.

There. Smoke, maybe? It was hard to tell in the gray winter air, clouds hanging low over the forest. Tai turned that direction, wind whistling in his ears. A hunch was better than nothing. Yes, definitely smoke.

Anticipation rose up in him and he slowed his waft, reaching into a side pocket to pull out more *mavenstym*. He ate the sour purple blossoms on the off chance his *uai* would do anything if Nauro attacked. Feynrick had given it even odds the man would try to kill him, but Tai thought it was better than that. Why would Nauro wait out here for months in the cold if he was so powerful, and wanted Tai dead? For that matter, he could have easily done it while Tai was under Naveinya's spell. No, Nauro couldn't be trusted, but he didn't seem to want Tai dead.

Which made things much more complicated.

Tai touched down in the center of a field of white, boots sinking in past the knee, forest silent after the howl of wind in his ears. Blue-green needleaves swam in the clearing, frosted in snow, with bare branched leatherleafs sticking through here and there. He stilled resonance and waited through the bends, world spinning and stomach rising from using so much *uai*.

When it passed he traced the smoke to a tent of hides tucked back in the trees, not so different in design from an Achuri *guyo*.

"Hello the tent!" he called, not wanting to startle the man, hating the old feeling of uncertainty and danger. He'd gotten used to the power of his resonance, to his ability to fight or escape anything, but the sense of uncertainty and danger was still there. It had kept him alive on the streets.

There was no answer, so Tai wafted up and inward, following a depressed trail in the snow—it looked like Nauro left regularly, likely to hunt or forage. It would be a lonely existence this far out. The man must really care, to be willing to wait out here for Tai to come to him.

The area immediately around the tent was hard-packed snow

covered in wood shavings. Half an elk carcass hung frozen from a tree. Tai dropped to the ground, called out again, and pulled back the door flap.

Heat rolled out, almost unearthly after hours of cold. Nauro stood to the side of a blazing fire, bare to the waist, his tailored slacks and tidy quarters a strange contrast to the wilderness outside. "Tai," he said, seeming totally unsurprised. "It's good to see you. Come in?"

Tai had been braced for an attack but Nauro was unarmed, hands at his sides, though that meant little.

"Yes," he said, voice muffled under his wraps. "I think I will." The warmth from the fire felt wonderful, and his skin ached from the cold.

"Care for a cup of mavensytm? Or dreamtea? I still have a bit left." Nauro gestured to an elegant bench along one wall, on which a few earthenware cups and bottles were arranged in clean lines.

Tai pulled the flap closed, and immediately started to sweat. "Mavensytm, yes. Thank you." Was the man offering it to show he was unafraid of Tai's resonance?

"Apologies if it's warm in here," Nauro said. "I haven't spent many winters in the south, and I'm afraid my northern blood isn't up to it."

Tai unwrapped his face and hands, then moved to his three layers of coats. "Where are you from, anyway?"

"Worldsmouth," Nauro said simply. "Though Worldsmouth before it was named Worldsmouth. The Yersh pronounced it more Worlds*mout*, but of course the merchant houses changed that once they successfully won their freedom."

Tai paused in unwrapping. "How old *are* you?"

"One hundred and thirty-eight, at last counting," Nauro said, sitting back on his cot with a sigh. "Winters like this make me feel it."

He looked thirty.

There was just one other chair in the room, and Tai took it, wondering how the man got all this furniture out here. "One hundred and thirty-eight? How is that even possible?"

Nauro gave him a level gaze. "You defeated Naveinya, yes? So, you are a mindseye now?"

Tai nodded, feeling foolish. He still wasn't used to the resonance—he could have been reading Nauro this whole time. He struck and tried, but Nauro's mind was a river under ice, thoughts too far down to read.

The fyelocke man grinned, pouring steaming water from a pot over the fire into a clay mug. "I didn't mean for you to check the veracity of my statements by reading my mind. I try to stay protected against such things. But you must have read Semeca's mind, in the end. Seen how old she was."

"Yes. I don't know exactly, but at least a thousand years."

Nauro nodded. "And we believe there are archrevenants who are older. Some who are original, even. There are ways to tell but," he shrugged, "you would need to have captured her revenant to do so."

Tai leaned in, accepting the mug. Good. This was the kind of information he needed. "So, is that what you do? You—capture revenants?"

Nauro took a sip from his own steaming cup, revealing the tattoo of a circle pierced by nine spears on the inside of his wrist. "I have longed for human conversation, Tai, but there are still things I cannot reveal until we have an agreement."

An agreement. *Tutelage*, Nauro had called it in his note. Joining his team, whatever that was, and studying their ways with the aim of defeating Semeca. "And how does that agreement change in light of the fact I've already killed your target?"

Nauro smiled. "Very little. You will still need to learn our ways to stand any reasonable chance of defeating other archrevenants, and that will still take time."

"So now that Semeca is gone, you just move on to another archrevenant? Is your goal to kill them all?"

His raised his eyebrows, in the cultured way Tai had seen lighthairs raise their eyebrows, a controlled show of surprise. "Kill them? Oh no, our goal is not to kill them. It's to *become* them."

Ydilwen's words came back to him. *I can't risk you taking Semeca's power.* "You want to—become them? But you're already immortal."

Nauro twisted his lips, setting his mug down with a muted thud on the long bench. "Immortal, no. Not even Semeca was immortal, as you proved. But I do have some longevity, yes, and a bit of power to heal myself. All things that would be available to you, if you joined us."

An evasion. Tai let it slide—he had more important things to learn here. "You spoke of dangers in your note. Of the archrevenants coming after me, and other ninespears."

"Shamans, we call ourselves. But yes. The dangers are real. Which I'm guessing you know, as you've been recently attacked."

Tai started. He'd been keeping his mind defended against mindsight, using the hundred conversations defense. "How did you know?"

"There are... traces left, from such an attack. I would love to explain more, but," he shrugged. "That's up to you. Stay here, and die, and waste the potential you have to change the world. Or join me."

"Does joining you mean becoming your thrall?"

Nauro's brows shot up further this time. "Is that what they tried to do? Fools. It must have been a journeyman at best. No, friend, if Naveinya could not manage to keep her hold on you, I have little faith any attempt at thralling you would work."

Tai shook his head, feeling too hot in the narrow tent despite having shed his outer layers. He needed to understand all this, needed to know how to defend himself against it. But Nauro had spoke of studying for years, and he couldn't leave Ayugen that long, couldn't give up his friends—give up *Ella*—to go help Nauro fight immortal beings. He had to do this on his own terms.

Tai shifted on the chair. "In your note, you said I had done what your society has failed to do for three hundred years. You've admitted that I can't be thralled. And yet it seems you are still trying to fit me into your old model of tutelage. That won't work. I don't have the time and space to leave and study with you for years on end."

Nauro met his eyes, the man's cool and brown. "You remember our talk of the revolutions of the wheel?"

"Yes. Of it all seeming pointless when looked at from a longer scale of time. But I saw into Semeca's mind too, Nauro. I have seen the life that you seek, and it's empty. She was holding on to power for its own sake, had long ago lost anyone she cared about. What she was really fighting was the realization that she was ready to die, that she had nothing left to live for."

Nauro shifted, looking uncomfortable.

"I'm not living that life," Tai went on. "I *have* things to live for, people I care about. And if learning the secrets of your society means giving those up, even for a year, then I'm not doing it. I'd rather die now than spend a thousand years powerful and alone."

Nauro held his gaze a moment, then looked down. "Fair enough. You are not our typical apprentice, and the system doesn't fit you. But you still need me."

Tai shook his head. "In what way? I defeated this man that came after me. I defeated the revenant you put on me, supposedly one of the most powerful the world has ever known. What more do I need?"

"You need to be able to defeat *gods*," the bare-chested man said, voice loud against the crackle of the fire. "The archrevenants are not ignorant of each other. We don't know how much communication they have, but most scholars agree they've had some sort of pact for the last five hundred years, which means they keep an eye on each other. When we attack, we try to do it in secret, with as little fanfare as possible, in the hopes that once we ascend, we will have a few years to prepare ourselves for their counter-attack."

He laid another branch on the fire, wet bark hissing. "You have no such options. Word of your battle with Semeca will have spread all over the continent by now, and likely beyond. Thousands witnessed the Broken in Gendrys, and while less will have escaped Ayugen having seen Semeca in her power, do not doubt that some have, and that the tale will grow in the telling. The other archrevenants know of you now, and they know you are a real threat to their power."

Tai wiped the sweat from his forehead. *Gods?* Is that what Semeca was? "Won't they also know that I didn't take her power? That maybe I just got lucky?"

Nauro glanced at him, then back to the fire. "No. I don't think you just got lucky. But yes, they will know you didn't take her power. I don't know how they will interpret that. I'm not sure it's ever happened before. But any deicide, after so long without one, will raise their hackles. And the archrevenants are not ones whose hackles you want raised."

A chill ran down Tai's spine, despite the heat. "Why? What would they do?"

Nauro shook his head. "Anything. Everything. Semeca was the least example of these, and still she commanded an army of insane resonators, threw giant bridges at you, duped one of the world's most powerful governments into thinking she was daughter to a Counciliate House. Their power is not limited, Tai, in the way that yours or, to some extent, mine is by the revenants we have overcome."

"And they would destroy my friends to get to me?" It didn't really need to be asked, but he had to know.

"They would destroy cities to get to you. Whole peoples. Archrevenants think on the scale of millennia, not years or decades as we do. They view people like we view the insects of summer, dead now for months with no one to mourn them. So would your city be. So would *all* our cities, if they had reason." He looked back to the fire.

Tai took a moment to let his breath catch up. He was in real danger. That was fine—was normal, really—but it meant he was a danger to his friends, to Marrem and Feynrick and Aelya and Ella. At least he could do something about that. "And this tutelage you offer," he said quietly. "It would give me a chance against them?"

Nauro rolled a log, flashing the tattoo on his wrist again. "For most people, no. But you are not most people. Which is likely why this journeyman tried to thrall you."

"Ydilwen," Tai said. "A Yatiman."

"Yes, well. What you need to know is that as much danger as you are in from the archrevenants, you are in even more from my people. Make no mistake that *they* have heard you defeated Semeca, and that you do not know our ways. No decent journeyman, no *initiate* would have let her revenant escape."

"Which means they know I can't defend against them," Tai said. The words reminded him with a chill that Nauro was very capable of such an attack, if he wished. That he had only defeated Ydilwen, apparently of low rank in their society, by dumb luck and a knife throw.

"Yes. And that you are either a threat or an asset, but either way not to be ignored. Ydilwen saw you as an asset—thralling you would have given him access to your *uai* stream, increasing his own power. Others will see you as a danger to their own efforts and want you gone."

Tai raised an eyebrow, trying to find some humor in the situation. He couldn't trust Nauro, but he had no other options. "I take it you are in the first camp?"

"Yes," Nauro said simply. "And I have been patient in my offer, but your grace period is over. More shamans will come, with greater skill than Ydilwen's. Eventually, the archrevenants will come too. If you don't start tutelage now, there is little hope you can save yourself."

A warning with an offer. Powerful, but Tai had spent too long scraping coins on the streets not to know he had power here too. "Seems like your grace period is over too. I imagine many will come seeking my talent, once they realize thralling me will not work. I will likely have my choice of who to study with. Some who will be more pliable than you have been."

"I have been *duly* pliable!" Nauro growled, then took a deep breath. He continued in a more even tone. "You do not know how this usually happens, how apprentices usually *beg* to begin real tutelage, so I will give you leeway. But you cannot deny I have done nothing but help you and give you time, living out here in this wasteland when there are important things going on right now elsewhere, waiting for you to see the urgency of the situation."

Tai relaxed some inside, seeing how much it meant to Nauro. He raised an eyebrow. "You *did* sic Naveinya on me."

"Yes, I did. I tried to force the matter, as I thought your death not far off. You accomplished the impossible once. Do not expect to do it again."

"You were wrong, you know," Tai said. "Semeca was not archrevenant of fatewalkers, as you told me. She ruled the mindseyes."

"Yes," Nauro said, looking back to the fire. "I realized my mistake when you released her power. Our knowledge is not complete, even now. Or especially now." He refocused. "But it is still leagues beyond what you know. You need me, Tai."

"As you need me," Tai answered, "or you would not be waiting out here in the cold, hoping that I came by. So let me propose a different agreement, something that might work for both of us."

Nauro's knuckles tightened on his cup, but he nodded.

"I will study under you. But you will stay with me, go where I go, and if we fight it will be on my terms. I am not interested in the power you seek. I will fight more archrevenants if need be, but what I care about is keeping my friends safe."

"And if that safety involves leaving? Involves fighting the gods themselves? Will you refuse the power they offer?"

"The question you are asking," Tai said, meeting the man's cool gaze, "is whether I will refuse *you* their power. I know what you seek."

Nauro inclined his head. "Fair enough, yes. I am not donating my time to you in the hopes that you live a long and prosperous life, or that your little rebellion becomes the next Councilate. If we *do* fight more archrevenants, or shamans who have gathered some power of their own, I will need my share of the rewards."

Tai did not miss the change in tone. Nauro was close to an agreement, an agreement Tai desperately needed, all question of the man's mad quest for power aside. If Ydilwen was only a low-powered ninespear and he nearly bested Ayugen's best two fighters in combat, Tai needed to know how. To make defenses against it. Learn how to attack with it.

Which meant trusting a man he could not trust.

"And you will have them," Tai said. "I take it you expect we *will* be facing more archrevenants at some point?"

Nauro inclined his head. "I would not be so motivated to agree to this otherwise. But your potential demands its own exceptions. I will accept your terms, Tai Kulga of Ayugen, if you will in matters of shamanic wisdom and practice take me as your master and agree not to leave my cell until such time as we are both satisfied with your power."

"Agreed," Tai said, the moment feeling too weighty for a sweltering tent in the middle of nowhere. "Do we lock arms now? Or go through some other ritual?"

"Normally yes, there is a formal process, and I would attach a new revenant to you. But given our history," he said with a slight smile, "perhaps a simpler ceremony will suffice." He held up a hand, fingers spread wide. "To defeat death."

He showed Tai how to pierce the five fingers with four of his own, forming nine. "To overcome life," Tai repeated, wondering again what he'd gotten himself into.

They met eyes, Nauro's deadly serious. "The gods must die."

3

We know of four waystones: the At'li stone sticking from the ice, the Seingard rock, the Wanderer in the Yati hinterlands, and the stone at the center of old Aran. If Semeca's stone is not one of these, or the stone rumored to exist in the Minchu peaks, the journey to find it will be long. But what is time to a shaman?

—Meyn Harides, *personal journals*

Ella trudged back to town trying not to think about Tai. She loved him, but she hated how much power he had over her emotions, especially at moments like this. She would worry about anyone going to see Nauro, given what she knew of the man, but Tai? It was like a butcher held her raw heart in one hand while he juggled cleavers with the other. Drunk.

How had this happened?

She knew she was odd for not having had more relationships, but there'd never been time. Not in the whirlwind since she came to Ayugen. Not on the ship, despite Ralhen's urgings, because she'd had too much to hide. And certainly not in her parents' house, where the whole reason she'd been locked up had been her refusal to get involved with suitors. Not since Poddy, and as much as she'd loved him, they'd just been children.

So apparently love was like Rider's Pox—the older you got it, the worse it was.

Which meant a sick stomach every time Tai went into danger. Which, with him, was most of the time. She hitched the bag of wintergrass higher on her back. Damn the man.

Ella pushed out of the trees, shivering in the bitter wind. At least she had plenty to do to distract herself. With the key role resonance harmonies had played in defending against the Broken, and the relative lack of other things to do, her fledgling school was suddenly flooded with students.

And they were making progress—leaps and bounds compared to before. She could never think of Semeca's attack as a good thing, not with all the people they'd lost, many of them her students and friends. Still, it had been the push she needed to break through the mystery of why only some students were overcoming: sympathetic resonance and harmony. Everything in the month since then had been refining that, testing it, and putting it into practice.

She took the long way around the bittermelon field, world silent save for the crisp sound of her steps. They'd gotten a *lot* of practice. Not least because many of the students who overcame their first revenant came back as soon as their second revenant made itself known. Revenants seemed to choose an identity from the person's past with the highest emotional attachment, and in this city that meant they were mostly people dead only a few weeks. Students were coming to the school just to escape the pain of talking to them, especially as the realization spread that, cherished as the Achuri notion of spirit guides was, revenants weren't who they said.

Ella nodded in greeting to the man shivering at the entrance to the school. Her school still met in the caves, despite everything that had happened there, for the simple reason that the bluffhouses were full of beds and people, and no other buildings remained that were big enough. But in a nod to what had happened, they kept a guard outside the front entrance, rotated every half hand in the cold.

Not that the Broken would stand much chance now, against her school.

The familiar feel of damp air greeted her as she descended the rough-hewn stairs, along with the scents of woodsmoke and *aletegang*, the main dish the Achuri made from wintergrass. It tasted like cat vomit, but it kept them alive. At least the Achuri agreed it was disgusting.

Marea sat at the bottom of the stairs, wrapped in a thick fur coat even in the relative warmth of the caves, making notes in a ledger. With the influx of students, Tunla had needed help making the rounds, and Marea was the perfect option—well-trained in math and literature, fluent in Achuri and Yersh, and already done with both her revenants. She had turned out to be a blank, one of those rare few whose resonance had no effect, but she still understood overcoming.

Maybe more importantly, she was a lighthaired orphan in a darkhaired world, daughter of wealthy Councilate parents killed in the rebellion, stuck amongst the people who killed them. She needed someplace to belong until she could get back to Worldsmouth, someone to be friends with, and Ella was the only one in the city with a similar background. So Marea had started helping out, quickly becoming indispensable.

Not that it made her any easier to deal with.

"There you are," the young girl said, marking her place in the book. "Done making out with your boyfriend?"

Ella raised an eyebrow. "Jealous?"

"Of him? Never." Marea pushed back a few silvery locks that had escaped her tight bun. "Still don't know what you see in him."

This was an old discussion. Tai was part of the original rebellion, so for Marea he was the worst thing imaginable, and yet Ella was in love with him. "Maybe you'll figure it out sometime. And no, we weren't making out. We were attacked, actually."

Marea's face brightened, her features that strange fifteen-year-old mix of cherubic childhood and mature woman. "The army? Have they come back?"

The girl had a recurring fantasy that the Councilate army would come back and save her, though all reports from Gendrys said the Councilate had more or less pulled out for the winter. "No. A ninespear."

Marea's eyebrows rose. In the course of their time together, Ella had told her about Odril and Sablo. "Did you kick them in the shatterhole?"

Ella grinned. "Close enough. We killed him." Was it okay to grin at a man's death? Especially in front of an impressionable girl? She didn't care. He'd threatened Tai.

"Pearly. Where's your lover then?"

"He—had to go see someone for a while." She tried to ignore the pit that opened in her stomach at the thought of it. She should be there, but he insisted on going alone. "How are the students today?"

"Two overcome just this morning," Marea said, tapping the page. "Gylen and Waglea. Finally realized Gylen needed an augmented triad if he was going to get anything done."

That was the other great thing about Marea—she'd trained in classical music, and knew all the vocabulary for things Ella, who'd never had much of an ear, struggled to hear. "Augmented… that's the one that sounds kinda dreamy?"

Marea raised an eyebrow. "It sounds *augmented*. Your parents seriously never brought in tutors?"

"I told you, I scared off every tutor that taught anything even *remotely* making me a more suitable candidate for marriage."

"And now you're hooked up with a darkhair, not even a citizen. Bet they'd love that," Marea smirked.

Ella... didn't know how they'd feel. Or how she'd feel about how they felt. It'd been a long time.

"I did some math, while you were gone," Marea said, glancing back at her notes.

"What did you come up with?" For all that she hated showing it, Marea had a brilliant mind. And she needed approval, much as that was the last thing she would ever admit. Had Ella ever been like that?

No. She'd been trying to make sure *no one* approved of her.

"The city," Marea said, flipping her ledger to a different page. "I went through our latest census, and marked off who's overcome, and whether they've done one or both, then calculated how quickly we've been getting them to overcome, and extrapolated that out with a little bit of acceleration assuming we continue getting better at this, and—"

Ella glanced at the numbers, her calculor's mind juggling them. The math looked solid. "And?"

"And I think we can be revenant-free by winter's end."

"What?" Ella lost the numbers she was juggling, gaping at Marea's beaming face. "You—we could get *everyone in the city* overcome?"

"Not just overcome. *Both* revenants. Completely free."

"Marea, that's amazing!" She'd thought they were working through them quickly, but all of Ayugen?

Marea beamed. "Just in time for me to go back and teach it to my house."

Ella's smile faltered. They hadn't directly discussed this, but she doubted Tai or the rest of his council would like the idea of Marea teaching the Councilate how to overcome without yura. And yet the academic in her, the researcher that bubbled at the thought of *everyone*, not just Ayugen, getting free of their revenants, was all for it. Thankfully the snows kept them from having to decide that one for a while. "Right. I'll be sad to see you go."

Marea cocked her head. "You don't want to go back?"

"Ayugen's my home. I never fit in the Mouth, and now?" She shrugged. "There's nothing for me there."

"What about your parents?"

Ella shook her head. "They—were never really parents to me. Just managers. Like I was some kind of House asset that needed special assistance."

Marea shrugged, looking back at her notes. "Maybe that's just because you were young. My second voice was my mother, and even though it was a fishscat revenant and not her, she still helped me realize a lot about how I was to them, before they died." She shook her head, closing her ledger. "I had no idea how much they cared about me."

"My parents kept me locked in a bedroom for five years. They fed me through a door. I hardly knew them."

"Okay, okay," Marea held up her hands. "They were scatholes. Don't need to get all defensive on me."

Ella cleared her throat. "How's everyone else doing?"

Marea flipped open the ledger and they spent some time going through the list of students, over seventy of them at the moment. The process had come down to making sure the student was willing to overcome, gauging what their relationship with their revenant was, then trying different triads of resonance on them, interspersed with reflection time. "How about this one, Eacham?"

Marea grimaced. "Says he wants to overcome, but every time

I try to help him he starts lecturing me. Think he doesn't like it that I'm young, and a girl. Or that my hair's the wrong color."

Ella nodded. Some of the Achuri still held a grudge against lighthairs. "As I recall Tai said he was a curmudgeon. Had his grain stores raided in one of the first attacks."

Marea glanced up. "Speak of the devil."

Ella's heart leapt. She spun and saw Tai coming down the long stairs.

Nauro the ninespear walked at his side.

4

"Tai!" Ella cried, barely resisting the urge to run and fling her arms around him. He was *safe*.

"Hey." He smiled, but she didn't miss the lines of worry around his eyes. "You remember Nauro."

Her excitement cooled. "I do."

"Ellumia," the thin mixed-hair man said, voice cultured and smooth. "A pleasure."

"Hardly. You going to try to pump me for information again, then run when I refuse?"

"My apologies," the man said, face still cool. "Time was short, and I was worried for Tai's wellbeing. I needed information."

Tai's wellbeing. Not, you know, hers too, or the people of Ayugen. "And now?"

"The situation is no less dire, but he at least understands the dangers."

"And you're not planning to sic some evil revenant on him again?"

"Not without his wishes, no." Nauro quirked a smile, directed at Tai, and anger welled up in her. This was the man who'd tried to *kill* Tai, to take him from her, and now he was trying to *smile* at him? It was all she could do not to strike resonance then and there.

Aside from the fact he could probably stop her as easily as Ydilwen had.

Tai was looking back and forth between them, eyebrows up. Ella realized with a start how defensive she probably sounded. "He's going to teach me," Tai said. "On my terms. Show us what Ydilwen did, and how to defend against it, for starters."

"Do we have any reason to believe there will be more?" Ella asked, searching for some hole in the man's logic.

"Yes."

"And they are?"

Nauro sighed. "These are not things we normally discuss with the uninitiated, but I see we are in a unique situation here. To put it in the simplest terms, Semeca was queen of a large amount of revenants."

"An archrevenant," Ella said.

"Yes," Nauro said. "Normally those spirits pass some small portion of the *uai* they take from their hosts on to the archrevenant above them, giving Semeca the powers you witnessed in her attack—control of the Broken, using any and all resonances at a high level, moving giant structures—"

"The power to control Broken," Ella cut in, half wanting to catch him in a lie and half because she hadn't been able to figure it out. "That was a form of mindseye?"

"No," Nauro said, appearing annoyed at the interruption. "That was no resonance at all. When you are being fed *uai* directly, as shamans and archrevenants are, you are not limited by those shapes. If your belief is strong enough, you can make that *uai* do anything."

"My feet," Tai said, meeting her eyes. "Ydilwen stuck them to the ground somehow, when I tried to attack him."

"Good," Nauro said. "Yes. He had likely been out hunting loose revenants, and thralled enough to have some simple abilities like that."

"Then why haven't we seen this kind of thing before?" Ella asked, far from convinced. This man was a snake.

"As I said," Nauro said, clearing his throat, "everything changed with Tai's defeat of Semeca. Normally, when someone defeats an archrevenant, they thrall their revenant, and through it take all the revenants thralled to it. Tai did not. This means that all the revenants she held in thrall—say, thirty or forty thousand—suddenly had nowhere to send their *uai*. And the targets for shamans like Ydilwen and I went from a few souls that never conformed to a resonance to those loose forty thousand."

"So Ydilwen was hunting… revenants?" Ella asked. Tai had seen something like that in mindsight.

"I imagine so, yes. Thralling their *uai* stream to his own to harvest their power, now that Semeca isn't taking it. I don't doubt that most shamans have realized what happened, and even as we speak they are gathering up loose revenants, replacing Semeca with a host of power-drunk shamans. The war between them could last centuries, if we don't do something about it."

"Why would you?" Marea cut in. "We'll all be long dead before it matters."

Nauro glanced at her, mouth twitching. "Because Tai is involved in that war. He started it. And they all know, no matter how much power they gather, that he defeated someone who had all of it."

"Semeca," Marea said.

"Yes. So he has the power to defeat them too."

"Unless they kill him first," Ella breathed, fear spreading in her belly.

"Kill or thrall him, if they are foolish or powerful enough to try thralling," Nauro said. "That, I gather, was Ydilwen's quest."

"And he nearly did it," Tai said, popping his neck. The lines of worry were back around his eyes. "But shamans aren't all we have to worry about."

Fear spread further in her core, a snake made of ice. "What do you mean? Who else is after you?"

"Semeca's peers," Nauro said. "Teynsley. Alenul. Gyelon. The eight other archrevenants. As much as Tai poses a threat to the shamans now gathering up power, he will seem like more of a threat to those *in* power. Semeca is the first to die in more than three hundred years, and her power was not claimed. This is a break in a pattern of millennia. They will fear for their safety."

"This power," Ella said. "Whatever Semeca left. Why don't the other archrevenants just take it for themselves?"

"They cannot," Nauro said. "Each can only hold one resonance. Or in the Trinity's case, pairs of second-level resonances."

"So where is the rest of it going, while Semeca's old revenants float around unclaimed?"

"Ah," Nauro said. "Now *that* is a good question. You are familiar with waystones?"

Markels had spoken of them in his travels, strange standing stones in different parts of the continent that looked remarkably similar—one in the wilds of Yatiland, another sticking from the ice sheet among the At'li, a third in the holy city of Aran.

"Yes," she said. "What do they have to do with this?"

"According to our histories," Nauro said, "and they are admittedly spotty, these stones were created during the Prophet's time, to seal away the power of the archrevenants he defeated."

Ella sucked in a breath. "You have histories going back to the time of the Prophet?"

Nauro smiled. "We have histories going back much further. Things existing only in translation. But yes. Our organization is very old."

"So, it didn't work," Tai cut in. "Sealing away the power of the archrevenants. They are still here, still powerful."

"It worked for a time," Nauro said, tone warmer toward Tai. "Centuries, if the histories tell it right. But people have always been hungry for power, and the Prophet wasn't able to entirely suppress our knowledge." He smiled at this. "Shamans chipped away slowly at the revenants feeding the stones, until little to no power was going to the stones at all, and new archrevenants rose up."

"But because I didn't take Semeca's power," Tai said, "one of the stones has started—what? Sucking up power?"

"Redistributing it," Nauro said. "Buried in each of these stones are the spears the original archrevenants had thralled their power to. With Semeca gone, the *uai* streams from all her thralls return to those weapons, and the stone sends it back into the world."

"How?" Ella asked. She had never heard of *uai* coming from anything other than digestion.

Nauro shrugged. "How does the star send *uai* to the winter plants that capture it? Or how do those plants convert its light into *uai* instead of the sugars of summer fruits and vegetables? We don't know. But histories tell of cities built around these waystones, places where people were able to use enormous amounts of power at any time. So we can assume it's just there to be taken."

"And somewhere in the world there is a stone now radiating all of Semeca's power?"

He nodded. "The power of all her revenants that haven't been gathered up yet, at least, and I would guess that is most of them, as the process is not easy."

"What happens when you get the spear out?" Ella asked.

"Then all the power goes to you," Nauro said, eying her cooly. "You are instantly a god."

"And I suppose the only option is to go? That this is part of Tai's tutelage?"

"No," Tai said, to Ella's relief. "We're not trying to get into this game. We're trying to stay out of it."

"But you are already in it," Nauro said. "You started it. If you do not finish it, someone else will. And once they have Semeca's power they will come for you. To secure their position."

Ella clenched her fists. Of *course* Tai had to go. Of *course* there were all these dangers. It all made sense, didn't it? And in the end, it dried out to Nauro getting Tai alone. Like he wanted.

"Then why haven't they come already?" Ella snapped, thinking fast, trying to find some hole in the web he was weaving. "It's been a month or more."

Nauro looked displeased. "The stones are not broken easily. In fact, it's said they are unbreakable, that they have remained smooth and unweathered for thousands of years."

"So we're safe then," Ella said, changing tack, trying to keep Tai from danger. From Nauro. "Someone would have broken them already and taken the spears if they could."

"There was no point, before now," Nauro said, meeting her eyes. He knew she didn't trust him. Fine. Let him know. Not everyone had to be friends. "With Semeca alive, all the power went to her. Now that the power has returned to the stone, to her spear locked in the stone, there is every reason in the world to try to find it, and break it open."

"And whoever does," Tai said, almost as if talking to himself, "instantly becomes an archrevenant."

"Yes," Nauro said. "And they will come for you, and your city."

Tai took a deep breath, and Ella's heart sank. She knew what he was going to say already.

"Then we have to go," Tai said. "We have to find the stone, and break it."

5

"Not without me," Ella said, just as Marea did. She looked at the younger woman and grinned.

Tai glanced between them. "Marea, I'm sorry, but I can't let you come. And Ella, it's going to be dangerous and—"

"And?" Ella demanded. He knew she could handle danger.

"And we'll need to move quickly," Nauro said.

"I can move quickly," Marea said, not giving it up.

"I'm a timeslip," Ella said in the next breath, loading on the scorn. There was no way she was letting Nauro take Tai away from her. She loved him, and he was smart, and powerful, and lots of good things, but Tai could be too trusting. And Nauro wanted something.

Nauro opened his mouth, but Ella cut him off. "Tai. Can I talk to you privately?"

The fyelocke shaman looked perturbed, but Tai nodded. Was it crazy that she felt relieved, that she was still more important to Tai than Nauro?

She took the stairs with Tai. They climbed them in silence, steps echoing from the rock. His hand found hers, and the world started to feel better.

"You don't actually trust him," she said when they crested the top, back into the blustering cold. No one was around, and the star's blue light cast a pale glow over the snow. It would still be a sunny afternoon in Worldsmouth. She missed it sometimes.

"No," he said. "But if even half of what he's saying is true—and it all makes sense with Ydilwen—I need to know what he knows. *We* need to know."

"But he'll only teach *you*," Ella said, unable to keep the bitterness from her voice.

Tai scoffed. "Doesn't mean I can't then teach it to you, right?"

"So—you *will* let me come?"

He looked confused. "I wouldn't go without you."

She would have kissed him, if it wasn't so shatting cold their lips would freeze together. She settled for a hug, squeezing the solidity of his body through their layers of fur. "Good. Yes. Well then. What about Marea?"

Tai hesitated, rolling a shoulder. "I know she's your friend, but—"

Ella nodded. "She's also still a child."

"And just looking for the quickest way back to Worldsmouth, if you're right about how much she hates it here. A boat once the river thaws would serve her better."

"And be safer," Ella said. "Do you really think they'll come after you?"

Tai shuffed a boot into snow. "Ydilwen did. I can't just sit here and wait for someone to ambush us with Semeca's power. We got lucky once, but I don't want to count on it happening again."

She nodded, not liking it but determined to go if he was. How did this happen again? "So you, me, and a strange, probably evil, man with unknown intentions. It'd be good to have someone else."

"I can carry two," he said. "Three would be a stretch, long-distance."

"We can't fly with Nauro, anyway."

Tai frowned.

"Ydilwen took away our *uai*, right? And Nauro's more powerful than Ydilwen?"

"Seems like it." Then his eyebrows went up. "Oh. You're saying if we're five hundred paces up in the air and he suddenly attacks us, we're both in trouble."

"We're both dead," she said. "Which is probably not what he wants, but maybe he just takes me out, or hurts you in some way that you have to depend on him. I mean, he's probably got the same unshaped power Ydilwen did, right? He could heal himself like a brawler. Fly like a wafter. Don't tell me he's been quietly waiting in the woods ignoring all these free revenants Semeca released."

Tai popped his neck. "He wasn't just waiting there. There were tracks leading from his tent out into the woods."

"Hunting," Ella said. "Like Ydilwen said he'd been hunting. For power. Have you considered that even if we do find the stone and open it, he might turn on us once we get the spear? That he won't teach you as much as you need to know to defeat him if he does?"

"Yes," Tai said. "And I don't know what to do about it. We still need him, need his knowledge."

"Well if we're not flying, we should at least take someone else with us. Someone reliable and smart about fighting the *regular* way."

Tai looked off toward the forest, eyes searching. "Feynrick," he said at last. "He's great with his resonance, used to fighting without it, and good at strategy. He'll get our back, and see things we missed. But I think that's all we can do. The more we take, the slower we go."

She nodded. Feynrick was a good choice. "Okay. So, we're really doing this? Really leaving and going on some mad quest to destroy an unbreakable stone?"

He met her eyes. "Yes. As long as we're together."

Prophet's *piece* the man was lucky it was freezing out here, or she'd have to strip him naked and have her way with him right now.

"As long as we're together," she said back, squeezing his hand. "Now let's get the shatters back inside? I'm freezing."

He grinned. "There's going to be a lot colder days if we do this on foot. Sure I'm worth it?"

She gave him a considering look as she pulled him back toward the stairs. "We'll see."

6

Then where is the woman, I ask you? And where is my cousin Tayo? House Fenril cannot continue to mask its losses at Gendrys, nor the extralegal commandeering of Councilate forces. Let them be assessed and pay restitution as per our codes. And if they can't cover it, cede their seat on the Council. I've always said their rise was more serendipity than solvency.

—Lady Asra Mettelken, *Speeches of the Day, Yiel 112*

Marea wrapped the furs tighter around her, the best she'd been able to scrounge from the ruins of Newgen. It was cold, a deep biting cold she'd never known in Worldsmouth. The kind she spent winters trying to avoid.

And now she was walking out into it, Ayugen already hazy behind her, cheeks going numb.

If her parents had been alive, they would have bought her thicker furs. Would have hired her carriages heated with coals to make the long overland trek to Gendrys. Would have sent porters and attendants with her, to see to her every need.

But they were dead, and she was done living with their murderers.

A cold wind skirled across the burned fields of the river valley, kicking up a spray of hard snow. She shivered and pressed on.

Life in the overcoming school hadn't been bad. She liked working with Ella, liked what they were discovering with the resonances. But there was always that moment after someone overcame, when their eyes would focus again after being lost in struggle, when the *uai* raging through them would push them to shout, to celebrate, and their eyes would jump to her hair. To her skin, too dark for any southerner. And then they would look for someone else to share the news. Someone like themselves.

And then there were the rebels. Tai, Aelya, Dayglen, Lumo. The people who had been inside the walls of Newgen that day, when her family had heard the rebels were attacking in force and fled the enclave. Her mother hadn't been fast enough, caught inside the gate as the rebels took it. Her father had run back, trying to pull her through. The rebel who'd cut them down had been so casual. Two strokes to end three lives.

She would never forgive them.

And now she was following rebels out into the wilderness. Marea kept her feet carefully in their tracks, following them to the edge of the valley and up into the waving needleaves beyond.

Ella, at least she didn't count as a rebel. She'd been involved with them, but her focus had always been academic. She'd had no part in the tactics, no part in the attacks. Had done her best to end them, even, and she'd been Marea's only friend once her mother was gone. Been the only one willing to help her build her mother a proper pyre, among the droves of Achuri burying their dead in water or earth.

And it was on Ella that she depended now to take her in. That, and the surety the cold would kill her if they left her alone.

The sun sank low in the sky, days bitterly short this far south. The star still hung overhead but she hated its blue half-light, a dim sun that gave illumination without warmth. Even here, among the rocky bluffs and packed trees, the wind gnawed at her face, pushed fingers of ice through the seams in her furs. She should have worn more. Her feet were frozen despite layers of socks, her knees aching desperately.

And this, maybe, was the flaw in her plan: she had no doubt she could follow them until dark. Could catch them even if it took all night. But if she lost their tracks, once the star set too? If the path in the woods faded out, and she was alone in the bitter cold night?

Marea walked faster, cursing herself, lips sluggish from cold, chewing dried bittermelon, the only food she could find. She *would* find them. She had to.

There was nothing left for her in Ayugen. Would she even have a place in the caves without Ella? Marea had seen the lighthaired bodies laid out, the last time Ella and Tai had left the city, the angry glare Aelya and her Blackspines had given her. What if they decided Marea was a threat? There was no one to stop them.

And even if they didn't, she was done living with her family's murderers. Done helping them overcome their problems while hers only seemed to mount. She had watched the snow fall, watched the river freeze over. No boats were leaving the docks. No travelers attempting the road to Gendrys. The only way out was on foot, and Tai's party the only one taking it.

So she had to catch them.

At least, that's what she'd thought last night, when they'd told her she couldn't come and made their own plans. Now, with even the starlight dimming and the blotchy shadows of trees beginning to hide four sets of footprints in the snow? Now she was not so certain.

Full dark came, the moon rising cold and distant above the trees. Fires burned in its dark half, tracing the round sphere against the dark. Her footsteps crunched, solitary and echoing. How far could they have walked? Did Nauro use some shamanic trick to speed their steps?

It didn't matter. She would catch them now, tonight, or she would die. She was too cold to possibly survive out here, and there were no villages this direction. Only snow and trees and the mountains that split Ayugen from Yatiland.

Marea stumbled, banging her knee against a stone hidden under the snow. She cried out, sucking in air—and stopped. The air carried a scent, something other than the dead cold scentlessness she'd been breathing all day.

Smoke.

Marea broke into a smile and started shuffling on, sniffing like a dog with her nose, tears freezing on her cheeks. Smoke. A fire. Ella, and her friends. Safety. *Warmth*, gods praise it. *Warmth*.

Around a bend she found firelight spilling from the top of a dark conic tent of furs, two elk hitched to a tree nearby. "Hello!" she called, all guile forgotten in panic and hope and a cold that had sunk to her marrow. "It's me! Marea!"

"We can't keep her, obviously," Nauro was saying, stirring a copper pot of something that smelled like heaven. Marea huddled in the cramped tent, furs shed to absorb as much heat as she could, body shaking uncontrollably. "She's a liability."

"She's almost *dead*, Nauro," Ella retorted, one warm hand rubbing Marea's back. "We can't send her back like this. It's not safe for Tai to waft her back, and we can't spend the days to walk her back, not if you're right about other shamans seeking the stone."

This was the rationale Marea had been counting on. Compassion for someone facing death. Looked like Nauro didn't have any.

He was as bad as the rebels. Prophet send Ella could talk sense into them.

"And if she comes," Nauro said, "you think she has a better chance of living? Even if we open the stone unscathed, knowledge brings its own risks."

"Far-off risks," Ella said. "This one is immediate. She comes."

"You would risk the fate of your whole city for one girl?" Nauro asked, still gazing at the soup. "Send her back."

They both looked to Tai, and Marea's heart dropped. This was the flaw in her plan: the ultimate decision would rest with Tai. With a friend of her family's *murderer*. And from what she'd seen, he'd always listen to the different sides of an argument, but when he made up his mind, it was final.

He looked at her, eyes black and cold.

"She stays," he said, and for a shocked second she couldn't believe what she'd heard. Then Nauro scowled and Ella smiled and Marea relaxed like she hadn't in months. She was going home.

"But you have to abide by our rules," Tai said, looking her in the eyes. She met them with difficulty. *Murderer.* "We have a long ways to go, so you have to keep up. We discuss collectively, but I make the decisions here. And you may see things that you don't understand. You are not to speak of them to anyone, once you are safely back in Worldsmouth. Agreed?"

Marea nodded, too relieved even to feel humiliated by the way he was talking to her. Like a child. His friends had ended her childhood a long time ago.

Feynrick slapped her back from the other side of the cramped tent. "Happy to have ye, for my part. Though this little tent was going to be tight with four. With five? We might all be getting to know each other better than we want."

"As long as we're warm," Marea said.

She learned to regret her words, cramped between Ella and Feynrick's hairy, smelly, snoring form. Sleep took its time coming, but it didn't matter: she was safe, she was warm, and she was going home.

7

It can mean only one thing—the Achuri boy killed one of the nine, and he didn't know to take their power. But he must have known something more than yura and wafting, to take down a god. And whatever that is, I'll wager it's key to unlocking whichever stone holds the god's power.
—Meyn Harides, *personal journals*

Tai heard the dead man two days later.

I had a mother, you know. Have one, in Yatiport.

Tai knew the voice right away, though he'd barely heard the man talk, and then only as he was dying. The shaman they'd killed in Ayugen. Ydilwen. His new revenant.

"He's here," Tai said, breaking a silence that had lasted since their cold lunch of grasscakes and leftover roast ptarmigan.

"*It's* here," Ella and Nauro said at once, then shot looks at each other. They'd been frosty since Nauro put a shamanic revenant on Tai, then denied he had another to give to Ella.

"It, right," Tai said, trying to ignore the feeling that had come with the voice. The sense of a life unfulfilled, the promises made to a lover long dead, the mother freezing in an upstairs apartment.

Was that all real? Or was the revenant planting ideas in his head even now?

You saw when you read my thoughts. You know it's true.

"Who's it pretending to be?" Ella asked, tone casual. That was the thing with revenants—it was so obvious when it wasn't in your head. But when it was...

"He—it's the shaman, from Ayugen. The one that attacked us."

Feynrick guffawed. "How's he feeling with that hole in his side?"

"It's not *actually* him, Feynrick," Ella said. "This is just the persona Tai's new revenant chose to be most effective. Though it *is* an interesting choice."

Tai could just see her hands itching for a quill and notebook. He was glad for once she didn't have one handy. He'd been of scholarly interest to her from the first moment they met, and had never really gotten used to it, even after her interests had gotten more... personal.

"Agreed," Nauro said. "Well. We might as well start training."

Training. Is that what you killed me for? To get a shamanic spirit?

Tai started. He hadn't thought of that—to be a shaman, the dead man would have to have shamanic powers, and Nauro had stopped intentionally on the way back to Ayugen to gather his revenant. Which meant Nauro either hadn't had a shamanic revenant ready before Ayugen, or he was lying about not having one for Ella, since he'd taken up the dead man's too.

Ydilwen. My name is Ydilwen. Or was.

"Prophets, but it's hard not to take this thing seriously," Tai said.

Ella made a sympathetic noise. "You want us to just get rid of it? We could probably work up enough of a chord to do it."

"No," Nauro said sharply. "It needs more time to seat, and to attract a secondary revenant. Remove it now and he won't have access to the second resonance, which is the whole point."

"Secondary revenant?" Ella asked, looking caught between dislike and curiosity.

Nauro sighed. "Yes. His current revenant is shaping an *uai* channel, but they can't capture all the *uai* taken thereby—some streams back to their archrevenant, if they have one, and enough escapes that another revenant can survive on it, waiting for their chance to be primary."

"And that's why, after you get rid of your first voice, the second takes a while to show up? Because it's been just barely surviving, and now needs time to feed and make a plan?"

"To seat, yes, is how we put it. We will have to wait long enough for Tai to attract a higher level shamanic revenant before we can think of taking this one out."

Tai glanced at Ella, who was looking at him. What Nauro was saying could be true. But now that Tai had more or less caught him in a lie about how many revenants he had, this again sounded like a convenient way to put off training Ella. Still, he was too much of a street child to mention it right away. Better to watch and wait. Like it or not, they *did* need to learn defenses against shamans, and Nauro still seemed like the best way to do it.

Even if the man wouldn't teach Ella.

"So how do we start?" he asked. At least at the moment, if he didn't have the secondary resonance, whatever Nauro had him do the rest could too.

"Very simply," Nauro said. "Close your eyes."

Tai glanced at the path ahead of them. It was fairly smooth, but walking with snownets still took a lot of balance. "What?"

"Close your eyes," Nauro said again. "Just for a few moments."

"Okay," Tai said, glancing at Ella then doing it. Hers were already closed—she must have realized this training didn't take a revenant too. He closed his eyes. "Now what?"

"Now focus on your stomach."

"My *what?*" Ella said beside him. Tai was thinking the same thing.

Nauro sighed. "Your stomach. The sensations there. Are you full, hungry? Is it upset, calm, tense, what? Tell me."

"Normal," Tai said. "Well, maybe a little tense."

"Okay. Ella?"

"Tense. Sick of wintergrass. A little empty, if truth be told."

"Good," Nauro said, voice sounding much too young for his hundred and forty years. "Now continue paying attention."

Tai fluttered his eyelids a moment to make sure he wasn't going to walk into something. "To what?"

"To *this.*"

Nauro's voice sounded a touch strained, but nothing else happened.

"To…what?" Ella asked.

"Open them again," Nauro said.

The world looked unchanged.

"Few people notice anything their first time," Nauro said, though he looked disappointed. "Let's do it again."

"Notice what?" Ella asked.

"*Again,*" Nauro said. "Close your eyes."

Tai dutifully did, making sure the path was clear ahead.

"Now *feel* your stomach, everything about it. In three…two… one."

Ella sucked air, and Tai frowned. He had almost felt—what? Hunger?

"Open them," Nauro said. "Anything?"

"I felt a—coldness," Ella said. "Like a chill?"

Nauro twitched his lips. "Tai?"

"Nothing. Or, maybe a hunger? But nothing, I think."

"Fine. Again."

"What are we doing?" Ella asked.

"*Again.*"

They did a few more rounds of this, Nauro offering no explanation, until finally Tai couldn't stand it either. "What does walking blind and feeling our stomachs have to do with anything?"

"He's just keeping me and the girl entertained," Feynrick said in a stage whisper, from where he and Marea led the animals. "You look mad."

"You are learning to sense revenants," Nauro said.

"In their stomachs?" Marea asked.

"The stomach is a good place to start. We are too used to our eyes, our ears, our nose, our regular senses. Used to filtering out any information that doesn't make sense, or doesn't fit into our worldview. Like the way we tend to believe a voice in our heads, because they *sound* so real, even though we know they are not. Same with our senses."

"But not the stomach?" Ella asked.

"Well. We have our familiar categories of understanding for the stomach too, but it so happens that most people will feel something there, when they touch a revenant."

"*Touch* a revenant?" Tai asked. "I thought they were, y'know —" He didn't know this word in Yersh.

"Incorporeal," Ella supplied.

"Yeah. That."

"They mostly are," Nauro answered. "Just as we are mostly flesh, but have nonphysical components, such as the *uai* our bodies create, vibrating on use but otherwise incorporeal. You can sense revenants in a number of ways, even without shamanic sight. How they do varies some on the individual revenant, and on the sensitivity of the person touching them."

"So you just… walked revenants through us?" Tai asked.

"More like you walked through them, but yes."

"Do it again," Ella said at once.

They did it again, Tai paying extra close attention to his stomach as they walked blind. Yes—there *was* a sensation. Almost like hunger, or hunger if it was also angry. Tai said as much.

"Good," Nauro said. "Yes. I could see that with this one. Now I will switch the revenants I have been using. See if you notice the difference."

They closed their eyes and felt. Ella gasped the same moment Tai's eyes popped open. "That wasn't hunger at all, it was like a chill, or a cold needle—"

"And mine *did* feel hungry!" Ella cried. "This is amazing!"

"Okay, okay," Marea said, pushing up from where she'd been walking with Feynrick. "I want in too. Put a ghost on me."

Nauro's face went flat. "No."

Marea's face went angry. She'd been showing more emotion the last few days. "*Yes*. I'm hearing it all anyway. Not like I couldn't repeat what you're doing with someone else."

"You couldn't, actually, because you're not a shaman. And it would be dangerous to try and repeat this without having a much firmer grasp on the forces in play."

"Excuses." She glanced at Tai, but like usual wouldn't actually meet his eyes. "Ella? Tell him I have to learn too."

Ella raised her eyebrows. "That's—not really my call to make. Although for my part, yes, of course you should learn. And as soon as I can do what he's doing I will teach you."

"The girl can learn," Tai said, turning to Nauro.

"Think about what you're saying," Nauro said, voice calm as ever but mouth starting to twitch. "This is not one of your people. She's with us for the express purpose of *leaving* us as soon as she can. Foolish enough that you let her come, knowing what she knows of your insights into harmonic resonances, but to send her back to your enemies knowing something of shamanism too?"

Tai rolled his shoulders, glancing at Marea, who was glaring at Nauro, still refusing to meet his gaze. Did she hate him so much? He knew Nauro was right, that it was already a mistake to let her go knowing what she knew, but he also wasn't going to keep an innocent girl prisoner. What would a few days stumbling into ghosts change anything? And maybe if he did this, she would let go of whatever she was holding against him.

"She can learn. That's final."

Nauro worked his jaw for a moment. "Fine. Then we resume."

Marea's face lit up. "Thank you."

Tai smiled. "You're welcome."

"I was talking to Ella," Marea said, not looking at him.

Ella opened her mouth but Tai waved her off. It was disappointing, but maybe it was justice too. That he meet at least one of the widows and orphans he'd made during the rebellion. That he deal with never being forgiven the way he would never forgive whoever had taken Fisher and Curly from him.

They continued trying to sense revenants as the sun set and the star's light cast everything blue, Nauro switching out revenants and making them guess which they had run into. Ella showed particular aptitude, and Marea wasn't far behind, though Tai held his own.

It was fascinating and exhausting. During a break near starset Marea cleared her throat. "I never got a chance to ask this but… where are we going?"

Tai glanced at Nauro, who'd taken him aside to advise telling the girl as little as possible. "To the closest waystone."

They walked in silence a few moments. "And that's where,

exactly?" Marea asked. "North, at least? The direction of Worldsmouth?"

"It is a few days more," Nauro said.

"A few days more would be the Yati hinterlands," she said. "And across a low mountain range, if I remember my topography right?"

So much for that secret. Tai opened his mouth to answer, and Nauro cleared his throat, and Tai closed it again.

"Oh, Prophet's piece," Ella said, "you two really think we can travel together for weeks on end and just keep her in the dark? What if she gets lost? What if *we* do and she remembers her maps better? The girl is Worldsmouth educated. She'll know where we are when we get there anyway."

"I just want to go home," Marea said, keeping her face forward. "Or to a port that's not frozen. I can make my way from there."

Tai answered her over Nauro's frown. "We're headed to the closest waystone, which is somewhere in the Yati valley beyond the divide. Nauro doesn't know exactly which one was tied to Semeca, so we need to check them all, and this one is closest. After that we'll take a boat downstream to Yatiport, and you can book for Worldsmouth from there."

She tilted her head. "How will you know if it's the right waystone or not?"

"There will be an energy to the place," Nauro said. "I don't know exactly what, but it will be obvious."

"An energy," Ella said. The two made a vicious combo. "So this is what all your great knowledge comes down to, is that you'll just kinda *feel the energy* when you get there?"

"I have been there before," Nauro said coldly. "I've been to all the waystones on this continent, including the one buried in the ice sheet. I know how they feel. If forty thousand souls are suddenly feeding one of them *uai*, we will be able to tell."

Ella raised an eyebrow. "And then we what, tap it and ask it nicely to break open so you can take its power?"

"And then we start experimenting," Nauro said. "The book is unclear about how they can be opened, but there are only so many possibilities."

Marea raised an eyebrow. "You don't know how to open it? Aren't you, like, three hundred years old?"

"*One* hundred," Nauro said. "And thirty-eight. Don't believe all the rumors you heard in Ayugen. And if you know what's good for you, don't go repeating them once you get back to Worldsmouth."

"Because you don't want your precious secrets getting out?" Ella asked.

"No," he said, eyeing the forest around them. "Because there are plenty of people in *Worldsmouth* who don't want those secrets to get out. Who have spent their lives protecting them. Don't assume the death of a minor House daughter would mean much to them."

Marea's face paled. "Are you threatening me?"

"I'm preparing you," he said. "I warned you, knowledge has its costs. You wanted to know more, and now you need to be prepared to protect yourself. Speaking of which, if you don't mind I need to watch the air. We could be attacked at any time out here."

She paled further, and Tai rolled his shoulders against a knot there. They couldn't have left the girl in the forest, and she obviously wanted to come. But was she really ready for where they were going?

They set up camp in a hollow between two large boulders, the land growing rockier and trees thinning as they climbed toward the pass that separated the Genga river valley from Yatiland.

Feynrick and Nauro busied themselves with the fur-and-poles *guyo* while Marea saw to the elk, a task she seemed to enjoy. Tai raised his eyebrows at Ella. "Help me gather wood?"

Feynrick chuckled without looking up. "Is that what you Achuri call it?"

Tai blushed and pulled Ella out, unable to think of a response.

"Interesting lessons today," Ella said when they were back in the trees. "Who would have thought you could sense revenants without being a shaman?"

"I didn't know you could sense them at all until a few weeks ago," Tai said, "but I'm starting to feel like the more I learn, the less I realize I actually know."

Ella laughed. "Try reading old Yersh scholarship. If you don't start with the ancients you'll have no idea what's going on, and even then," she shrugged. "I guess there was a reason I always preferred ethnography."

Tai bent and shook off a fallen tree limb. "Did you find anything strange about Nauro only having one revenant that's fit to put on us?"

"Strange, no. Infuriating? Yes. Another excuse to only train you, even if he's tolerating Marea and I. He was only really paying attention to your answers."

Tai nodded. "He does seem pretty single-minded. But think about it: he was waiting outside Ayugen for me to come to start training, so surely in that time he had gotten a revenant ready for it, and would have taken it with him when we went to the city, and then on this trip."

Ella nodded. "Yeah. So?"

"So Ydilwen was a shaman too, and Nauro took his revenant on our way back to Ayugen. He said not all revenants would 'serve,' but you'd think the newly-dead revenant of someone who'd *been a shaman* would work."

"Stains," Ella said. "Well it just means he really doesn't want anyone but you to learn shamanism. No surprises there."

Tai shrugged, using the limb to poke at a fallen cragbark. "And that he's comfortable lying. Makes me wonder how much we can believe what he's teaching us, other than what we can actually test."

Ella leaned into a dead branch to break it from the tree. "I guess it comes down to what his actual goal is. Maybe he has his reasons for only teaching you. Or maybe he wants to make sure we can't overpower him once he turns on us to take the spear."

Tai nodded, scanning the sparse trees for more dead wood. "Right. I've been thinking about that, but I still don't have a good answer. If I don't get to the stone, someone will, and they'll come for us. If we do get there, it will be before I'm Nauro's equal in shamanic power. He'll see to that. So I guess we have to have some kind of plan on how to keep him in check."

Ella broke another branch off. "A plan we can't even make until we know what he's capable of."

Tai took it from her. "A knowledge he's in control of."

"Looks like he's outmaneuvered us this time."

"Well he *is* seven times our age. Or maybe six, for you." He bent down to work at a fallen tree.

"Hey! I've got twenty-three summers, you know that!"

He wasn't always sure. He didn't think she'd *lie* about her age, but... "You know I don't care how old you are."

"I'm twenty-three," she said flatly.

"Okay, okay!" He held his hands up. "Anyway, I think the point is we'll have to watch what we tell him, and really think through what he's teaching us."

Ella kicked off a smaller branch on the tree. "Some of us have lived that way for a long time. Trusting people as much as you do is what seems crazy to me."

He paused. "Do you think I made a mistake with Marea?"

"No. She's young, and she's angry, but I don't think she actually wishes any of us harm. She just wants to go home."

"Probably too much to ask that she stops hating my guts."

Ella stacked her branches and turned back for camp. "Put it this way, if you can win her over, you can probably win over anyone in the Councilate. And if you can't, that would just make one small part of you a normal human being."

Tai smirked. "Hope you're not thinking of the part I'm thinking of."

She raised her eyebrows in mock surprise. "I couldn't say. Sleeping in a fur tent with three other people hasn't given me much chance to explore how all your parts are doing these days."

He raised his eyebrows. "Seems like we're pretty alone right here."

"Well," she said, dropping her armload with a clatter, "maybe a little exploration is in order."

8

*M*area was an icemonger.

At least, that's what she felt like: constantly cold, constantly wet, constantly walking without getting anywhere. Only here, instead of having a nice Worldsmouth sun shining down on her and the colorful trappings of civilization all around, she walked most of the day by frigid starlight surrounded by strangers and rebels.

And Ella, of course. Ellumia Aygla was the one redeeming aspect of this whole trip. By the time they climbed through the rocky gap at Ninefingers Pass, three days after she found them, she felt like she knew Ella as well as her best friend. Better, even, since it'd been hard to keep a best friend the last two years, with everyone in Newgen coming and going all the time.

"So you really kicked him in the cockwattle?" she asked one day, around the time the sun was setting, two past noon by a proper hourglass. Tai and Nauro were off somewhere being shamans, and Feynrick was back with the elk.

"Yes, I kicked him in the wattle," Ella said back, grinning. "My parents ran through all the good suitors pretty quick. By the time I turned fifteen, I swear, they were throwing merchant's bastards at me just in an attempt to get rid of me. And some of them thought, well, because they kept me locked up there, maybe I was crazy. Maybe I was desperate."

Marea snorted. "Bet that one learned his lesson."

"And a few of his friends. As I recall, I didn't have to put up with another suitor for a month and a half after that."

Marea whistled. "So you just didn't want to get married?"

"I didn't want my *parents* to get me married. To do *any*thing they wanted. It was a war of attrition: they kept me locked up, I kept their plans on hold. Someone had to give in, eventually, and it wasn't going to be me."

"So they did, eventually? Let you go?"

"No," Ella said, looking away. "I got away on my own."

"You *ran away*? Descending *god*scatter Ella, that's amazing!"

She pursed her lips. "You might not think so, if you were there."

"Why?"

"I had to hurt someone I cared about very much. And there's no taking that back."

"But that's always how it is in the stories! At least you've done something *interesting*."

This trip was probably the most interesting thing she'd ever done, and so far it was pretty boring. Except for the shamanic exercises.

Just then Feynrick trotted past them. "Mind the elk, would ya?"

Feynrick was nice, for a hill tribesman. Had funny stories to tell too, when he opened up, but right now he looked pretty serious.

"What's going on?" Ella asked.

"Tracks," he said briefly, way too nimble for his heavy form in those snownets. "Going to make sure Tai saw them."

Marea shared a glance with Ella. "I didn't see anything."

"Me neither."

Tai and Nauro came back in a bit, and Feynrick had them stop to look at some depressions in the snow.

"There are tracks here?" Marea asked. "I don't see anything."

"That's because you grew up in the city, lass," Feynrick said. "Three or four days old, I'd say, and someone moving like they wanted to watch but didn't want to be seen. See how the tracks stay behind that first row of trees?"

Tai nodded. "Still a long way from anything out here, though. Sure it isn't just some hunter from an outlying village?"

"Hunter would use the road," Feynrick said. "Easier."

"It could be a monk," Marea said, remembering her cartography lessons.

Everyone looked at her like she was stupid.

"What? There's a monastery near Ninefingers. Two, three days that way," she pointed west, "along the top of the ridge. Who knows what those monks could be up to?"

"Meditating on the saints, ain't they?" Feynrick asked, poking at one of the supposed tracks with a stick.

"The monasteries don't follow Yati beliefs," Ella said. "Or any belief system, as far as I've read. Though there isn't a lot of scholarship available on them."

"Monks come through Ayugen sometimes," Tai said. "I think on their way between here and somewhere in the ice sheet. If that's who this was, I don't think we need to worry. They seem pretty harmless."

Nauro rubbed his chin. "They might be more of a threat than you think, if their ire was raised. But still, no, I doubt this was the renunciants. As I recall they spend most of the cold months in meditation, rarely leaving their compounds. This was more likely a journeyman or other shaman, searching for revenants to thrall somewhere away from competition."

A shiver ran down Marea's spine, which was pretty amazing

since it was already freezing. "Like the one that attacked Tai and Ella?"

"Could be like that, yes," Nauro said. "Or it could be something different entirely."

That was helpful. They started walking again, but by common agreement Tai and Nauro stayed close, which was great because it meant she could listen in on Nauro's lessons. Tai's ghost had seated a few days ago, and Nauro had been trying to get him to see the ghosts ever since.

It was fascinating and infuriating. She was good at the exercises that didn't need a revenant, better than Tai as far as she could tell, and she was dying to try doing what he was, with a shamanic revenant. But according to Nauro they were hard to find, and he didn't have any, and on and on. She didn't believe a word of it, but what was she going to do?

She *hated* that feeling. Powerlessness.

So instead she listened along and tried to imagine what the revenants looked like as Nauro taught Tai, tried to overlay ghosts on the otherwise never-ending sameness landscape of snow and trees and broken rocks.

"It should look like a human figure distorted by water," Nauro was saying. "Elongated, maybe, and perhaps glowing on the edges. This one is Needles."

Marea smiled at this—everyone had taken to using her names for Nauro's ghosts.

"It's a relatively recent death, which means it hasn't had much time to emaciate. Something like Chill, on the other hand, has been without an *uai* stream so long it looks insubstantial even to a full seeker."

Tai grunted, eyes strained and resonance humming faintly from him.

"Why do you keep it then, if it's so starved?" Marea asked.

Nauro looked peeved, which was one of the reasons she interrupted him so often. She might be powerlessness, but she could be *annoying* at least. And maybe learn something.

"Because this is one of Semeca's old thralls," he said.

"Meaning if you can sic it on someone, then it'll start feeding you power?"

"Yes. Now quiet, Tai is trying to concentrate."

"Wouldn't it be easier to find someone to sic it on if we weren't in the middle of nowhere?"

"Yes. But there are a lot of sacrifices I'm making on this journey."

Meaning having to put up with her. Very funny. *Gods,* she wished she had a revenant like Tai, so she could beat him at his own game. Or that she had any resonance at all. Maybe Nauro would think twice about insulting her if she could get as strong as Feynrick, or as fast as Ella.

Instead she was a blank. And an orphan. And barely being allowed to tag along, even if they were taking the slowest and most ridiculously roundabout way to get home she could imagine. It would make a story to tell her cousins when she got home, at least.

If they cared. She'd never been close with them, and it had been years now. But who else did she have?

They are family, her mother would say. *The only people you can rely on in this world.*

Mom. Marea shoved down the twinge of grief in her and shut up. The second revenant she'd defeated, in her stupid quest to try to prove that she *wasn't* a blank, that maybe yura just didn't work for her, had been pretending to be her mother. It was awful, but she hadn't really been nice to her mom before she died, so it'd been good too. Forced her to realize she'd been a brat to a woman who meant well, despite her shortcomings. So now she still heard her mom sometimes, in her head, but not as a revenant. Just as a memory, something she hadn't appreciated when it'd been real life.

They made camp that night right by the side of the road. Marea gave Bellows and Farts their daily ration of precious barley before finding a patch of wintergrass to tie them up in for the night. Much as she was ready to be done with this journey, she was coming to love their daily routines: Nauro setting up the *guyo*, Feynrick scouting the area and laying his little traps, Tai and Ella going off to 'gather firewood' and probably make out. Much as the thought of kissing Tai was disgusting, she still envied Ella. A lover would make this trip *so* much better.

Or so she imagined. She *would* find someone when she got back to Worldsmouth. Especially now that her parents wouldn't have any say on who.

They shared a pot of hare and wintergrass soup around the fire that night, *guyo* pleasantly hot after another freezing day. The thing was basically a tent made of furs with a hole in the top for smoke, but it was as warm as any house she'd ever been in. It probably helped that it was designed for two, maybe three people max, so they slept more or less on top of each other all night. She quickly discovered Feynrick was a heat box, even if he snored.

"So what's our story?" Marea asked, after one of Feynrick's extended and very likely made-up stories of personal bravery in the Counciliate army.

"What's that, lass?" Feynrick asked, seeming stirred from his own dreamland. The man took his lies seriously.

"When we get to the waystone," she said. "Or anywhere bigger than a village, really. You don't want other shamans to recognize Tai, right? So what's our story? You don't see two lighthaired ladies traveling with a bunch of darkhaired men every day."

Feynrick cleared his throat. "That's *red* hair, young miss. Not to be mistaken for dark."

Same difference. "Right. But still."

"With any luck," Nauro said, still holding his cooling bowl of soup, "there won't be anyone there, and we can just be who we are."

"With as much as you've been talking up the waystones and how power-hungry all your friends are, that seems unlikely."

Tai set down his bowl. "When we went to Gendrys, we said we were all guards for the Lady Aygla—" Ella snorted at this "—and that seemed to work fine."

"Really? I heard it ended up with the town burning and you almost dead."

"Not our fault," Feynrick said. "It was a good story."

"But you're right," Ella said. "If there *are* people at the waystone, they are likely to be well-educated, and suspicious of anyone showing up who *isn't* aware of recent, um, shamanic events."

Marea looked around. "So we tell them we're the Ayugen cell?"

Nauro cleared his throat. "I don't think that would be wise. Cells can be... aggressively competitive. But sometimes the best lies are those closest to the truth."

"Meaning what?" She swore the man said the most vague thing possible on purpose.

"We tell them Ella and I are scholars, writing a treatise on the waystones, and investigating reports of a disturbance recently. Ella and I can speak scholarly Yersh, we stand out most in terms of hair color, and it will put other shamans at ease while allowing us to gather information, should they know any of interest."

He sounded doubtful about this last. "And me?" Marea asked, annoyed that she wasn't even included in his obviously well-thought-out plan.

He rubbed his chin. "Ella's daughter, perhaps?"

Ella's back went straight at this. "My *daughter?* My younger sister, more like."

Nauro raised his eyebrows noncommittally. "Younger sister, then, perhaps by marriage. The Ayglas are known for frequent divorcings, are they not?"

They certainly were, or had been in the last few years, but Ella didn't blush at it. "I suppose," she said noncommittally.

That was strange. The Ayglas were also known for their fiery defensiveness, one of the reasons Marea hadn't brought it up to begin with.

"That settled, then?" Feynrick asked. "Got a mind to get some shut-eye while the star's down."

They all settled in, Tai banking the coals as Ella painstakingly undressed beneath a large sheet—all part of their nightly ritual. Marea was shattered if she was going to undress in a tent full of men, so she slept in her clothes, even though the fabric was starting to itch. Thank the prophet she was between moons, at least. Her eyelids grew heavy.

She was just in the middle of telling a handsome and roguish young man she'd rather have sweet tea than flavored ice, given her recent encounters, when Feynrick twitched, startling her awake. She jerked her arm back from him—how had that gotten there?—then realized Tai was standing with a dagger in his hand.

"What's going on?" she asked, and was met with furious stares from Tai and Feynrick.

Scatters. Something not good then. Snow crunched outside and a chill shot down her back. Who was out there? It could be anything. Attackers. Shamans. Wolves. Tribesmen.

Thoughts were still shooting through her brain like wildfire when Nauro rose, bare chest muscled in the dim glow of the coals. He held up a hand, then a voice spoke outside.

"I know you are in there," it said. "I can *see* you."

"Whattheshatters," Marea whispered, clutching at Feynrick's leg.

"And I can see you," Nauro replied, voice raised but calm. "An impressive little collection you've built, friend, but I advise you to move on."

"And I advise you to *kneel*," the man said, growling the last word.

The *guyo* ripped apart around them, frigid air rushing in, revealing a single figure floating in the moonlight. At the same time something pressed down on Marea, hard, and Tai and Feynrick stumbled down.

Marea screamed, trying to push up, but her blanket had turned to stone. Stone that pressed down, like it was growing heavier by the second. Furs flew like a spooked flock of gulls, though the night was dead still. The torn pieces of the *guyo* had a will of their own, wrapping Tai and Feynrick, piling onto Ella, pressing down on Marea.

Only Nauro remained standing, somehow impervious to the furs circling him. "I advise you to move *on*—" he was saying, till a fur wrapped his face, muffling his voice.

Oh, Gods. They were going to die. She was never going to see home and they were going to die, right here, right now. This guy, whoever he was, had taken their *uai* like the other attackers, and he was going to kill Nauro and Nauro was their only chance and—

He is an amateur, Nauro's voice came in her mind, clear as a bell. *Powerful but simple. I can divert his* uai *stream, but it will take time. Use your resonance. Fight him. It will get easier.*

"I don't have a resonance!" Marea screamed, just as she felt two resonances ring her bones like a struck bell. Tai and Feynrick —they must have heard the voice too. Nauro probably wasn't even talking to her. She struck anyway, needing to do *something*, able to do that at least. Maybe her resonance would help with a chord, even if she *was* blank.

Feynrick roared beside her, and she could feel him pushing up, even as more furs slapped down on him.

"*Kneel* I said!" the man cried, and even through her fear Marea could tell his voice was a little too high for the tone he was using, like a man pretending to be a god. It was just the slightest bit pathetic, even if she *was* going to die.

Marea focused on that. Anything was better than this crushing fear, than the feeling her lungs couldn't draw breath. Pathetic. The man was pathetic.

In the dim light of the swirling embers and moon, she saw Feynrick struggle to his feet, shouting something about being rude, swinging his axe wildly at furs flying from the darkness. Tai was faring worse, in the air now but being buffeted around by furs, trying to pull him back down.

"No!" she shouted. She had *seen* Tai in action, the man was amazing, and Feynrick was great, so much better than this pathetic thing attacking them. They *needed* to win. She *needed* to not die, and oh Gods there was the fear was coming up again—

"Kneel *now* or the women die," the man shouted, still in his pathetic voice, and suddenly the weight on her was double. The breath squeezed from her lungs. Across the scattered coals Ella screamed, furs pressed down on her too. Timeslipping wasn't much use in this situation, a detached and rational part of her brain noted. You needed raw strength.

She had neither. Then panic clawed through even those thoughts. She tried to scream but there was no air.

9

Tai slammed sideways, another fur tearing at him. He restruck his *uai* and tried again to push forward. If he could just *reach* the man—

A fur tore at him, wrapping around his neck and squeezing. Tai responded with a shove of his own, air intended to blast the thing off, but there was no air between it and his skin.

Use your resonance, Nauro had said. *Fight him. It will get easier*, he said.

Easy to say when you weren't choking.

Tai shot himself left and up in the air, spinning, two furs pulling at one leg while others slammed into him like stone hammers, managing to loose the fur from his neck. Whoever this man was, he didn't play by normal rules, like Ydilwen hadn't, but he wasn't invincible. Tai wafted air again, creating a swirling sphere around himself, trying to keep the furs tangled and off him.

It sort of worked, but he made no progress forward. Below him Feynrick bellowed, swaddled almost too thick in furs to make out the man, but still struggling forward, arms completely trapped at his sides.

What was *taking* Nauro so long? Was the man actually not any good at shamanism?

Tai shoved forward again, but the furs pressed in despite his attempts, stopping him, buffeting him, forcing him ever downward.

"Kneel, I said!" the man shouted. "Kneel now or the women die!"

Below him Ella screamed, and for a moment he almost lost it all in fear. She was going to die. He couldn't kill this man in time and Nauro didn't care and Ella was going to be crushed to death, or smothered.

Maybe that was Nauro's plan all along.

Anger sparked hot, that anyone would try to harm her, that she who was so precious would end just a pawn in the games of men too powerful to be stopped.

No. This man was powerful but Tai had killed a *god*. He just needed to get smarter. Wafting wasn't working. So what? Shamanism? But he could barely see revenants, let alone try to control them.

Mindsight. The resonance Naveinya had left him. Semeca's resonance. Tai struck it even as he kept swerving and dodging and spinning air around him, trying desperately to stay off the ground, because he knew it was over if he was forced down. Struck mindsight and *peered*.

There. Amidst the waves of fear and anger and resolve was something like glee. *Glee?*

Tai peered in closer, stream of thoughts rushing under his eyes, but yes, the attacker was gleeful. Drunk on power. Cedrig, his name was. A minor Galya functionary stationed in Seingard. A secret ninespears member. Someone who had left everything as soon as he heard Semeca was dead, realizing the potential.

A man who wanted to be a god.

Tai slammed down, a fur blasting through his vortex to hit

him in the face, pushing him toward the swirling bed of coals. He responded with his own blast, sideways, twisting, ripping free.

Not good enough. He pushed deeper into Cedrig's mind, upstream, back from his thoughts to his intentions, his plans. Ella screamed again, but it was muffled, Marea's voice almost inaudible in the roar of wind and flood of thoughts. They were dying. He needed something better, some trigger, needed it *now*.

There. A face Cedrig feared, a stern-faced Galya higher up, shouting at him. Teterwel. Shaming him in front of the entire Seingard contingent. The latest in a long line of men shaming him. The last. The reason Cedrig would become a god.

"Teterwel!" Tai shouted, trying to shock the man, trying to get past his façade. "You are no god! I know! *Teterwel!*"

For just a moment, the winds stopped. The furs dropped. The man's mouth opened in an O in the moonlight. Tai shot forward, seizing the chance, pulling the dagger he kept on him even in slumber.

Then Cedrig responded, screaming something lost in the confusion, and a hundred furs flew at Tai, surrounding him, wrapping him in crushing stone.

10

One moment Ella couldn't breathe, stars dancing behind her eyes as her lungs collapsed, ribs unable to push against the crushing weight. The next it was gone. Her lungs sucked frigid air, and her racing mind took in the scene in an instant.

Marea, sprawled in the remnants of the *guyo*. Nauro, standing tall and straight, deep in concentration. Tai, vanishing under a ball of furs, the attacker screaming at him.

He was going to kill Tai. Nauro was too slow, Feynrick too slow, they were all too slow.

Not Ella. She struck resonance hard, the wind stilling around her, furs freezing in air. She stood, every bone and muscle aching in her body. She would not lose Tai. Now or ever.

She ran, straight over the coals, heat barely touching her feet, skin insensitive to the cold, pulling the axe from Feynrick's stilled fingers. Ran straight for the attacker and swung.

And missed. He was wafting too high. She couldn't even hit his feet.

Shattercocks. Find something to stand on?

She looked around wildly, furs drifting in air, knowing time was limited, even with the amount of *uai*-filled wintergrass she'd eaten. The *guyo* was scattered, elk off in the trees, firewood burnt. Nothing.

"Shatsickles," she cursed, looking up again. Her knives—if she could find them she could throw them, but their packs were scattered too, indistinct from furs and everything else in the dim moonlight.

No time. "Here goes nothing," she muttered, wishing she'd taken Feynrick up on those axe lessons.

She swung the axe back and hurled.

It wobbled up in the air, bouncing harmlessly off the attacker.

"Cockstains," she cursed, crunching through the snow to retrieve it. Tried again, failed again. A few furs drifted toward her.

How much longer? Her back was starting to ache, and she hated seeing Tai buried in furs up there, even if this was all less than a single breath's time for him. Threw again. Missed again.

"Stains!" she screamed, world dead and cold around her. "No! Shatter this! This isn't happening!"

She threw again, and this time managed a deep cut on the man's forehead, her slip so deep she had the axe back in her hand before it started to bleed. It was a start, but her spine was truly aching now—time for maybe one more throw. She hauled back and hurled the thing skyward, hopes not high at this point.

It turned, and tumbled, and stuck handle-first into his eye.

11

*T*ai stared at the axe, sticking blade-out from the dying man, blood still pounding in his ears.

"What in bloody boarscock?" Feynrick asked beside him, looking from the dead man to Ella. "You're lying. Don't know why ye are and don't mean offense, miss, but that throw's impossible."

Ella looked baffled. "I guess I just got lucky?"

She also looked freezing, standing there in her shift. Tai summoned the *uai* still in him and began sweeping the scattered furs together, looking for any large enough to cover her.

"Thank ancestors you did," Tai said. "The rest of us were too busy dying."

There. He found a large scrap where three pelts were still stitched together, and draped it over her bare shoulders. *Distractingly* bare, even in the freezing cold. Something about almost dying always made him want her more.

"Speaking of which," Marea said, trying to stand and keep her pile of furs on her, "what are we going to do? It's freezing and we don't have a fire and it's the middle of the night."

"Got to gather the furs," Feynrick said. "Won't last another night without them, and take too long to hunt down this many animals. Stitch 'em back together once it warms up."

"And until then?"

"Until then we walk," Tai said. "You don't stay warm standing still, and a fire will do us little good without the *guyo*, even after we gathered wood and lit it." Prophets knew he and Aelya had spent enough winter nights walking the streets to keep warm, when they had no place to sleep or no fuel to heat it.

They got to work, Feynrick going after furs in the woods and Marea going to check on the elk, tied up a few hundredpace away.

Nauro stood in the same place he had since the beginning, furs fallen in a pile around him, face a mask of concentration. Gathering up the revenants the other shaman had thralled?

"What *was* that, Nauro?" Tai asked, picking through the snow for their belongings, scattered in the fight.

"Journeyman," the fyelocke answered, eyes focused in the distance.

"The lowest in your order?" Ella asked, finding her clothes and dropping furs to pull them on.

"Middling," Nauro said, like he was dream talking, "but this one had a healthy *uai* stream. Likely been out here a while."

"He was insane," Tai said, remembering the quick sight he had into the man's mind. "I—read his thoughts, before he died. Thought he was a god or something."

And that was reason to kill him? Ydilwen said inside. *The man was abused all his life. You saw that.*

Ella wrapped a beaver pelt around her head. "Makes sense, with him telling us to kneel."

Tai opened his mouth and closed it again. They'd *had* to kill him, right?

Sure. Like you had to kill me.

"Not uncommon, unfortunately," Nauro said, turning from his

distant stare. "An increased *uai* stream without preparation can make one feel... more than human."

"How're you feeling, then?" Ella asked, Tai recognizing the too-casual tone of her voice. She saw the danger: whatever Nauro had been before, if he'd just taken all the attacker's revenants, he would be at least that powerful now. Enough to kill them all, in other words. "You just thralled his revenants, didn't you?"

"I added them to my stream, yes," Nauro said. "But this is not a new experience for me, and I was prepared for it as a journeyman, before I ever increased my *uai*. This man, I doubt he had risen that high in the training."

"He was a bureaucrat," Tai said. "Mid-level in Galya. Came here from Seingard, seeking souls."

Is Nauro any different? Why do you not kill him too? Or anyone seeking power? Because these are your friends?

Yes, Tai thought back. Because they are not trying to kill me.

Yet. Give Nauro time—once you stop being useful to him, you will be a threat.

Nauro nodded. "Smart then, at least. Plenty of revenants out here to take. He was likely gathering them in the wild, then traveling to the cities to attach them to new hosts."

Ella pulled a rucksack from the snow, voice still casual. "So you can do all the things he was doing? Control objects, float?"

"I could already do all that," the fyelocke said, bland as if he was talking about a second helping of soup. "But yes, now I can do it better."

"Then why did it take you so long to stop him?" Tai asked, unable to keep the anger in his voice. They had almost died. *Ella* had almost died, while Nauro was doing what? Increasing his own personal power? Was that all he was after?

He's a ninespears. That's what they are.

"A battle between shamans is not primarily a battle of *uai*," the man said, sounding again like a teacher. "It is a battle for control of revenants. He either didn't know this, or thought he could overwhelm me too quickly for it to matter."

"Looked to me like he was just better than you," Feynrick said, coming in from the trees with a pile of furs. "If Ella and the milkweed hadn't fought him the way they did, we'd probably all be eating dirt about now."

Nauro paused a full breath. Deciding what to say? Choosing a lie?

"Yes," he said at last. "The man *was* stronger than me. Not more knowledgeable, or more skilled, but while I have been waiting in the woods for Tai to make his decision, others have been actively gathering Semeca's power, and have done in the space of a month what it took decades to do previously."

"And we're to believe," Ella said, sounding as hot as Tai felt, "that you weren't also spending a lot of that month in the wild like this man and Ydilwen, gathering up unclaimed revenants?"

"I was," Nauro said. "But unclaimed revenants do little until they are attached to a host and begin harvesting *uai*. And there was no one in the southern forest to attach a revenant to, and precious little time in Ayugen to find hosts."

"So you risked it all," Ella said, voice softening. "You knew others would be outstripping you, journeymen like this one, and still you risked it on Tai agreeing to tutelage."

"Yes," Nauro said. "I am not one of your Cult of the Blood, but I have faith in Tai. There have been many who have become powerful in the last few centuries. Many who have made their tries at the gods. Only one who has succeeded."

"Then you will remember the terms of our deal," Tai said, dropping another stack of furs and standing up straight. "Any power that we gain, we share. That means this man's power too."

Ella and Feynrick stopped gathering furs, the clearing suddenly getting very quiet.

"You are not ready," Nauro said. "I can't share these with you if you don't know how to take them."

"Then teach me."

"The—thralling revenants is not something taught until the journeyman stage at least. You are barely an initiate."

"And as we agreed, this is not a normal training. You don't teach it to initiates because it's impossible, or because it's customary?"

As he asked, he struck mindsight and pushed hard at Nauro's mind. The man was normally impenetrable, the current of his thoughts flowing deep underground, but just in case. He needed to know how much he could trust this man. *If* he could trust him.

He caught a bare glimpse—not of frustration, or calculation. Of fear.

What was Nauro *afraid* of?

"More of custom," Nauro said at last. "We can try. But I can't promise it will work, or work out the way you think."

"Story of my life," Tai said, relaxing some. Fear was better than calculation—it pointed to an honest motive. And the man had agreed, at least for now. Good enough.

And so, you will take on power too, as I did, as the dead man did. How long will you deny what you are?

Tai opened his mouth to respond and found he had no answer. He bent back to the furs.

12

The Yati are the only people accounted little faith in the Prophet. I wonder, did he skip their rocky valley in his pilgrimage from the ice sheet to Aran? Or did his tales, preserved everywhere in their own cultural inflections, get absorbed somehow into the Yati mythos of the genitors? Markels speaks of one genitor unlike the others, not renowned for violence, fertility, or bawdy wisdom, theorizing this was the Prophet. Markels, however, was no ethnologist, and his account is likely apocryphal.
  —Eylan Ailes, *Treatise on World Religions*

The weather warmed some as they descended the slopes from Ninefingers Pass toward the Yanu river, trees thickening and bare patches of ground beginning to appear. For Ella it was like walking into Markels' classic *Among the Yati*, the descriptions she had pored over in her youth coming to life in tidy Yati terrace gardens and hilltop villages. These were still sparse and often so hidden behind forest Feynrick had to point them out to her, but it was exciting nonetheless. After the Achuri, the Yati were the most recently-colonized people, and this far upriver their lifestyles would still be similar to what they'd been before Councilate influence. Unspoiled.

She took a deep breath, catching the scent of burning dung and roasting meat on the air as they passed near another village. "I have always wanted to come here."

Feynrick barked a laugh. "To the hinterlands? These people are savages."

"Aren't you... one of them?" Marea asked. The girl was starting to open up, slowly.

"Sure," Feynrick said, "if one of your saltmarsh peasants is the same as a city-dwelling House daughter. I grew up in the warring counties, just upriver from Yatiport. People up here? They're still breeding with dogs and building with mud bricks. Barely call 'em Yati, if you ask me."

Ella shrugged at Marea. She doubted very much that the people here bred with dogs, but it was good to remember that what looked like one culture and people from the outside always had divisions within it, not least between rural and urban.

"How far from here to the waystone?" Tai asked.

"Piss if I know," Feynrick said. "A day, maybe two?"

It turned out to be more, but the going was easier once the land flattened out, and though they kept watch at night they saw no sign of other shamans wandering like the one they had fought. The land was stippled with steep hills, the highest of these cleared of trees and planted in stepped terraces fed by an intricate system of waterways.

"How could savages build something like that?" Ella asked, gesturing at another terraced and fortified Yati settlement. Feynrick insisted they not make contact, for their own safety.

The burly red-haired man snorted. "That's nothing. Wait till you see the warring counties."

Tai's lessons continued on apace. Nauro had either relented or given up fighting Tai on letting her and Marea listen in, which was both frustrating and gratifying. Frustrating because she couldn't *see* what Tai was seeing, could only feel the occasional revenant that passed too close. It was like learning to play fox-and-rat with a blindfold on. Only this fox and rat was much more than a game.

Gratifying too because it was still *learning*. She'd read about none of this, heard of none it, in years of studying the resonances and cultural understandings of them. The ninespears really had managed to keep their arts a secret, for centuries if Nauro was telling the truth.

Which made sense, if you considered the archrevenants would kill anyone with the knowledge. According to Tai, that was why Semeca had risked attacking them directly.

The arts themselves were fascinating too, like learning a new way of seeing. She practiced what she could of the skills Nauro taught Tai, determined to be ready for when she finally got a revenant.

Because she *would* get one. One way or another. If Nauro didn't want it, then she did.

This morning, their third since the night attack, Nauro was pushing a revenant into the trees and challenging Tai to find it. Because Tai needed *yura* to see revenants with his resonance, and they hadn't brought much with them—mainly to use in barter—they often practiced without his new resonance. Which meant Ella could do it too.

"There," Nauro said. "Where is it now?"

Ella searched the trees, unfocusing her eyes like Nauro had taught, looking for any kind of smudge or disturbance. Theoretically you could see revenants without resonance, they were just much more indistinct, like details in starlight instead of day.

"High up, about thirty paces ahead," Tai said, before she'd seen anything. "In the yewleaf."

"*Cock*stains," Marea cursed, following the lessons just as closely as Ella and much more competitive about it. "I almost had that one."

"Again," Nauro said. "Find it and name it."

Weighted silence. Ella's eyes flew over the draw they were passing through, trees clustered around a wide, shallow creek. There?

"The rock outcropping," Ella said. "To the right of the dead needleaf."

"Yes," Nauro said, sparing as ever with his praise. "And its name?"

"Chills," Marea said without pause. She'd given most of the revenants their names.

"No."

"*What?*" She sounded indignant, though it was difficult to name the revenants without feeling them.

"Ashes," Tai said. "Winding around the lower branches."

"Good," Nauro smiled. "Now the touchings. Two and you're out."

This was a separate exercise, one of Ella's favorites. Rather than try to identify the revenant, which was still easiest for her by touch, the goal here was to be the last one touched, which meant seeing the revenant and dodging it. Not to mention not tipping off your competitors if you did manage to see one.

"What are the stakes?" Ella asked casually, already unfocusing her eyes to try seeing the revenants. Or *un*seeing them, as Marea said.

"Stakes?" Nauro asked. "The stakes are will you get better at this or not."

"Oh, come on," Ella answered. "Make it interesting. Say, I'm the last one standing twice in a row and you give me a revenant?"

Nauro smiled. "Very well. But those are only one side of the stakes. What's in it for me, if you don't win?"

Tai eyed her and she shot him a frown. She wasn't going to gamble Nauro with *that*. "*Guyo* duty," she said. "You're free and clear the next two nights if I fail. I'll gather wood *and* put up the tent."

The strange man raised his eyebrows. "High stakes indeed. Very well. You're on."

"Me, too," Marea cut in at once, and Ella smiled despite the banter that followed. Smiled because the fyelocke had basically admitted he had a revenant to give her, after denying it.

Not so ancient and wise after all, Mr. Ninespears.

"Begin!" Nauro snapped, and Ella ducked left on instinct. Nauro would be trying to eliminate her even more than usual. She unfocused her eyes and spun in a circle, listening for watery rustles, sniffing for dead leaves.

There! Maybe? She dodged right, heart pounding. If she could get a revenant, she could finally put this all in practice.

She could finally *do* something to protect Tai.

Ella heard a rustle and ducked, feeling a faint chill along her back. Nauro was definitely pushing revenants at her. Of course. It was unfair, but her whole life had been unfair. She knew how to use that.

Ella stood abruptly and ran for Tai, as fast as their clunky snownets would let her. Nauro wanted to target her? Fine. She'd use that. Behind her Marea cursed—good, one touched. Now if she could just get Tai—

A chill washed over her. "Shat it!" she cursed. "Again!"

They went again, and this time she was more careful, running for Tai every time she caught hint of a revenant, dodging around them but cutting it close enough that the revenants would hopefully brush *him* as Nauro tried to herd them toward her.

It worked—the next round she got Tai out first, and eliminated

Marea soon after. Then Nauro started to wise up to her tricks, and it seemed like as soon as he said *start*, the air would be a rush of blurry shapes coming at her from all sides.

She got touched first the next three rounds. On the bright side, she was really learning to see the things.

"Enough," Nauro said at last, far too soon, when they were all out of breath and Marea was flat on her back in the snow after tripping over a log, and Feynrick was hoarse from laughing. He, of course, thought the pack of them running away from invisible monsters was hilarious.

Nauro siccing the revenants on her on purpose, to keep her from winning? Not as hilarious, but nothing she could do about it.

"Two nights without *guyo* duty," Nauro mused, mouth twitching in a smile. "What will I even *do* with all my time?"

Ella stayed silent, having learned by now she only made herself look stupid when she spoke in anger. But she *would* get a revenant. She *would* learn shamanism. Maybe if there were other shamans at the waystone, she could convince one of them to give her a training revenant.

Without revealing their real identity, of course.

"So why," Marea asked Nauro between pants, as Feynrick put together some leftovers for lunch, "isn't your head a cloud of revenants? Surely you've got a bunch of them thralled."

"Thralled, yes," Nauro said. "But *with* me? No. What's the point? Once a revenant is tied into your *uai* stream, there's no need to be physically proximal to each other. Otherwise you'd have to keep all your thralls within walking distance, or risk losing the *uai* they're feeding you."

"So you just—left them somewhere?"

"Mine are nearby," Nauro said. "I gave them instructions to fan out in the woods and look for hosts. I'd rather not tip any other shamans off to my *uai* stream, and I certainly don't want to show up with a host of revenants about me, if there's company at the waystone."

That made sense. "But what about us?" Ella asked. "If we meet shamans, surely it will look strange to have five adults with only Tai attached to a revenant, and even then only for his lower resonance."

"I'm glad you brought that up." Nauro cleared his throat. "Unpleasant at it might sound, I'm afraid I'm going to have to attach revenants to all of you for the rest of the journey, so that we don't stand out. A single revenant is fine, as in the north many people barely put off enough *uai* to feed one, but having none is unusual indeed."

"Another ghost?" Feynrick bellowed. "On me?"

"No," Marea snapped.

"Fine," Ella said. "One on condition."

Nauro raised an eyebrow, but he knew what she was going to ask for. He had to.

"Put a mosstongue spirit on me. Make me an initiate too."

"I told you, I don't have any that are fit for training."

"But you agreed in the last exercise to put one on me if I won. Meaning you have one you can do it with."

Nauro smiled. "I did agree to that. But not to *when* I would put it on you. Didn't you say you were a calculor once, my dear? I'd expect more attention to detail."

Ella clenched her fists and held her tongue. The man could be *insufferable.* "Then put one on that's not fitting. We'll work it out. I find it hard to believe that in all the revenants you captured in the forest, and all those you took from the last shaman, that there aren't any mosstongue spirits."

Nauro sighed. "This is why we train acolytes and initiates for years before giving them a revenant. You are smart, Ellumia, but you do not have all the information you need to draw conclusions in this matter. The revenants I have been gathering, that the other shamans are gathering, are *mindseye* revenants. Entirely. There is no point in taking on other revenants—they are still thralled to an archrevenant somewhere. In fact, it is highly dangerous to do so."

"Why?" Ella asked, unable to stop sounding petulant.

"Because when you thrall a revenant, its *uai* goes to you rather than the archrevenant. And if that minor subtraction from their *uai* stream happens to draw their attention, your death will be sudden and swift. They do not tolerate shamans, because we are the only true danger to their power. This is why we train journeymen for years before teaching them to thrall. A single mistake could destroy an entire cell."

Descending Gods—draw an *archrevenant* down? That *was* serious. And yet— "How then did you have a mosstongue spirit to put on Tai? Wouldn't taking it also draw the ire of the gods?"

"No. Not so long as I didn't try to thrall it, to take its *uai*. Which is why you can all feel very safe—I am not going to put mindseye revenants on you, so your *uai* will not be entering my stream. Instead you'll be feeding the old gods just as surely as humankind has been since before the Prophet."

Ella clenched her fists. "And these other revenants you are able to easily find, but not a mosstongue for me?"

Nauro's mouth twitched—a sure sign he was irritated. Good. Maybe she would wear him down through sheer strength of will. "Again, you know enough to sound intelligent, but not enough to actually be that way. Not just any revenant will do. I will let you know when I find one that fits."

"We already have one that does. Tai's revenant. Surely it's seated by now. Take it off and put it on me."

"It has seated, but for whatever reason he hasn't attracted a secondary revenant yet. I imagine a mind as—experienced as his does not look as attractive to a revenant seeking a stable host."

Or because Nauro was keeping any secondary revenants away —but Ella didn't say that. Enough. She would find another way.

"Fine. Give me a brawler, if you can. I've always dreamed of having a brawler's strength in slip."

"Timeslip brawler slips are fearsome indeed," Nauro said. "Very well. Prepare yourself."

Ella did, but very little changed, just a slight tingle in her forehead. Marea, however, gasped.

"I can see it!" she cried, staring at Ella. "I can see your revenant!"

Tai stared at her a moment, then his eyes widened too. "I can too!"

"Yes," Nauro said. "Revenants are more visible and most vulnerable the moment they attach. For many of them, it is like being woken from a deep sleep, and they do not have their wits about them enough to hide. Marea, Feynrick? Preferences on your ghosts?"

"Anything," Marea said at once. "Everything. A slip. Make me a timeslip." Her eyes cut at Ella.

"I'm afraid I don't have any of those—they *are* quite rare. A wafter, maybe?"

"Fine. Yes." She looked lit up, and Ella could understand it. Marea had worked for months in her school, helping other people come into their power, and knowing the whole time she was a blank. How exposed must she feel, how vulnerable, being out here without even a resonance?

If nothing else, even if Nauro abandoned them, they knew how to overcome revenants. In fact, if they timed it right, the power they offered on first overcoming might be very useful.

"Wafter for me too, then," Feynrick said. "If ye have to." He grunted as the revenant hit him—Ella could see it clearly as it attached, a drawn-out wavery form, like looking up at someone from beneath the surface of a murky lake.

"And for yourself?" Ella asked, eager to see it a third time.

"Oh, a mindseye, I suppose," Nauro said. "I've actually kept my original revenant all these years. Comes on and off like an old coat."

"How far are we from the stone, anyway?" Marea asked, after the novelty of the visible revenants had worn off. They didn't seem to be doing anything but clinging to their host's backs, sort of like a worn-out cape. Made of smoke.

"I'm hoping to reach it today," Nauro said. "I recall a few low draws like this near the site."

"Well, thank the Prophet. I for one am looking forward to *not* having to walk for a day or two."

"Just do not get lazy because of it. Remember most of the world's shamans will be thinking of visiting this place, and the archrevenants will be taking special interest too. Watch your tongue. You have still seen little, in terms of what these people are capable of."

"I saw Semeca," Marea said, but her voice had gone quiet, and they didn't speak again until they saw the stone.

13

Tai almost missed it, blue starlight drawing long shadows over the snow-white valley ahead, as they crested a long saddle between two rocky hills. It looked like one big shadow—except for the tip of the stone, catching the star's failing light.

Marea sucked in a breath. "Is that—"

"It is," Nauro said. "The Yati Waystone, also known as the Wanderer, named by some the Sounding Stone, though reasons why are lost to history."

What surprised Tai, though, was not the size of the stone—it did stand double the tallest tree's height, but he had seen larger boulders on the way here. It was the snow.

There wasn't any.

"It's—warm?" Tai asked. "Where's the snow?"

The stone stood in the center of a circular bowl perhaps two hundred paces across, free of snow. There was green grass, even.

Nauro shook his head. "It shouldn't be warm. Unless—"

Tai met Ella's eyes, a shock of excitement running through him. "Unless this was Semeca's stone," she said.

"Unless there's *uai* pouring from it."

"Too bad if so," Feynrick said, axes clinking on his belt. "Because someone beat us to it."

Tai focused on the miniature valley, still small in the distance. Yes, there were tents—fifteen, maybe twenty of them. Ella drew in a breath, and Nauro gave an uncharacteristic curse, though it was in no language Tai understood.

"What would you estimate," Tai asked the Yati militiaman. "Thirty people? More?"

Feynrick grunted. "More like forty I'd say, judging by fire rings. A lot more than we can battle, is the short of it."

Worry wormed its way up Tai's spine. "If that's the stone, we have to get down there. Get to it before they do."

"Calm yourself," Nauro said, sounding peaceful despite his earlier outburst. "If they knew how to get the stone open, they would have done so by now. There is no guarantee this party even knows of Semeca or the real purpose of the waystones."

"Be a piss of a coincidence if not," Feynrick said.

Tai nodded. "Maybe better if one of us goes down alone and feels it out."

The Yatiman shook his head. "This main of a road, if they've got any kind of training they know we're here. Might as well all go."

"I'll stay here," Marea chimed in. "No need for us all to get killed, right?"

Tai glanced at her, not wanting to put the girl on the spot, and not needing more than a glance to read the fear in her eyes. No wonder. She was physically weak with a blank resonance—all the danger of the past few months would have been double for her. It was a wonder she'd made it through all the Broken attacks on Ayugen.

"You can stay if you want," was all he said. "We'll come back when it's safe."

Her chin shot up. "Oh, no. You're not leaving me behind. I'll be fine."

Prophets, the girl was harder to read than Aelya drunk on dreamleaf. "Alright then. But let's go slow, make lots of noise, be sure if they don't know we're here yet, they figure it out before we're on top of them."

Feynrick nodded and they made their way down, rattling the bells on the elk and Ella beginning to talk like he rarely heard her, in Yersh so thick with scholarly words he could hardly parse it, falling into her supposed role of researcher. Nauro joined in with Yersh just as thick, and Tai let the language wash over him, focusing instead on his other senses.

No fresh tracks in the snow—the other party had been here a while. No scouts, no visible ambushes—they were either very good, weren't trying to keep people away, or didn't know the true nature of the stone.

Nauro had said he would know if the stone was active, that it would feel different. Tai glanced at him. The man seemed unfazed —but then, he always seemed unfazed. Maybe it was a product of long life—he had gotten the impression little affected Semeca either, in those few eternal moments he'd spent in her mind.

Hard to imagine. Life had been nothing but surprises and danger as far back as he could recall.

The road had a small spur turning toward the bowl around the stone. They were nearly to the edge of the trees before someone called out. Feynrick held up a hand to halt them as a chorus of shouts rang through the other camp.

Tai felt inside for his resonance. No need to strike it yet, but he could feel the *uai* there, thick and heavy from all the wintergrass they'd been eating. Forty men. Forty *fighters*? Even with their abilities, that would be a hard battle to win.

And for what, Ydilwen asked inside. *For the right to touch the stone? Is that all the justification you need to kill men like me? That we are in your way?*

Tai shook his head. The revenant had to speak up now, when he most needed his concentration.

A pair of men detached themselves from the camp—not an orderly one of straight rows and uniform tents, like the camp they'd seen at Gendrys. Not military at least, then. With any luck, not overtly Councilate at all. Though they certainly weren't a ring of *guyos*, like an Achuri party would make.

The hazy blue of starset made it difficult to make out the men's features until they were close. One was lighthaired, the other dark with the fine strands of a Seinjialese, both dressed in ornate Councilate waistcoats with straps and buttons down each side. Tai shifted the heavy furs on his own shoulders, making sure they covered the scar on his neck. Aside from his height, that was his most recognizable feature.

And if Nauro was right, the last thing they wanted was these men recognizing him.

"Ho, travelers," the darkhaired one called out in plain Yersh. Not of Worldsmouth, then, though his companion could be. "What brings you to the hinterlands?"

"Scholarship," Ella replied. "We—that stone. Descending *Gods,* but they are so much more impressive in person, don't you think?"

Her voice had gone breathless and a few degrees higher than her normal tone, playing the highborn lady.

The two men exchanged glances, appearing to take each other as equals despite the differences in hair color.

"They are," the Seinjialese one said. "You are... scholars of the stone?"

"Of the waystones generally," Nauro said, for his part sounding exactly like he always did. He held out a hand in the Councilate fashion. "Nauro Eddinsley, of the Landley-Hafyen

Institute. We have traveled long and through many dangers to arrive here. It is good to see some friendly faces."

"Likewise," the Seinjial man said, though his companion didn't look as friendly. "Ollen Firstblood, of Seingard. I see you haven't brought much; are you not staying long?"

"Oh, I'd guess not," Ella said in the same breathless tone. "The tribesmen are too fierce for that. Honestly, I'd feel much safer just knowing you and your men were nearby. Have you had any trouble with them?"

"We know how to handle them," the lighthaired one said, in the slurred tones of a Worldsmouth native. At least he and Ella could bond on that. If this conversation didn't go well, they would be hard-pressed to fight their way to the stone. And what then? Even if they did, it sounded like Nauro and Ella would need time to figure out how to open it.

"What's the cause of your hurry?" the Worldsmouthian went on, looking far less welcoming and trusting than his partner. "I would think summer a more hospitable time to visit the stones."

Tai's shoulders knotted—here was the crux of it. Why indeed would someone travel to a forgotten stone in the dead of winter, if they didn't know about Semeca and the rest? He hated not being able to speak, to add his voice, but he had the wrong accent, and so far the men had barely glanced at him or Feynrick, which was all for the best.

"Scholarship," Ella jumped in. "There are theories that the ancients placed the stones at cartographic and astrological points relating to the stellar orbit. According to Nauro's mathematics, and I do think he's correct, the only way to truly verify that is to be here during the solstice, which as you must know is rapidly approaching."

"Is it," the lighthaired one said flatly. Tai's shoulders knotted again.

"Are we welcome here, friends?" Nauro asked, a little more

bluntly than Tai would have done. "We don't intend to interrupt whatever it is you are after. These sites, after all, are our shared heritage, and we believe all should have access, whether you are an academic or not."

"We are petitioning for it, actually," Ella piped up, before the men could respond. "In the chambers of the Counciliate itself! Do you know that the Gyolla have certain sites protected as Historical Preserves, for anyone to visit? Don't you think us terribly backward, for destroying such cultural relics as are still available here, among the less civilized races? I mean, imagine a few of these tribal hilltops made into heritage parks for others to come and examine! How much more so these stones, our last remaining inheritance from the Prophet himself!"

Ollen glanced between Ella and Nauro, eyes skipping the rest of them. "You two are… partners of some kind?"

"Oh yes!" Ella said. "Or, well, not—you see, I have always had a love of ancient history, and the stones in particular, but never had the freedom to study in an academic sense. My husband, you understand. But when he passed, well, Nauro's been good enough to let me take some small hand in his research, and the *least* I could do was bring together an expedition to visit them all."

The men's eyes softened then, glancing again between Nauro and Ella. She was good at this—not only had she convinced them she was a harmless fool, but in tying Nauro to such a fool had made him seem like a second-rate scholar as well, and implied they could only afford a few retainers. Far from a threat. Brilliant.

"You—have visited them all then? Recently?" the Seinjialese man asked, interest lighting in his eyes as the tension left his shoulders. It left Tai's too—the Seinjial believed them, and strange though it was, he appeared to be the one in control here. They were safe.

"Unfortunately, no," Nauro said. "Just the one on the Yersh plains, and of course the Seingard rock on our way here."

"And did you—find what you were looking for?" the lighthaired one asked, pinched eyes looking just as greedy.

No doubt about it—these were shamans, they knew about Semeca's power, and they were trying to take it for themselves.

Which meant if they figured out who he was, they'd try to kill or thrall him.

Great.

"Oh, yes!" Ella cried, once again playing the bubbly Councilate lady perfectly. "The stones are *truly* fascinating. Did you know their width is always in golden proportion to their height? The one in Yershlands was excavated in the time of Lucian the Fourth, and it holds that golden mean all the way down, hundreds of feet so it's said, though much of that earthwork has been covered up again. Isn't it just amazing?"

Ollen's eyes had gone flat. "Indeed. Well, you are certainly welcome here, though I'm afraid we don't have much to offer in the way of food or shelter."

The lighthaired man cleared his throat. "A word, Ollen, if you would please?"

Tai rolled his neck as the two men withdrew and spoke in low tones, the lighthaired one gesticulating forcefully. Ollen had clearly written them off as not a threat to his attempts to take the power, but lighthair looked unconvinced. What was the relationship between the two? Who would make the final decision?

The group stood in awkward silence, all of them too aware the outcome of the strangers' conversation would mean everything to how the rest of this went. Whether they would be able to set up their *guyo*, or be forced to fight for their lives.

The two seemed to reach some kind of agreement, and came back with the lighthair in the lead. Tai checked his resonance again, eying the trees, planning out how to make the best of this. If they were able to take these two hostage...

"My apologies," the lighthaired one said. "I have been unkind, and to kindred spirits, in the middle of the wilderness. My name is Credelen, and we too are here for academic purposes, although different than your own. You are most welcome here, and I look forward to getting to know you better. Now if you'll excuse us, the hour grows late, and I'm sure you have your own preparations to make for the night."

Tai relaxed, and saw a similar tension leave the shoulders of Feynrick and Marea. They were safe, for now. The men's story was a flimsy one at best, and it was impossible to know how much they believed the tale Ella and Nauro had spun, but either way they wouldn't be fighting tonight.

"Look to the revenants," Nauro said in low tones, as they led the elk into the bowl and settled on a site to make camp, across the unnaturally circular depression from Ollen's camp.

Tai unfocused his eyes, and nearly stumbled. The site was *full* of them, air positively muddy with watery forms. No wonder the shallow bowl reeked of dead leaves, despite the fresh green grass underfoot. Similar gasps came from Ella and Marea.

"Are they attracted by the stone?" Ella asked, keeping her voice low.

"They are attracted by initiates, journeymen, and seekers," Nauro said, "of which I would guess their party is at least half."

"Shamans," Tai muttered, leading them to a relatively level area. "But they haven't figured out how to open the stone yet? The power is still here?"

Nauro's mouth twisted. "The power's not here."

Ella stopped in her tracks. "What do you mean it's not here? We're too late?"

"No," Nauro said. "This isn't the right stone."

14

"Not the right stone?" Feynrick bellowed. "Then what in the piss—"

Marea hissed at the giant oaf, jerking her head toward the other camp. He went on in a lower tone, thank the Prophet. She was not about to get murdered by shamans in the middle of the Yati wilderness.

"Not the right pissing stone?" Feynrick bellow-whispered. "Then what are we doing here? Let's get away from these soulsuckers while we can."

"It is not the right stone," Nauro said, "but it is *a* stone, one of only nine in the world, and relatively unpeopled and unguarded. There are things we can learn here."

"If what we're learning is how to get our souls sucked," Feynrick said, "ye can count me right out. I'll swim the pissing Yanu river first."

"I'm with you," Marea said. The sooner they turned back toward civilization, the better. And civilization was always downstream.

"Nauro's right," Ella said. "If we can practice here, it will make the real one much easier. And Ollen's party may know something we don't."

"Which wouldn't be hard," Marea said, "because we know basically nothing, right?"

Ella and Nauro had talked about this some on the journey here, and it had sounded like Nauro was making the best of basically having no idea how to open an ancient and indestructible stone. Which kind of made the whole trip seem pretty stupid, when they could have just used the rivers and been nearly to Worldsmouth by now.

"Not *nothing*," Nauro said. "And this is not the time or place to discuss it. Let's get the *guyo* up first, and talk once I can deaden the air a bit."

No one explained what *deaden the air* meant, but that was pretty par for the course. Feynrick wouldn't know, Tai wouldn't have the words to explain, Nauro would think she was too stupid, and Ella would be too lost in her own thoughts to remember Marea might want to know.

"That's fine," Marea whispered to Bellows, sliding the *guyo* furs from his back and rubbing him down. "I can figure it out." Farts snorted because he still had his pack tied on—he *was* the jealous type. Marea went to work on him.

The conversation continued once they were all in the *guyo*, Ella looking particularly exhausted because she'd had to do Nauro's work plus her own.

"I'd advise we stay here a few days at least," Nauro said. "They seem to have accepted our story for the time being, and we may not have this kind of chance to practice when we get to Semeca's stone."

Marea cringed, all too aware of the all the people that would want to kill them on the other side of the circle, if they overheard. "So, I guess you *deadened the air* then?"

"Yes," Nauro said, sipping at his cup of broth. The man

seemed to eat basically nothing. "A little trick we use to keep anyone from overhearing."

"Does it stop mindseyes too?" Tai asked.

"Yes," Nauro said, sounding put out by a stupid question. Marea hid her grin in another ladle of wintergrass soup. Nice to see the teacher's pet getting his fair share once in a while.

"This is one of the things you can do with *uai* that are outside the resonances?" Ella asked.

"Exactly. One of many, which our friends will be able to do too. I know of two cells in Seingard, and both had respectable power, at least when last I made contact."

"Which was?" Marea prompted.

Nauro gave a pained smile. "Eighty years or more, I expect."

"Eighty *years*?" she cried. "Seingard wasn't even a *protectorate* that far back!"

"It wasn't," Nauro said. "Things have changed a lot recently. Still, there might be a member or two I know still alive."

She still had trouble believing the man was a hundred and forty—he would have been sixty already when he was visiting them!—but he had no reason to lie.

"All this to say," the shaman went on, "that we must stay vigilant. I can deaden the air around us so long as you stay in close proximity, but Tai and Feynrick, you might do well to stay distant or practice mindseye defenses, if you know them. Just because they accepted our story doesn't mean they won't be double-checking."

"Ollen accepted it," Tai said, popping his neck. "Credelen I'm not so sure about."

"What's their deal anyway?" Marea asked, thanking the Ascending God she was hungry. There was no other way to eat wintergrass soup. "Pretty strange to see a darkhair ordering a lighthair around."

"Not so strange among us," Nauro said. He set his bowl down, half-drank. "If I had to guess, I would say Ollen is a seeker, the highest of their cell, and so he is in command. Credelen is likely a full shaman or advanced journeyman, but providing much of the financing, and so he's used to special treatment because of his money."

"Always are," Feynrick mumbled, stretched out as best he could in the tight confines.

"Probably part of the reason they bought our story so well," Marea said, seeing the connection. "In the story you told them, you two have the same kind of scholar-patron relationship."

Nauro's eyebrows went up—the old goat hadn't thought of *that*, apparently.

"Even so, Nauro's right," Tai said. "We need to watch our mouths, watch our movements, watch who we talk to. The less contact the better, because Nauro and Ella are outright lying, and there's no reason for any of us to be coming from Ayugen."

"And the second they recognize you," Nauro said, "We will be in a lot of trouble."

Fear spread like spilled milk in Marea's belly. "And it's really worth staying here despite that?"

Ella's face softened, and Marea hated that Ella felt bad for her, even as some other part of her liked it. Feelings were confusing.

"I'm sorry to have to put you through this," Ella said. "I will keep you safe if anything happens."

"Aye," Feynrick spoke up. "Ye can swim the Yanu with me."

Tai and Nauro chimed in too, and Marea shifted uncomfortably. It was nice, but she wasn't kidding herself about how it would actually go down: Ella would protect Tai, Tai would protect her and whatever they needed to win, Nauro would do whatever was best for himself, and Feynrick would probably try to help them all and end up stuck to the earth or plastered in furs as all the shamans unleashed their powers.

"Thanks," she said. What else could she say? These people

were not her people. She couldn't really ask them for more, even if she wanted to.

"And in the meantime," Ella said, "we need to try to open this stone without tipping our hand. There are too many of them to wait for a time when no one's around, so we'll just have to disguise it as part of our research."

"And once it's open?" Marea asked. "Won't that be kind of... obvious?"

"Once it's open," Nauro said, "We play our parts. Act surprised. Answer their questions with misdirection. And leave, as soon as we can."

"What are we trying, anyway?" she asked. *A woman's best protection is knowledge*, her mother used to say. "Nauro, you said all you know is that it's something about *uai*, right?"

"*He who seeks uai from the stone must first give it*," Nauro quoted. "That's all I've been able to uncover, but my resources have been admittedly sparse in the month since, ah, Semeca's death."

Even here he wouldn't say Tai's name aloud. Gods. "So it has to be a man?"

"No, that's an artifact of translation. The original doesn't specify gender."

"Okay," Marea said, drawing it out as she thought through the implications. "So we just resonate at it?"

Ella gave a rueful smile. "That's my first guess. Or maybe strike resonance but not use it, so our *uai* is available. Maybe it needs a critical amount of *uai* to open, or—" She shrugged. "We'll just have to try and see."

"While making sure they don't figure out what we're doing, don't mindread that we're from Ayugen, and don't realize who Tai is and then shaman-slay all of us?" Marea asked. "Great. Who's ready for bed?"

15

Better to swim in unknowing than drown in truth.
—LeTwi, *Reflections*

*E*lla woke to worship songs. The songs continued through breakfast, through getting dressed and making plans, unperturbed as they emerged from the *guyo* and approached the stone to play their part of second-rate researchers. Tai had left for the morning to hunt, not wanting to give the others any more chance to recognize him.

Almost the entirety of Ollen's party stood in a circle around the stone, colorful Seinjialese garb in stunning contrast to the unseasonably green grass, strange and massive rock rising from their center. Ella was eager to get a closer look at it, but she and Nauro stayed behind the line of singing shamans, not wanting to disturb them.

Not that it was hard to see: the stone was massive, rising perhaps forty paces from the smooth green lawn, and thick enough at the bottom that she doubted all ten people could clasp arms around it.

It was strange too—*stone* almost seemed the wrong word for it. While the rock was gray and appeared slightly weathered, its surface had a depth to it, looking smooth at a distance, but on closer inspection revealing intricate lines and whorls covering the entire surface, without marring it. Instead they seemed to run just under the scuffed surface, like quartz veins laid in intricate designs.

Most powerful of all, though, was the thing's presence. While Nauro swore this was not Semeca's stone, that they would feel something much more if it were streaming all her unclaimed *uai*, still there was an almost holy feeling as you approached, like you had reached the ocean after a long journey, or the highest mountaintop, or the bottom of the sea. An undeniable uniqueness to the thing.

Part of that might have been the unnatural heat. It was warm enough in the bowl that she hardly needed her furs, a welcome break from the week of bitter cold. "Prophet's patience," she said, playing the role of a breathless Worldsmouth lady in case someone was listening. "The stories just don't do it justice."

"Agreed," Nauro said, sounding his normal self, though she trusted him to play his role. She might not trust him otherwise, but self-preservation she didn't doubt he did well. "The Sightfarer is much as I've read and yet so much more."

"Have you read the theory," Ella asked, using the time to scan the people around them, "that the heat is caused by the stone acting as some kind of pump, to pull the energy of our sphere up and outwards, as one experiences in deep mines?"

"Oh yes, my lady," Nauro said, his eyes also casually roaming the crowd. Ollen's party was entirely men, but beyond that a true mix of personages: old and young, light- and dark-haired, muscled and fat, with expressions ranging from educated and wise to rank and shallow.

They were united in one thing: singing. Old Eschatolist hymns, apparently.

"And do you believe it?" she asked. The hymns had to have something to do with the stones—but what?

Whatever it was, it wasn't working.

"I don't disbelieve it," Nauro said. Prophets, if they could just talk openly. What was he thinking? Could the stones even be opened before the spear inside was putting out *uai*?

Ollen seemed to think so.

Presently the hymn ended, and Ollen approached them, wearing a casual Seinjialese waistcoat and fur cap. "Blessings on the morning," he said to them. "I'm afraid I never got an introduction to the fairest of your party." He nodded to Marea.

"Marea Fetterken, if it please you," she answered, the soul of Councilate courtesy, with the hint of condescension that usually accompanied it. Ella loved the girl, but she was Worldsmouth through and through.

Ollen accepted Marea's offered hand, brushing lips against it, then turned to Nauro. "We don't mean to impede your work, but it is our tradition to begin each morning with a round of song."

"Are you so religious, then?" Nauro asked, leaving unsaid the question of how such mixed company could possibly share a faith.

"Just myself, I'm afraid," Ollen said in an affected tone. Ella doubted the man believed in much but power, if he was a ninespear. "The others don't have much of a choice."

His story was so flimsy it felt intentional. Ollen could make up better excuses, but he had no need to. He was in control here, and almost seemed to be inviting them to question it, to give him a reason to want them gone.

"Would there be time for us to approach the stone, then?" Ella asked. "I'm pining to lay hands on it. It has *such* a presence."

"Feel free," Ollen said, sweeping a possessive hand at the stone. "We'll likely break for tea now, and pursue more individual avenues of study the rest of the day."

Excellent. While she *was* curious to touch the stone, what she was dying to do was push some *uai* into it. To learn what they could through experimentation.

Though she had a nagging feeling what they stood most to learn from was whatever Ollen knew, that was driving him to sing to the stone. He wouldn't be so committed if he didn't have a solid theory.

The trouble would be finding it out.

First things first. "Well," Ella said, adjusting the parka around her shoulders. "Shall we?" She took balls of yura from an inside pocket and distributed them.

Ollen watched with interest, the devil. Likely curious to poke holes in their story too.

"For resonances," Ella explained. "Nauro has a bit of mindsight, and I dabble in resonating too. We thought it might help in experiencing the stone, which some theorize was created from the Prophet's own powers."

Ollen raised his eyebrows. "An interesting theory. I'll leave you to it."

Ella tongued her moss—they didn't have much, but certainly needed to keep up appearances. If Ollen knew they had overcome their revenants it would raise all kinds of questions they didn't want to answer.

"All together then?" Ella asked, then squeezed her eyes shut, as though striking resonance took all her concentration. She didn't actually strike hers—timeslipping would come in handy for digging through their camp, but would do little here—but felt

Nauro's high-pitched tone and Marea's higher whine in her bones. Blanks had the highest-pitched resonance of all.

They walked slowly to the stone, Ella watching it for any changes with her heart in her throat. She didn't know what to expect—a line opening somewhere on its smooth length, or a sudden shattering, or a spear floating whole from the rock?

A spear put there by the Prophet himself. A spear with the power of a god, if that god died.

This one would not have that power, and if the stone did start to open, their plan was clear: act surprised. Stop doing what they were doing before anyone could take the spear—better it stayed in the stone than Ollen's party force it from them. Then leave as soon as they could.

Ten steps closer, fifteen, resonance humming, but the stone looked unchanged. When they reached it she struck her resonance in earnest, in case the stone needed more *uai*. Still nothing, though it took longer to see that in slip.

She dropped back out, glancing at Nauro. His face was impassive, but this obviously wasn't good. "Try striking secondaries?" she asked in a low voice. He said he would be deadening the air around them the entire time, but it still felt vaguely suicidal to say things that could turn the 40-odd men at their backs against them.

He gave a brief nod and they did, Ella placing her hand on the stone as if she might feel something that way.

Nothing, still.

They tried various iterations for the next fifteen minutes, striking resonances, using them, trying different combinations, adding Feynrick to the mix, with nothing. All while talking nonsense about their studies, inventing various justifications for what they were doing.

Ollen's camp, for their part, seemed only vaguely interested, the younger and rougher of the bunch watching flat-eyed over their tea.

Watching Marea, mostly. After Ella got over her initial beat of jealousy—when had men stopped watching *her?*—she worried for the girl. She was undeniably beautiful, in an elfin kind of way that men no doubt found attractive. And, as far away from anything as they were, she could likely look like a female Feynrick and still draw stares. At least, that had been Ella's experience working on the *Swallowtail Mistress*, and those lechers were usually paying for company in ports besides.

Eventually Nauro cleared his throat, after the fourth or fifth time attempting a combination of all their resonances. "Some tea of our own, perhaps?"

A few of Ollen's camp had wandered over, their own tea done, and the shaman likely just wanted to be sure they wouldn't be overheard the old-fashioned way while they talked. They found Tai in the *guyo*, on edge for news of their first attempts.

"Nothing yet," Ella said, trying to think positively about it. "Nauro, do you think the problem could be that the spear inside *isn't* activated? That this might work with Semeca's stone?"

The fyelocke shook his head. "Of course I don't know for certain, but I doubt it would make much difference. Tracts have been written about attempting to open the stones pre-emptively, to get the spears out, as a way to double-cross other cells. Their authors presumably had studied enough of the stones to believe it possible."

"So the stones might be empty?" Marea asked.

"This one might be," Nauro said with a shrug. "Hard to tell when it's not putting off *uai*. We can be sure Semeca's is not, or none of her revenants would be free to get thralled."

"Because her power would be flowing to whoever held the spear," Ella said, still trying to wrap her head around shamanic power.

"Yes," Nauro said. "If someone held her spear, they would become an archrevenant the instant Semeca died. And likely then hunt down any who tried to thrall the revenants in Semeca's stream."

"If we know one spear is still intact," Tai said, "doesn't it stand to reason they all are? If someone had figured out how to open the stones, you'd think in all the years since these were made they would have taken all of them."

"Especially easily-reached ones like these," Nauro said. "Yes. That sort of reasoning is what I'm banking on."

"So no one's figured out how to open them in thousands of years," Marea said, slumping to a seat. "Great. How long were we going to stay here?"

"We have to try at least a little more," Ella said. "Ollen's camp obviously knows something we don't, with the singing they're doing. Maybe if we know what they know, we'll be able to do it. This new incentive for power is drawing old knowledge out of the woodwork. We can't leave until we have it, even if it's still not enough."

Marea raised an eyebrow. "And how are you going to get it, if you can't admit you know anything about what they're doing?"

Ella pursed her lips. "That's the hard part."

"Well," Marea said, standing abruptly. "Let me know what you find out. I'm sick of this *guyo* and all our endless talk about theories."

Ella frowned, but she really couldn't make the girl stay. And she should be safe enough if she stayed close. "Watch yourself, okay?"

Marea gave her a frown. "Sure, mom. Nauro, we good?"

"I can keep your thoughts deadened, yes, so long as you stay within the bowl."

"Fine." She pushed out the tent flap and was gone.

"What's gotten into her?" Tai asked.

"Pining to get home, I expect," Feynrick said, ceramic mug

dwarfed in his thick hands. "You can't keep a girl her age fenced in."

"And she has no stake in what we're doing here," Ella said. "It's just a setback on her journey home, and she makes a good point that the information Ollen has will be difficult to retrieve."

"Even if you timeslip?" Tai asked.

Ella shrugged. "I don't know the layout of their tents, or where to start looking. Even at my speeds, I'd eventually draw attention."

"And that is the last thing we want to do," Nauro said.

Feynrick guffawed. "Then meaning no offense, Miss Ella, we might not want to send you in. Last time you tried to slip in to gather information seems like an army tent ended up on fire with Broken shooting out of it."

Ella reddened. "As I recall things were made a little less easy by you punching your old commander in the face."

"Me?" Feynrick's brows shot up in mock outrage. "You were the one starting a catfight with some lady you knew from your Newgen days."

Tai held up his hands. "Enough! Okay. Maybe slipping in isn't such a good idea. But what else is there? Nauro?"

The fyelocke grimaced. "Any attempt I make would be noticed by an experienced shaman, as I expect at least Ollen is."

"Okay," Tai said. "Other ideas?"

Silence. Ella looked around the room and saw only consternation on the other faces. Not good.

16

Marea pushed out of the *guyo* doing her best not to scream. Seriously? Not only did they trek eight days through frozen wilderness to get to this stone, but now that they knew it wasn't the right one they wanted to *stay*? Even though they had no idea how to open it? And they'd be in danger the whole time?

Stains, it was enough to make her want to slap the bunch of them, even Ella. Marea paced the edge of the bowl, frustrated that she couldn't leave it, couldn't talk to the other camp, couldn't just go home—it was too dangerous. Danger all the time.

Danger got boring. She hadn't even *earned* this danger, it wasn't like she'd done something fun and now she was paying for it. She'd just taken the only way out of a rebel city, and here she was still stuck in their schemes. Stuck more than ever, sitting out here in the middle of nowhere no closer to Worldsmouth than she'd been when they left.

Prophetscock, it was enough to make her pull her hair out. Instead she found herself wandering down to the stone, running her fingers along its side. The thing had a power, she would admit that much at least, whether or not it was the key to someone's godlike powers or not. If she could just open it herself, maybe she could leave this scatting place, get back to somewhere someone actually cared about her—

"Pretty amazing, isn't it?"

Marea started out of her reverie. One of the other camp's men stood in front of her. Leaned actually, broad shoulders to the bare stone.

"I—yeah," she said, caught off guard. "And you are?"

"Avery," he said, pushing off to brush lips against the back of her hand. "I'm with Ollen's crew."

"Not many other people you could be with," she said, trying to regain her composure. He wasn't handsome, exactly, but there *was* something about him. A freedom in his eyes. "You're from the Mouth, though?"

His brows went up. "Yeah. How'd you know?"

She smiled. "Because you talk like a decent person. First one I've met in months, other than Credelen."

Avery glanced toward their camp. "Credelen. He's…"

"An ass?"

He smiled, brushing back rakish fyelocke hair. "Yes. Exactly."

She was smiling back, then suddenly the moment got awkward. Say something, Marea. "So what do you—do, here?"

Awkward too, but better than silence.

"Who, me? Oh, I just haul things for Ollen, watch the camp, you know." He shrugged. "Easy stuff."

Her certainly *looked* like he did a lot of heavy lifting. Thick forearms came from the ends of his shirt, muscles stretched his pants, and he just looked *solid*, standing there. Solid and refreshingly real, after everyone lying to each other all the time.

He was looking at her expectantly. Stains, did she miss something? "Sorry, what?"

He smiled. "I said, what do *you* do in your party? You're all, ah, researchers, right?"

"Oh. Yeah. I—I'm a relative. Of Miss Ella's." It sounded stupid the moment she said it, but what was she supposed to say? They hadn't even really made a place for her in their lies. Just some orphan tag-a-long girl.

"From the Mouth?"

"Yes. Upper east side. Near Widow's Hill, you know it?"

"Oh, I know it," he grinned. "I used to push casks up Widow's Hill from the docks. On the way to the snobs at the Downs."

She snorted. The Downs was where councilors and their rich supporters met to talk policies and contracts and generally show off their wealth. She'd been there once, with her father, who'd spent half their monthly income on two glasses of Gyolla liquor to impress a new association who didn't end up investing anyway. "Should have pissed in the casks."

He grinned. "I was tempted, a time or two. To replace what we drank on the way up." He winked.

She laughed. "It's really nice to talk to a real person, you know that?"

He shook his head, still grinning. "What do you mean? Your people aren't real?"

"No, I just—" she flushed, hating that she had to watch what she said. "We've been on the road a long time, and you get tired of the people you're with, you know?"

"Oh, I know," he said, raising eyebrows in a way that seemed to say *don't even ask because I've got stories*. "And I've got forty of 'em to get tired of. I can't imagine what a tiny group like yours is like."

"It scats," she said, "but at least we're here now." At least she had met one person worth talking to. Who actually wanted to talk to her back, instead of just tolerating her.

"Avery," an older lighthaired man snapped. "Aren't you supposed to be felling trees?"

Avery ignored the man, but gave her a grimace. "The only

thing more boring than having nothing to do is having a lot of boring things to do. See you around?"

"Yes," she said. "I'd like that."

He turned to go, then turned back. "Hey, if you wanted, you could come around tonight. We always do a big meal on Ascension, and I'm sure you'd be welcome."

Welcome. Didn't that sound nice? "Okay. Yeah, I think I will."

"Great. Till then, then?" He gave her a mock bow, sweeping an arm out in highborn style, then winked and strode off toward the older man.

Marea watched him go, feeling better than she had in weeks. In *months*. It didn't hurt that his backside was as pleasant to watch as his front.

The others came out eventually and they did more of their farce, pretending to measure out angles and things while Ella whispered instructions about resonances, and the stone continued to just be a stone. Marea caught glimpses of Avery in the crowd now and then, and found herself blushing and smiling.

How long had it been since she'd done *that*?

Eventually they gave it up, star's light stretching shadows over the bowl and hinterland chill coming down even through whatever strange heat the stone gave off.

"I see you made a friend this afternoon," Ella said on the way back.

"I did." Marea smiled. There was really nothing to talk about, but still it was nice to talk about it with someone, like she used to do in Newgen with whoever was her best friend at the time. "Avery, is his name."

"Avery. And what does this friend do?"

"Oh, I don't know really. He's just one of the other camp's workers, I think."

"Mhm. A very handsome one of the other camp's workers, as far as I could see."

Marea smiled. "He is, isn't he?"

Ella glanced around them—Nauro was a ways behind, and Feynrick up ahead, helping Tai clean some hares he'd caught. "Just be careful, okay, Marea?"

She frowned. "What do you mean?"

"I mean we are two women in the middle of nowhere with a bunch of men, and we don't know their intentions."

That was annoying. "Avery's a nice guy."

Ella gave her that infuriating smile she used sometimes, like *oh to be that young and innocent again*. "Lot of men seem nice, till you figure out what they really want. Nauro said half of their party were shamans or training to be. He could just be using you to get to Nauro, or Tai."

Anger flared up hot in her belly. "Or he *could* just be interested in me for *me*, Ella, did you ever think of that? I know I don't mean anything to you guys, but that doesn't mean everyone in the world feels the same way!"

Ella started. "Marea, I—"

She didn't want to hear it. "No, it's fine, whatever, I get it. You've got Tai and you've got your big secret mission. But not *every*thing has to be about that, okay? Can't you just be happy for me?"

Ella didn't answer.

"What, no answer? Just admitting you've treated me like scat?"

Marea stared at her, waiting for something, ready to attack it, but she still didn't speak. And then scats take it she started to feel bad. Ella hadn't really treated her like scat, she'd been nice. But it *was* infuriating how the only time they noticed her was to remind her how young and stupid she was.

"I don't think this is necessarily all about our mission," Ella said finally, speaking slowly. "And I'm saying this because I care about you. I worked around a lot of men like Avery at the docks, after I escaped my parents. Hard men, who'd been at sea a long time. He doesn't have to care anything about who we are to hurt you."

"You mean that he might possibly want to have sex with me?" Marea asked, loading on the scorn. "I'm not a child, Ella. I get that. And what if I want it back? Are you going to turn into one of the Councilate chaperones you hate and tell me I have to wait until an arranged marriage?"

That seemed to catch her off guard. Good.

"No, I am definitely not. I just—I do care about you, Marea, and I think Avery only looks good because of the circumstances. But I trust you. Just—let me know, if you want to talk about anything. Okay?"

She *had* wanted to talk, before now. Ella was a good friend. Her only friend, the last few months. But still ultimately a couple decades older, whatever she said about her age. "Sure."

She remembered Avery's invitation then—she wouldn't really be able to leave without them all noticing, so might as well get it out of the way now. See if Ella was serious about not turning into a chaperone.

"Oh, and he invited me to dinner tonight," Marea said, "so I won't need any of whatever Feynrick's making. Just so you know."

Ella's brows rose. "He—oh wow. Okay."

Marea held her breath, waiting for her mother's words to come out of Ella's mouth. *There's no way in hell I'm letting you go over there with some boy you've barely met and a bunch of darkhaired louts.*

But Ella said nothing of the sort. In fact, she had that thoughtful expression that meant she was coming up with a plan.

"What?" Marea asked. "You're thinking about something, aren't you? A plan to stop me?"

"Who, me?" Ella asked, looking genuinely startled. "No. I—" She turned and met Marea's eyes. "What would you think if I came too?"

17

"Absolutely not," Tai and Nauro said at once, when they were back in the *guyo*.

Ella had expected as much. "Think about it," she said. "What we're doing to open the stone isn't working. They're doing something different, which means they have some other information. Ollen is never going to share it with Nauro the scholar. But Ella, the ditzy trophy wife?"

Tai looked uncomfortable at this, but Nauro spoke first. "Every moment you spend with them is a moment more for you to slip up, for them to see through our plans. And then it's a battle just to escape with our lives."

"I think she'd be good at it," Marea spoke up. "Better than any of you, at least. *She's* the one that got Ollen to buy our story last night. Nauro, you lie like a second-rate mummer, and they can't even know Tai exists."

"I think someone just wants to go see her new boyfriend," Feynrick grinned, turning the hares on a spit.

Ella grimaced at Marea's expression, wishing she hadn't shared that part.

"Yeah," Marea shot back, "maybe I do. I'm going to go either way, so wouldn't you at least I had somebody to watch me?"

Ella spoke up before Feynrick could crack some kind of lewd joke. "I'll be careful. And being Marea's chaperone is the perfect excuse to look like I have no other intentions."

Which worked doubly—because much as Ella wanted to learn what they knew about opening the stone, she also wanted to feel out their shamans on getting her a revenant. Since Nauro never would.

"These men are not idiots," Nauro said. "Whatever story we've given them, they will still be watching us for any signs we are competition in opening the stone first. If you go, you're putting all our lives at risk."

"They already are," Ella countered. "They have been since we got here. Since we left Ayugen! This could be our only chance to get information. Prophet knows we don't have the men to force it out of them. So we go to dinner, and you three quietly get ready to cut and run if things go wrong."

Tai shifted his legs. "I don't like it. But I think you're right. You should go."

And that was why she loved him—he didn't try to control her like a Counciliate man would. He *trusted* her. Ella smiled and snuggled closer into his shoulder. "Thank you."

Nauro still looked sour, but the man was beginning to accept that he couldn't actually go against Tai. "Fine. I will be watching from here, making sure the air is dead around you."

"And listening in, I imagine?" Ella asked. "Maybe you'll hear something I miss."

"And listening in," Nauro said. "He may say something only a shaman would understand. If everything falls apart, I can likely get you out alive."

"And I as well," Feynrick said, not looking particularly intimidating stretched out on his back with his knotted toes exposed.

"We will be fine," Ella said. "If worse comes to worse, shamans still seem as susceptible to timeslips as anyone else. I will get us out."

Tai rolled his shoulders. "Let's hope it doesn't come to that."

18

Wild beasts they are, wild beasts. The Yati war and kill and procreate with all the abandon of a pack of curs. A man could grow to love it.
　—Seamon Twelvehands, *Among the Dark: A Travelogue*

Marea's stomach was a bundle of nerves, which was stupid. *He'd* invited *her*. And she was the most attractive woman in this camp by default, at least for someone his age. Probably in the hundred thousandpace area. And it was *just a dinner*.

Still her stomach felt like Brinerider paper art, cut and twisted and folded a hundred times into something it absolutely shouldn't be.

Ella, for her part, seemed entirely calm beside her, walking across the springy green grass toward the fires of Ollen's camp in the near-dark blueness of starset. She was the one who should be nervous—she'd be spying, trying to get their secrets without letting on she was trying. Marea just had to keep her story straight and she was good.

Still her breath caught when a tall and broad-shouldered man stepped toward them, silhouetted in firelight. "Marea?" he called.

"Yes!" she cried, then immediately was glad for the darkness as she blushed. "Yes. And, I brought my aunt. Ellumia?"

"Great." Avery's features came clear as they reached him, broad cheekbones and that wild light in his eyes. He took Ella's hand and kissed it like any Councilate gentleman. "A pleasure, Miss Ellumia. How are you liking the stone?"

"Oh, it's just fascinating," Ella said, voice higher and breathier. "I envy you men the freedom to stay here weeks and months, just soaking in its presence."

Was that supposed to be a reminder of their earlier talk of lonely isolated men? Marea brushed it off. "Well. What's for dinner? I love a good Ascension day feast."

Avery gave a rueful grin. "Well, it's probably not *good*. Definitely not by Mouth standards. But for the middle of Yatiland we do okay."

He took her hand then, and—Gods, he *took* her *hand*—nodded to Ella to follow, pushing deeper into their maze of tents and cookfires. Unlike the Achuri, they had the sense to keep their fires *outside* their tents, where they wouldn't all breathe smoke all night long. A long table was laid out in a clearing between the tents, lumpen candles illuminating an entire roast venison, trays of roast tubers with fragrant herbs, and a drunken Seinjialese man ladling something awful-smelling from an earthenware cask.

"Lager!" he called. "Yealon's finest! Drink up ye dogs, it's feast day!"

Men moved about the table, joking and calling, tearing into the meat with bare hands, many appearing well into their cups.

"Seinjials," Ella muttered beside her. "The Prophet himself couldn't keep them from their drink."

A hush fell over the rowdy men as they gradually noticed her and Ella. Forty-five pairs of eyes fell on them, and Marea suddenly felt like a piece of meat. Gods. *This* was what Ella was talking about.

She was all at once glad to have the woman along.

"Relax!" one of them called, standing up. Ollen, the camp leader. "Did ye forget what women look like?"

"Reckon I did!" one of the others called, and their general mirth started up again, twice as loud if anything, though plenty of the men kept staring.

Thank the Prophet Avery wasn't one of them. Neither was Ollen, who approached looking quite steady on his feet. "Miss Aygla, what a pleasant surprise! Avery, you invited the women over?"

He didn't sound happy about it, but he also didn't sound like a master talking to his worker. Ella was worried Avery wasn't a good person, but if even his *master* respected him…

"He invited Marea, actually," Ella answered. "And though we are far from Worldsmouth, I still didn't think it appropriate to let the girl go alone."

Marea tamped down on her frustration. Did they have to talk about her like she was a child in front of Avery? She was an adult. Had been surviving for months now among enemies of the Councilate, and knew secrets about the resonances few people could claim.

She was *not* a child.

Marea tugged on Avery's hand, his fingers calloused. "Come on," she said. "Help me get a plate?"

He did, thankfully pulling her away from Ella and Ollen and any further conversations about how she was incapable of taking care of herself.

"Here we are," he said, sweeping an arm grandly at the rough-hewn table. "This is as good as it gets in the hinterlands."

"It looks amazing," she said honestly. "Have you ever heard of wintergrass?"

Stains. Was that only something the Achuri ate? She didn't think Avery would care, but... everything *could* go terribly wrong from some minor slip here.

Which she also hated.

Thankfully, he grimaced. "Wish I hadn't. The stuff is supposed to be full of whatever powers the resonances, but personally, I'd rather go hungry."

She laughed. "Me too! We've been basically living on it. So, deer and tubers? Yes, please."

He helped her dish a plate—thankfully, they had a few. She did *not* want his first impression of her eating greasy meat with her bare hands.

Stains. Was that something her mom would think?

"Lager?" Avery was asking.

Marea wrinkled her nose. "That stuff the Seinjials drink? I don't think so."

He shrugged. "I thought it was nasty at first too, but it's kind of grown on me. Here. Just try a sip."

And he held up *his* glass. Marea had read about this in her novels: the first sign you wanted to kiss each other was sharing the same glass, or fork. It was even a ritual among some of the peasants apparently.

Well she couldn't really refuse *that*, could she?

"*Shattercocks*," she choked, once it was down. "That's dis*gust*ing."

Avery shrugged. "It'll grow on you. Want to sit?"

19

*E*lla watched Marea go with dismay. The girl was obviously still angry about their conversation earlier today, even if she'd agreed to Ella coming. Prophets send she didn't get careless and let something slip.

"Can I offer you a chair?" Ollen asked. "Some dreamtea or lager?"

"A chair, yes! I'm afraid I never took to dreamtea or your, ah, cultural beverages."

At this Ollen smiled, directing her to a seat near the fire. "To each their own. I confess I have tried your ginseng beer and, well, it's difficult to forget one's roots, isn't it?"

A clever play on words. Too clever for her persona to catch—was he testing her? "I'm sure it is. Oh, what a lovely chair! Did you drag this all the way out here?"

"Oh no," Ollen said, sitting in a similarly well-made wood chair. "Some of our men have woodworking backgrounds, and we have nothing but time out here."

"I'm sure. You have so many people here—are they *all* involved in your research?"

He paused, and she cursed inside. Baby steps, Ella, baby

steps. She was dying to know what he knew, but this needed baby steps.

"I will admit many of them are here just to keep the rest of us comfortable. We have the luxury of a well-funded expedition, and Credelen thinks this could take some time, so we made some allowances for creature comforts."

Ella gave a dramatic sigh. "Nauro's research really deserves better than what I can give him. And even so, this cost me a second mortgage on our Yersh estate!" She put on a bright smile. "But isn't it all so worth it? I never thought I'd get a chance to see these stones, and here we are!"

"Yes," Ollen said, eyes glazing a bit at her exuberance. Excellent. Let him take her for a fool. "Did you find anything noteworthy today?"

Ella put on a frown-pout. "I'm afraid not. Nauro has some theories about the proportions of the stone in relation to the moon and star, but it's all terribly mathematical. I'm really an idiot when it comes to that sort of thing! My interests lie more on the spiritual side of things."

Hint, hint. How did you bring up shamanism if you weren't supposed to know about it?

Ollen raised his eyebrows. "I see. This is part of the theory around astrological alignments?"

"Oh, yes. You know some old texts talk of the stones having resonances of their own, and of course the star is the ultimate source of our resonance, so I am hoping, well—"

"Yes?" He looked interested but unthreatened. Perfect.

"It must sound so foolish. But hoping that the stone will come to life, and that we'll be given a new resonance, or—I don't even know what will happen! There are so many hints in the old texts, but no direct answers."

Ollen leaned in, mug of lager forgotten. "What sorts of hints?"

Aha. Got you now. Ella suppressed a smile. "Well, Nauro

would really be the one to talk to about that, I just read what he points me to. But some sections talk of spirits, or our ancestors, coming to life, and giving us power. Honestly I was so excited when I saw you here because I thought maybe you'd have clearer answers. The hymns—did I mistake that those are dirges for the dead? Does your research speak of any similar things?"

His eyes darted for a moment before settling back on hers. *Tell me*, she willed him. *Tell me what you're doing.*

"Our... knowledge has come at great cost," he said finally, fingers toying with the rough clay of his mug. "I wish I could share it with you, but it would be a disservice to the work we've already done."

Stains. Or was he hinting at a trade? She had no knowledge she was actually willing to trade with him, but he didn't have to know that. And what harm if another pack of ninespears was thrown off course by some plausible lies? Their whole goal here was to get Semeca's spear before any others had a chance.

"Perhaps we could arrange a trade then," she said, struggling a bit to keep her façade up. "A scholarly trade! Our insights for yours?"

Ollen gazed into his glass, swirling the liquid. The man was interested—and if he was a real scholar, or just really hungry for power, he would take the risk. Time was limited, and she had tempted him enough with talk of the stone giving power that his ambition would be peeked.

Then Credelen laid a hand on Ollen's shoulder, from where the man sat a chair away. He had clearly been listening. Ella waited for him to say something, to deny the deal, but he just laid his hand on Ollen's shoulder.

And Ollen's eyes grew distant—they were talking! Ella felt a chill creep down her spine—this was no resonance she knew of. Mindseyes would have no need for physical touch, and what was the likelihood they were both second-level mindseyes? No, they were shamans with *uai* streams, which meant they could do anything. Like have conversations through touch.

Across the clearing Marea tittered, leaning in close to Avery. *Don't ruin this for me now, girl*, Ella thought, recognizing the timbre of her voice. Marea was getting drunk. But Ella needed more time to learn what they knew. Especially if Credelen was involved.

The lighthair's hand dropped, and Ollen took a drink. "I'm afraid I can't, Miss Aygla, much as the scholar in me would love to. But thank you for the offer."

Meck meck *meck*. Ella glanced at Marea, still grinning foolishly at her boy toy. The girl wasn't stupid. She could keep her mouth shut, even tipsy on Seinjial lager. She had to.

Because Ella wasn't leaving till she learned *some*thing.

20

Marea laughed, leaning into Avery. He was so *funny*. And so *solid* on her arm.

"So I told him," Avery said, grin wide in the firelight, "*you drink the scatting pondwater, if you like it so much!*"

She lost it in another fit of laughter. A distant part of herself wondered, *what* was so funny?

"Are you a mosstongue?" she asked between gasps, though it came out more like *moshtongue*.

"No," he said, grinning back at her. "Why?"

"Cuz you're just so funny," she said. Was he *naturally* this funny? Or was he just so handsome she was laughing from nerves? Because he *was* handsome.

"Have another drink," he said. "It'll help with the giggles."

"Will it?" she asked, and took another big swallow. Lager was still dis*gust*ing, but she was getting a little more used to it. Or maybe everything was just so funny—

"I'm a brawler," Avery said. It took her a second to remember *why* he said it. Right. She'd asked. Stupid. "Not that I get much chance to use it. Moss was always too expensive, even in Seingard. You'd think this close to the rebels there'd be some cheaper, but the Yati—" He shrugged.

"Savages," she said. "Or—that's what Feynrick says. But he's a Yati, so—"

That was funny too. Was it though? It seemed like it shouldn't be—

"So what are you?" he asked, their hands still twined together. It was just a hand, but *prophets* it felt good to hold it. To feel his eyes on her.

"A blank," she said, a second before thinking maybe he'd think badly of her for it. "I mean, I—"

"Hey, no worries," he said, giving her hand a squeeze. "I know lots of blanks. Thought I was one for a long time too. Turned out I just wasn't eating enough bitter foods."

He looked at her like he was expecting a laugh, but somehow she suddenly felt very serious. He was so *kind*. He didn't care that she was a blank. Because he wasn't some southern barbarian who all had all kinds of resonances. He was just a *normal* boy from the Mouth. Or, well, a *man* really.

There was no denying that.

"I like you," she blurted, then blushed fever red. Oh meck-stained *cock*wattles what did she just say?

But he just smiled, like it was the most normal thing in the world to say. "I like you too," he said, and leaned in closer.

He was going to kiss her. Holy Gods mecking *stains* he was going to *kiss* her right here in front of the whole camp and Ella and everyone—

But he didn't, he just leaned shoulders against her. "I'm so glad you showed up," he said. "Can I get you more lager?"

21

Talk had turned to more mundane topics—the state of Councilate politics, the rebellion in the south, their journey here. Ella had to think fast to lie convincingly a couple of times, and she worried about Marea on the other side of the fire, looking ready to start making out with Avery then and there. What if Avery was more than he seemed? Another shaman like Ollen and Credelen, sent to squeeze information out of the weakest of their party whatever way he could?

Ella took a deep breath. Marea could handle herself. She would have to. There was only so much they could do here without getting Ollen's secrets, and only so much time they could stay before they needed to keep searching for the real stone. Every night was precious. And the longer they stayed the better chance Ollen's camp had of discovering who Tai was, or their real purpose in coming here.

Her attempts at weaseling Ollen's information out through talk had failed. But there was more than one way to learn what they knew.

"If you'll excuse me," Ella said, standing, "I'm afraid I need to attend to some business in the woods."

Ollen started up. "Let me accompany you. The night is dark, and there are predators this far out in the woods."

He could be a gentleman. Or he could be worried she'd see something she shouldn't in their camp. Either way, she couldn't let him come. She put on her mother's best smile. "Oh, there's really no need. I'll just step over to our side of the bowl. It's not entirely ladylike, but I guess it's become routine after this long on the road."

Ollen appeared as though about to say more, then nodded. "You'll come back? I was so enjoying our conversation."

Ella glanced at Marea. "Oh, yes. I wouldn't want to leave her unattended."

And I have more I need from you, shaman.

She wandered as much as she could on her way out of their camp, looking in the wavering shadows for tents that looked bigger or more luxurious. They were of all shapes and sizes, but she marked a few that would bear closer inspection on her return.

Then walked across and did her business, as she *had* actually needed to go too. Damn soup.

"You need to be careful with what you say," a voice spoke behind her.

Ella started up, pants around her ankles, striking resonance. She spun in slowed time to find Nauro a few paces behind her. The ass. She dressed herself and dropped resonance. "You did that on purpose."

He shrugged. "You need to remember shamans are not regular people. If I want to approach without alerting you, I can do that. As could Ollen, or Credelen, or likely any other number of them. I don't think they've seen through my deadened air, but there's nothing I can do about your foolish attempts to draw information out of them. Asking for a *trade*?"

Ella shrugged her coat closer around her. "I wasn't going to actually tell them what we knew."

"Still, you're playing a dangerous game."

"And it's mine to play," Ella said, growing tired of the man's superiority. "You are not the only one invested in this, Nauro. Nor are you likely even the most invested in it."

"Never doubt my investment in this," the shaman hissed. "I have waited *decades* for such a chance. Many times longer than you have been alive. And I doubt such a time will come again. So disagree with me on methods if you will. But never doubt my dedication to the cause."

"Easy words," Ella said, glad they were being honest now. "We'll see when it comes time to act."

"I will defend Tai to the death," he said, voice still angry.

"As will I," she said. "Against *any*one who threatens him." Let him interpret that how he would. "Now if you'll excuse me."

She left without waiting for a response, turning her back on the snake. Could Ollen be convinced to join their cause? Even Credelen would likely be better than Nauro. They needed someone to teach them shamanism—they didn't necessarily need Nauro. But no, the risk of revealing themselves would be too great, with no guarantee the men wouldn't kill Tai outright.

Not that she didn't think Nauro would too, if he decided it was in his best interests.

Ella struck resonance well before she reached Ollen's camp. The man would be watching for her, probably several of them would, so it would be better to slip out here, where it was still near pitch dark, in case her figure stuttered between where she started and ended her slip.

The world slowed, and she walked quickly to the nearest fine tent, taking care to avoid brushing anything or anyone. Fortunately, most of the men were clustered around the central table and fire, though there were a few huddled around smaller fires here. Were these the actual laborers of his camp? Or evidence of divisions among their cell?

No matter. She pulled back the tent flap and ducked inside, hating that she couldn't bring in light. *That* would be obvious, a sudden flash of light from a tent flap that shouldn't even be open.

The inside was dark, a few low pallets and some heavy bags arranged against one wall. Ella went to the largest of these, not much more than an outline in the darkness—curse her eyes for not adjusting. If she were a shaman she could just use her *uai* stream to do it, most likely. She felt only clothes in the pack, and time was passing. How long before her pause out in the dark would be noticed, or someone would see the tent door flip rapidly open and closed?

Cursing, she went out, closed the door and peered at the few men who could see her. They didn't seem to be reacting. Good.

She didn't seem to have found anything either. Bad.

She searched the next tent, and then a third smaller one, with similar results, cursing all the while at how much time she was taking. Finally, she had to abandon the project with nothing to show for it.

Great spy *she* was.

She ran back to where she'd struck, finding her mark in the dirt, and dropped resonance, then strode back to the camp. Thank Prophets timeslipping didn't have any kind of after effect, like the breaks for brawlers or bends for wafters.

"Everything alright out there?" Ollen asked, his mug refilled but otherwise looking just as she'd left him.

Did he know? Was he implying something? Nothing to do but play it straight. Which was even harder to do knowing that Nauro was watching and judging her every word.

Too bad for him. He wasn't going to like what was coming next at all.

Ella sighed, sitting back down. "If you can call freezing cold alright. My charge still behaving herself?"

Ollen cocked his head. "I don't think she's had lager before. But considering that, yes. Her antics make for something interesting to watch, at least."

Antics meaning the way the girl was draping herself all over Avery, apparently. Prophets curse it girl, just hold off a minute! "Ah, to be young again. Tell me, Ollen, have you ever been in love?"

He started. "What?"

"Love. Have you ever been truly in love? Ready to give your life for someone? Felt you would give anything to make them happy?"

He shifted. "I—well yes, I suppose, once or twice. Though it didn't last."

She sighed. "Mine did. Until his heart gave out, that is. That's why I'm here, to tell you the truth."

Ollen took a swallow of lager. "I'm sorry. What?"

"My husband. He died three years ago, and ever since I've been obsessed with scholarship on the departed. It's how I found Nauro's work, honestly, attending a lecture at Landley-Hafyen. You're a religious man. Do you think there's any truth to it?"

Delicately now, Ella, delicately. But not so delicately he doesn't agree to give you a revenant.

Ollen didn't look particularly surprised, but then the man wasn't much for showing emotion. She pitied his partner if he ever *had* been in love. "That would depend on the content of the scholarship, I suppose."

Oho! Here we were getting somewhere. "That's the frustrating thing—there's no particular area of study on the departed, other than religious texts. Instead I find scraps here and there, especially in the older tomes, as if the ancients knew more than we, but the knowledge was lost, or buried. But I just—I can't get over the idea that there's a way to contact him, still."

How did one become a ninespear? Who did they accept, and why? Surely the power-hungry shamans at the top would not want their underlings to be too ambitious. Perhaps a moneyed but lovelorn Councilate flimsy would be just right.

Ollen shifted. "You know, the Achuri believe the voices we hear are ancestors, come back to guide them through life."

Ella gave an indulgent smile. "Yes. And the Yati think them saints, do they not? I don't wish to cast aspersions on your Seinjial traditions, but I have never put much stock in all those beliefs. Voices in your head are like dreams, I say: interesting but ultimately meaningless."

Across the fire Marea giggled, Avery gesturing at something in the night sky.

"And yet you want to contact your husband?" Ollen asked.

"More than anything," Ella said, making sure to sound breathless. Should she also mention how much money she had? Surely the man appreciated money, to keep Credelen around.

The Seinjial's eyes twinkled in the firelight. "What if I told you his spirit was still out there somewhere, likely searching for a new home?"

No need to feign her excitement at this. Marea, stay sober. Nauro, stay back at the *guyo*. This conversation was going exactly where she wanted it to. "Do you really think so? That he's still out there somewhere?"

Ollen smiled. "I know so."

"How—how can you know?" Ella gasped, playing the fool even as she thought desperately through what his game was. Did he want sex? Information on their party? Or just to lord superior knowledge over her?

He eyed her speculatively. "Tell me, Miss Aygla, what would you give to be with him again?"

"Anything. That's love, as far as I'm concerned." That part was true, at least. Prophets, ancestors, and saints send she was never parted from Tai. Which was the whole point—Nauro was a danger to Tai, and she couldn't counter it until she learned shamanism. Which meant she needed a revenant. A revenant this man could give her.

For that? She'd give a lot.

Ollen savored her words, swirling the liquid in his mug. "I have read of ways to contact the dead. To *see* them."

Ella gasped again. "Where? Which scholars. Point me to them, sir. I will pay you anything."

The Seinjial shook his head, silver hair clasp glinting in the firelight. "This knowledge is not in books. It is too dangerous. Too powerful. We keep it in our memories."

Her heart was beating fast. Across the table Marea gave a drunken giggle, and it was all she could do not to snap at the girl. Ollen had as much as *admitted* he was a shaman. "And how does one—get hold of these memories? Will you give one to me?"

He sucked in a breath.

Stains—had she gone too far? Had she said *give one* when she should have said *teach them*?

The silence stretched. "I would desperately like to learn," she tried again, worry welling in her stomach. "Whatever it takes."

But Ollen's face had grown cold, his fingers white-knuckled around his mug. Stains stains *stains*.

"I think you and your friend should go," he said.

"I'm sorry," Ella said, struggling to act the breathless fop through her fear. "Did I say something to offend you?"

He narrowed eyes at her. "I don't know how to take you, Miss Aygla. But I think this has been enough for one night."

Fear and hope roiled in her belly. *Had* she tipped her hand? Play it cool, Ella. "Yes. Well, I think it's likely time for Marea to go, at any rate."

Marea was understandably angry and resistant, and it was just the thing Ella needed to cover up whatever had just happened.

Easy to fall into the role of chaperone, to make apologies, to use Marea as excuse for leaving.

But it wasn't Marea that had given them away, even stumbling drunk as she was.

No, that had been Ella. The fool.

22

Ella and Marea weren't halfway across the bowl when Nauro appeared in front of them. He was furious.

"Look, I—"

He grabbed her arm and the wind stilled, Marea's wobbling gait pausing suddenly under Ella's hand.

Ella's eyes went wide. "What did you do?"

"The question is what did *you* do?" Nauro snapped. "This is nothing. A little twist of *uai* so we are both in slip, instead of just me. Marea's outside of it, so she'll understand nothing."

"You can do that?" Ella asked, dread forgotten for a moment in wonder.

"Of course. You could too, if you'd bothered to explore your own resonance. It's your higher resonance."

She shook her head. "Every time I try to use my second resonance, my *uai* just vanishes." Though that wasn't true—she had used it once, the day Tai saved her from the Councilate prison. She'd given *him* her slip somehow. Like Nauro was doing now.

"That doesn't matter. We don't have forever, even with my *uai* stream. Do you realize what you've done?"

Ella bit her lip, all her dread turned to defiance in front of this man. "Yes. I've done my best to give us an option, because you refuse to give me a revenant, and I don't trust you as far as I can spit."

"And in so doing turned forty shamans against us," Nauro said. "Do you have any idea what they're capable of?"

"Yes," she snapped. "The same things Tai and I could be doing, that Marea could be doing, if you weren't *intentionally* holding us back. Waiting for your chance to snatch whatever power we get at Semeca's stone."

"Fool girl." She had never seen him this livid. Good. She'd rather fight than pretend to be friends. "I *told* you I am committed to this. That I'd do anything to protect Tai."

"Right. Like you told me you were a member of the Cult of the Blood. Remember that? Or that you don't have a revenant to give me when you obviously have the one you took from our attacker? Do you see now why I might feel protective of Tai? Or have a little bit of trouble trusting you?"

Nauro's mouth worked. "You wouldn't understand. Sometimes lies are necessary."

"Well they sure as stains don't do much to get people to trust you. You'd think you'd have figured that out, if you've really been alive a hundred forty years."

Nauro looked over her shoulder, but the world was frozen around them. "We don't have time for this. If Ollen decides we're too much of a threat, the only option is to run. Even *I* can't defeat this many at once."

Ella snorted. They were in danger and she should feel worried or sorry but she just felt furious. "You couldn't even defeat *one* at once. Or have you forgotten how close that attack was back at the pass?"

He waved a hand. "Because I wanted to take his thralls, not just kill him."

"So we could *all* be taking thralls here, if it came to that. You know what I've done with resonance harmonies. What Tai can do with his natural resonance. Don't you realize the talent you're wasting, holding us back like this?"

"I have already taught you far too much. Shamans are not made quickly."

"And the longer you stretch it out, the more indebted he is to you. The more he needs you. Why *would* you teach him quickly? When we get to the stone you're going to need him to stay weak, so you can take the spear for yourself. Right?"

There. She'd said it. His eyes went wide.

"That's what you want, isn't it?" she pressed. "What you've tried to do for a century and a half, what your whole little organization is all about? Becoming a god, or a god of ghosts at least? And then you think we're going to believe you when you say you'd give it up because Tai is *special*? You'll drop us the moment you get the chance."

His face had gone white with rage. "I may not love him as you do, but Tai is precious to me. *Worth* giving up ascension for. What he's capable of—it's so much more than taking the power of one arch-revenant. He could take it all."

But all she heard was love. "No," she said, "you *don't* love him. So whatever your end game is, taking Semeca's power or all their powers or whatever, he's still just a tool to you. Well I *do* love him. More than I could ever love power, or some self-serving goal. He's worth more than all that."

Her eyes burned, and she didn't know if it was from anger or love or something else. It didn't matter.

"Then you should thank me," Nauro said quietly, a gleam in his eyes.

Ella frowned, taken off guard. "What? What do you mean?"

He shook his head, the only thing moving in a frozen world. "You really don't know, do you? The cost of slipping?"

"I—thought it didn't have a cost." Though a voice inside her said that was stupid. That of *course* it had a cost.

"All power has a cost, girl. Brawlers have the breaks, mindseyes get the mud. And slips?"

Dread formed in her belly, hard and heavy. "Have what," she asked, her voice near a whisper. But she already knew. "What do we have?"

"Oh, I think you've figured it out by now. All the comments about your age? People's confusion when you tell them you're twenty-three, but you look thirty-five?"

"No—"

"Timeslipping shortens your life. Every second in slip costs weeks in regular time."

Ella stared at him in horror. "You're lying."

"Am I?" He didn't smile, but she could see his lips twitching, the bastard. "Look at your hands. Do they look as they looked a year ago? Do they look more like Marea's or Marrem's?"

She couldn't help but look. And yes, even in the dim light, they were aged. There was no denying it.

She looked up at him. Of all the people to tell her, it had to be him. It had to be now. A barbed knife in the wound. "I'm dying?"

He scoffed. "Most people are dying. But yes, every time you use your resonance, you die a little faster than the rest of us. And I'm guessing you've used your resonance a lot since coming to Ayugen."

Pain clutched her—the pain of her own death, and the pain of leaving Tai. Of losing so much time they could have shared. She'd already wasted the first part of her life, and now she was losing the rest of it, just as she'd found him?

"How much," she asked, voice barely a whisper. "How much have I lost?"

"Hard to say," Nauro said, unaffected. "Ten years? Twelve?"

Twelve years in the last few months?

"So you see," he said, unperturbed, "you should be thanking me. I am as dedicated to Tai as you are, if in different ways. And when you are gone, I will still be here to take care of him."

When you are gone. When all this is gone. When old age claims you too soon, and you leave your school and Tai and this life you just started building behind.

It was too cruel, too much, too awful to bear. Ella ran from the man, weeping.

23

In the square you find at the end of this winding lane is the Statue to Porscetta, an unusual blend of old Yersh and Brinerider artwork. Rumored to be built at the time of the fourth expansion, it is a mystery how it got here overland, and who might have created it with such a blend of traditions. Either way, it is one of the best sights in this part of the city, and just a few steps on you'll find a delightful old Yersh bakery. I recommend the lingwal tea.
—Arenia Melthesan, *A Walking History of Aran*

The mood in the *guyo* was grim the next morning. Ella had been up half the night crying with Tai, and he'd been wonderful but there was no taking the edge off the truth. She was already seeing him as younger than her, and couldn't stop thinking about when she was an old woman and he still young, and would they even be able to have kids—

And then they had stayed up even later talking as a group about what her slip-up meant. If they should flee in the night or stay and try to brush it off. They still needed to learn what Ollen knew, and there was more to be gained from their own attempts at the stone. Feynrick had been for leaving, Nauro grudgingly for staying, Tai and Ella willing to risk it, reasoning that Ollen's party would have attacked already if they were going to. Marea had been passed out.

She woke now, rolling away from Feynrick with a groan. He chuckled. "Someone taste a little too much mountain man lager last night?"

She just groaned again. Ella could relate—between the revelation of her resonance's true cost, her regret over putting them all in danger, and the worry about staying despite the danger, she'd hardly slept. *I probably look forty-five this morning*, she thought darkly, resisting the urge to hide her face from Tai as he sat up. He had been so good about it.

He won't be for long, a voice said inside.

Ella started. She'd been waiting for the revenants Nauro gave them to wake up, but she *knew* that voice.

Of course you do. You wouldn't forget your old master?

"No," she groaned. Was Odril even dead? Apparently her revenant thought so.

The others looked at her, and she blushed. So much for hiding her old-woman's face. "What?" Tai asked.

"Nothing—just my revenant. It finally seated, and it's pretending to be Odril."

"Trade you for feeling like I'm dying and going to be sick all at once," Marea said from the other side of the tent.

"No," Ella said. "No, I don't think you would."

Nice to see you again, too.

Feynrick chuckled, but Nauro looked distinctly unamused. "Because of Ella's little prank last night, we are all on thin ice. I am deadening the air, but as a precaution we should all stop talking about anything incriminating. No knowledge of revenants.

No Tai. No Ayugen, no hidden purposes. We are who we told them we are, only."

"And if we get any signs they are gearing up to attack, we run," Tai said. "More knowledge on the stones will do us no good if we die here."

Was it wrong that the thought of dying *with* Tai was somehow comforting?

Yes, Odril said. *But then, you've always been a sick little girl.*

Not a little girl, anymore, Ella thought back at him, missing LeTwi and Telen for a moment, even if they'd been lies. Didn't this revenant realize how much she *despised* Odril? *I'm an old woman, remember?*

A sick old woman. Even worse.

They went through the motions of morning, Feynrick stirring coals and heating leftovers as they took turns using the woods and dressing. Marea was badly off, refusing breakfast and fretting about Avery, if she'd made a fool of herself last night. How wonderful it sounded, to have those be the biggest stakes of your life.

But then, that's what she got for falling in love with someone like Tai. Sure, they had relationship problems sometimes. But they also had to fight gods.

The star was high in the north when she climbed from the *guyo*. Ollen's people once again stood in a circle around the stone, but they were silent today. She looked a question at Nauro, hating that she still needed him, that they had to work together, but he seemed to bear no ill will toward her this morning.

Of course not. He had basically ruined her life last night, so he was probably feeling great.

"The skies," he mumbled. "Look to the skies."

Meaning revenants. Ella unfocused her eyes, watching the peripheries, but the smell hit her first: dead leaves, but not the slight whiffs she'd gotten during their training sessions. Overpowering autumnal rot, like the salt marsh forests at the beginning of wet season, thick and humid and pungent.

Then she saw them, at first fleeting, then filling in as her eyes adjusted. The air was rife with revenants: hundreds, maybe thousands of them, all spinning around the central pillar of stone, a vortex of dead souls in strange order.

Marea gasped behind her and Nauro hissed. "Don't look. Act normal, keep walking. You can't see them, remember?"

Ella started out of her reverie too, trying to go about her daily motions, but it was so hard. Now that she was looking, they streamed everywhere through her vision, flitted cold and sour through her stomach, overlaid the normal scents of needleaf and cookfire with dead leaves.

And the strange thing was they were so *orderly*, the whole mass of them dipping or twirling or reversing direction in sync, as if they were a huge school of fish, or a troupe of dancers under careful choreography. And yes—there was Ollen, back to the stone, directing the revenants like a ghostly orchestra.

Not trying to hide it, then. The reason they had decided to risk staying was that they reasoned Ollen didn't see them as a threat. Apparently he saw no reason to try to hide what they were doing now. Or maybe this display was to draw them out, a spectacle so grand they couldn't help but react. And they were tied to their lies now, needing to act as though nothing was amiss, despite the stream of souls rushing around them at all times. Gods.

But what else could they do? They played their parts, Feynrick tinkering about the camp as Tai went off into the woods—though not too far. She, Nauro, and Marea made their way toward the waystone, taking measurements as they went.

It all felt like such a farce. She wished to scat she knew if Ollen's sudden change last night had been from realizing she knew about shamanism, or realizing he was giving away too much information. If it was the first, they were in real danger. If the second, not only were they safe, but the man might seriously be considering initiating her into their cell. Which she had no intention of going through with, but it might get her a revenant—because Nauro certainly wasn't giving her one now.

I would have given you one, Odril said.

Sure you would have, she thought back. Too bad you *are* one now.

For half a second, hope sprung up—Odril had been a shaman. So wouldn't his revenant be a shamanic revenant? Then she remembered, this wasn't Odril at all. This was some other revenant reading her memories and taking on the persona of Odril to try and control her. Though it was a damned odd choice.

No, I—

Don't even try, she cut him off. You know exactly as much about shamanism as I do, because all you know is what's in my mind. And I would never trust you to teach me anyway.

That shut him up.

They kept a respectful distance all morning, consulting over books and discussing theories and generally trying not to be overwhelmed by the amount of revenants streaming through them at all times.

"What do you think they're doing," Ella asked in a low voice, when it seemed unlikely anyone would overhear.

"I don't know," Nauro said, nodding and pointing to a place in his book. "That sort of combined effort is not easy, and there's no reason I know of to do it otherwise so—"

"So it must have something to do with the stone," she finished, excitement mixing with disgust in her belly. She hated that she had to work with him on this, but it was too important to let personal difference get in the way. Thank the Prophet he seemed to feel the same.

"An agitation to stir the stone?" he asked.

"Or just a critical mass of ghosts," Marea said, looking a little better as the morning wore on.

"We won't know until we're at the right stone," Ella said, "but for now I don't see how it relates to *she who seeks uai from the stone must first give it*. Revenants don't give *uai*—unless they're being thralled to the stone somehow?"

"Impossible," Nauro said, though he looked a little doubtful. Ha. Did the master of shamanism just learn something from the upstart young lady?

Old lady, you mean.

Ollen's circle broke up around sunrise again, and he and Credelen made their way up the bowl to where she and the others were stationed, looking through their notes. Fear uncoiled like a waking snake in her belly, and Ella tamped it firmly down. She had to be bubbly, bright, stupid. If they were going to attack, they would have already.

"Blessings of the morning to you," Nauro called. "I hope my patron didn't upset your revels too much last night. She can be— hot-headed, at times."

There was no need to fake her blush, but she *did* have to swallow her pride to agree. "Yes, I am so sorry! Marea and I should never have come. We will leave you in peace from now on sirs."

Ollen merely looked between them. "No need for that. It was —enlightening to have you around."

That could mean he enjoyed it, or he was enlightened as to their real purpose here. Damn the man!

"Did Avery say anything about me?" Marea asked, then immediately went scarlet. Good. Perfect. Her teen drama was just the kind of diversion they needed.

Credelen gave an indulgent smile. "I imagine he made a few cracks to his friends, but no dear. A drunken young lady is always welcome in our tents."

The lecher. Odril chuckled.

Nauro cleared his throat. "I trust the morning has been beneficial to you?"

Scat. The man accused *her* of prying too much?

Ollen gave the hint of a smile. "It has. Will you be needing access to the stone this afternoon?"

"Oh, yes," Ella put in, pouring on the ditz, "if it's not too much trouble to you sirs."

"On the contrary," Ollen said, "I'm quite interested to see what you do."

So there it was. Not only were they not a threat, he thought maybe they knew something worth finding out. And so he was tolerating them—at least until he decided to force it out of them.

Great.

They wasted the afternoon in misdirection, coupled with a few of their own experiments, but really Ella was out of ideas for how to interpret 'giving the stone *uai*,' and wasn't about to try copying what Ollen had done, lest they blow their cover.

Sometime after the sun dipped below the trees—it rarely got above them these days, while the star seemed to make almost a full circle in the sky—Avery walked over to them, and he and Marea chatted a while, the girl blushing occasionally. Ella left them to it—the burly youth was the least of their concerns at the moment, and the way they drew eyes gave her a chance to try a few more things on the stone.

Still, by the end of the day it was clear they either needed to find out what Ollen knew, or go to the next stone. There was little left to learn here on their own.

Nauro concurred. "It isn't safe staying here," he said, pulling boots off in the cramped *guyo*, "and my sources aren't clear whether an unactivated stone can even *be* opened. So unless we come up with a better plan than Ella's to learn what they know, we would be better served moving on."

"We could kidnap him," Feynrick said, pulling the flap closed against the chill air. "We do it all the time in the hills. Wouldn't even have to hurt too many people, just slip in and grab him and tie him up."

"He's a shaman," Nauro said. "You might find him harder to tie up than your average hilltribe wench."

"Not to mention our nine-to-one ratio if it came to a fight," Ella put in.

"Mindreading," Tai said. "They've been—fuzzy, every time I tried, but maybe if we can surprise them, catch them just waking up or sleeping."

Nauro shook his head. "They must be deadening the air in shifts. And like as not, they are old hands at keeping their thoughts veiled, even without deadening the air. It's a way of life for shamans, because our knowledge puts us at risk."

Silence for a moment. "Marea," Ella said, hating to bring it up, but having no better ideas. "I'm only asking this if you're comfortable with it, but Avery—"

"What, you want me to spy on him?" she asked, eyebrows shooting up.

"Not on him," Nauro cut in. "On his camp. His superiors. See if he knows what they know."

"Or if he can find out," Feynrick said. "Maybe you could work out a trade?" He wiggled his eyebrows suggestively.

Marea blushed and frowned at once.

Idiots. That was *not* how Ella would have approached the topic.

"No way," Marea said. "Not only am I not going to put that on Avery, but that would just make us stay here longer, when all I want to do is *go*."

"Even if it means leaving your dogleg behind?" Feynrick asked, still grinning with teeth.

Before she could answer, Nauro had sat bolt upright, eyes

glazing. "Someone approaching," he said. "Unarmed, but from Ollen's camp."

Tai struck resonance, Feynrick laid hands on his weapons, and Ella readied herself to slip, hating it now that she knew the cost. But she'd rather get old fast than die now.

Footsteps sounded and the *guyo* flap opened, letting in a cold breeze.

A stocky young man stood in the doorway.

"Avery?" Marea cried.

He glanced at her, then his eyes took in the rest of the cramped space. "No time," he said, sounding older than he looked. "They're coming for you."

"What do you mean," Nauro barked. "Who is?"

"Ollen, Credelen, the whole camp," Avery said, meeting the man's eyes. "They know."

"Know what?" Nauro barked, but it was too late for that, obviously. Avery had figured it out somehow.

"That you're a shaman," Avery said. "That you're all from Ayugen, and you've been lying, and that man there," he levelled a finger at Tai, "is Tai Kulga, Godslayer."

24

It was all Tai could do not to strike resonance then and there, get a headstart on whatever attack was coming. Nauro had said if the shamans knew who he was, they would either try to thrall him or kill him.

Not without a fight they wouldn't.

Tai raised his voice over the sudden din in the tent. "What do you want?"

"Standard cut," Avery said. "I'm a journeyman, and sixth in position among your cell, if this is a cell, so a fifth of a half. We can negotiate later. We need to go *now*."

Avery was a shaman too, or an initiate at least. He had to be, to know the language. And he'd figured out their secret somehow.

"No," Tai said. "Feynrick, Nauro, see to the girls. I'll hold them off. I appreciate the warning, Avery, but you should run. You'll only slow us down."

"You need me," Avery insisted as Tai pushed past him out the flap.

"Why?" someone inside asked. Shouts sounded from the other side of the camp. It was true then. Ollen *was* coming.

"Because I know what Ollen knows."

Tai stopped in his tracks. Meckstains. There was no time for this. "Prove it," he snapped. "Why were they singing hymns?"

"An *unholy chorus*," Avery said. "I can recite the whole passage. But only if you take me!"

Tai glanced at Ella and Nauro—they were the experts, and they seemed to accept it.

"Done," Tai said. "You know the closest path to the river?"

"He does," Nauro said, pushing out of the *guyo*, "and you should go with him. Let me handle Ollen."

"We'll stand together," Tai said, squinting across the moonlit bowl, where Ollen's camp appeared a mad scramble of men and torches.

Nauro put a hand on his shoulder. "You are brave, and noble, but that is foolish, Tai. You cannot yet fight as these men do. Save your party. Go."

"This *is* saving my party. I'll stick to the edges. Keep them off the others at first."

"Fine," he snapped. "But when I tell you to go, you go." He began walking toward the other camp.

Feynrick had Ella on his back, and Avery Marea on his. They stood there with resonances struck, watching him. Waiting for orders?

"Go!" Tai cursed. "I'll keep them off you."

"No," Ella said. "You come with us."

The first of Ollen's camp was charging across the bowl, air suddenly alive with resonance.

"I'll follow as close as I can," Tai said. "I will catch you at the river."

"You promise?" Ella asked, intense despite being slung over Feynrick's shoulder.

"I promise. Now go."

The brawlers ran, and Tai ran with them, not wanting to give away his resonance, give them a clue which one was Tai Kulga, Godslayer.

Were they really calling him that?

The brawlers were pulling ahead by the time they reached the trees, and Tai slowed. Their tracks would be easy to follow in the snow—part of the reason he needed to make sure no one followed. That if Nauro *couldn't* handle twenty shamans, someone kept Ollen's party away from Ella and the rest.

Twenty shamans? The man had barely handled one on the way here. What was he doing?

I can handle them, a voice came in his mind, *but only if they're focused on me. Stick to the woods, they will try to flank me.*

Nauro. Using mindsight to speak directly to him. Even as he did Tai saw the first line of Ollen's men go down with muted thumps, like invisible boulders had dropped on each one, mangling them.

Ancestors. Was *Nauro* doing that?

A contingent of them split off toward him, no doubt told off to track them down. Tai struck resonance and wafted into the trees. Maybe Nauro *could* handle them. It looked like ten men were coming after him.

Nauro was taking thirty. Could he handle ten?

Yes. Unless they were shamans.

They will attack like Ydilwen did. Use your shamanic sight. Avoid the revenants.

Easier said than done—he could barely see them in broad daylight. He unfocused his eyes all the same, seeking with his senses.

More screams sounded from the clearing. How Nauro was fighting a clutch of shamans and still calmly sending him thoughts, Tai had no idea. It didn't matter. A pack of men rushed underneath him, resonance roaring, crying out when they found Feynrick's trail. Brawlers, then.

He could handle brawlers.

Tai dropped from the branches, silent, his resonance no giveaway in the roar of theirs. The men moved at brawler speed—but at the front, two carried other men slung over their shoulders. Shamans, then, or some other resonance. Tai grimaced. He would have to be careful. Pick them off slowly.

The first he took down with thickened air to trip him and a dropkick to the head to knock him out. This worked for the second and third as well, Tai choosing the slowest in their team, the ones at the back of the pack.

Then the rest of the pack noticed and slowed, shouting to each other while he shot up to a treetop above.

Good. The whole point was to slow them down.

And bad. Because the non-brawlers were starting to perk up, which probably meant shamanic attacks.

Which meant losing all his resonance if he wasn't careful.

Tai unfocused his eyes, straining at the peripheries, the star's blue light dim among the trees. Shimmering shapes appeared, elongated, smoky—yes. Revenants.

One of them was streaming for him, and he dropped under it, then struck his higher resonance and slammed a boulder of air down into the center of their pack.

Clever, Tai. But don't get caught. I may not be able to help you from here.

Nauro's voice sounded strained, but there was no time to think about that. The boulder attack had scattered them and Tai swooped in, straining his eyes for revenants, smashing about him with fists of air.

Focus on the shamans. You can handle the rest.

Right. Tai shot up at the faintest hint of something shimmering off to his right, then righted himself a few paces above the trees and shot back down, locking his legs to slam into the nearer non-brawler with a crunch.

Tai felt the impact, though wafting seemed to strengthen the body nearly as much as brawling did. He shot back up, narrowly dodging a pair of revenants that came at him from both sides. Lose his *uai* now and he'd been dead or worse.

Still at least one more shaman then—and not easy to pick out who, as the surviving fighters crowded together. That they hadn't kept going meant they'd figured out who he was.

Well. Brawlers who were standing and defending didn't get much chasing done. Tai shot higher up, hoping they couldn't see him through the trees, and sped west following the trail Feynrick and Avery were breaking through the snow. Found them a few thousandpace on, as his back was starting to ache.

They were alive, and safe. Good. As much as he wanted to go down and reassure them, Tai knew it would do no good. They should be able to keep ahead of the brawlers for a while now. But if Nauro didn't stop Ollen's main force, they would be in serious trouble.

So Tai crunched down dried mavensytm blossoms and sped back the other way, swinging around the brawlers to head for the waystone.

There was no mistaking it in the night: fire jetted up from the clearing, and claps of thunder sounded from below.

Tai slowed, the first real pangs of fear pushing through the rush of battle. Whatever was happening there, it was beyond anything he'd seen. But what had Nauro said? They would try to flank him. Meaning powerful as he was, he couldn't handle a flank attack.

Not that Tai could either, if the attackers were all shamans. But surprise counted for a lot, and according to how the first party of brawlers had acted, he would guess they spent more time reading old volumes of ninespear lore than training in drills.

He hadn't done those things either, but you didn't defeat an army of Councilate soldiers, and then another one of Broken resonators, without picking up a few tricks.

Tai circled around the clearing, some of the trees ringing it burning despite the cold. What he saw in the shallow bowl almost made him lose resonance: a single man, illuminated in firelight, facing down a pack of shamans. Jets of flame roared and lightning crackled and stones flew through the air. Nauro stood like in the heart of the maelstrom, arms raised, deflecting every attack, sending out waves of his own, the area around him littered with bodies.

Gods. He was doing it.

For now. Concentrate on those near the stone, if you can.

Nauro sounded breathless, even in mindsight. Maybe he wasn't doing it as well as Tai thought. He wafted the canopies around the clearing, some of them burning, waves of heat and smoke rolling through the trees. There—a cluster of shamans near the stone. They appeared to be the ones calling forth lightning, raising arms to the sky to call down blinding blue-white streaks.

How was that even possible?

No matter. Nauro needed help, and the shamans wouldn't be expecting any. He could do this. At least one attack. And every shaman he stopped here was one less than would come after him later. Come after his friends, and after his city.

But this needed a different approach than battling soldiers or Broken. Attract the attention of the whole party and he'd be incapacitated in moments. No. He needed to be careful, subtle.

Tai dropped to the forest floor on the far side of the stone, its shadow flickering and moving with the flashes of fire and lightning on the far side. For a crazy moment he thought the stone was burning, that he could see the spear hanging buried inside. But no. It was as solid as ever.

He crept across the empty side of the bowl, dropping resonance, sticking to the shadows, until he was hard up against the stone, opposite the shamans and the rest of the battle.

Then he struck resonance—not wafting but mindsight. Struck it and peered through the stone, seeking the minds of the men on the other side. There. They were predictable muddles of anger and fear and determination, battle minds, but one among them stood out as calmer than the rest. He would be the most dangerous.

Tai crept around the side of the stone, seeking the body that fit the mind. Heat washed over him as he peered around the side of the massive stone. This would all end fast if any of the shamans looked his way. He had to count on Nauro keeping their attention, on seeing a revenant attack coming if they did, though the air was awash in spirits. He sought deeper with mindsight.

There. Ollen's mind was the most calm. No surprises there. Tai struck his higher wafting.

And this is where you kill him? Ydilwen asked, silent this whole time.

Tai ignored him. There was no time for questions of right or wrong in battle. Survival was right. And the survival of your friends.

He struck, focusing all his resonance on two tiny blades, closing in around Ollen's throat. Air was not solid, could not be solid, but a wind had force. Enough force to choke a man, if you did it right.

Ollen doubled over, calm shattering as his airway crushed. Tai kept on him, adjusting the blades, pressing in harder, until he felt something break, somewhere between mindsight and his wafter's push. Ollen fell and Tai moved to the next one, his companions too caught in the battle to notice.

A battle Nauro was losing, Tai saw from the corner of his eye. The sphere of protection around him was getting smaller, the projectiles flying closer to their mark, his clothes smoking from the heat of a near-constant gout of flame from a red-haired man on the far side of the shallow bowl.

Ancestors. Was this what true shamans could do?

The second shaman fell to more blades of air. Before Tai could move to the third the man's head snapped over, taking in Tai and his fallen companions in one quick motion.

He raised his hands, and a cloud of revenants rushed in.

25

Ella called a break as Feynrick stumbled a third time under her weight.

"Pissing whoredogs," the thick brawler wheezed once he'd set her down, "you think we've come far enough yet?"

Ella looked to Avery, the young man breathing heavy too. She felt bad for needing to be carried, but her slip wouldn't take her nearly as far as brawling did, and they needed to stick together.

Besides, that feel-bad was pretty much drowned out in worry for Tai, who still wasn't back. What was he *doing*?

"Did Ollen find out what Tai looked like?" she asked Avery, dread gnawing at her stomach.

"Yes," he said. "I don't know how, but he knew. They all did."

Marea pursed her lips. "Could have been a lucky mindread, a failure of Nauro's screening, someone who'd seen a sketch of him."

The girl looked pale, her eyes a little wide, but still holding together. She was strong, for sixteen.

Ella glanced between the men. "Do you think they could follow us this far?"

"Some of them," Avery said. "Ollen, Credelen, a few of the others. The brawlers and journeymen."

"And how many journeymen among you?"

"Among *them*," Avery said, already catching his breath. "I was never part of their cell, I just joined at Yatiport."

"But you *are* a shaman?" Marea asked, face shadowed under double hoods.

"Well, a journeyman. But yes," he said. "I *will* be a shaman."

There was something in the simplicity of his speech and gaze that made you want to trust him. Ella did not like having a stranger in their party, but then, Nauro had been that at the beginning too.

And now he was dying for them, or at least putting himself in serious danger. Prophets. She had misjudged the man.

"How much farther to the river?" Marea asked.

"I haven't been since we came up," Avery said, "but maybe another eight thousandpace?"

They were more than halfway there, then. Good. "Can we arrange passage from there?" Ella asked.

"Just the five of us?" Feynrick said, breathing less heavily but hands still on his knees. "Oh aye, some jackal will want to make some change from us, visit the pleasure houses in Yatiport. Trouble's going to be finding a worthy boat."

"And Nauro," Marea said. "We'll have to wait for him, right?"

Ella hesitated, not wanting to admit Nauro might not be coming. Because Tai was with him.

Marea's chin stuck out. "What, we're just going to abandon him? After what he did for us?"

"He did it so we could get out," Feynrick said gently. "We can't waste that by waiting for Ollen and the rest to catch up."

"And our tracks are easy to follow," Avery said, gesturing at the snow. "We need to get on a boat and get downstream."

"We'll still be easy to follow," Marea said. "Isn't it obvious?

If we were interested in that stone, we'll be interested in the next one. They'll just follow us there, if they don't catch us first."

"Problems for later," Ella said, hollow. What did later matter when Tai wasn't coming to them *now*? "Avery is right. We need to go."

Though just as much of her screamed they needed to go back, needed to find Tai, needed to *do* something to make sure he survived. What was the point of all this without him?

26

Tai shot backwards, rolling, knowing any one of the revenants screaming toward him would mean death, or worse. He hooked through the trees, shot through the canopy, unsure if losing revenants was like losing regular people. Could they still follow after their shamans lost visual sight?

Apparently not—he hung a few hundred paces back from the bowl, night flashing with the battle there, and saw no revenants.

He should leave. If he was smart, he'd accept Nauro's sacrifice and go. But the man was dying for them down there. For *him*. And there were still things he could do to help.

Tai dropped below the crackling branches and circled back the way he'd come, checking the woods for anyone trying to flank Nauro. Nothing here—watching through the trees Tai could see the subtle way Nauro was shifting, moving himself like a Ninekings piece and deflecting attacks in certain directions to keep his attackers on one side of him. Whatever he was doing to defend himself must get a lot more difficult if he couldn't physically see his attackers. Tai worked his way around the far side, fresh lightning crackling across the bowl. One caught a tree a few paces ahead, and in its bonfire burst Tai caught movement to his deeper in—yes. A man there, creeping through the woods.

Tai dropped lower, striking his higher resonance. He was about to strike when the firelight revealed a second man a few paces beyond him. And a third.

Stains. He couldn't attack one without the others seeing and turning on him.

Nauro, he said inside, hoping the man was listening. *Shamans coming to flank you here. More than I can handle.*

In the clearing Nauro dodged boulders and deflected lightning and strode through pillars of flame, apparently untouched, but the boulders came closer, the hair was burned from his head, and no response came to his thoughts.

Tai tried again, as the three shamans crept closer to the edge of the clearing, and closer to him. *Nauro. If you can distract them I can take one or two at least.*

Still nothing, though he got a sense of exhaustion, of stress, of danger. Then one of the three in the woods summoned lightning from his hands, a blue-white bolt that left a red afterimage in Tai's eyes. It stretched from the shaman's hands to Nauro's back.

Nauro stumbled and Tai screamed, even as two more bolts flew from the other shamans, one of them again striking Nauro, who'd fallen to his knees with the first.

Tai struck and shot out, burying his knife in the throat of the first even as a fresh bolt flew from him. The thunderclap was deafening, but Tai was already coming around for the other two.

Who were turning to him, arms raised, the periphery of his vision starting to blur with revenants.

Go, came Nauro's voice, weak and pained but unmistakable. *Go now.*

Tai took one anguished look back at the bowl, where Nauro lay under a hailstorm of rock and fire. Looked back to the revenants rushing at him like the floodwaters of a broken dam. Death on all sides. Nothing he could do.

With a roar of frustration Tai shot up and out, lightning cracking after him, blood roaring and back aching. Stay and die with Nauro or go and live.

He shot out into the night. Behind him the waystone stood from the burning bowl like a tombstone in a grave of flame and death.

27

They found the river around the time the star was rising again, and a few thousandpace downstream a cluster of huts along the bank. Feynrick went first, negotiating passage in rapidfire Yati while they shivered in the cold. He managed to get passage, rations and a promise of silence in exchange for a single ball of yura.

The value of moss had gone up.

There was no sign of Tai or their pursuers, though they had walked most of the rest of the way to conserve *uai*. Ella was exhausted, worried sick, and frozen to the bone, climbing into the narrow wooden boat mainly through force of will.

No one spoke, but the same question was on all their lips: where was Tai? Could he find them if they left without him?

Was he alive?

"Shall we go, then?" Feynrick asked, avoiding her eyes. Their meager gear was loaded and he held the oars.

Ella knew what she needed to say, knew it was only practical, only making the best of what he and Nauro had done for them, but her was lead. Stone.

"I'm staying," she started to say. Marea gasped.

Ella's head cracked around, stone heart racing. She didn't see it at first, then Marea pointed, saying "There."

But there was no need—she felt the thrum, the sweet, familiar bone-shaking resonance of her lover, as he dropped from the sky a few feet from the boat.

Ella leapt from it and pulled him close. He smelled of smoke and ozone and she shoved him back, looking him up and down. "Are you hurt?"

"No," he said, "but we should go."

"Nauro?" Feynrick asked, but the sorrow in Tai's eyes was enough of an answer. He shook his head.

"He sacrificed himself for us," Ella said, her voice dropping.

Tai nodded though it wasn't really a question. "He really was what he said he was. He held back Ollen's entire camp, Ella. The things he did—" he shook his head. "But we should go. I can waft faster than they can run, but they will still be after us."

"Where are we going *to*?" Marea asked as they climbed back in the boat, carefully avoiding the frigid waters.

"Downstream," Tai said, looking as exhausted as she felt. "Yatiport. The next stone, though you can—you can book passage wherever you want from there."

Ella shook her head, Nauro's loss sinking in. "How will we even know which stone to go to? Nauro was the only one who knew what to look for."

Avery cleared his throat. "I might be able to help with that. I know some people in Yatiport."

"And you know something about the stones," Tai said, nodding to Feynrick, who shoved them off the shore. "The information Ollen was using."

"Yes," Avery said. "That too."

Tai just nodded, shoulders slumped. "We'll talk more when we get down the river some. For now, Feynrick, if you'll watch the boat?"

"I'm a Yatiman," he said. "I could do this in my sleep."

"Let's not test that one out," Marea said, though there was a note of affection in her voice Ella hadn't noticed before. She would miss the girl when she left.

Ella laid her head into Tai's side as the current took them, Yanu's waters dark and tree-lined shore darker in the star's pale light. She hated this life of constant danger, that as much danger likely lay ahead as behind. But she loved Tai for being the one who cared about it, and the chance they had to start something new, to discover old secrets and live their lives to the fullest. This was she'd always wanted, what she thought she'd never have, locked up in her parent's house in Worldsmouth.

She just hoped they lived long enough to enjoy it.

28

The hilltop settlements are for more than aesthetic beauty, though: they allow for the careful channeling of rainwater, the natural distribution of waste among terrace gardens, and successive walls of defense against invaders. Because invasions are like blizzards in the warring counties: you can count on a few every year.
—Markels, *Travels Among the Yati*

Marea fell asleep leaned against Avery's solid shoulders, which made it possibly the best sleep she'd ever had despite the noise of the water, the frigid cold, and the images that kept coming up of those men running at Nauro and getting crushed, blood gouting from ripped skin in the chaotic firelight. Against all that Avery was solid, and real, and warm.

And he *liked* her. Enough to want to come with them. To save all their lives.

She kept cracking her eyes to look up at him, or gaze at his arms around her waist, or just watch the water as the sun rose and savor feeling comfortable for the first time in what felt like years.

Since her parents were murdered, at least.

"What are you thinking about down there?" he murmured one of those times.

Marea started. "Me? Ah, nothing. Just—I'm glad you're along."

"Me too."

"Me three," Feynrick said from the back of the boat, which was about a pace and a half from the front of the boat. "Avery. You look like you could work an oar. Give an old man a break."

"Yup," he said, giving her a last squeeze before getting up. She sighed, wanting to follow him and knowing everyone would stare. That they were probably already staring at her leaned against him. What she'd give for some privacy.

Feynrick thumped down next to her, and she immediately caught a whiff of his beard stink, poor replacement for Avery's cedar-and-woodsmoke scent.

Tai cracked an eye. "Where are we?" He'd been cuddled up with Ella since they shoved off. No one looked twice at *them*, of course.

"Gariba, near as I can tell," Feynrick said, shifting himself around trying to get comfortable, boat rocking wildly under his weight.

Tai cleared his throat. "Which is?"

"About halfway down the Yanu," Marea said, remembering the trade routes her father had made her memorize. They were mostly water, which made sense now that she'd realized walking somewhere took *forever*. "It's a Yati county named for the medium-sized market village along the river, known for its black fleshed salt pork."

Feynrick and Tai both stared at her, and she shrugged. "What? I told you I knew my maps."

"So how long does that put us from Yatiport?" Tai asked.

"Another day," Feynrick jumped in, shooting her a look. He obviously wanted to be the expert about his own nation. "Long as we don't see trouble with the warlords."

"Warlords?" Ella asked, voice mirroring the sudden dread Marea felt. First shamans and then warlords. How had the Councilate ever conquered anything?

Feynrick shrugged. "They get bored sometimes, start to shoot at boats, or pirate 'em. You never know."

"Well, you sound pretty scatting casual about it," Marea said, trying to scoot herself further away from his beard stink in the cramped boat.

"Don't you remember? You've got Tai-barking-Godslayer with you," Feynrick said, waggling his eyebrows. Tai scowled but Avery nodded at the back, as though it made a lot of sense.

She was going to have to tell him what kind of guy Tai actually was.

"The real question," Ella said, "is what we do when we get there. Avery, you said you know some people in the city?"

He nodded. "I—was part of the cell in Yatiport, for a time."

"You said you were a journeyman?" Ella pressed on. "That's above apprentices and initiates?"

He nodded, and Marea felt an irrational surge of pride. Her boyfriend was a *shaman*, or almost.

If he was her boyfriend, that was. It seemed like it, but in books you always had a talk. Swore your love to each other, that kind of thing.

Marea started. Did she *love* him?

Ella was still talking. "—refused to give me one, but if you have any shamanic revenants around, maybe you'd be willing to do it?"

"Sure," Avery shrugged. "I can do it now, if you want. Or, as soon as someone takes these oars for a second."

"And me, too," Marea said, a little more quickly than she probably should have. No way she was letting Ella get private lessons from Avery, the woman was too old for him. "If you have two, that is."

He shrugged. "I do, actually. We had a lot of time to gather spirits while we were out there."

"Great," Ella said. "And we need to continue training. Nauro showed us some of the basics, but we need to know more." Tai nodded at this.

Avery leaned on an oar, steering them around an outcropping of rock like it was second nature. "I've never taught anyone before, but sure, I could give it a try. Teach you the basics at least."

Sudden fear stabbed into her, as deep as any moment of danger they'd been in so far. He was talking like they'd be together a long time. "But you're—coming with me, right? Back to Worldsmouth?"

Avery glanced between her and Tai. "I—didn't know you were parting ways."

"Worldsmouth," Marea said, though the dread was already forming in her gut. "I need to get back to my family. My cousins—"

It sounded so stupid when she said it out loud. So childish. *I need to go home. Can you take me home?*

Avery licked his lips. "I guess I had thought to go on with Mr. Kulga. Earn a place in your cell. At least, if this is a cell?"

"Close enough," Tai said. "I'd promised Nauro a similar share to what we promised you. And we could use your help."

Dread pounded through her stomach now, working its way up her chest. She'd just *met* Avery, and now they were going to get split up? She couldn't let that happen.

But keep traveling with Tai and their ridiculous quest?

"Marea?" Ella asked, voice gentle. "Are you still thinking to book passage from Yatiport?"

"Well, it's not really any different I guess, anyway," she said, mouth suddenly running with a mind of its own. "I mean, if I take a boat from Yatiport, or we wait and figure out where you're going. Maybe it'll be the same direction, right? Isn't there a stone in Worldsmouth? Maybe we could go there."

It sounded so stupid. *She* sounded stupid. She glanced at Avery, whose steady eyes were on her, and her cheeks burned. Why did they have to be having this talk *now*, with everyone staring at her? When she and Avery hadn't even really *talked* yet? Descending *Gods* what she'd give for some privacy.

"There's not a stone in Worldsmouth," Ella said, "but some of the other stones would need us to take waterways north."

And some of them would not. Most of them, if she was reading Ella's face right.

Avery cleared his throat. "Well, hopefully we'll all be going in the same direction."

Marea's face lit up, and then it fell, and then her emotions were such a rush she had to just stare at the water and pray they talked about something else, *anything* else. Did Avery mean he hoped she would come with them? Or that he hoped he could stay with Tai a little longer because he was definitely coming with her? Did he not care at all?

Ella said something about Nauro and thank Prophets they moved on. Marea kept staring till she felt like she could at least trust her mouth, and her cheeks weren't burning, though she still couldn't bring herself to look at Avery.

"—do think he's gone," Tai was saying. "There were ten or fifteen shamans still standing when he fell, and the lightning bolt—"

He choked. Did Tai actually care about Nauro? Someone not from his precious rebel city?

Ella put a hand on his shoulder, even though she'd obviously never liked Nauro.

"Then I guess the question, me dears," Feynrick said, pushing himself up from his sprawl with another dangerous rock of the boat, "is how we're going to know *where* to go, without Nauro along. He said he'd be able to feel it, though pissed if I know what that meant." He turned to Avery. "Can you feel the stones, boy?"

"I'm not sure what he meant by that either," Avery said. Marea still couldn't look at him, but he sounded uncomfortable. "But you all know about Semeca's—well, obviously you know about it, with Mr. Kulga and all. I figure that much *uai*, anyone nearby has got to notice it. The Wanderer doesn't have many people around it, but most of the other ones do—the Seingard Rock, the Ascension Stone, and the Minchu Stone. Even the At'li make regular trips to their stone, I hear."

"And if the stone isn't on Saicha?" Ella asked. "News won't travel fast across the seas. If the Brineriders tell us at all."

"Well we'll have to go to Worldsmouth to find out," Marea said, perking up. Riders rarely left their ships, and weren't allowed past the Worldsmouth delta.

"I think we'll see what we can learn in Yatiport first," Tai said. "It's a major Councilate port so there should be plenty of talk, and Feynrick and Avery, you both said you have people there. Hopefully someone will have heard something unusual, and we can make a plan from there."

Make a plan from there. The weight in her stomach since Avery said he wanted to stay with Tai solidified into a solid rock of dread. What if they heard it was the At'li stone, way out on the ice sheet? Would she go? Was she never going to see her family again?

But what were a bunch of cousins compared to *Avery*?

Her mind spun on it the rest of the day, as Avery then Feynrick oared their way west, Yanu's current slowing some as it widened. More villages began appearing along the coast. Yatiland looked much like the land around Ayugen, only with more stone, the river often running against gray granite cliffs or rushing around jagged outcroppings of rock.

There were more people, too—Ayugen seemed pretty isolated, but the lower they floated on the Yanu, the more red-haired people Marea saw doing their wash or trading or just watching the water. The forests patched out too, replaced with open farmland, and by the time the star was sinking low most every hilltop they saw was settled and fortified, and they were far from the only boat in the water, others laden with saltpork or hairy tubers headed downstream. The chill air carried the scent of smoke and human waste carried in the dirty streams flowing from the fields.

Feynrick and even Tai spelled Avery at the oars throughout the day, but he never held her as closely as he had during the night. She didn't know if it was because he didn't want everyone to stare or had a change of heart or something else, and hated that she couldn't talk to him about it without talking to *everyone* about it. She ached for his touch, for some reassurance things were still okay between them.

That he would go with her and not Tai.

They shared a last round of stale bread and Yati saltpork—it was delicious, after weeks of wintergrass—as the star dipped low. Fires spangled the hillsides and water slushed against the oars. The air smelled of needleaf sap and burning dung.

Tai cleared his throat from the back of the boat. "Feynrick, aren't you from this area? Any chance you know a safe place to put us up for the night?"

The Yatiman had been unusually quiet that afternoon, watching the shoreline pass and rubbing his beard. He rubbed it now then dropped his hand with a sigh. "Wish I did, milkweed, but things change fast around here."

"Don't you—have family here? Come from one of these villages?" Ella asked gently. She must have noticed the Yatiman's melancholy too.

"I did have," he said. "Now? Probably better to go on to Yatiport. Plenty of inns there."

"Is that it?" Marea asked in the uncomfortable silence that followed. The horizon glowed, like Worldsmouth did at night.

"It should be," Avery said. "We're getting close." He sat next to her, their arms interlinked, the single spot on her body that didn't feel frozen.

"You're still willing to ask around your contacts tomorrow?" Tai asked him. "See if anyone's heard anything about a waystone?"

"Yes," Avery said. "First thing. It's no good for any of us if someone beats us to it."

It'd be fine with her. What did she care if someone became a secret immortal being?

"If they did we would know about it by now," Ella said. "At least, Nauro seemed to think we would."

Avery licked his lips. "We would—all the *uai* I've gathered would be suddenly gone. But I doubt no one's gotten there yet. They must just not know how to open the stone."

"Neither do we," Marea said. Avery *knew* that, right?

Ella resettled her furs. "Well it's not the first mystery about the resonances I've solved," she said. "I just hope we have all the clues we need. Speaking of which, Avery, what do you know of what Ollen was trying?"

"Just that it was based on a scrap of old text his cell had," the muscular youth said. "*Spears nine fall not before an unholy chorus* was how most of them translated it. Or *fall in time with*, Credelen thought."

Ella flexed her chin. "Not a lot more to work with."

Tai leaned into an oar to steer them around a train of empty boats paddling back upstream. "Hopefully, it's more than anyone else has," he said, voice annoyingly casual about all the danger. "If someone figures it out first, well—"

He shrugged.

Shrugged! Because he didn't want to say *then we're all instantly dead* out loud?

No one else said it either, and the next bend in the river revealed the lights of Yatiport spread out like a landed colony of fireflies. Marea sighed and snuggled herself into Avery's shoulder. Prophet send the gossip pointed them toward Worldsmouth tomorrow. And that she could convince him to leave this whole stupid thing if not.

Because if he didn't want to, she'd have to choose between love and survival.

And what kind of choice was that?

29

The very currents themselves seemed to guarantee Worldsmouth's ascendancy. Lying at the end of all rivers, even barges stacked high need little propulsion to travel downstream, beyond steering. And once we have lightened them of their load, they row easy against the current to fetch more.

—Telen Fostler, *Empire Reconsidered*

Yatiport was a city of towers. Not massive towers, like the Counciliate had built in Ayugen, but miniature ones all over the city, each surrounded by its own wall and guarded with a surly-looking man out front.

"Not enough hills," Feynrick said with a wink, when Tai asked him about it. The man was back to his jolly self after some heavy rounds of dreamtea last night. "Yati don't feel safe unless we've got the high ground, but you can't build a port on a hillside. So every clan and tribe has their own tower, and they watch each other as close as we do out in the counties."

Tai was feeling better too, after a night in a real bed and a meal of something other than wintergrass. "Is that why you didn't want to stay out there last night? Is your clan at war?"

"Clans are always at war," the grizzled man said, stepping out of the way of a porter with a goat on his back, its bleats echoing from the high wood walls. "That's what they do. But no. Regular war I could deal with, especially since the Councilate outlawed vengeance killings. Most they do is shoot a few arrows these days."

Tai nodded, pulling his furs closer about him. It was warmer here, but the air still carried a chill. "What then?"

Feynrick worked his beard for a second, then brightened. "Did I ever tell you about the bottomless inn here?

There was something there the man didn't want to talk about, which was fine. Everyone had their secrets. "No. Is that where we're going to get information?"

"Information?" the man guffawed, drawing no attention in the noisy street. Turned out Feynrick wasn't the only loud Yatiman. "Hounds no, man, you don't go there for information. Though I don't doubt those ladies know a thing or two. No, I know some houses I can stop, places people might still think kindly on old Feynrick of Rotwen. But you'd do better to stay out front, keep that hood up. I don't doubt word of the Ayugen Savior has spread this far."

Feynrick turned in to a sag-roofed tavern a few blocks down and Tai took his advice. It felt very strange, to be known this far from home. Even in Ayugen, the attention of the cultists and the way everyone looked at him had felt odd, but these people didn't even *know* him.

They knew me, once upon a time.

Ydilwen. The voice had been mostly silent since the battle at the waystone, but Yatiport was his home, after all. Or, the home of the person his revenant was pretending to be, anyway.

You don't think I'm real? Let me show you my mother's house. Let me see her.

Tai did his best to ignore it, to keep his eyes on the street without drawing attention. Fortunately, this was something he had years of practice in, even if the streets of Yatiport felt different than Ayugen's, with stone gutters and slate roofs and a humid breeze carrying the scent of burning dung. By the time Feynrick emerged Tai had identified the kids begging for change, the keepers minding them from a distance, and had guesses about which ones belonged to different gangs.

He pushed off the wall, raising eyebrows at his friend. "Learn anything?"

"Red Dogs are hunting Bent Stakes across the city, and Gealon Banewillow is trying to scrub an army big enough to take Splitsap and Bentow counties. But about what we're looking for? Nah." He spat green. "Drank enough dreamtea to last me a week, though."

The next place they tried was a stone-faced restaurant on a wide street, though Feynrick entered through the back door. Tai took up position next to a pile of broke-staved barrels nearby, again spotting beggars from a gang he assumed used facial scarring to get sympathy, and a team of boys about Curly's age working to pick pockets.

Would have been Curly's age, anyway, if he'd survived.

And you still think you can kill whoever you please, in the name of your mission? Isn't that what the Councilate did to your kids?

"I don't kill kids," Tai said under his breath. "And you might have noticed I didn't kill most of Ollen's brawlers in the forest, just knocked them out."

And Ollen himself? Did you just knock him out?

Tai had choked the man with air—it was hard to know what

had become of him. He rolled his shoulders. "He was attacking us."

And that gives you the right to kill *him?*

"Yes," Tai muttered, glancing around. "He was trying to kill us."

Because you lied to him and were trying to find out what he knew.

"No. Because he found out who I was, and that was all the reason he had to want us dead."

And can you blame him? After everything you've done?

Tai shook his head, trying to remember the thing wasn't real, that it was just taking whatever tack it thought would give it the most sway over him. And that the persona it'd taken had attacked *him* first.

Only because you—

Its reply was lost in the shock of recognizing a face in the crowd. It took Tai a moment but yes, he knew that face—a sandy-haired man with a pinched expression, walking down the far side of the street with a determined expression on his face. And scorch marks on his furs.

Credelen. That was *Credelen*, Ollen's second in command from the waystone.

Tai ducked his head back, slouching to drop his height, striking up conversations in his head to hide him from mindsight. What was Credelen doing here?

There could be only one answer. One reason he would abandon the stone and his wounded companions and take boat or waft here.

Tai's heart pounded. He was hunting them. Hunting *him*. And if Tai understood shamanism well enough, the man might have thralled some of Nauro's revenants, meaning he'd be much stronger than he'd been. And Tai *still* didn't know defenses against shamans, could barely even see revenants. If it came to a fight...

Tai risked another look. The man had passed, was still striding down the street like he had no time to lose. Did he have some lead? Some way to find them? Nauro had had tricks no resonance was capable of, shielding conversations and seeing through walls and who knew what else. Did Credelen know some trick like that?

Tai took a deep breath. No. The man couldn't, or he would have attacked. Still, there was no doubt why he was here.

Which meant they needed to leave.

30

I have seen the weighty vessels, swaying into port—
  Seen them leave with empty bellies, men hungry-eyed.
  How long will this city mouth the world
  Fore starving peasants rise on rulers fat and weak?
    —Etrimus the Houseless, *Dirges for Adeline*

Ella took a deep breath, smelling sweat and river and roast goat. They were on the Yatiport docks, gulls wheeling and men calling in the crush around them. There was something about a city, any city, that made her feel alive, but Yatiport more than most. This had been her first real taste of another culture, her first experience outside Worldsmouth, when she'd taken passage on the *Swallowtail Mistress*. She smiled, watching barrel-chested Yatimen loading casks onto a wide barge, remembering her mix of fear and excitement at finally meeting the 'wild beasts' of Yatiland, and finding they were no more beastly than the Councilate. She'd come back many times on her trips up and down the Ein, gradually coming to know the brick-lined streets and open-air restaurants within walking distance of the port, savoring the city's transition from strange to familiar.

Strange to think that for all that had happened since her last boat trip up the Ein, it had still only been a few months since she'd been here. About the usual interval.

It felt so much longer—though maybe that had to do with her resonance. How many life-years had she burned since meeting Tai?

Avery cleared his throat, nodding to a pack of dockworkers leaning against a brick warehouse, heads a mix of red, black, and fyelocke. "I'll try over there. You're sure you're okay with me doing this?"

He had half their supply of yura on him, forty balls. Ella nodded. "But don't take it if they're scalping you on the rate."

He nodded and pushed off, growing more of a swagger as he approached the men. They needed to sell the yura if they were going to stop sticking out—no one had yura to barter outside Ayugen—and a lighthaired woman like her would get an awful rate. It was a slight risk letting Avery take that much of their money, but she didn't think he'd run. The mixed-haired youth seemed committed both to their mission and to Marea.

Ella glanced over at her—the girl was still scowling, had been all morning. "You okay?" she asked.

"Fine," Marea snapped.

They hadn't had much chance to talk since their argument over Avery, and Ella had no idea where they stood. Still, she was serious about wanting to be there for the girl. It would be hard to go through all this so young. Prophets, it was *still* hard.

"You want to talk about being fine?" Ella asked, leaning against the solid stone railing that bordered the Ein, Counciliate stonework pleasantly modern after weeks of tents and woods.

"What's there to talk about? When you're fine, you're fine."

If only she could see herself, scowling about being fine. Had

Ella ever been like that? Probably. Probably worse—that was about the age she'd run away from home.

Ella cleared her throat. "You're worried Avery's not going to go with you."

Marea blushed scarlet, glancing to where the bulky young man had blended into the crowd of workers, then scowled deeper. "Yeah, I am, okay? It's all fine for you that you want to follow your boyfriend around fighting gods or whatever, but some of us might not want that."

Poor girl. It must feel awful, but the last thing Marea probably wanted was pity. "Maybe he wants that too. Have you talked to him about it?"

"No, I haven't talked to him about it, because there's always a million people around listening to everything we say."

The inn had been crowded last night—Tai didn't want to draw attention by bartering too much yura, so they'd traded for a single room and dinner, and ended up sharing beds. Thinking back, the girl wouldn't have had a chance on the boat either, and obviously not before then.

"Well, I plan to do some asking around today," Ella said. "I'll make sure to give you some space."

Marea only looked more miserable, an expression out of place on her elfin features, made more delicate from the long walk and poor food they'd had the last few weeks. She was obviously dreading the talk as much as she wanted it. "Thanks."

Ella wanted to reach out a hand to her, do *some*thing to make the girl feel better, but maybe there was no escape from the misery of youth. None that she could offer, anyway. In the awkward silence she noticed a high whine in her bones—the tone of a blank. "Are you using your resonance?"

"My *blankness*? Yeah. It makes me feel better." Marea glared at her as though daring her to tell her it was stupid or childish.

Fortunately, Avery had left the crowd of men, and Ella nodded to him. "Here he comes."

The muscular youth walked up with pockets bulging, a grin playing on his lips. "Stuff is worth its weight in solium," he said once he reached them. "Two hundred marks a ball, and I know they were all planning to turn around and make more than that."

Marea's eyes bulged, and Ella worked to keep hers from doing the same. "So you've got... four thousand on you?"

Avery nodded once, face getting a little more serious and glancing around. "I do, and most of those men know it. So maybe we wander on?"

If it came to an attack they could probably handle it, but the attention that drew would be the last thing they needed. Especially if Tai was back by then. "A great idea. Give me half, then I'll seek out the richer travelers, if you can make the rounds of more dockworkers."

She hesitated, because lighthaired Marea would obviously stand out in Avery's crowd, but the girl wanted time with him, so—

"Marea, walk with me a bit?" Avery asked, digging in his pockets. Smart man. He half-turned and passed Ella two wrapped rolls of coins, his palms surprisingly smooth for a day laborer.

Ella nodded good day to them, silently wishing the girl luck, then made her way along the stone-and-plank boardwalk that lined the Yanu's confluence with the Ein. Along the way she struck resonance just for a moment, seeing no better way to do it, and stuffed the coin rolls down her front. As the world slurred back to speed, she wondered how many minutes or hours she'd aged in that time. How many days?

Curse Nauro for ever telling her about the cost. LeTwi was right: better to swim in unknowing than drown in truth.

She spotted a well-dressed couple taking tea at one of the

open-air restaurants built along the dock's south side and made her way over.

"Excuse my forwardness," she said, "but I've been many days away from civilization and am dying for some proper conversation."

"By all means," the man cried, jumping up. "We've ourselves been cooped up with the same passengers two months now, and would love a fresh ear."

They knew nothing, beyond the mundane scandals of the higher Houses and the usual discussion of how recent Council policy might affect trade. It sounded exactly like the conversations she'd heard every day about *The Swallowtail Mistress*, with different names and Houses swapped in.

She hadn't missed it a bit.

The next couple was the same, as was a svelte gentleman she talked to in front of the lawkeeping station. Few had any mind for events outside Worldsmouth, though there was some talk of a poor sweetleaf harvest this year, and unsettled peasantry in Yershire. More interesting was the discussion of Semeca Fenril's death and the withdrawal of the Councilate legion at Gendrys. Most people she met blamed Ayugen for her death, some going so far as to mention Tai by name, and very few had any idea what had actually happened.

No surprise there, as Semeca had attacked only with Broken, a program not well-understood even within the Gendrys army camp. But it did not bode well that across the board they were frustrated at the Councilate for not taking more decisive action, and the slowdown in business as yura supply dwindled and costs skyrocketed.

"Don't understand why we don't just smash them," the svelte gentleman was saying, Aeson Jeltenets of the Jeltenets hides and tanning division. "Send more legions in than they can handle and take our moss back."

"The river is blocked, from what I understand," Ella said.

Aeson snorted. "A few stones. That's going to stop us from the most lucrative trade in the history of the Councilate? Byaldsden and Deyenal just want the Houses materially involved to fund it. And I don't disagree with them, but you have to consider—"

And on and on. Ella was glad when Marea rejoined her, because the girl had a knack for keeping the people they talked to on topic, but after another few conversations Ella was beginning to doubt Semeca's waystone was on their continent. Surely an entire stone lighting up with *uai* would make *some*thing worth talking about, especially to these people who had so little of value to say?

Marea agreed, though her heart obviously wasn't in the search.

"How did your talk with Avery go?" Ella asked, after they escaped a portly grain trader with wandering eyes. They were near the south end of the docks, where the land rose in steep granite outcroppings, wind brisk off the wide river.

"Awfully," Marea said. "I mean, it was great, and he's great, but—"

"He doesn't want to go," Ella said. She'd suspected as much —all the ninespears she'd met seemed dedicated to their cause, and youthful or not she didn't doubt Avery was any different. Besides, a man like him probably was used to pretty young women coming into and out of his life. None of which she could say, of course.

"No," Marea said, the word loaded with disappointment and confusion. "But he says he wants to be with me. And asked me if I would come with, wherever you end up going."

Ella took a moment to adjust her loops of braids. "And what did you say?"

"I—don't know. I said I don't know what I want to do."

She said something more, but Ella only half-heard her. Was that—her old ship?

"Ella?" Marea asked, when she'd missed the beat to respond. That *was* her—the *Swallowtail Mistress.*

"Yes, sorry, I—come on. I may know someone we *can* get information from."

31

Tai filled Feynrick in with low tones when the man emerged a few fingers later.

Feynrick just grunted. "You sure what ye saw, milkweed? We would've seen Credelen on the river, like as not, if he'd taken it at the same time."

His breath stank of floral dreamtea. "He could have wafted," Tai said. "Or come through the ground, I don't know, shamans aren't limited like we are. Or not in the same ways." He rolled his shoulders, frustrated again that he didn't know more. And now that he finally knew he could trust Nauro, the man was gone. And Avery didn't seem to know nearly as much.

"Well, the main thing is he didn't come for you, and I doubt he's after Avery or the girls if he doesn't care about you. That or he's got no way of finding us, and in that case Yatiport's a big town. Come on."

Tai followed him, shouldering his way through swelling morning traffic. The sun hung rosy to the east, casting everything in the purple of a winter dawn. "You learn anything good back there?"

"More of the same. People here are too pissing concerned

with their own noses to see much of the outside world. Doesn't help that I can't talk about a waystone without them looking at me like I'm crazy. But some word of trouble on the plains, for what it's worth."

The plains—that meant old Yersh country to the north, the Counciliate's first conquest after independence. Nauro had said there was a stone there, but the Yershire looked huge on maps he'd seen—it could be totally unconnected to the stone. Still.

"It's something at least," Tai said. "You got more places to talk?"

"One more," Feynrick said. "Though if they feed me any more dreamleaf I'm like to turn into a shaman myself."

This time Feynrick went into one of the towers, a leaning five-story wood structure surrounded with a fence of sharpened stakes and armed with guards. Tai stayed well back, fading into the shadows and watching the street. Ella, Avery, and Marea were down by the docks, hoping to gather information and seek out ships traveling up or down the Ein once they'd made a plan. He didn't like leaving Ella with someone he'd known as briefly as Avery, even though she was more than capable of protecting herself. And the man seemed trustworthy, if young.

And if he hadn't crossed the bowl to warn you that night, you'd have been just as happy murdering him. Right?

Tai rolled his shoulders, watching the guards outside Feynrick's tower share a steaming cup of dreamleaf. "I would not have been *happy* about murdering him," he answered, despite knowing he should just ignore the voice. "But yes, if it meant protecting my friends? I would have done it."

What does protecting your friends mean when you're fighting people who could *be your friends? You would protect Avery now, wouldn't you?*

He likely would. They needed the man to teach them shamanism, he was good for Marea, and they'd need all the help they could get when they found the right stone.

Wouldn't Ollen have been even better help?

Tai shook his head, watching a pair of pickpockets work the crowd—young girl to draw their attention, older boy to check their pockets. They looked like siblings. "Ollen was never an option. He wasn't willing to share his information, and attacked us without even knowing our intentions. He just wanted power. Like all you shamans, as far as I can see."

Did he?

Images came up then, the fire and stark shadows that night at the stone, but as if seen through darkened glass, with Tai's thoughts loud and on the inside of the glass, his determination and worry for Nauro.

"What are you doing?" he muttered, resigning himself to looking totally mad. There were hermits on the streets sometimes, people too involved with their voices to really interact with others. It was as good a cover as any other.

I'm helping you remember. You had a lot on your mind during that time, but I didn't. I saw everything when you looked into Ollen's mind. All the things you forgot, or couldn't see in the moment.

More images came up then, dreamlike against the darkened pane of the battle, Tai creeping closer to the stone as he sought the minds of the men on the other side. Ollen had stood out, his thoughts calm and focused.

Regret was the first thing that came up. He hadn't wanted to kill Nauro, had understood by then what a rare and talented shaman he was.

Unlike you, who seems to kill anyone standing in their way.

"He was still trying to kill him," Tai muttered, but the revenant was having an effect on him. He needed a distraction.

What I say isn't less true because I'm dead. You kill at the drop of a hat, which means that I have to do that with you now. So I want you to at least know who you're killing.

More images came up them, the mindsight he'd only glanced at as he crept around the side of the rock, sighted on Ollen, and pushed air against his throat to suffocate him. Images of Ollen's tidy stone home in Seingard, the gray-haired wife he feared not coming home to, the plans he had for the power once he got into the stone.

He wasn't planning to come after you, or anyone. He wanted the power because he trusted himself to use it wisely. Sound familiar?

A knot formed between Tai's shoulder blades. That was *his* reason for pursuing Semeca's stone, or close enough. To take the power before someone more dangerous did, to prevent it from hurting anyone.

But who was to say he was better suited to it than Ollen? Ollen, who had been kind to them up to the end, who appeared in those brief moments of mindsight to be a decent person?

Who might also have been Tai's friend, in different circumstances?

Tai shook his head, unable to tell for a moment which thoughts were his and which Ydilwen's.

"The *revenant's*," he muttered. "It's not Ydilwen. It's just a voice mecking with me."

Tell yourself what you want. You know that I am right.

"And if you are?" Tai snapped. "What then? Do I just let the next person that threatens my friends hurt them? Do I give up and go home and let the greediest shaman take the spear and destroy my city to protect themselves? What difference does knowing all this make?"

Silence, then a cleared throat behind him in the alley.

Tai spun, striking resonance. He'd forgotten the street, forgotten to keep an eye out. Stupid.

Feynrick raised his hands quickly, "Easy, milkweed! Didn't mean to interrupt you."

"You—didn't interrupt," Tai said. "I was just—" He shrugged.

"Don't worry about it. Yer lady might have her theories about the genitors, but I never minded having Gleesfen around. No shame in getting a different opinion."

Except when that opinion made you question everything you'd been doing. "Right. Did you—learn anything, in the tower?"

The Yatiman snorted, and only then did Tai notice he was a little unsteady on his feet. "I learned the Rotwens still brew their dreamleaf pissing strong. If Marrem could see me now."

Tai took his shoulder, grateful for the distraction, and steered him back into the street. "She'd snap at you, for sure. I never really said thank you, for leaving her to come with us. I got to take Ella along."

"She would never'a come," Feynrick slurred, stumbling just slightly as they retraced their steps. "Too good. Too kind a woman. Not her kind of fight. Too good for me, really."

Oh, no. Tai knew this kind of talk, the talk men deep in their cups would get into. He'd never seen Feynrick get purple, but he didn't want to. Especially not with Ydilwen pushing him to do the same. Credelen was somewhere in this city. They needed to learn what they could and get out before he found them.

"Anything about the trouble in the Yershire? Or something else about the stones?"

"Oh, aye," the thick man said, still sounding melancholy. "Uprising, they're calling it. Regular rebellion, right in the belly o'the empire."

Shouldn't that be where they liked the Counciliate best? Tai had never heard of uprisings outside Ayugen and Yatiland, the newest protectorates. "That definitely sounds odd. Any idea where exactly it is on the plains?"

"Califf," Feynrick said, "or near enough. South plains. Supposed to be a big thing. Whitecoats are keeping everyone back."

South plains. Nauro had said the Yersh waystone was centered in the old capital, the one built before the city of glass on the coast, that itself was built many centuries before the Councilate. "Califf," Tai said. "Is that the old capital?"

"Nah," Feynrick slurred, eyes following a buxom woman on the far side of the street. "That's Aran, nother twenty or thirty thousandpace upriver."

Tai almost stopped in his tracks. Twenty or thirty thousandpace? That was nothing. Could it be a coincidence that this uprising was happening a day's walk from one of the possible waystones?

Tai took Feynrick's arm and steered him toward the docks. "Come on. We need a boat for the Yershire."

32

aptain Merewil Ralhens looked no different than Ella had left him, three months and a lifetime ago. He stood stiff-backed aboard *The Swallowtail Mistress* as his wealthy passengers disembarked via the teakwood ramp. She smiled despite herself, remembering all the times she had been one of them, then called "Master Ralhens!"

His eyes passed over her at first, swaddled as she was in furs, then picked her out when she pulled her hood back to show her hair. A smile broke out on his face, and he strode closer. "Ellumia Aygla! Is that you?"

"The very same," she said, genuinely glad to see him, and glad too that he didn't still seem angry about the false calculism license she'd used aboard his ship, and the debacle of her exit. "Didn't expect I'd see you here."

"What are the odds! Of all the ports and ships, and all the days. Only make it up here every once in a blue moon, these days."

It *did* seem a strange coincidence. But then, stranger things had happened to her in the last few weeks. "Perhaps the Prophet willed it. It's good to see you, sir."

"And you, Ellumia. Working a different ship these days?" he asked, climbing down the portside wale and leaping onshore as casually as any deckhand.

"Ah, no," she said, thinking fast about what might have brought her here. He obviously hadn't heard about her role in the troubles at Ayugen. "I—took passage back here, actually, once I'd earned out my debt, and have been working under a calculor since. Saving to get my real licensure."

"Good! That's good. I was sorry to see you go, everything else aside," Ralhens said, shaking his head. "Never liked Odril. And this is?"

"Marea Fetterken," Ella said, holding her tongue on Odril. "A fellow student here in Yatiport." She glanced at Marea, who was chewing on a strand of hair, resonance still humming. Poor girl.

"Well, what brings you to the docks? Surely not looking for a familiar face."

Ella smiled. "Oh, no, I just like to take my air in the mornings. And I find a few conversations with passengers is generally more informative than all the broadsheets you can buy in the city. News comes so slowly up the Ein."

Ralhens nodded, rubbing his beard. "You get out of Ayugen before the troubles then?"

"Yes," she said, trying to summon the proper amount of fright and relief. If he only knew. "I'm guessing you don't sail that far south anymore?"

"Last port of call, right here. Used to run to Gendrys now and then, but no passengers for it on this voyage, nor do I expect many more, what with the legion pulling out. Damn shame about all that."

She nodded, hoping to forestall more of the crush-the-Achuri talk she'd heard all morning. "I liked Ayugen, the few chances I got to see it. Any word from up north, beyond the usual?"

Ralhens rubbed his beard, working the glass beads there.

"Some trouble in the home country. Whitecoats have got the area locked down, passage up the Oxheart stopped past Califf. Bad business, that."

Home country would be the Yershire, for Ralhens. She cocked her head. "What sort of trouble?" There was never news or trouble from the Yershire, just grain and meat and an endless supply of peasants flooding into Worldsmouth, seeking a more interesting life. Ralhens had likely been one of them, once.

"Rebellion," the captain said darkly. "You know we never—well, some of the Yersh never took kindly to Worldsmouth rule. Based in Aran, y'see. Boats down from Califf say you can't hardly see the commonfolk for whitecoats."

Aran was the ancient capital of the Yersh Kingdom. A likely place for a rebellion, if there was going to be one.

And the location of a waystone. Ella's stomach lurched.

She schooled her face to casual interest. "Sorry to hear it. I don't suppose you're headed back that direction?"

"Nah, up the Zein after this. Started running to the falls, trying to expand business what with the south route cut off." He narrowed his eyes. "Didn't you say you were working here now?"

Ralhens had never fully trusted her, and with good reason. She gave him a breezy smile. "I just like to run home now and then, and it would have been fun to sail with you, for old time's sake. Well," she glanced around, noticing Avery a few paces away, "I have taken enough of your time. Take care, captain, and thank you again for your hospitality those two years."

Ralhens puffed up. "Oh aye. My pleasure, young miss. Anytime. You come and see me, once you've got your papers in order. It'd be a pleasure to have you back."

Strange to think of going back to that life. Would she even be able to, anymore? Would she even want to?

"Thank you captain, I'll do that."

"Did you really live on a boat for two years?" Marea asked in low tones as they walked away.

"Yes. You thought I was lying?"

"No, I just—scats, Ella, that's amazing!"

Ella shrugged. "It probably sounds more glamorous than it was."

Avery separated from the crowd and walked over to them, looping a casual arm around Marea's waist. The girl lit up. "Learn anything good?" he asked.

"Yes," Ella said, "at least I think so. There *is* a stone in the Yershire, isn't there?"

He smiled. "Yes. And some very suspicious trouble based right around where it's supposed to be."

Ella smiled back. "Then I think we need to book a ship."

They went through a few before they found one headed up the Oxheart, a cargo barge with enough spare quarters abovedecks that the captain was willing to take them on. "I'll need six hundred marks, though, and ye'd best be paying up front," Captain Selwin said, a bone-skinny Yershman with a nervous air.

Ella paid him, and still he looked suspiciously at the money. "Not one'a them rebels, are you? Got a contract to bring supplies to the legion there. I don't need any trouble."

Not that kind of rebel, anyway, Ella thought. "I'm a broadsheeteur, actually. I've been in Yatiport covering the fallout from the Councilate defeat at Ayugen, but things have quieted enough I thought I would see what's happening in the shire."

"Broadsheeteur," the man snorted. "Well. Six hours to departure. Your friends better make it by then, cuz this boat waits for no man. Intend to make it to Dalhaven tonight."

Marea raised an eyebrow once the man had limped off, shouting to a crewman. "Broadsheeteur? How many stories are you going to make up today?"

"As many as I need to," Ella said. "I'm a writer, remember?"

The girl's blank resonance whined in Ella's bones—she must still be feeling unsafe, which was no wonder with the chaos of the port and her uncertainty with Avery and their plans to sail into a rebellion.

A voice called out from the docks and Avery stiffened. A man was striding toward them through the crowd, waving an arm "Harides!"

Ella glanced at him. "Someone you know?"

"No, I—just a second." He strode down the gangplank to meet the man, making small shushing motions with his free arm.

"Harides?" Ella asked, looking at Marea. "Is that his family name?"

"I—don't even know, actually," Marea said. "Could be."

Avery leaned in, talking to the man in low tones. It was an older Yatiman, dressed well. Odd that he should recognize Avery, but then the youth had apparently spent some time in Yatiport.

"Trouble?" Ella asked, when Avery had returned.

"Just an old employer," Avery said, then turned to Marea. "Do you still have your resonance on?"

She started. "Yeah, you can feel that?"

"Yes. Maybe you—"

Shouts sounded from the docks, and a splintering crash. As one the three of them looked over the side of the ship. Tai wafted there above the crowd, a toppled line of barrels bounding into the crowd below him.

"What the stains is he—"

Three barrels picked themselves up from the mess and hurtled toward him. Ella's stomach clenched. Tai dodged and the barrels arced out into the crowd.

Wafters, then, or shamans, or archrevenants. It didn't matter. Ella struck resonance. They were attacking Tai, which meant they needed to die.

Tai and Feynrick took the long way back to the docks, the grizzled Yatiman muttering to himself about shamans and pulling Tai through muddy alleys and barrel-clogged side streets. Tai hated the delay, but as much as they needed to get out of the city before Credelen noticed them, they needed even more not to have the shaman see them as he strode the streets doing whatever it was he was doing. At least the man had been walking away from the docks when last Tai saw him.

"The Yershire," Feynrick said. "Never thought I'd want to go there."

"Why's that?" Tai asked, turning sideways between a pair of three-wheeled vendor's carts blocking the end of a narrow sidestreet.

"Piss on the Yati, is all they do. Even when I ran my own company, the Yersh thought they knew better than me, just because they lived closer to Worldsmouth. Is the thigh better than the paw because it's closer to what stinks?"

Tai had no answer for that. They came out onto the docks a few minutes later, following a long narrow walk between two bark-sided warehouses, emerging into the sudden noise and stink of the docks. It was like Ayugen times ten, or times one hundred: shouts of merchants and grunts of porters, stink of spilled fish and sour wine, crush of passengers and handcarts with mangy dogs threading their way underfoot. They were supposed to find Ella in all this?

"Head for the ships," Feynrick said, pulling him along a long stack of weathered barrels. "Anything northbound. We'll book something first then get our crew."

Tai rounded the end of the stack only to run face-first into a pinch-faced lighthair. He rebounded off the man, then looked closer.

The apology died on his lips.

"Credelen," Tai managed. "Long time."

"Tai Kulga," the narrow man hissed. "Godslayer."

Feynrick had turned, eyes widening. Good. Keep Credelen talking. "I prefer Savior of Ayugen, actually, but sure, you can call me Godslayer."

"I don't care what they call you," Credelen said, thrusting a hand behind himself without looking. Feynrick blasted backwards, knocking down people as he went. "You killed my friend. My *seeker*. And you know something about the stones. Surrender and I'll spare your companions."

Why didn't the man attack? Tai remembered at the last second to unfocus his eyes. Revenants wriggled from the stones around them.

Cursing, Tai struck resonance and shot up. Thralling. The man was trying to disable him, not kill him, which meant he wanted to thrall him. Too bad for him Tai could see ghosts.

Tai dodged the first that rose, wishing he was able to fight back, but he had other means. *Plenty* of other means. With a snap of air he knocked the chock out from the line of barrels, sending the whole line of them rolling and bounding toward Credelen

With barely a glance Credelen swept an arm at the oncoming tide, and barrels leapt from the ground toward Tai.

Tai dodged again, having to watch both the barrels and air, then grimaced as shouts and screams sounded behind, a space opening rapidly around them as the docks cleared. Tai focused his higher resonance and slammed a fist down at Credelen, meant to crush the man as he had seen Nauro do at the waystone.

And kill him, Ydilwen said. *Again without cause.*

Tai gritted his teeth, looping around revenants and airborne barrels. "If this isn't cause, what is?"

Credelen sidestepped the air attack, then again struck Feynrick with an invisible hand as the Yatiman tried a second attack. Tai struck as the shaman was distracted, sweeping down for a kick to the head that should stun if not end the man.

He slammed to a halt as if into a wall, insides lurching at the sudden stop.

"What," Credelen said, turning calmly to him, ignoring the screams crowd and shouts of sailors pulling up anchor around them, "do you hope to accomplish with this? I have Ollen's power, and the power of all the men your friend killed two nights ago. You cannot resist."

Tai pushed hard the opposite direction, then up, then down, trying to dislodge himself any way he could, but he was stuck fast. And as Credelen spoke the revenants reformed, swirling in a dead mist around him. The shaman considered them, then chose a particular one.

"I'm trying to save my people," Tai said. "End this insane war I started."

Credelen smiled. "Oh, you didn't start it. But you could be my key to winning it."

He raised a hand and the revenant slammed into Tai.

34

Time slowed and Ella sped up. Barrels bounding through the crowd slowed to a crawl, the cries of alarm shifted to a rumble, and the stench in her nostrils faded to just a smell.

She leapt the ship's rail, landing awkwardly on the pier, and started to run. Shaman, wafter, archrevenant, she didn't care. A slip that struck without warning was as good as a heart attack, she'd heard someone say—maybe Karhail. She'd killed him in slip, a former Titan, and his entire pack of Broken, sent to destroy Ayugen. This would be nothing.

Except for the staining *crowds*. People were running away from the scene, pushing against each other, and the crowds had been thick to begin with—all the merry chaos of a dockyard that she normally loved. Now they were all just in her way, and about as moveable as stone in the slowed momentum of slip.

So she climbed. First just on an upended barrel to get her bearings, but then onto the shoulders of a shorter woman nearby, and from there on the backs and shoulders and heads of the people in the crowd. They would likely barely feel it in regular time—she had run across water not a month ago, again seeking to save Tai's life, so each individual footstep had to be light.

This was why she had to come—because he was always getting in over her head. Even if her resonance killed her in the process, she'd rather die fast with him than live long alone.

She leapfrogged closer, watching the drama play out ahead, hating how long it was taking. She'd had to climb up and down a few times where the crowd thinned, and the docks were long, but she was close now. Tai appeared to be paused in air, Credelen saying something to him.

No matter. She didn't need to hear the words. She'd seen the man attack her lover. That was a death warrant. Ella drew her knife, dropping from the shoulders of the last panicked porter and sprinted across the empty space.

She unfocused her eyes as she did, remembering Credelen might have some shamanic defense in place. And saw a revenant streaming into Tai, half-buried in his chest. Prophets. He would lose his resonance, ten paces up. She'd have to catch him after she killed Credelen.

The things she did for love.

Then Credelen turned to her, head moving at regular speed despite the slip, and flicked his fingers.

The air gelled around her, going from the warm honey of slip to something much, much colder. And thicker. Ahead of her Credelen froze, and the basso rumble of the crowd dropped to something so slow it felt like individual waves, like the tremors of a giant beast's steps.

She was trapped. Ella tried to push forward, but the air was thick as clay. She leaned into it, leveraging her weight, and made it a half-step further.

No. No, this couldn't be happening. She had always wondered what would happen if she slipped deeper, if the sheer resistance of air would eventually be enough to keep her from moving. How the laws of physics would change at super slow speeds. She stilled her resonance, with no change. The *uai* was coming from Credelen, then. How did she stop it?

At least she still had time—Credelen had just barely begun to turn his head away from her. She drew a breath to calm herself.

Or tried to. The air was clay in her lungs too. She couldn't breathe. Her lungs hitched against, but the air was too solid, too slow. Panic set in, the scream caught in her lungs. She would die of asphyxiation, trapped between seconds, alone.

35

One minute Ella was there, the next she was gone. Marea looked to Avery, heart pounding, barrels flying and people screaming on the docks, some of them leaping into the water. The captain of their ship was shouting, telling his men to shove off, to get out.

He stood like an island of calm in the storm. "What do we do?"

He took a deep breath and blew it out. Ahead of them Ella appeared, suddenly frozen in the middle of the empty circle around Tai and Credelen. "I think we can do this," he said, "but I'm going to need your help."

A hundred thoughts flew through her head. She took his hand. "What if we just stayed on the ship? Let them fight their fights. Avery, you could die."

Avery shook his head. "I won't die. I know Credelen. I know what he's doing. I can stop him."

"But why? What's the point?" Ahead Tai jerked in air as though stabbed. Ella was still frozen.

"The point is saving our lives, Em." His eyes gazed into hers, deep and earnest. "I betrayed Credelen, and he knows we're here. He'll come after us next. And if he doesn't have Tai and Ella as a distraction? I don't know if I can beat him then."

Em. He'd called her *Em*, his own name for her. Did he realize that was all she really needed?

"Okay. What do I do?"

He took her shoulders. "I can explain all this later, but just listen. You're not a blank. You're something rare, and wonderful, and powerful. And right now I need you to focus all your thoughts and all your feelings on Credelen. On something bad happening to Credelen. Okay? Something *bad*."

Rare? And wonderful? She wasn't a blank? Tears started in her eyes, but she nodded. "Yes. Okay. I can do that. What are you doing to do?"

Avery glanced toward the fight. "I'm going to kill him."

And before she could so much as clutch his arm he blasted off, as fast as she'd ever seen Tai waft, shooting over the crowd toward Credelen. Fear seized her, and she shook her head. "No Marea, don't be *stupid*," she muttered, almost like she was talking to her mother-revenant again, "you've got to *focus*. Something bad. Credelen. Something *bad*."

But all she could think about was Avery, about how much she wanted him to live. *Needed* him to. In the distance he swooped in, catching Tai as he fell, then landing and raising hands at Credelen. Why didn't he attack?

They were shamans. Right. Marea unfocused her eyes, and suddenly the air around them was a maelstrom of revenants, spinning around their heads.

"Stains stains *stains*," she whispered, trying to concentrate, knowing any one of those could knock out Avery like it had Tai. He was just a journeyman, and Credelen was probably a full shaman. Isn't that what Nauro said? Something bad. Something *bad* happening to Credelen.

Barrels flipped behind Credelen, flying for Avery. He dodged, but more came, lifting out of the crowd like a swarm of wooden insects drawn to blood.

Avery ran, weaving impossibly between them, barrels smashing into the ground and each other all around him, making a terrible mess. Was *she* doing that? Saving him? *You're something rare, and wonderful, and powerful*, he'd said. So why couldn't she just end this?

"Friends don't look like they'll make it, missy," a voice croaked behind her. Marea startled, seeing a wizened old deckhand looking at her as he untied ropes. "Pushing off, we are."

His left eye was glass, and something about the strange glassy stare, about the intensity of his one good eye, made her forget everything for a moment.

She heard a shout, and looked to see Avery on the ground. "Yes," she said to the deckhand, squashing the fear that rose. She could do this. Bad things to Credelen. "They *are* going to make it."

The shaman kept advancing on Avery, smashing more and more barrels on top of him, arms raised. Tai and Feynrick were attacking as they could, but Credelen batted them off like springmoths.

Prophets. Prophet's *tits* he was going to kill Avery.

No. She would not let that happen. *Could* not. *Bad things.* She imagined fire and hail and arrows and plague, every death she could dream of, hitting Credelen at once. "Bad things," she muttered again, glaring down the length of the docks, resonance buzzing.

And then Credelen fell. Not from a sword, not from a triumphant sweep of Avery, who was still buried under a mountain of shattered barrels and salt fish. From a random shard of shattered barrel, struck straight through his neck.

A *barrel* shard. What the shatters?

Credelen fell, blood fountaining around the wood.

Did Avery do that?

Did *she*?

The deckhand whistled through his teeth. "Might make it after all, huh?" He clapped her on the shoulder hard enough to make her stumble. She didn't care. Credelen was dead. And Avery was pushing out of the broken barrel heap, Feynrick giving him a hand. Alive! Thank the prophets, he was alive.

Had she done that? Did she do anything? What *was* she, that was so rare and wonderful?

Gods, it had felt good to hear him say it. Marea went to run down to them, needing to get her hands on him, only to find water where the gangplank used to be. The ship was pushing off. The crowd's roar crashed in then, panicked people still fleeing the battle, porters and nobleman alike leaping into the Ein to escape, other ships pushing off the docks in a wave of wood and oars.

And a gap of water growing between the railing where she stood and the stonework of the docks. She was leaving them behind.

"No!" she cried, spinning, looking to the ship's captain. "No, you have to wait for them!"

"This ship waits for no man," the toothy Yershman grinned. "Sides, they already paid."

She was just about to snap something back, about to start wishing bad things happened to *him*, when she saw Avery floating above the crowd, three grown people in furs clinging to his back, heading for the ship.

Relief replaced anger in the blink of an eye. "Over here!" she called, waving her arms even though he probably knew exactly where to go. "Avery! Over here!"

He turned for them, coming much slower than he'd gone but still wafting as strong as she'd ever seen the famous Tai do it. Pride welled in her breast. Avery was *amazing*.

And he thought she was *rare and wonderful*.
Maybe she *could* go to the Yershire.

36

Marea ran to Avery as soon as they touched the deck, Tai and the others piling off while the hum of resonance left Avery. He was hurt, one arm cradling his right elbow and blood staining his pants. "Are you okay? What happened?"

"What happened," Feynrick boomed, "is the milkweed ran face-first into the last person he wanted to see in Yatiport."

"I'm fine," Avery said. "Just give me a minute. I can—heal this."

Avery could battle shamans and brawl and waft *and* heal himself. "You were amazing," she said, then realized she sounded like a star-eyed seven-year-old. In front of everyone, of course.

Stain it. What was it about Avery that made her sound so *stupid*?

He shook his head. "You were the one that did it."

Ella cocked her head at them from where she was seeing to Tai, but before anyone could say anything else Captain Selwin pushed into their circle. "What's this, now? Off my ship! I said no trouble!"

"We don't intend to bring any trouble," Ella said, "and we've already paid passage."

"What do you call that back there?" Selwin demanded, waving his hand at the receding port.

"Trouble, no doubt," Feynrick said, standing up straight and eyeing the narrow Yershman, "but nothing *we* brought. You should feel lucky we took care of it. Shaman like him, coulda sunk your whole ship."

"Lucky? We'll be lucky if we make it out of this Prophets-cursed mess without sinking," he barked, gesturing at the mass of ships pushing into the Ein around them. "Eddlen, to port! *Port*, ye goatlover!"

A reedy youth at the tiller swung it around, a heavy slave barge clattering oars against them.

"We trust you," Tai said, standing straight with a wince. "And you've already taken our money, so you're bound to give us passage."

The skinny Yershman spat. "I oughta turn around and drop you all back at the docks for the whitecoats to take care of. Ye know they'd have something to say about it."

"I don't doubt they would," Ella said, "but you and I both know this is an unpowered barge. You can no more turn upstream than a fish could walk on land."

"Dalhaven, then," the Yershman said, "Turn you in at Dalhaven, and there's an end to it."

Avery straightened under her arm, his muscular frame making a powerful addition to Tai's height and Feynrick's width. "You want to talk about trouble," he said quietly, "trying to take our money without giving us passage, that's trouble."

"You've seen what we can do," Tai said, gesturing back toward the docks. "Is this really a fight you want to pick?"

"Criminals," the skinny man said, eyes flitting away from the blood but not backing down. "Soon as I hit port they'll come for me, say I was aiding you. Part of whatever that was."

"News only travels as fast as the current, Master Selwin," Ella said. "They'd have no way of knowing."

"And if it comes to that," Feynrick said, "you tell 'em we hijacked ye. No choice of yours."

"Basically true, ain't it?" Selwin barked, though his eyes were starting to dart.

"We paid you," Tai said, "and we don't mean trouble, we just want a little privacy. You give us that, and no reason for us to *actually* hijack you."

"Which we would," Feynrick said helpfully.

"Privacy," Selwin spat. "Shatters little of that to be hard on a barge. Ye've got the common room and we'll mess on the deck, but there's only one scatseat and ain't much a man can say anywhere on board but the others can hear it."

"Then ye'd best not be listening," Feynrick said, laying a hand on his axe and offering a toothy grin.

Selwin's eyes darted between them once more, then he said something under his breath. "Best be keeping your noses down in Fenschurch. And soon as we're to Califf you're gone and I ain't knowed ye."

"Then I think we have an agreement," Ella said, though the captain looked none too happy about it. "That common room you mentioned?"

He showed them to the front of the boat, where a second and third story rose above the main deck. "This here's my room, this here's the crew, and this here's you," Selwin said.

You turned out to be a room not much bigger than the *guyo*, stinking of woodsmoke and dried fish.

"*This?*" Marea asked, knowing she probably sounded like a spoiled Councilate girl and unable to help it. Just *one little bit* of privacy, for once? Was that too much to ask?

"This." Selwin grinned. "Lap o'luxury."

They moved the table and chairs off to one side, Ella saying she would see about getting them some bedding in the next port. They did their best with the food droppings dried to the floor.

"Avery," Tai said in low tones. "Nauro—the shaman that was traveling with us—knew a trick to mask our conversations. Can you do that?"

Avery pursed his lips. "I should be able to. Give me a second."

They sent Feynrick outside while Avery and Ella chatted about the differences between the Worldsmouth docks and Yatiport. Marea found herself wanting to interject, disliking Avery enjoying conversation with Ella. The older woman *was* beautiful—though she also had a spate of new lines and wrinkles following the fight at the docks.

Was it bad that that made her feel good?

Was this love?

Was she *jealous*?

Feynrick came back in shaking his head. "Were ye talking? Couldn't hear a thing."

"Good," Ella said. "Because we need to talk about what just happened. Tai, you just *ran* into Credelen, out of all the people on the docks?"

"Literally," Feynrick said. "Face first."

"And for the second time that day," Tai said. "We saw him earlier on the street."

Ella shook her head. "And I ran into my old ship captain, just as soon as I got close to the ships."

Marea looked at Avery, something between dread and hope in her chest. "Did I—have something do with that?"

Avery cleared his throat. "Yes. You've all heard of mosslucks?"

Mossluck? Is that what she was? What *was* that?

Ella and Feynrick shook their heads, but Tai frowned. "Yes. I think so. Nauro said something about a sixth resonance. Fatewalkers?"

Avery nodded. "Another name for them. Marea is one of them."

Marea flushed, hope rising inside. "So I was never a blank?"

He turned and smiled at her, like the sun breaking through clouds. "No. You have the rarest resonance of all. Some say the most powerful."

"But I—but she," Ella spluttered. "Timeslips are the rarest!"

Marea grinned. Not a blank. Rarest of all the resonances. Able to make *bad things* happen to people. It was the best thing she'd heard in years.

"Second rarest," Avery corrected. "Most of the vulgate—ah, regular people that is—don't know about fatewalkers because they assume they're blanks, like they'll call mosstongues blanks, till they notice their persuasiveness. Nothing really changes when a fatewalker strikes resonance. A few more coincidences, maybe. Nothing like floating up into the air or stopping time."

"So she… can make coincidences?" Tai asked. "Like me running into Credelen?"

"Exactly," Avery said. "Em, you had your resonance on since we got to the docks, didn't you?"

Em. He said *Em* again. "Yeah," she said, cheeks getting hot under everyone's gaze. "I—strike it sometimes. Makes me feel safer."

He nodded. "It does make you safer. Strengthens your body and speeds your mind like the other resonances. Of course you use it. And since she does, I'm guessing the rest of you have noticed some strange coincidences since you started traveling with her?"

Ella, Feynrick, and Tai frowned at each other, then Ella's eyes widened. "The axe handle. That night we were attacked, and that throw I made that killed him even though I was nowhere close."

Feynrick's brows lifted. "That was an impossible shot."

"I had my resonance going," Marea said, a chill running down her back, remembering suffocating under all those furs. "I was trying to do something. *Any*thing."

Avery squeezed her arm. "Sounds like you did something."

"We would have been dead that night," Tai said quietly, "or all thralls to that shaman, if it wasn't for you. Thank you."

Her grin got wider, if that was possible.

"Prophet's piece," Ella whispered, staring at her. "And what just happened with Credelen? She—"

Avery nodded. "I asked her to focus her thoughts on him. Knew I was going to need a little luck to get it done."

Feynrick let out a long whistle. "So our little lady's a scrapper too. I *thought* it was barking strange when that one piece of barrel took 'im right in the throat."

"Barking strange it was," Avery said, sounding for a moment older than his twenty-two years. "And the only reason we got out of there."

The looks she got then were vindication for all the time she'd felt like a fifth wheel on this trip, as the useless tagalong little girl. She hadn't been useless. She'd *saved* them, twice now.

It was gratifying as hell. She opened her mouth to say so then stopped, because the odds were high she'd probably say something stupid and ruin the whole thing. She shut it again.

"And you knew this whole time?" Ella asked, turning back to Avery.

He looked uncomfortable, the expression out of place on his normally confident face. "Yeah. I thought you all did, too."

"No," Ella said. "At some point you had to realize we thought she was a blank. Marea, did you never tell him yourself? Surely it came up."

"I—" Marea thought through her time with him, caught off guard. It had been so short. "I don't know. Maybe I did. But he told me when it mattered. And told all of you. Isn't that enough?"

Ella glanced at Tai. Marea liked her, but the woman was not good at trusting people. Ella looked back to Avery. "Anything else you want to tell us about ourselves we might not know?"

Avery shrugged. "You've all only got lower level revenants in except Tai, and that stands out because people usually have two? It's hard to know what you don't know."

"My second level seated?" Tai asked. "I can get rid of my first?"

"Looks like it," Avery said.

"Anything else?" Ella pressed.

"Hey," Marea snapped, "do you really think he's trying to hurt us? Did you forget *he's* the one that warned us when Ollen was coming, and *he's* the one that got us out of the last mess, when you all got shattered fighting Credelen? Why would he be holding anything back?"

Ella opened her mouth and closed it again. Good. Marea had gotten used to people not trusting her in the last half year—she was the Councilate girl who hadn't run when everybody else did—but she wasn't going to stand for it with Avery. She squeezed his arm again, loving how solid it was under her fingers.

"The real question, I would say," Avery said after a pause, "is why your friend Nauro didn't say anything about Marea. He had to know."

More glances around the room. Marea swore Ella and Tai had some kind of personal mindsight that involved looking into each other's eyes. She needed to remember to never do that with Avery.

"He was against her coming," Tai said at last, talking about her like she wasn't there. "Even when leaving her meant she'd probably die. Maybe he was afraid of what she could do."

"He refused me for my resonance," Marea said, not sure how she felt about it. Other than powerful. "And he didn't want to tell you guys."

Ella gave a secret-mindseye glance at Tai again. "Looks like it. Though I don't know why he wouldn't say anything."

Tai shrugged. "He must have had his reasons."

"More importantly," Ella said, "we'll have some time now, before we get to Aran. About eight days if I remember right, to float down to Fenschurch, and probably that many to paddle up the Oxheart to Califf. We need to keep studying shamanism, and Marea and I need different revenants. Avery, you said you could help us with that?"

"I can," he said. "I don't know what Nauro taught you, but I used to train initiates in our cell in Yatiport. I'm sure I can at least get you ready for the kind of attacks we might face around the stone."

"And no... reservations about doing that?" Ella asked.

Avery frowned. "No. The better you can protect yourselves, the better chance we have of getting the stone open. Right?"

Another mindreading look from Ella to Tai. "Right," she said. "Well, no time like the present, right?"

Avery glanced back toward the docks, though the door was shut so there was nothing to see. "Right. But I'll need to concentrate for this, so watch what you say, I won't be able to shield us."

"And y'know them rat-cockers got their ears to the walls," Feynrick grinned.

Marea unfocused her eyes, and felt inside as Nauro had taught them. Being a fatewalker was pearly, but she was determined to be a good shaman, too. To show Avery she was more than just lucky.

And to keep him from spending all his time with Ella and Tai.

When he turned to her, blue eyes intense, there was just a slight peeling sensation, none of the roar and drama of the times she'd overcome her revenants in the caves. None of the rush of power, either—guess you had to do it yourself for that. But she felt something gone, like the lightness on her skin once she'd shed her furs after a long day.

Then a cool sensation, almost a cutting—she remembered this from before, when Nauro gave them revenants. And yes—there! She could see the thing, wafting through the wall toward her, *feel* it latching on to her somewhere where her head met her neck, starting to feed.

Panic struck her. What if this wasn't what Avery said it was? What if he was trying to thrall her, to thrall all of them?

But no. This was *Avery*, not Nauro. Marea watched with fascination as he repeated the process with Ella, a drawn-out wisp drifting out of the ceiling, almost like heavy smoke, then seeping partway into her back.

"There," he said. "Give them a few days to seat and we should be ready to really begin. Till then we can practice the five senses—Nauro showed you those, right?"

Marea frowned. "He showed us how to see and feel them," she said. "And smell them, I guess. Can you taste and touch them too?"

"You can," Avery said, eyes a little distant. "There, barrier's back. Revenants are just barely physical, but it's enough to feel them, if you're paying attention. And they get stronger the more *uai* they're fed. If you've ever met a hermit who's losing control to their revenant you can almost *see* the other person in their eyes."

"Prophets," Ella shuddered. "And this is all common knowledge? Something your initiates would know?"

Avery gave an apologetic smile. "More like aspirants. Initiates have usually been practicing this stuff for years."

"So, we're a long ways from being able to defend ourselves, in other words?" Tai asked.

"Especially against what we're likely to face at Aran?" Ella asked. They were always finishing each other's thoughts.

Avery licked his lips, and a rock formed in Marea's gut. He was looking for the nicest way to tell them they were all going to die.

"Ollen wasn't the strongest shaman," Avery said, "but he was smart. He knew he couldn't stand up to many of the elders, so he took his cell to the Wanderer stone, knowing it was a long shot, so there'd be less competition there. He mentioned thinking the Yershire stone was a better bet, and not going because other shamans were likely to be there."

"Stronger shamans," Ella said. "Older ones. Elders, you said? Like Nauro?"

"I didn't get much chance to meet Nauro," Avery said, "but yes, if he held off Ollen's party that long, I would guess he is an elder. Was."

Tai's face went pale. "So we'll be facing worse than what Ollen's party did?"

Avery pursed his lips. "Yeah. Probably."

"And we have half a moon to get ready for that," Ella said flatly.

And her man was determined to go into the middle of it. The rock got heavier in Marea's belly. Still, there was no way she was leaving him. Maybe she could still convince him to give it up.

"Well then," Feynrick said, rubbing his hands. "Up and at 'em. Best not be wasting any time, right?"

37

News comes on the current—swiftly downstream and slowly up. Even the richest Councilor cannot learn faster than the Ein flows.
    —Sewto Talweth, *A Captain's Tract*

The Wandering Argot was not nearly so grand as its name: a tarred and patched rectangle of wooden barge, forty paces long and twenty wide with a weathered stack of room on the prow. The deck stank of Yati cured pork at the moment, sweet and smoky, but the wood had a deeper smell, of salt and brine and spice and all the thousand things it had hauled in its long career. Of river life, in other words.

Ella breathed deep. Ralhen's ship had not smelled nearly so strong, but still it reminded her of her old life, of mornings spent on the back rail watching the world slide by, reading books and dreaming about what was out there. She knew some of that now, had experienced some of the wonders, witnessed sights strange enough even Markels and LeTwi would marvel. She'd had that wonder tempered by cruelty too, by a knowledge of how dangerous the world was. In fact the more she learned of its mysteries, the more dangerous it seemed: Broken, shamans, archrevenants, waystones—even her own resonance was a danger to her.

Ella sighed, remembering again the face that had stared back at her from the bowl of water that morning, as she held it still aboard the rolling vessel. Her face, and yet not. A face somewhere between her and her mother. A face she didn't want to be hers, with its sagging skin and spreading lines and faded spots where once there had only been smooth complexion.

How long had she been stuck in Credelen's super-slowed time? How many months or years of her life had passed as time stopped and the air turned to clay in her lungs? Would she have choked or died of old age first, if that barrel stave hadn't speared Credelen?

She shuddered, not wanting to think about it. Everyone died, but she did not want to die alone, did not want to die *now*, when she had finally found a person and a calling she loved. But if she hadn't used her resonance, hadn't distracted Credelen even for that half-second, who knew if any of them would have survived?

So she had to keep using it, at least as long as they were up against shamans and gods. But she wouldn't kill herself doing it. She had a plan.

An arm circled her waist. "Deep thoughts this morning?" Tai asked, following her gaze out to the rocky western shoreline, Seinjial peaks rising in the distance.

"Deep enough," she said, leaning into him. "Is that... real food I smell?"

"Real enough," he said, waving a bowl. "Millet porridge with goat's fat, a little crunchy but a lot better than wintergrass soup."

She laughed. "Anything is better than wintergrass soup. They serving it up top?"

He nodded and glanced at her. "You sure you're fine?"

"Never better," she said, offering him a smile. Wondering if he still saw her smiling, or the old woman that was taking her place.

Sunrise found Ella standing on one of the tight-stacked barrels lining the aft deck, in a rough circle with Tai, Marea, and Avery. The chill wind whipped her hair straight back, but it felt good, made her feel alive, made her focus.

Avery started their training much as Nauro had, guiding them to see the wisps of revenants and smell their dead-leaf smell, moving quickly on to feeling them internally as they passed through, then to extend that sensation to their skin and hands, chill or friction or occasionally heat.

His tests were different than Nauro's, though. "I'm going to test your touch now," the young man said, eyes distant as he called forth a revenant. "Close your eyes, and remember what I said: shamanic battles are not all about speed. Each revenant has its own strengths and weaknesses, and needs its own approach. You need to be accurate as well as fast. The first to feel the revenant gets one point. The first to describe it accurately gets two."

Ella closed her eyes, glancing as she did at Captain Selwin, who scowled at them from the rudder. He had to wonder what they were doing, even if Avery's power masked their words. No matter. By the time he had a real inkling they'd be gone.

Ella felt something in her left hand, but before she could react Marea was crying "There! A—chill!"

Tai called out "Chill!" at the same moment, while Ella was still searching for the word.

"Cockstains," she growled as they opened their eyes, the last wisps of the revenant retreating.

Marea grinned and patted her on the shoulder. "You'll catch up, don't worry."

The girl had been sharp before, nearly her and Tai's equal, but she was a razor's edge today. Ella felt dull in comparison, her reactions always too late. Tai gave her a sympathetic smile and she ignored him, bending sideways to stretch her hip. They'd been at it for hours, and her joints hurt.

Prophets. Like her mother's used to during wet season. She really *was* getting old.

Avery glanced at her. "Should we take a break?"

"No," Ella snapped, angry they had noticed, angry there was anything to notice. "Again."

They pushed on through the morning, Ella keeping up with the others through sheer determination. Avery guided them through increasingly difficult tests, using more and more ephemeral revenants. She was exhausted when Feynrick came from the fore with lunch. She didn't argue when Avery glanced at her and called a break.

They sat in a circle on the stout wooden barrels, southern breeze pulling away the *Argot*'s stink to bring them scents of forest and river and a chill that made her glad for her furs, even if the air had warmed from Yati country. Tai and Marea were joking about their tied scores, the competition apparently overcoming Marea's frosty attitude toward him, but Ella couldn't bring herself to look at Avery's chalk tallies. She was woefully behind.

How was she ever going to learn what she needed to if she couldn't keep up?

"So what's next?" she asked Avery, trying not to sound too interested. It helped that the morning's practice had worn her out. "Thralling revenants?"

The fyelocke's eyebrows rose. "That's a long ways off. You have to be very precise about what you thrall, even with all Semeca's revenants. Thrall the wrong thing and—" He shook his head.

Ella nodded. "Nauro talked about that. Said you could draw an archrevenant's attention."

"Draw your own death, more like," Avery said. "I saw it happen once. Was in the front range hunting spirits with a cellmate, and he thought he'd found an unaligned revenant. Those were all you could safely thrall, back in the day."

"And?" Marea asked. She was pressed against him on the same barrel, slender legs sticking from her furs to rest on a separate barrel. Interesting choice of dress for a chilly day, but Ella guessed the girl had other priorities.

"And he was dead in thirty seconds," Avery said soberly. "I never even saw it coming. He just—fell over. The arch-revenant could have taken me as well, maybe didn't realize we were together." He shuddered. "So since then I've been pretty careful about what I thrall, and I'd advise you to do the same."

"Did you get any of Credelen's revenants?" Tai asked. "The man seemed pretty powerful."

Avery grimaced. "There was no time. Thralling a revenant is like luring a wild animal. You can't do it fast, and once the host dies they get spooked, streaming off in all directions."

"Which is why Nauro always took so long," Ella said, thinking back. "When we were attacked on the road, he just stood there. I thought he was just bad at what he did, but he was probably trying to thrall the other shaman's revenants."

"Very good," Avery said. Marea scowled.

"When you are in a position of advantage," he went on, "if you have a larger *uai* stream, or a lot more knowledge, thralling away their power is usually the best option. When you're not, a direct attack and a little support usually works better." He winked at Marea, and she blushed.

"And there's no way you can thrall revenants before you get your shamanic resonance?" Ella asked.

Avery hesitated. "Theoretically thralls can be given to

someone else, but I've never heard of anyone doing it. Before, ah, what happened at Ayugen, most shamans could only hope to thrall a few revenants in their lifetime, so it never really came up."

Good. Because Ella didn't have time to wait for her first revenant to seat, then her second revenant to attach from somewhere, and to seat, and to overcome both of those. She needed power *now*.

So after a few more rounds in the afternoon, when the sun set and the wind grew bitter, she stayed out on the barrels, unfocusing her eyes, listening with every sense in her body, seeking for the souls that were drifting out there, that were drifting everywhere once you learned to look, even in the water. She was exhausted, but Avery had said it was possible, and that was all she needed. All she'd ever needed.

"Hey," a voice said, startling her from deep concentration, watching the shreds of something no longer alive drift through the needleaves along the rocky coast.

Tai. "Hey there," she said, voice a little rough. How long had she been out here? The star was nearly set to the west, fires coming out on the Yati hilltops.

"You—coming inside soon? Selwin brought us some coals, it's nice and warm."

"Yes! Soon. I just want to—" Wanted to what? Prophets, she was tired.

Tai crawled up on the barrel next to her. "You still practicing what Avery showed us?"

She nodded, shame rising. He'd figured out her plan, or he was going to.

"Plenty of time for that," he said. "Revenants take days to seat, and then even if we use the harmonies—"

She nodded. "A week at best before we could access the shamanic resonance without yura. Probably more like two."

He shook his head. "The trip'll take longer than that. We have time. Come inside, love."

"We don't have time," she said. "I don't, anyway." She couldn't keep the bitterness from her voice.

And that was all he needed to figure it out. Tai went still beside her, then she felt his shoulders slump. "The *uai* stream," he said. "The longevity. You want to start thralling so the cost of slipping doesn't kill you."

"So it doesn't kill *us*," she said, ashamed he'd figured her out but still passionate. "I don't know how much more I can slip before I'm—"

"Before you're old?" he asked. "Before you die?"

"I almost did, back there," she said. "You can see it on my face."

"I think you're a long way from dying, still," he said. "Unless it's from cold out here."

"I'm a long way from living too, if I want to keep up with you and Marea," she said bitterly. "You saw how I am today. How my reactions are slower, my senses duller, how my bones hurt. I'm *old*, Tai."

"You're not old," he said. "Not to me. You're *Ella*. The woman I love."

"Even if you don't want to see her naked?"

He laughed. "Small chance of that happening on the ship anyway."

Worry warred with love in her, one side wanting to stay out all night and one side wanting to smile with him, to trust that it would be alright. Her mother would have stayed out, would have held on to her fear and shame.

Ella sighed, letting go of it. What was shame anyway, between them? "You're too good for me, you know that?"

He laughed. "How do you think I feel? When my woman

would stay out in the dark and cold just to look a little younger for me?"

"To keep you alive when you fight shamans and arch-revenants more like."

"Thank you," he said, meeting her eyes, his smile dropping a little. "But freezing out here and losing sleep is not going to help with practice tomorrow. Come inside?"

Ella took one last glance at the water. Her spirit was still ready to sit out here all night, but her body said a brazier of coals and some sleep was definitely the best option.

"You win," she said. "Help an old lady down from these barrels?"

38

The days passed quickly aboard the *Wandering Argot*, Tai taken at first with the novelty of ship travel, and then just with the *size* of the world. Ayugen, Ninefingers Pass, the Yati hinterlands he could understand, could walk there with his own feet—that was a scale to the world that made sense, like the distance to Gendrys. Even the float down the Yanu hadn't seemed that different than a long waft over the southern forests, searching for Nauro.

But the Ein river was endless.

They'd been floating it for days now, Selwin and his two men often working day and night, shoreline passing by at the pace of the current, faster than a man's walk if slower than a fast waft. But it passed *day and night,* for almost a quarter moon now, and Ella said they were barely out of Yatiland and into the Yershire. A few days back they had passed the bustling port of Hafeluss, along a milky-blue river Ella said lead to Seingard. *Seingard,* a place he had only ever heard stories of, as foreign to him as Worldsmouth itself.

And every port they stopped, people had heard of the rebellion at Ayugen, the battle at Gendrys. Heard of *him*. The man who dammed a river. Titan-killer. The Achuri menace. Savior of Ayugen. The names went on and on. *His* names.

The fame felt strange, unreal, so Tai threw himself into the training, into something he could understand and control.

And good thing, too, because Ella was throwing herself in just as hard as she had the first day, and Marea hadn't slowed down in her wild attempt to impress a man who, as far as Tai could tell, was already quite fond of her.

Maybe because of it, because Ella was desperate and Marea love-sick and Tai needing an outlet, every day Avery remarked on how fast they were progressing, how it took normal initiates years to learn what they were learning.

"Well we're not stilt-legged calves," Tai said a day after Hafeluss, during a break in their morning session. "We've all overcome resonances, fought wars, killed Broken and worse."

The words felt strange in the bright sun and gentle roll of the river, the morning warm enough to strip off their furs. Ella leaned into him with her eyes closed, breathing deep. She didn't have the stamina she'd had before the battle at the docks, and the sessions left her exhausted. But the woman didn't let exhaustion stop her.

"Still," Avery said. "You're all seeing as well as many do *with* the resonance, and Ella is close to getting a grasp on Fattie."

Ella smiled at this, but Marea grinned. She'd taken to naming Avery's revenants like she'd named Nauro's. "Too bad she's way behind on the leaderboard," the girl said.

That was what she called the barrel top Avery chalked their scores on, with daily and cumulative scores. Tai grinned back. "Too bad you are, too."

She was actually only four points behind him, which was a single test or two, but Marea gave him a false scowl. "I'll defeat you yet, God-slayer."

He false-scowled right back. "I am Tai Kulga, destroyer of worlds. The lighthairs must pay for their crimes."

The girl was still cold to him outside of the training sessions, but something in her competitive spirit meant they got along when they were learning. It was a nice change from how things had been before. She probably still blamed him for her parents' death and still hated everything they stood for, but at least they could laugh about something now.

"Speaking of which," Ella said, her eyes still closed. "Avery, do you think Tai's second revenant is seated well enough? Could we start getting rid of them and get him actual shamanic power?"

"I don't see why not," Avery said, "though you have to overcome the second revenant on your own to get the power. It can take years."

Ella opened her eyes and smiled. "Oh, I think we can get it a done a little faster than that."

They convened in the cramped cabin that night, Avery looking doubtful but promising no one would overhear as Ella briefed them all on what to do. Ydilwen had been mostly quiet since the battle on the docks—the revenant seemed to pick only the worst times to speak up—but Tai would still be happy to have him gone. What would shamanic power be like? Would he see revenants all the time?

Feynrick struck resonance first, a low buzz, then Marea, hers a whine almost too high to hear, quickly tuning her pitch to Feynrick's. Avery came next, striking his higher brawler's resonance, and three worked for a while to get them in tune. Tai had been a little hesitant about revealing the harmonic secrets to Avery, but Ella for once had been trusting, arguing he'd saved their lives, and the harmonies were something everyone deserved to know.

While they worked Tai searched inside. "Well, old friend," he said quietly, like he'd spoken to Hake and Fisher and even Naveinya, "you ready to move on?"

Move on, Ydilwen's voice came immediately. *Is that what you think happens? That we live forever in some happy garden until a fresh host comes along?*

"I don't know what happens," Tai said, "and I don't care. You're a parasite feeding on my *uai* and using lies to try to control me. You need to go."

What lies have I ever told you? The harmonies had synced now, and Tai could feel the synergy, the coordinated buzz rattling his bones.

"That you're Ydilwen, for one thing," Tai said over the buzz. "That you have anything other than noble intentions in feeding off me."

I am Ydilwen. I told you to visit my mother's house in Yatiport. I could have proved it, but you refused.

"Yes," Tai said, willing the thing gone. He was done with this voice. "And I will refuse you everything you ask, because you are not Ydilwen."

And this is why you need me. You act like you owe the people you've killed nothing. That you can kill them whenever it suits you. What do you think death is like? That we just fade away? Join the ancestors?

"I don't know," Tai said, feeling an edge of frustration, "and I don't care." In the background Ella said something about it not working, had Marea adjust her tone down to a melancholy harmony.

And that is why you need me. Because we don't *just fade away, especially the ones you kill. We stay here,* are *stuck* here, *slowly starving unless we get a host.*

"Then give it up," Tai said. "Let go."

You think it's easy to let go of your deepest hopes and dreams? Of the widowed mother you were supporting in Yatiport? Of all the hopes you had to find your wife's revenant? How would you feel about Ella if you died today? At peace?

That caught Tai off guard. The resonant harmony was thrumming through him, and yet Ydilwen felt as real as ever. "I—don't know. I'd miss her, I guess."

Yes, you would. You would pine for her. You would want to see her, to talk to her. Do anything for more time with her. And that alone would keep you from truly dying, would lock you into the hell of being a revenant. Not to mention what would happen to your friends and your city, once someone else takes Semeca's power.

The horror of it struck him. Life on the streets had taken away his fear of death, but he'd never thought about what it would be like to stay here, to see everything, but not be able to touch it. Not talk to Ella or Aelya again. Not keep the Counciliate from taking back everything they'd fought for.

That's right. And every person you kill has lovers and aspirations just like yours, so they are all doomed to come back to this hell. Ollen. The shaman who attacked you. The others in my cell. Me. All the people you killed in the rebellion—all revenants now. All doomed to suffer because they were in your way.

Ella had switched harmonies again, but the air in the cabin was suddenly too hot, too close around him. Tai stood. "I have to go."

Her eyes widened. "Tai, wait!"

She reached for him but he pushed out and pounded down the stairs, needing to get out, the walls closing in on him.

He paced to the edge of barge, blood beating hot in his ears. The air was blessedly cool, slush of the river peaceful in the blue of the setting star. He took a deep breath.

I am still here. And the more people you kill, the more you doom to my fate.

"Shut *up!*" Tai shouted to the night.

. . .

Ella cleared her throat. "So," she said carefully, the others in the cramped cabin avoiding his eyes since she'd brought him back. "That didn't seem to go so well. Maybe you weren't totally ready to get rid of it?"

Tai hated this. Hated the feeling of powerlessness, hated the hold Ydilwen had over him. He'd defeated *Naveinya* after all, one of the most powerful revenants the ninespears knew. And yet—

"I *am* ready to get rid of him," Tai said. "I just can't."

A silence followed that, and he hated admitting it, but it was true.

Avery cleared his throat. "Well. That was all very interesting. But I *can* get rid of him for you, Tai."

"He just won't get the resonance," Ella said. Somewhere outside his frustration Tai could tell Ella was upset her harmonies hadn't worked, but they didn't always work.

Especially on people who aren't ready to get rid of their spirit guides. Isn't that right?

"Shut *up*," Tai muttered, then nodded at Avery. "Good. Do it."

The shamanic way was a lot faster and easier—all Tai felt was a cool slice, like someone sliding an icicle along his neck, and then nothing.

Tai looked up. "Is he gone?"

"Is *it* gone," Ella corrected. He didn't need mindsight to tell she was worried. Thought he'd started believing in the revenant. Felt like she'd failed.

And it hurt his pride, but was she wrong?

"It's gone," Avery said. "A healthy revenant, too. But then I guess that shouldn't be a surprise, given your native amount of *uai*."

"Right. Well. Just don't stick it back on me."

"I won't," Avery said. "Can't, actually. No one really understands why, but a revenant can't attach to the same host twice. It's why thralling takes so long, because you can't put the revenant back in the host you took it from."

"And they never repeat personas," Marea said. "Of all the people we helped overcome in Ella's school, no one ever heard the same voice twice."

Well that was a relief. Even if Tai felt like a total idiot for not being able to defeat a simple revenant by himself. Ydwilwen was gone, and he wasn't coming back.

"It's okay," Ella said, laying a hand on him. "This happens to lots of people. It must have just—picked an effective voice."

"It must have," he said, not wanting to think about it. "How long before the next one comes up? A couple days?"

"At most," Avery said. "Given your *uai* stream, maybe less than that."

"And with that," Ella said, reaching for the lantern, "I suggest we call it a night."

Marea and Avery stood up—the two usually went out for some privacy, after everyone else turned in. That was good. Life was short—let them enjoy it.

Ella snuffed the lantern and lay down next to him, snuggling in close, but sleep wouldn't come. Ydilwen was gone, but his words still rattled in the darkness.

How would you feel about Ella if you died today? You would pine for her. And every person you kill has lovers and aspirations just like yours, so they are all doomed to come back to this hell. Every person.

And you still act like you owe them nothing.

39

The barge pulled in to Fenschurch the next morning, Tai feeling groggy and out of sorts from a night of no sleep. Ella, Avery, and Marea stepped out into town to buy provisions—anything to improve Selwin's youngest son's endless pots of saltless porridge—but he stayed back in the cabin. The further north they traveled the more his hair stuck out, and with his height and scar combined, he didn't want to risk anyone guessing who he was.

Especially with the number of white-hulled Councilate ships and white-coated Councilate soldiers he saw out the cabin door. The docks were crawling with them, reminding him of the day he'd overcome his Hake-revenant, pushing a legion of white-coated soldiers down Ayugen's docks on the back of an unstoppable *uai* wave. He had no such wave now, not even a revenant to overcome.

And would he be able to, when the revenant did wake up?

"Milkweed," Feynrick said from the other corner of the cabin, leaned against the wall with his fur blankets heaped over his knees. "What's got ye mopey?"

Tai rolled his shoulders. "I'm not mopey. I'm just—thinking."

"Like I said," the grizzled Yatiman said, blowing on a cinder he held with a smoker's tongs. "Mopey."

He touched the cinder to his pipe and inhaled, sage crackling, then exhaled in a cloud of fragrant smoke. He held the pipe out. "Want some?"

Tai had never smoked before—no money for it, then no time. But you know what? "Sure," Tai said, taking the pipe. Lumo smoked like a chimney, and he always seemed peaceful.

Tai drew a breath, sage crackling, then instantly started coughing, puffs of smoke leaving his mouth.

Feynrick cracked up—of course he did—and took the pipe back. "Just hold it in your mouth, lad," he said, once Tai had recovered. "Enjoy the flavor. Selwin's like to take all morning arguing prices for a tug up the Oxheart. Might as well pass the time."

There were probably a million other things Tai could be doing, like practicing shamanic sight or watching the docks for clues about what they were going into, but he took the pipe back, tried again and managed not to cough. The smoke was actually kind of pleasant, rolling out of his mouth.

They passed the pipe in silence a while, watching the sun rise —it'd been rising earlier and earlier, the further north they traveled—then Feynrick exhaled a cloud and said. "Now. What's got ye mopey?"

Tai drew a long breath and added his cloud to Feynrick's, feeling more relaxed than he had since the waystone. "My revenant," he said. "The one Avery cut out. Ydilwen."

Feynrick nodded. "Seemed like a piss-barker."

Tai laughed at the word. Were all Yati curses based on dogs? "He *was* a piss-barker. And then not being able to get rid of him last night—" He shook his head.

Feynrick paused, about to take a puff. "Took me forty-two years to get rid of Gleesfen, and you're complaining about having yer voice a week?" He pulled on the pipe, sun's rays catching in the smoke through the open door.

"It's just—I've gotten rid of voices before. I understand what they're doing, and usually I can see through whatever they're trying to get me to believe. Hake wanted me to feel guilty for not saving his life. Fisher did the same thing, and Naveinya was trying to convince me I was unfit to lead. But Ydilwen?"

Feynrick nodded, watching him.

"Ydilwen wants me to make it up to everyone I've ever killed," Tai said, though that didn't feel right either.

Feynrick repacked the bowl and passed him the pipe, soapstone warm from the sage. "So he's using guilt too. Sounds like a pattern."

Tai drew in smoke. "Maybe. But it's more like—he wants me to stop killing. Like he's trying to convince me that being a revenant is hell, and everyone I kill goes there."

"Wouldn't that be nice," Feynrick said, "if you didn't have to kill. But that's what this world is. Ye kill millet for breakfast. Pigs for dinner. Whitecoats in battle. We all got to make our peace with it, whether it's ancestors or afterlife or not believing any of it. Maybe that's yer problem. Ye don't really believe in the Achuri ancestor bit, do ye?"

Tai shook his head, handing the pipe back. "I can't. That's all *belief*, which is fine if you don't know something. But we *know* about the revenants now, and we're learning more every day. They're not ancestors. Just like they're not saints either, or whatever you call them."

"Genitors," Feynrick said in a wash of smoke. "And it don't matter that much, what they are or aren't. You kill someone, you're making orphans and widows and grieving parents and lonesome friends. That's just what it is, and there ain't many of us strong enough to take that full-weight and keep fighting. S'why so many soldiers drink, I guess."

"Or smoke?" Tai asked, knowing Ella would say something about the stink when she got back.

Feynrick snorted. "Sage? That's like comparing bittermelong to *mavenstym*. This ain't nothing but a way to kill some time."

Voices sounded on the deck below, unfamiliar. Tai tensed. He had Selwin and his sons' voices memorized by now. Was it the Councilate? Had the captain figured out who he was, and tipped them off?

Feynrick nodded at him, the old warrior sitting up straighter. "Use your mindsight."

Tai did, hating how often he still forgot he had the resonance, and peered through the walls. He found three minds close: one was Selwin, one his son, and one a stranger, thinking in Yersh. His thoughts—it seemed to be male anyway—were a wash of impatience and fear and images of a leather satchel and pale stone chambers open to the breeze, a city cut through with rivers.

"Worldsmouth," Tai said, speaking low, trying to focus in on the new mind. Selwin's was always a clamor of negative thoughts and long figures estimating his profits. "A—messenger of some kind. Booking passage, I think."

"Messenger," Feynrick said, pipe forgotten. "The kind that speaks with a sword?"

Tai looked harder, thinking again he needed to spend more time learning mindsight. Maybe Avery knew something of it. "I don't know, it's hard to tell. I can only ever see what they're thinking about right now, which is mostly doubting whether Selwin's is the right ship to take or not."

Feynrick eyed him a moment longer, then settled back. "Going to put a hitch in your little practice sessions, having someone else along."

Tai shifted uncomfortably. It would put a hitch in a lot of things—like his ability to even leave the cabin, for fear of being recognized. "Maybe we can practice in here."

"And maybe this messenger is just looking to make some quick change wherever there's trouble. Always a pack of 'em, following the Councilate's wars. Plenty of money to be made, fighting or cocking or stealing what's left after the army's done. Running messages. Could be harmless." Feynrick held out the pipe. "Smoke?"

Tai stood. "No. I think it's time for a talk with Captain Selwin."

"Shatters you want?" Selwin cursed, when Tai found him haggling over prices on a sack of millet.

"I want this ship to ourselves," Tai said, turning so his back faced the bustling docks. "How much do you need?"

Selwin's eyes narrowed. "Messenger boy. Don't want him on board?"

"I don't, actually, and I know it's all just money to you. So what do you need?"

Selwin wiped his hands on his pants. "Might be I'm doing civic duty. Don't care about the money."

"Might be five hundred marks lets you do something civic in your spare time."

"Five hu—" Selwin's eyes narrowed. "Awful lot of money if you got nothing to hide."

"We're private people," Tai said, mind spinning for some rational excuse. They hadn't really bothered since their first talk with Selwin, but they'd need to tell the passenger something. "Our religion is not—well, you've seen what we do. We'd rather not draw attention to ourselves."

"Religion, is it?" Selwin rubbed his hands again. "Not

believers?"

Believers to a Yershman would mean Eschatolists, the Yersh church of the Ascending and Descending God. "We're a smaller sect," Tai said. "On a pilgrimage to Aran, to see the stone."

Tai had no idea what Eschatolists thought of waystones, but he'd heard Beal and Ilrick talk of Aran with pride, the capital that never fell.

Selwin seemed to soften some. "Sight to see, it is. Shatters better'n Shatterbrook at least. Lend your weight to the fight, are ye?"

That was dangerous territory. Selwin was bringing supplies to the Councilate army, but that didn't mean he was personally rooting for them. The Yersh had been the first people the Councilate conquered, one hundred years ago or more, but that didn't mean they liked being ruled. If the Yati Troubles and the Blacksmith Rebellion in Seingard were any measure, no people did. Still, better not to commit, in case he guessed wrong.

"Just pilgrims, headed for the stone."

Selwin narrowed an eye, gazing at him. "Sure you are. Might be I earn a little favor with the whitecoats, carrying their messenger. Boy stays."

Tai rolled his shoulders, but there was really nothing he could do short of threatening the man, and that would just make him more likely to report them, with all the whitecoats around. Tai nodded. "Be good to have him on then."

Ella came back a few hands later, talking of all the Councilate soldiers in town and excited for the bakery she'd found, with fresh pear tortes. She took a huge bite of one and sighed. "The one thing the Councilate gets right."

Marea and Avery showed up toward sunset, the girl's face glowing and a smile playing about Avery's lips. They'd snuck off at the last port too, and good for them. Tai'd be doing that as well, if he could risk it.

An echo of Ydilwen's words came up then, and Tai shoved it down. The voice was gone. It didn't matter.

"Who's the new guy?" Marea asked as they all settled in to wrapped packets of a fiery riverfish curry with fresh herbs and cassava cake.

"Messenger," Tai said. "From Worldsmouth."

Ella and Avery looked up sharply at this. "Councilate?" Avery asked, mouth full of curry.

"Hard to tell," Tai said. "From Worldsmouth, but I don't know whose messages he's running. I didn't talk to him, just read his thoughts."

"I'll go and feel him out, once we push off," Ella said. "Whatever he doesn't tell me, maybe you can learn in mindsight."

Tai nodded. "Good. But be careful, he could be a mindseye too, for all we know."

Avery gazed through the wall a moment, toward the captain's room where the messenger was now staying, Selwin having moved in with his boys. "Not a mindseye. A brawler, though doesn't look like he's overcome any of his revenants."

"A *normal person*, then," Marea said. "You're all so used to shamans and yura and overcoming revenants you forget that most people up here don't even eat enough winterfood to *have uai*, much less know how to use it."

"Except where we're going," Ella said, "where we're likely to find shamans more powerful than Nauro was."

"Yeah. Except for that."

They stayed in the cabin savoring their meal as the barge bumped and jostled out of port, then Ella left to seek out the messenger. Tai told her about the pilgrim cover story, then looked intently for the thoughts streaming through the wall. Avery joined him, apparently able to use mindseye resonance too. Were all journeymen as skilled as him?

Watching a conversation with mindsight was a lot different

than hearing it out loud, but Tai did his best to swim through the emotions and images and word snippets that came up, following them through greetings and pleasantries and talk of Worldsmouth. The messenger—Eyadin—was a fearful fellow, thoughts often returning to a lattice-walled stone chamber on a particularly sunny afternoon. As Ella honed in on what he was doing, some half-formed images flashed up that Tai assumed were lies he was telling her, with the image of the leather satchel coming up more and more often, secreted now between Selwin's bed and the rough wood wall.

Tai glanced at Avery, who nodded, but they were both too intent on watching to talk. Tai tried following Eyadin's thoughts upstream, as he had for Semeca, looking for the deeper causes behind the fear, but kept coming back to that sunlit chamber, as though there were something there Eyadin didn't want to see either, some dam in the flow of his thoughts.

Two things were clear though, as Ella wrapped up in niceties that felt uncertain from her and relieving from him, to be done talking: Eyadin was no shaman or ninespear, but he *was* carrying a message intended for the commander at Aran. And he expected it to result in a swift and brutal crackdown.

Tai stopped watching as Ella came back into the room. "Learn anything?" she asked, slightly out of breath from the climb up the stairs.

Tai glanced at Avery. "He's definitely from Worldsmouth, and he keeps thinking back to a particular place and time with fear, but I couldn't see what happened there."

Avery nodded. "I'm guessing it was when he got the messages that he's carrying. That someone threatened him."

"Worldsmouth?" Ella asked. "Are you sure? He said he was from the saltmarshes."

"He's lying, then," Tai said, and Avery nodded. "What did he say about what he's doing?"

"He said he was hoping to enlist," Ella said. "Though now that I think about it, he could have done that at Fenschurch, or Worldsmouth for that matter."

Feynrick grunted. "Any outpost. The legions are always looking for fresh meat."

"So he's going to join the other side?" Ella asked.

Tai shook his head. "His orders are from someone high up in the Concilate. High up enough that they expect to be obeyed when they command the whole city of Aran be put to the sword."

"The whole city?" Marea asked, eyes widening. "They wouldn't."

Tai shot a look at Avery, who nodded. "That's what I saw too," the stocky youth said.

Silence fell on them. The Concilate had been brutal in forcing Ayugen under its control, but killing an entire city?

"They have no idea what they're doing," Ella said. "The ninespears there aren't going to go down without a fight."

"Unless they know exactly what they're doing," Avery said. "There are plenty of theories about which arch-revenants have seats on the Council."

"Smart," Feynrick grunted. "Use the legions as a first line of attack. Throw the soldiers at them first and hope sheer numbers get rid of the weak ones, then clean up themselves if they have to."

"They may be underestimating the shamans," Tai said. "What Ollen's party threw at Nauro... that could take out a lot of soldiers."

"And the shamans at Aran are likely to be a lot stronger than Ollen was," Avery said. "Elders."

"And this is where we're going?" Marea asked. "Right when they get the message to do it?"

A second silence descended, then Feynrick cracked a smile.

"Sounds like a party."

41

Sure, the odds are slim, and there is only one chance at this. But as the book says, patience means little without a decisive strike at opportunity. So I will strike. Patiently.
  --Meyn Harides, *personal journals*

Marea stepped off the long dock and took a deep breath, glad to be away from the stink of the tug boat. She'd gotten used to the rowers' smell during their three-month trip to Ayugen, but that boat had at least stayed a few hundred paces ahead. Flat-fronted barges needed the sleeker tug boats to break the current, and that meant all the sweat and dirt and feces stink of the indentured servants was lashed right to the front of the ship. It was almost worse than walking the whole way herself.

Almost.

The good thing about tug boats was they needed to stop frequently to feed and wash the servants, which meant more chances to be alone with Avery. She squeezed his hand and he smiled, stopping to plant a kiss on her lips. It still sent tingles straight through her. She felt so *grown-up* walking through strange towns on the arm of the man she loved, so far from anyone she knew.

The actual town of Clearspont was a few hundred paces away from the docks, connected by a long series of boardwalks through tall reeds and the keening wail of cicadas. The ground was bare here, far enough north that snow rarely stayed and plants grew year round. Marea breathed in again, smelling marsh and alfalfa and sweet clover from the fields ahead.

"Can you imagine living out here?" she asked him. "Just raising a family and working the land and never having to worry about the stuff we do in the city? Doesn't it sound great?"

"Maybe we can for awhile, after the stone," Avery said. "Just you and me."

The thought of it turned her knees buttery.

If there was an after, that was.

"You're not worried about Eyadin?" Marea asked, swatting at one of the giant blue-black flies buzzing lazily through the reeds. It'd been two days since they started up the Oxheart, but they hadn't really talked about the messenger or what he meant for their mission.

Avery shook his head. "It doesn't change what we have to do. Honestly, I'm surprised Tai and his crew aren't excited about it."

"Excited?" Marea asked, looking up at him. "Why would they be excited?"

"Less competition," Avery said. "If they were smart they'd let the messenger get through, watch the army do its work, and then slip in afterwards. Not all the shamans would get killed, but some of them surely would. The rest would be easier to deal with."

Marea gave a little laugh. Was he joking? "And just let the city of Aran die?"

He glanced down at her, breeze ruffling his peppered locks.

"A lot worse could happen if someone else opens the stone. Sometimes you have to accept your losses."

She squeezed his hand. He was so *confident*. "Where did you even learn all this stuff?"

He shrugged. "Here and there. You learn a lot, growing up in the ninespears."

Ahead of them Clearspont's Shrine of the Ascending God rose up, steep roofs and ornate windows in stark contrast to the single-story buildings and cobbled streets beyond. "What if we just stayed here? Let the whole thing blow over."

"And lose my chance? Lose *our* chance? We've talked about this. What if one of Ollen's friends ended up taking the spear? He would find out about me, find out I betrayed their cell. Come after us. No. This is the only way that we're safe. For good."

Marea sighed. She hated it, but he was probably right. "Well, at least we have the afternoon. Selwin said we wouldn't shove off until sunset. Where shall we go, my love?"

It would be a lie if one of her first thoughts wasn't the copse of goldbark they'd found outside Fenschurch, and the things they had done there, finally alone. She blushed, but Avery just said, "It looks big enough to have a bakery. Maybe we can get some real food, and practice your walking."

"Sure." This was another thing they had been doing with their private time, practicing fatewalking. Turned out it was not as simple as wishing bad things would happen to people, though that was the heart of it. Avery had been showing her concentration techniques, and ways to focus her resonance to make more particular things happen.

The amount of things he knew was amazing. Her parents had kept up with her education, but Avery must have been reading nonstop when he wasn't working the docks.

Clearspont did turn out to have a bakery, with a few simple Yersh-style stools out front, built of bent and braided wood with three legs and a straight back. Avery ordered them a pair of apricot tarts and glasses of honeyed chamomile. They sat out front, inhaling the aroma of baking bread and watching the slow-moving traffic on the street.

"Something bad," Avery said in a low tone, though he always used his shamanism to make sure no one could understand what they were saying. He was watching a stout woman with baskets on both arms, delivering eggs to nearby houses. "Bird droppings, maybe. Remember, don't strike until you're focused."

Marea nodded. This was one of the techniques he'd shown her, to not strike her resonance until her mind was focused, until she was imagining the thing being real, in this case the bird swooping down to meck on the woman. On one of her baskets, Marea decided, though it often didn't go exactly as she wanted. Still, she imagined the look of the bird, a blue-winged marsh jay, the smell of the air, the sound of the meck landing, all the fine details he'd said would focus the resonance, focus her desire for it to be real.

Then she struck, resonance whining in her bones, eyes boring into the woman.

A jay squawked and swooped, leaving droppings half a pace from the woman. The woman startled and cursed, then made the rising sign of the Ascending God and hurried about her way.

"Good," Avery said, "you're getting it. Try closing your eyes next time, once you've gotten the scene, to focus your imagination more. See it all, hear it, feel it, touch it, *taste* it."

Marea nodded, wanting to do him proud, wanting to master her rarest and most powerful of resonances. To be his equal in at least one way. "Who's next?"

They tried making a carpenter trip next, then a farmer's cartwheel break, then an alley cat step in the path of the one of the town's ministers. Each time something like the intended effect happened, but no matter what they tried, she couldn't make it happen *exactly*.

"I'm sorry, love," she said, after the minister ended up kicking the cat—Eschatolists were notoriously wary of cats. "I just can't seem to get it."

"You're doing great," he said. "It's not easy, and we've only been at it a few days. You'll get it."

Then he leaned in and kissed her, to the raised eyebrows of the egg matron passing the other direction. Marea smiled, not caring, *wanting* the woman to see. To be envious of her, who had only been an object of mistrust or pity for so many months.

Avery broke off suddenly, eyes looking intently over her shoulder. "Ready for a real challenge?" he asked, voice low.

"Yes," she said. "Anything." She *would* get control of her resonance. She *would* impress this man who knew and could do so much.

Because otherwise, eventually, he'd realize he was too good for her. And leave.

"Good," he said, still looking over her shoulder. "Don't look, but the messenger from the *Argot* is coming. Eyadin. He's got his satchel with him. I want you to make it open, make his documents fall out."

That was a lot harder than anything they'd tried so far—a lot less *likely*—but she nodded, wanting to do it, believing she could do it. Marea focused on the idea of her doing it right, trying to sway the odds. Then glanced at Eyadin and started visualizing the worn leather satchel, a weak spot in the shoulder strap giving way, the flutter of papers spilling out, the gentle wind they would make as they see-sawed through the air, his startled cry, the blue sky, the smell of yeast and alfalfa—

Avery squeezed her shoulder. "You can do this. In three."

Her eyes were still shut, imagining every detail of the slip as clearly as possible, *desiring* it to happen as strongly as she could. Two. For Avery. For her. For their future.

One. She struck resonance and opened her eyes, *willing* fate to bend, willing the weakest point in his strap to break, the papers to flutter out.

And they did. Not exactly as she'd thought—the bag slipped from his shoulder and flapped open, but still.

Avery was already there, walking casually toward the messenger when it happened. He must have stood up after squeezing her shoulder, must have started walking toward the man.

Eyadin blanched, and Marea saw Avery *stutter* for a moment, as if his whole body snapped left, or as if he'd timeslipped. She'd seen Ella do something like that, when she slipped for a moment.

"Let me help you, friend!" Avery was calling, bending to pick the scattered papers off the cobblestone.

Eyadin protested, face still white as lime, thrusting handfuls of papers into his satchel. He looked deathly afraid—and he should be, carrying the kind of messages he did—but Marea smiled, dropping her resonance and reveling in what just happened. In what she'd *made* happen.

"That was amazing," Avery said when he came back, his eyes alight. "I didn't think you could do it."

She smiled. "I wasn't sure I could, either. And did you *timeslip*?"

He nodded. Was there *anything* the man couldn't do? "I wanted to know what his message said. The one about Aran."

"And?"

He sat back down. "And we saw it right in mindsight. One of the Council members is ordering an attack on Aran."

"Is it—do you think it's one of the archrevenants?"

"Hard to know," Avery said. "But at least I have names now. That's more than any other shaman knows."

Marea took a bite of her pastry, savoring the mix of salt-crusted bread and sweet apricot. "What are you going to do with it?"

"Nothing, for now. But when we get the spear…"

She nodded. "They will be your enemies."

"Or our allies," he said, gazing down the street at a trio of dusty travelers, bags balanced on curved sticks over their shoulders. "As far as we know, no arch-revenant has attacked another in a long time. Possibly never. There are theories that one person can't master more than one resonance, but others think maybe they are in some sort of alliance."

Marea swallowed. "Do you think they'll be at the stone?"

"No," Avery said. "I don't think they'd have the army make such a big move if they were planning to do something themselves. But I *do* think it's a good sign we're headed for the right stone. If anyone would know whose power is in each stone it's the gods themselves. And they wouldn't waste political capital this way unless it mattered."

She shook her head fondly. "How'd you get so smart? Weren't you raised on the docks?"

"On the docks by the ninespears," he said. "My math and history might not be that great, but my archrevenant politics? Second to none." He nodded at the three travelers, likely pilgrims headed to Aran. They had seen many in the days since Fenschurch. "Make one of them stumble?"

It was mean, but fun too. She could *do* this. Marea focused her imagination, closed her eyes, and struck resonance. A shout sounded, and she opened her eyes to see two of the travelers down, a bag of clothes spilled open, the third looking befuddled.

"Nice work," Avery said. "That's the best you've done yet."

She waggled her eyebrows at him. "Better watch out. No telling *what* I can do."

He raised an eyebrow. "Is that an invitation?"

He paid for their pastries and they wandered out of town, finding a secluded spot by a stream to pass the afternoon in a pleasant tangle of kisses and touches and whispered words. Marea found herself playing with her resonance as they did, inviting his hands to slide higher up her arms, hold her more closely to his chest, whisper sweeter words when he spoke. He knew when she did it of course, and smiled, and kept on. He was amazing.

The sun's evening rays found them curled together in the mess they'd made of the late season meadow grass. Marea sighed, snuggling herself deeper into the warm, solid expanse of his chest. "Doesn't it all feel so unreal?"

"Doesn't what all?" he asked, one hand stroking her hair.

"Aran," she said. "The waystone. My resonance, the archrevenants, all of it."

He shrugged. "I guess I grew up knowing about all that stuff."

"But the danger," she said, pressing on. "I mean, the Councilate's planning to kill *all of Aran*. Right when we get there, probably. And after that we're going to battle the strongest shamans for the chance to open a stone and take the power of a god? It just seems crazy."

He nodded. "It *is* crazy. But it's something we have to do."

"Why?" she asked, frustration taking some of the shine out of the moment. He was so *determined.* "I mean, Tai's trying to protect his people, I guess, but why do *we* have to do it?"

"Because we're in danger too," he said. "*You're* in danger, after what happened at Yatiport. The cell there will know who we are. Know we're with Tai, and if someone else takes Semeca's power Tai will be the first one they go after."

"So we leave Tai," she said, pushing back to meet his eyes. "There's no guarantee they can open the stone anytime. Maybe we play it safe, wait for whatever happens at Aran to happen, wait to see if anyone takes the spear and goes after Tai, and if they don't, *then* we can make our move."

He shook his head. "I don't think it would work out like that, love. Maybe no one will open the stone, but I'll bet you Tai and Ella have the best chance of anyone to do it, based on what they've done. And if anyone gets that spear, we'll never be safe again."

"Even if Tai and Ella get it?"

He hesitated. "I—don't know what they'd do with it. But if they get it when we're not there, I don't get my share of the power. *We* don't get it."

Marea felt her cheeks getting hot. Was that really what was most important to him? Some power? "But if we *die* that doesn't mean anything. Is it really worth the risk?"

"We won't die," he said, quiet and sure.

For once his quiet tone didn't convince her. "What makes you so sure?"

"Because we have you," he said, stroking her hair again. "My lucky strike. The thing they'll never expect."

That was sweet, but she couldn't help thinking it was naive too. "But I'm just learning."

"I have faith in you," he said. "And once we open the stone, none of it will matter. No one can touch us again. We can live *forever*, Marea. Just you and me."

She wasn't sure she wanted to live forever after meeting Nauro, but forever with *Avery?* "I could handle that part, at least."

"We'll just have to keep practicing," he said, still running fingers through her hair.

She sighed, trailing her fingers down his chest. He was so *confident*. "What do you want me to actually *do*, when we get there? Wish the stone open?"

"Maybe," he said, catching her hand in his and pressing his lips to it. "We'll know when we get there. For now we just need to keep practicing."

"In secret?" They'd kept what they were doing from Tai and Ella.

"No one else needs to know," he said, then looked up in mock uncertainty. "Unless you... don't *want* to spend time with me?"

Marea let go of the last traces of her fear. It was so *easy* with him. So easy to trust him. "That's all I want," she said, and leaned into his embrace.

42

Do not heed the voices, nor the desires of the flesh. Heed the Eschaton, for only when all men live in harmony will the Descending God return to set us free.
  —Yersh Book of the Eschatol

Tai squared his feet on the planks, took a deep breath, and struck resonance.

"Remember," Avery said. "Revenants need your belief to stay attached. A revenant thrown at you as an attack has no time to build that belief. They just try to overwhelm you immediately, to take control of your body, but you'd have to be a simpleton to let it happen. What they *will* do is consume your *uai*. And in the middle of a battle—"

Tai nodded, his body aching, the ship's cabin cramped and hot. "I'm dead. Disbelieve in the pain. Disbelieve in the voice. Hold my *uai*."

They had been at it all morning: lecture, attack, pain, repeat. Ella had begged him to stop after the last—it was no fun to watch someone you cared about get attacked over and over—but he needed to learn this, to learn some defense against the ninespear attacks.

Tai closed his eyes and nodded. "Do it."

Something hit him, and then there was pain. Pain and a scream that drowned out all thoughts. *Not real*, Tai thought, struggling to stay conscious. *You're a revenant. You're not* real.

The pain went on, ripping up his spine, though Tai could feel resistance. He pushed harder against it, striking his resonance again, a trickle where it should have been a roar. But if he could just hold on to it—

"Enough!" Ella cried, somewhere on the far side of a sea of pain and screams.

The scream stopped. Tai found himself on the floor, breathing in gasps, spine hurting, *uai* gone. Like so many other times that morning.

"Close," he panted. "I was closer that time."

Avery nodded, offering him a hand. "You held onto your *uai*. That was good."

"And a practiced shaman could have kept all their *uai*?" Ella asked, pulling him close to her. As much as the attacks hurt, Tai knew this was harder on her. He'd get his turn when she started learning it.

"A practiced shaman dismisses this kind of attack like you'd wave off a nettle wasp," Avery said. "It doesn't affect us at all."

Ancestors. He had a ways to go then. "Again," Tai said, squeezing Ella's shoulder and pushing away from her.

Avery eyed him. "I think that might be enough for today. Too much and the insertion point can get raw."

"Thank the Prophet," Ella said.

Tai took a deep breath and let it out. The practice had done nothing to ease his mind about bigger issues. Made them worse, if anything. "I'm going to get some air. Avery, come join me?"

The thick man looked surprised but followed Tai out the door and down the stairs, a brisk wind swaying the goldbark stands along the Oxheart. The only space to walk on the packed barge was a gap around the outside of the barrels lashed to the top deck. Tai followed it, taking a few deep breaths.

"Was I—going too hard on you, back there?" Avery asked, following behind.

"No," Tai said, rounding the bend at the back of the barge, Oxheart's waters rolling in the ship's wake. "I want you to go hard. Whoever we meet at Aran isn't going to cut us a break."

Avery brushed the hair out of his eyes. "So, what's on your mind?"

"The revenants," Tai said. "The way they scream when they attack. Is that something you're doing to them?"

"No. Revenants like that, they're trying to overwhelm your senses. Screaming is part of that, along with pain, and losing sight, and whatever else they manage."

The man sounded like Nauro at times, though he couldn't be much older than Tai. "What do you know of their natural state? Are they—naturally unhappy? The spirits of people who died unfulfilled?" *Doomed to suffer* was the term Ydilwen had used.

"That's one theory. It's pretty hard to find out, because it's difficult to talk to a revenant who doesn't have a host, and all the attached revenants stick to their personas for dear life. And, I guess knowing that doesn't really change anything, so no one's really tried to find out."

That sounded too much like how the Councilate thought of Achuri people. What they felt about being conquered didn't really matter, so why would they worry about it? "And everyone who dies leaves a revenant?"

Avery considered, gazing at a herd of sheep grazing on the far bank of the river. "A woman from my village died once. She wasn't old, but she'd been sick a long time, a year or more. She had children, but she was ready to go. Bluefoot fever, a terrible disease. Anyway, I knew enough of shamanism then to watch her as she passed. And her revenant, it just," he shrugged. "Turned to air."

Tai nodded. "And the rest of them? They can die?"

"Slowly. Look at the south bank, if you can. Along that patch of burnt grass."

Tai unfocused his eyes, seeking the shamanic sight. And saw something among the waving grass, like drifting tatters of cloth. "Is that—"

"A revenant," Avery said, "or what's left of one. If they don't find a host to feed them *uai* they start to disintegrate. One that far along, it might not be able to attach even if you offered it a host."

Tai watched it until it rolled out of sight. "But if they get a host, then they come to life again?"

"More like they have a chance at life," Avery said. "The *uai* helps them survive, but what they want is control. They want a body. They want power."

"So they can do what they failed to before death?" Ydilwen had wanted Tai to visit his mother in Yatiport. To leave her money, probably.

Avery nodded. "That's why they try to isolate their hosts, to be their only friend, their lover, or whatever trick they're using. So that eventually they can get control over what their host does, where they go. The Book talks about revenants taking over, where the host becomes a revenant and the revenant gains control of the body. I've never seen that, but some of the hermits you meet in the woods, the *true* hermits, it's like their personalities have blended, driving them both crazy."

"I saw something like that. When we used to overdose people with yura."

Avery licked his lips. "Why do you ask?"

"My revenant," Tai said. "The one you cut out. He—it asked

some questions I didn't have answers to. And I wanted to know if it was telling me the truth."

"And?"

"It was." He stopped at the stern, watching the ship's wake roll back into the Oxheart's slow current. Could Ydilwen have really been Ydilwen? "Do you think all the people I've killed have become revenants? That they're out there somewhere, starving for *uai* or trying to trick their hosts, wishing they had their bodies back?"

Avery took his time about answering, learning his forearms against the worn lip of the barge. "Probably."

Tai rolled his shoulders. How many was that? How many ghosts made for his rebellion? Did the Broken count too?

"What happens if I take the spear? If we get there and open the stone and don't die and I take Semeca's power?"

Avery gazed out over the water. "You get the power of a god."

Tai shook his head. "What does that mean? I know I'll be getting *uai* from all her revenants, but what will I be able to do?"

"Well, for one thing, anyone who has thralled mindseye revenants since her death will lose their *uai*, so all the shamans there will instantly stop being threats. That's why they are in such a hurry to get it first. Once someone holds the spear, it's all done."

"Okay, but what about after that?"

Avery shook his head. "Anything. Anything you can imagine. Live forever. See the world. Bend the rules of reality. It's up to you."

"And the revenants under me? I would have control over them?"

Avery nodded. "From what I understand, archrevenants control the basic strategies their revenants use: what kind of person to attach to, what personas to use, that kind of thing. My cell had a book that was supposedly the translated journal of an archrevenant from just after the Prophet's time. He talks of controlling individual revenants when he felt like it, almost like shamans do, but from the inside instead of the out. Like wearing a glove instead of picking it up and moving it around."

"And if I wanted to release them?"

Avery frowned. "What?"

"Pull my hand out of the glove," Tai said. "Let them go. To kill them, I guess. I could do that?"

"You'd... lose all your power," the stocky man said.

"But I could do it. I could take her spear and destroy the revenants attached to it, and end their suffering. Liberate their hosts."

"You could. But you'd do more good *using* those revenants. Keep your people safe. Stop the Councilate. Remake the world the way you want it to be."

"At the expense of all those souls thralled to me. And every person I killed along the way would become another one."

Avery smiled, lines of his face looking much older in the bright noon sun. "There will always be more revenants. People are unhappy, and then they die. You can't change that."

Funny how Avery talked of remaking the world, but not this part of it. And how Sablo had talked of the revolutions of the wheel, of how pointless it was because it all repeated. Wasn't this the same, on a different level?

None of which needed to be said. Tai nodded. "Feynrick said something like that too. Thanks, Avery. I appreciate you taking the time to teach us. I know this knowledge is supposed to be kept much more secret."

He shrugged, a dockworker's shrug. "Anything I can do. And you *are* still planning on giving me my fifth of a half, right? Or is it a fourth, now that Nauro is gone?"

Tai nodded. "Those were the terms, and I'll honor them. A fourth of a half."

Avery thanked him and left to see to Marea. Tai turned back to the rolling waters, to the passing banks, to his thoughts of Ydilwen and Semeca and ultimate power. There was no guarantee they would get the stone open, or survive long enough to even try.

If they didn't, Ayugen and all his friends would die.

But if they did, what then?

43

They pulled into the next town near sunset, a simple semi-circle of huts around a long wooden dock jutting into the Oxheart. Ella stood at the back of the boat with Tai, who seemed to have taken roost there in the last few days. She didn't mind—it *was* the best spot on the boat to enjoy the scenery, as it had been on Ralhens's ship, but she worried about Tai. He didn't seem to want to spend any more time than necessary in their cabin the last few days.

She squeezed his arm. "It looks tiny. Come on land with me, just for a bit?" He hadn't left the ship since before Fenschurch, which she suspected was part of his melancholy.

He shook his head. "It's not worth the risk."

She made a disbelieving click with her tongue, like her father used to do. "There's hardly anyone there! I don't see any white coats."

"They don't have to be whitecoats to recognize me. And if the messenger finds out who I am, or the captain or any of his boys, this all gets a lot harder."

Him not leaving the boat also meant they'd gotten no time

alone together, which was frustrating because she watched Marea and Avery sneak off together almost every port.

Then again, Marea was young and beautiful.

Ella stamped down on that line of thought, stamped down on her fears. Tai said he didn't care that she'd aged and she had to believe him, or what was this all for? She nuzzled her face into his shoulder. "You just afraid to spend some time alone with an older woman?"

To her gratification he grinned. "Not that at all. I'd *love* some time alone with a perfectly young woman I know. But doing it under fear of attack isn't my idea of sexy."

She sighed, knowing Tai well enough to know from his tone she wasn't going to convince him. The man could be stubborn as a mule. "Some people are into that sort of thing, you know."

He gave her a rueful smile. "Let's try it again some time when the stakes are a little lower."

"That won't be hard," she said. "You want anything from town?"

He declined and she left him with a kiss, picking up Feynrick from where he was sharing a pipe with a few crook-toothed Yersh sailors.

"I'm surprised you aren't looking for some farmer's daughter out here," she said, taking his arm lightly as they climbed the bank to the little circle of huts. Prophets send it had a decent bakery—the last two towns had only sold unleavened millet cakes, which were a poor excuse for a pastry.

Feynrick grinned. "Aye, and that I might have, in a younger year. But Marrey and me made a promise, and I intend to keep it."

Marrey was his term for Marrem, the healworker back in Ayugen. She hated the name, as Ella recalled, but the two had shared a special connection after Semeca's attack. "Do you ever worry," she asked as they crested the rise, "that something will happen to either of you while you're away, and you won't see her again?"

His grin lost some of its mirth. "Aye, that I do. Worried about it since we left Ayugen, really, but I done enough bad things in my past, I reckon I need to do this to straighten them out."

"And Marrem? How does she feel?"

Feynrick snorted. "She's tough as an old goat. She'd probably be happy to be rid of me. But long as there's a chance of seeing her again, I'll let those daughters be."

Ella couldn't help smiling. Maybe he *would* be able to woo a farmer's daughter out here. If he did it'd be with sheer bravado and pluck, because Prophets knew his waistline and his age weren't on his side. Nor was his red hair, this far north.

The village consisted of a squat inn, a farm stand tended by a sleepy teenage boy, and a few scattered houses, flanked by steep-roofed shrines at east and west ends. No bakery.

There were still lanterns burning at the inn, so they made do with some watery dreamtea and a table with a view of the setting sun. Despite the size of the hamlet the inn was full, and patrons sat on the covered porch, sipping tea or talking quietly. As she had done in every port, Ella made her way to the other tables, gleaning what information and rumors she could without seeming too interested.

The people were pilgrims, as so many on the road and river were, and most of what she heard was familiar: uncertainty about the rebellion, worry about being able to enter the old city, platitudes about the ascending god. Some sects of Eschatology held that Aran was the historical site of the Ascending God, which as far as she could tell meant the place the Prophet had risen into the sky. It was a regular pilgrimage site for believers, part of a much larger circle that included Bydford, Hast-by-Waters, and Shatterbrook along the shores of the ocean. Most believers made it a point to visit them all before dying, believing it would help in salvation.

One table at the inn was different: though the people seemed genuinely to be believers—she had sussed out a few ninespear travelers posing as pilgrims, and quickly ended those conversations—they had heard tell of the old city waking up, of a holy force pervading Aran.

"S'why the whitecoats are there," an elderly woman at the table confided in low tones. She was traveling with her husband and their youngest child, sweetleaf farmers from the far side of the Ein. "Want to see if they can make money off it somehow."

"Best not be charging admission," the husband rumbled, a round man with a ruddy face. "It's against the Codes."

The Codes were a long list the Eschatolists kept, and kept adding to, of what was right and wrong, and what sorts of punishments in the afterlife you could expect for committing different sins. None of it actually came from the Prophet, so far as she could tell, but Ella hadn't spent much time studying Eschatology.

"I hope not," Ella said, making the sign of the Descending God to ward off evil. Thank the Prophet she'd met enough believers in Worldsmouth that she could fake it. "I do so hope they don't close off the town."

"Not so far as I've heard," the matron said, "and I keep an ear to the ground like you do, ma'am." She winked, and Ella realized with horror the woman took her as a similar age. "Prophet's peace on ye."

Ella returned the blessing and finished her circuit, learning nothing new but bubbling with excitement from the news. Avery had thought it likely Aran was the right stone, since it appeared an archrevenant had taken an interest in it, but this was confirmation.

And if Avery still had the power from revenants he'd thralled, that meant no one had opened the stone yet, or taken the spear. They still had a chance.

She shared as much with the rest of the group once they were back on the ship.

"That's great," Tai said. "Selwin says we'll be in Califf tomorrow night, and Aran is another two days on foot past there. With any luck we'll get there before someone with a better chance of opening the stone shows up."

"Which will be the same time as Eyadin," Ella said. "Do we really want to be there when the legion gets his orders?"

"I think what you mean is, are we really going to let the message get through?" Marea asked, looking around. "Thousands of people live in Aran, and thousands more visit every year on pilgrimage. We can't just let them all die."

She glanced at Avery as she spoke. What did the shaman think about it?

Feynrick rubbed his beard. "I don't reckon we do. I've seen my share of the Councilate making an example of a town or city, and there's no way we could get in or out of it without causing a scene."

"Unless we use that scene," Avery said. "If the legion already there is under an archrevenant's control, they'll have barricaded the stone. They wouldn't risk any shaman getting close enough to open it."

"Best way to get rid of your enemies is make 'em fight each other," Feynrick said, tamping sage into his pipe. "Maybe we let the shamans kill the whitecoats and vice versa. Worry about getting past whoever's left when they're done."

"Those orders say to kill *Aran*," Tai said, "not just the shamans. I can't let that many people die to make our cause easier."

"What if they die to make our cause *possible*?" Avery asked. "We all agree we're up against long odds. Shamans more powerful than Ollen, a legion of whitecoats, the attention of the archrevenants and the risk someone will figure out who you are.

Every one of those parties wants you dead, for different reasons."

"Then better to kill me, than let thousands of people die for me to live," Tai said, and Ella's heart dropped. "That's more than we have left in Ayugen."

"You're not dying," Ella said forcefully. "Or Aran. Better to kill the messenger. Make sure the whitecoats don't get the orders, and we sneak in like we were planning to."

Tai grimaced at this, and she knew it was about the idea of killing an innocent man. But if it was Eyadin or Tai? She'd kill Eyadin a hundred times over.

"I can't let Aran or Eyadin die," Tai said, looking like he did when he gazed off the side of the ship.

"I think those are the choices, milkweed," Fenyrick said gently. "Anyone mind if I—" he gestured to his pipe.

"Do *not* light that thing in here," Marea said, "or I'll fatewalk you off the side of this barge."

Feynrick held up his hands. "Peace, woman. You're as bad as Marrey."

Tai was still grimacing. She loved him for his idealism, but it wasn't always possible. "Well, no need to make a decision tonight," she said. "If anything happens to Eyadin before we get to Califf you can bet Selwin'll turn us at the docks. We have another day on the water. Time to think it over."

"I still say we let him through," Avery said. "The Counciliate's business is no concern of ours."

Marea frowned at him but didn't say anything. The girl was probably realizing she had the same opinion as Tai, a first as far as Ella knew. Or maybe she was just wishing they'd let Tai die, though she'd started warming to him a bit in the last week. Finally.

Feynrick stood. "Whatever the milkweed says, I'll go for.

Now if you'll excuse me, Ms. Whitecoat over here says I need to smoke outside." He pushed up and left the room.

"Love," Ella said quietly, pulling at Tai's sleeve. "Take me for a walk?"

He got up, following her out into the cool night, sun's last glow purple against the blue light of the star. Tai's forearm was tight under her hand, his pace quick though there was nowhere to go.

After two laps around the barge she squeezed his arm. "Come with me to the end of the dock at least? You need to get off this ship."

To her surprise he agreed, and they took the short gangplank down then walked to the end of the dock, Oxheart slushing quietly against the piers beneath. Ella sat, pulling him down to sit with her facing out over the river, feet dangling off the edge. Tai sighed deeply, and she pulled his head onto her shoulder, looping an arm around his back.

They sat like that a long time, star making its slow journey toward the western horizon. Toward Califf.

"I don't know if I can do it," Tai said at last.

"Do what?" Ella asked, stroking his back.

"Kill Eyadin," Tai said. "Or let him deliver his message. Either one."

Ella shook her head. "Sometimes there are no good options."

"I know. There were no good options when Semeca dropped the boulder on the Tower, no good options when Karhail wanted to kill the Councilate, so many times of no good options on the streets. I thought I was used to it. Thought I was up to it. But this feels different."

Ella shook her head, gazing down at him. "Why?"

He stretched his neck. "Something Ydilwen said to me. I know, he's just a voice. But I asked Avery about it, and it's true. Every time we kill someone before their time, we make more revenants. And the revenants are unhappy, Ella. Ydilwen described it as suffering, as hell, and it's probably the one thing you can trust a revenant on."

"What does that have to do with Eyadin?"

Tai shook his head. "I used to think revenants were spirit guides. Ancestors come back to help us, even though most people didn't seem to get much help from theirs. And then I just thought death was the end, that when we die we're gone, and it doesn't matter what happened in life. But knowing that everyone we kill has to spend however many years starving for *uai* and longing to finish whatever we cut off? That's awful."

It *was* awful. "Are you sure that's true?"

"I don't think Avery has any reason to lie to me," he said. "About that, at least. And from the conversations I had with Naveinya, yeah, probably."

She hated how troubled he sounded. This was Tai, the one person who never got discouraged, never lost heart. "Are you thinking it's not worth it? That we just shouldn't go?"

He sighed. "No. That's the hard part, I still know this is right. And if I do get the spear—" He shook his head. "No. If someone else takes the spear we're all in danger, and I don't know if I could fight them off like I did Semeca. We need to take it, or at least to try."

She nodded. "But?"

"But I don't know how any more. How do you fight without killing?"

"Maybe revenants are just a part of life. Maybe you can't save *every*one."

Tai nodded, eyes on the water. "My voice came back."

"Your second level? That's great. Maybe the harmonies will work better on this one."

"No, it came *back*. Ydilwen. He's my second level too."

Ella frowned. "But that's—impossible. It never happened, in

all the people we worked with at the school. Avery *said* it was impossible."

Tai shrugged. "Well, he came back. Or whatever revenant it is, they chose the same persona."

The pieces all clicked together—Tai's worry, the curiosity about revenants, the hesitation about their mission. "And it's got you convinced?"

"No. Yes. I mean no, I know it's just a revenant, that whatever it's saying it's saying because it wants me to do something, to abandon my friends, all of that. But yes. As far as what he's telling me is true, I *am* convinced we're doing this wrong."

Ella searched for words for a moment. She'd seen lots of people believe in their voices, even when they knew better. But Tai? "You realize that the answer to all these questions is to stop fighting. To run away. To give up on everything we've fought for, and rely on your voice."

"I'm not giving up. I just—the cost is too high. The way we're doing it, it's too high."

She shook her head. "What other way is there?"

"I don't know," he said. "That's what I need to figure out."

44

It is interesting to note that the most moralistic of the Prophetic traditions, the Eschatolists, are the only ones to remember the Prophet as female (leaving aside the At'li tri-gendered deities). Should we conclude those faiths without clear morality need a father figure to control their populations, following Gesthel's theory? Or simply that a mother is more likely to teach her child right from wrong?
—Eylan Ailes, *Treatise on World Religions*

The city of Califf straddled both sides of a great bend in the Oxheart river, shrines to the Ascending and Descending Gods rising like giant horns at east and west ends. Marea stood at the bow of the *Wandering Argot*, ignoring the smell of the tug boat as she watched the docks approach.

Dread rolled in her heart: dread for what would happen once they got off the ship. Of the danger they were in if Tai got caught. Of what would happen if Tai *wasn't* caught, and they made it to

Aran. Of the message Eyadin was carrying, slung across his back as he too watched the docks approach.

But most of all, dread of the quarrel brewing between her and Avery. There was no sugarcoating it: her boyfriend wanted the entire city of Aran to die, so they could get in easier. And as much as she loved him, Marea couldn't stomach the thought.

They'd fought about it last night, when everyone else was asleep and they usually exchanged little but kisses and affection. Avery insisted it was for their protection. Marea argued they should just give it up like she'd wanted to all along. He said they would never be safe if they did. She said he couldn't know that. And on and on.

She had never had an argument hurt like this one. Never felt a space as painful as the tiny gap that lay between their bodies when they shuffled back into the cabin, exhausted, out of words to speak to each other. Wanting only the warmth and solidity of his body and at the same time too angry to look at him.

And this morning had been no different. He'd risen before her, quietly packing his things. Stood talking with Feynrick now, who was blowing great clouds of sage and grinning like the whole thing was the most fun he'd had in years. The man was insane. Or else he'd been through so much even this situation couldn't faze him. She had seen him as just a goofy Yatiman, a darkhair, for so long on this journey, but he was more than that. Funny how sadness opened your eyes.

Tai and Ella came out of the cabin looking grim, Tai wearing his furs despite the relative warmth. They motioned to her and she reluctantly joined the group, not looking at Avery, wanting desperately to know if he was looking at her. Wanting him to just shatting *apologize* already and admit he was being a cockstain.

Because if he thought *she* was apologizing first, he had another thing coming. Even though another part of her whispered that maybe she just should, that even with her fatewalking he could find someone better any time, someone prettier and smarter and richer. And the thought of him leaving her was a cold abyss she couldn't look into. The same one she'd faced when her parents died.

"We all know what we're up against here," Tai said in a low voice, drawing her back to the real world. "There will be whitecoats everywhere, and the main road and river passage to Aran both lead through Califf, so likely ninespears here too. Avery, you can still block our thoughts in a crowd?"

Marea stole a glance at him as he nodded, so handsome, so shatting *casual* as if he wasn't getting ripped apart by the distance between them. Maybe he wasn't. Maybe she needed to just apologize right now and make sure this wasn't the end of them.

But apologize when she was *right*? Never.

"Good," Tai was saying. "Then we stick together, keep our heads down, get out of the city as fast as we can. Time enough to talk on the road."

"And Eyadin?" Avery asked. The messenger was just four paces away—it was still hard to get used to Avery's soundproofing. "You've made a decision?"

Tai rolled his shoulders. "Leave Eyadin to me."

They disembarked then, Captain Selwin muttering something Marea had no doubt was rude to one of his sons as they left, stepping onto the wooden dock. Good riddance to the man and his ragtag ship and his breakfast, lunch and dinner of millet porridge. If she never had to ride on a river barge again it would be too soon.

The docks teemed with soldiers and porters and sandy-haired Yershmen. It felt strange to be back among lighthairs—strange to not stand out for what she looked like. They passed a pack of white-coated soldiers, standing guard like lawkeepers would in the wealthier parts of Worldsmouth. It was odd to be around them too, to see the white gilded ships and crisp uniforms that had always brought her such comfort in Ayugen, a sense of belonging despite the danger. Now the danger was *from* those uniforms, even if none of it was her fault. But try though she might to convince herself she should just grab the nearest one and tell them everything, she couldn't. Because Avery wouldn't come with her. And even now, even with last night hanging over their heads, she couldn't not care. Couldn't summon an anger or a self-protection strong enough to overcome her desire for him. Her need to be with him. He was all she had.

Besides, rebels or not, she couldn't just turn Tai's party in. Not Ella, or Feynrick. And Tai was the only one likely to stop Eyadin's message from reaching Aran.

So instead she followed as they wound through the press of bodies, the stink of man sweat, the cry of porter and merchant and circling wagull. Ella lead the way because the woman looked every inch a Worldsmouth lady, and her age would make most authorities assume she was harmless.

If they only knew.

"You there," a voice barked as they were leaving the docks, wood planks transitioning to hard-packed cobbles. "What's your business in Aran? Where are you headed?"

Marea turned, but where she expected to see lighthaired soldiers in polished leathers, she found a well-dressed darkhaired man leaned against the stone wall of the lawkeeper's station, eyeing them each in turn.

Ella started, apparently expecting something else too, then said, "Just pilgrims, sir, on our way to see the stone."

"The stone, eh?" the darkhair said, pushing off to join them. "Keep walking, keep walking. The famed stone of Aran?"

"The stone of the Ascending God, sir," Ella said, folding a hand up her chest for all the world like she was an Eschatolist.

"Good, good," the man said, glancing around them. They were on a main thoroughfare choked with carts and peddlers with baskets of produce. "Closed to the public though, you know. Whitecoats everywhere. But I can get you in."

Marea's stomach twisted, whether with fear or hope she didn't know. If it was closed, maybe they would just give it up. Or maybe they would let Aran die, like Avery wanted.

Ahead Ella glanced at Tai, then kept walking. "The Prophet has seen us this far on the journey, good sir. We will trust him to get us the rest of the way."

"To the stone?" the darkhaired man asked, lowering his tone. "Or to the spear?"

Nearly everyone in the party started at that, including Marea.

"You know of it, then," the man said. "Are perhaps seeking more than just religious absolution?"

This was dangerous. This was not the kind of exposure they needed. If the man was a shaman, if he attacked on the street like Credelen had…

"The Spear of the Prophet," Ella said, excitement in her voice. "Third wondrous relic of the Holy Church of Eschatology. You know where it is?"

The man's enthusiasm dampened somewhat. "Not *that* spear. But I can get you in to the stone, if you wish. The whitecoats aren't letting anyone through otherwise."

"We'll take our chances," Tai said, cutting the man off. "Thanks for your time."

His tone carried more than a little threat and the man left off, though not before Marea saw him reevaluating their party. Not good. What if the man was just there to alert the real shamans of competition? What if no one had opened the stone yet because someone was laying in ambush at Califf, killing them all before they arrived?

What if the man recognized Tai and pulled the whole city of whitecoats down on them?

Dread rolled on inside. What was she *doing*?

You could just leave, my pepper.

The voice came out of nowhere. "Dad?" Marea gasped.

In the next moment she realized what it was, what the *voice* was, and fortunately the street was too loud for anyone else to have noticed. Ella steered them down a merchant alley, likely looking for supplies for the journey to Aran.

What do you mean, what I am?

A revenant, Marea thought back with determination. Of the mosstongue variety. The third one I've heard. Pretending to be my father this time. And I'm in a bit of a tight spot, so shut up until I have time to deal with you, okay?

A tight spot? What's going on?

Stains, the voice did a good version of her Dad. Then again, it was doing it based on her own memories, so of course it would seem good to her. Ella had stopped at a narrow stall stacked high with dried goods, and the rest of them stood in a huddle in the narrow street.

"You're letting Eyadin go, then?" Avery asked Tai. "Planning to make our approach on the stone during the chaos, or after it's done?"

"I'm not letting him go," Tai said, sounding perturbed. "I told you. I'm not letting the city of Aran die on the chance it'll make things easier us."

"It's not a chance," Avery pressed. "You heard the man back there—the stone is closed off. If we go before or after, there's no way we're getting through their line with enough time to open the stone."

This is the man you love, my pepper?

I—yes, she said inside, part of her not believing she was having this conversation. He's not—he really cares about the stone, okay? It's for us. To protect me.

It's for him, you mean, the not-her-father's voice said. *I raised you smarter than this, pepper. He is in league with the man who killed me and your mother. You need to go.*

Of course the voice would say she needed to go. That's what revenants did, tried to separate you from your loved ones. Her father probably wouldn't have understood in real life anyway. If he'd been alive.

Or you're the one who doesn't understand, sweet pepper. Doesn't want to understand, because you're plunged backwards for this fellow. It's my fault. I should have arranged someone for you before we ever left the Mouth.

They moved on, Tai telling Avery again to leave Eyadin to him, Marea doing her best to ignore the voice. She was tired of this debate, and there was no time for it anyway. She needed to pay attention to what was happening. No telling when she'd need to fatewalk them out of something.

This side of Califf was not huge, perhaps as big as Hightown and Newgen put together, and Ella lead them towards the edge on a narrow street, obviously wanting to leave town without attracting attention. Only to find a pair of whitecoats blocking the road.

"No exit from Califf here," one of them said, sounding bored but gripping his weapon. "Everyone leaves by the east gate."

Ella thanked them and turned that direction.

"We could breeder-tie those boys," Feynrick said in low tones. "Make our way out real quiet-like."

"Or fly out," Avery said. "Between Tai and I, we can manage it."

"We go by the main gate," Tai said. "Nothing with even a chance of attracting attention, or sending someone after us on the road."

Marea sucked in a breath when she saw the main road out, splitting around the shrine to the Descending God with a traditionally carved Yersh gate over it on the far side. The path was blocked with whitecoats, thirty or forty of them in formation around the gate, with more loitering in front of a nearby tavern.

"Oh, gods," she groaned. Two lighthaired ladies traveling with three darkhaired men, one of them a red hair no less, in the middle of the Yershire. How was that for not attracting attention?

Feynrick gave a low whistle beside her. "Looks like our friend's getting held up, too."

Eyadin was near the end of the line snaking from the gate, ahead of an elderly woman with two young children. They fell in behind.

"I can't block here, not well," Avery said in a low voice. "I can still shield your thoughts, but watch what you say. There could be more than soldiers listening."

He sounded so calm. So confident. Did he even care they'd fought last night? Did he care about her?

He said he did, but words were just words. You could believe in actions—that was something her Dad used to say. She started. Did you put that thought in my head? she asked inside.

Who, me? I'm just trying to stay quiet and pray my only daughter doesn't get arrested or worse for traveling with known rebels.

He had just the right tone of disappointment and worry to make her feel awful. And then she felt stupid because it wasn't him. And then she felt frustrated because she needed to watch the shatting situation, not talking to her voice like some kind of child. What was *taking* this line so long?

Ahead a farmer with an empty handcart was allowed out, and the line inched forward. Five more to go. One of the whitecoats ahead was reading a proclamation in a bored voice, something about aiding and abetting any known rebels, the punishment for treason, and the city and surrounds of Aran being under martial law.

Marea's stomach rolled, dread getting heavier at the moment.

This was it. This was where the guards recognized Tai, or figured out Ella's past, and she ended up in some prison for having rebel sympathies.

For a mad moment she wanted to laugh—rebel sympathies. There probably wasn't even a rebellion at Aran, just a bunch of power-mad shamans, and these known and confirmed Achuri rebels were the only ones trying to stop them, *and* an order to kill everyone in the city besides.

Aran should be welcoming all the rebels they could get.

"Business," the sharp-eyed officer at the front said, looking Eyadin up and down.

What would he say, *ordering you and your fellows to commit mass murder on Aran*?

"Ah, pilgrimage," the slender messenger said.

Pilgrimage? Marea glanced at Ella. If Avery had seen his documents right, the seal of a high Council member was all he would need to get through this checkpoint. They should have stolen it to use themselves.

"Not safe past Califf," the officer said. "No one's allowed to travel alone. Next."

"You don't understand," Eyadin said, leaning against a soldier's attempt to move him aside. "I have to get through. I— my family, in Worldsmouth—"

"Not our concern," the officer said. "Move aside or we'll do it for you. *Next*."

"He's with us," Tai said, stepping forward.

Marea started. *What*?

The officer looked Tai up and down once, eyes narrowing at his dark hair. "And who are you?"

"Pilgrims, sir," Ella said, stepping up as well. "I've come from Hafeluss, and as you can see I have enough protection for one more." She gestured at the men.

"Pilgrims," the officer repeated, eyes moving to Ella. Good.

The longer they stayed off Tai, the less chance he had of realizing this was the man who had killed so many Councilate soldiers and citizens. "You know there's a rebellion on?"

"We have no part of it, sir, and I am not worried overly. No one knows the day or the hour. If the Ascending God wants me, he can have me." She made the rising sign from navel to throat.

That was a quote from the Eschatol—Ella played a good pilgrim.

The officer didn't look convinced. "And her?" He jerked his head her direction, making Marea start. "Your daughter?"

Ella choked, then nodded. "Yes. Here to pay respects to my late husband."

Marea suppressed a smile. Nothing like grief to grease the wheels.

"I am sorry to hear of your loss," the officer said, "but our primary concern must be for your safety. These men you have with you, you are sure of their loyalties?"

Please, Marea thought inside. *Please* just let me and these totally illegal rebels go.

And then she realized, she had something more than wishes. She had a way to *use* those wishes.

Marea struck resonance, and returned to her thoughts with renewed force. *Let us go. Next people in line. Nothing strange here.* She visualized it like Avery had taught, heard the crunch of their boots walking away, smelled the reek of *tynsfol* incense smoke from the shrine as they passed, the bright sunshine and open road. *We* will *move on.*

"Loyalty's to coin, ye don't mind me saying so," Feynrick was saying behind her. "Doubt whatever rebels ye got over there are paying what the missus does."

"You realize the penalty for aiding dissidents is death?" the officer asked, returning his gaze to Ella.

Marea stomach flipped, dread threatening to overcome her

wishes for freedom. A vision of the men pulling weapons rose up, of the whole thing descending into a battle like it had so many other times on this trip. She clenched her fists, willing the dread away, doubling down on her vision of them walking free and clear. She had to think *only* what she wanted to happen, or she'd fatewalk the *opposite* into reality.

"And you would take this man on," the commander went on, gesturing at Eyadin, "without knowing more of him?"

Gods. The officer wasn't giving up. He knew something. He was going to figure them out, despite everything she was doing.

And just as the dread was too much, just as she couldn't hold it any longer, a strong hand took hers. A solid hand. *Avery's* hand.

He just took it and give her a squeeze, like he knew, and suddenly the picture seemed a lot clearer. They would get through this. She would *get* them through this. Walking free and clear in the sunshine.

"We shared a ship from Fenschurch," Ella said, "and if he is willing to face danger for his faith, that is enough for me."

The officer eyed them all a moment longer, brows furrowed like he wanted to find something wrong and just couldn't, then gestured at the gate. "Peace be on your journey then. Inform the legion if you see anything suspicious. *Next*."

Marea let out a breath, dread evaporating. And just like she'd imagined in her head, down to the crunch of their boots and the smell of the incense, they walked through the carved Yersh gate into the countryside beyond, free and clear, officer already interrogating the next party behind.

Marea beamed. It worked. Her fatewalking worked. Instead of fighting for their lives or ending up in jail, they were walking free and clear, because of *her*.

How was that for helpless?

45

*E*lla stepped through the carved gates with sweat beading on her brow. "What," she said when they were ten steps away, when they would have a reasonable chance of running from the Councilate men she was *sure* were about to descend on them, "was *that*?"

"I—" Marea started, then cut off, just as Ella remembered they weren't alone either. Could Avery mask their conversation with Eyadin walking right there with them? Better to assume not.

Tai cleared his throat. "The man needed travelling companions, and we are all headed the same direction. It seemed like a decent thing to do."

He apparently *wasn't* going to attack Eyadin straight off then. Probably a good thing with the soldiers just paces behind. But how were they going to do this? Ella gnawed one of her nails. They had too much to hide.

What was Tai *thinking*?

"And I thank you for that," Eyadin said, his strides long on the hardpacked road, "but if you don't mind, I'd rather travel alone."

Oh, thank the gods.

"With a rebellion on?" Tai said jovially. "Don't be silly. Plenty of room for you with us, and we'd be glad of one more sword should rebels attack."

"I—am headed for Aran with all haste," the slender man said.

"As are we," Tai said, his accent more noticeable now that they were among native speakers, "but take too many risks and you may not arrive."

"I—" Eyadin struggled with himself, then nodded. "Excuse me. You are likely right, and I owe you my thanks. I am Eyadin Mettek, of House Mettelken of Worldsmouth."

"And I am Tai," Tai said, "of Ayugen."

Ella barely kept the goggle from her face. Was the man *mad*? His name wasn't well known, but a tall Achuri man from a rebel city *here*, where no Achuri had any reason to go? He was probably the only Achuri man most people in the north had even *heard* of.

"And I am Ellumia Aygla," she said, unsure whether to continue the farce of her being the head of their party, or a pilgrim, or what. She read similar uncertainty on Avery and Marea's faces, though they hid it well. "Of the minor House Aygla, also of Worldsmouth originally, though I've been posted at Hafeluss these last three years, where the Fyalset meets the Ein."

"I know it," Eyadin said briefly, his clipped way of talking closer to Yersh than Worldsmouthian. "I run messages. For my House, mainly."

"And that is your true business here?" Tai asked. "I did not see you joining Captain Selwin's morning and evening ablutions, and you no doubt noticed we didn't either, so perhaps we can agree privately we are not the pilgrims we claimed."

A clever move—including the man in their lie to the Councilate made him more a part of their group. But to what end? Killing him would be distasteful, but it also meant saving the lives of an entire *city*.

"Yes," Eyadin said, rather quickly. "An urgent message, for those of House Fetterwel still inside the city."

Would Eyadin tell them, before he triggered the attack on Aran? He knew what his message said, else Tai and Avery would not have been able to read it in his mind.

"A brave thing on your part, going into the very heart of a rebellion," Tai said, strolling down the road as if this were all a casual chat to pass the time. "Do you know something of the rebellion? It is as bad as the officer back there makes out?"

Eyadin hesitated, shifting the simple pack over his shoulder. "It is bad. Or it will be, my House betters believe. Honestly, I would advise you to turn back. Unless your mission is also urgent?"

Shatters. Tai had just admitted they were not pilgrims—what could they possibly say that would warrant their own haste? Tai hesitated. *Shatters* they needed a story quick.

"Perhaps less savory," Ella said, lighting on the first notion that came to her, "but there is money to be made in wartime, and my betters see this as an opportunity. If I may speak plainly, we are scouting any opportunity for Aygla to provide a secondary stream of resources to the rebels. There are valuable antiques aplenty in Aran, if the rebels are willing to part with them."

That should be believable enough. She'd never imagined her time in Odril's calculism dungeon, and the revelation of Alsthen's proxy funding of rebels in Ayugen, would ever be useful information. But this was the true way of the Counciliate: profit before all.

Eyadin nodded as if this was to be expected, and relief mixed with an old hatred for the Counciliate in Ella's gut. "Business is business, I suppose," the man said in his clipped style, "though I fear for your safety, madame. The danger here might easily outweigh the gains."

She gave a light laugh. "And why do you think they've sent me, a woman, into such a place? My betters would not risk a more valuable asset to the House. Still, it is not the first time I've ventured into unsavory places seeking profit, and a living must be made."

Eyadin nodded, a cast of sorrow to his eyes. "Would that our living came from better means."

"Prophet send it will, though that has never been the way of my House. I believe Aygla hopes to vie for a Council seat, with Coldferth and Galya both hurt so badly on the yura trade."

Eyadin's brows rose. "This sort of... opportunity exploration is how Tai comes to join your party, I take it?"

"I spent my time in Ayugen, yes. Though he is here as much by my wishes as much as any protective role." She took Tai's hand in hers—let them at least be open about this. Their relationship made a good excuse for why an Achuri would be in their party, but moreso if Aran ended up as dangerous as they thought, she would not spend their last few days together pretending to be business partners.

Especially if she was forced to use her resonance again. How much life would she lose if they had to fight in Aran? Would the resonance let her survive into old age, or if she was meant to die in her fiftieth year, would she suddenly die mid-slip?

Such were the questions that had tormented her since Nauro told her of the costs. Curse the man.

Eyadin reddened. "I see."

Relationships between lighthair and dark were not spoken of in polite society, but she wouldn't let it bother her. It was one area among many the Councilate could use changing.

"Perhaps there could be common ground between your Houses on this?" Tai asked. "Is Mettelken interested in such things?"

Did he know Mettelken made their money from banking and loans? Still, it was plausible—rebels needed funding too.

The sorrowful cast returned to Eyadin's face. "I doubt it, sir, but perhaps if your party would wait for me outside Aran, I could make introductions once we are all safely back in Worldsmouth."

Ella's heart softened then. The man was clearly determined to deliver his message, but he was doing what he could to keep them out of it. If only they could accept.

"I would welcome that," Ella said, "though I fear I would not likely keep what position I've made for myself at Aygla if I did not first do my diligence with these rebels."

"More's the pity," Eyadin said. "Though at the very least the Councilate does seem to have quite a presence here. Pray they keep us safe." He nodded at a square of white tents erected at a crossroads ahead.

The knot that had begun to loosen in her belly tightened again. Just as she'd smoothed things with whatever Tai was planning!

"Well," she said, taking a deep breath. "Just a band of intrepid pilgrims, right?"

They passed the checkpoint without incident, however, and continued on in the bright Yersh sun, shedding furs for under layers, the air carrying some of the humidity she remembered so well from Worldsmouth, and just a touch of the swelter. The Yersh plains were vast, stretching from the Sorral Mountains in the south to Shatterbrook on its peninsula jutting into the ocean, far beyond Worldsmouth. The Oxheart was one its southern rivers, and Aran was likely only halfway from Ayugen to Shatterbrook. Looking at the well-kept earthen irrigation canals and moss-covered stone houses along the road, it was no wonder the Yersh Empire had lasted a thousand years: they had the best climate, soil, and navigability of anywhere on Saicha.

Which made them the obvious targets for Worldsmouth merchants, once the merchants learned enough Brinerider ship design to trade further upriver with their boats. The wealth they amassed—along with the disease they brought--had undermined the authority of the Emperor, once held to be a descendant of the

Prophet himself. Now he was what the Councilate called a 'cultural leader,' figurehead for a culture disappearing into the maw of history.

They walked mainly in silence, perhaps from mutual agreement that neither side say any more for fear of spoiling the lies they'd told each other. Ella was dying to corner Tai and ask him what in shatters he thought he was doing inviting Eyadin along. And then to forget all of this and just be together, after long weeks on a ship with scant privacy, and him so withdrawn these last few days.

Tonight. So long as the regular checkpoints they passed *granted* them another night. So long as Eyadin didn't suspect Tai's true identity and spill it to one of the whitecoats. Though the man seemed determined to keep his mission a secret.

Who had sent him, anyway, that he couldn't reveal himself even to the whitecoats?

The land had begun to roll as they moved away from the Oxheart, hillsides dotted with stands of goldbark and scarlet puceleaf, flatter areas separated into fields and pastures by low fences of stacked stone. She had gotten used to the bluish-purple plants of winter in Ayugen and the Yati hinterlands, but the weather was too warm here for them to grow, and the star never rose as high in the sky as it did in the south. She had barely seen it in her youth, just a low glow on the southern horizon during the dry season that passed for winter in Worldsmouth.

Because of that, they wouldn't be getting much *uai* in their diets, if any. She'd bought mavenstym in Fenschurch, the blossoms expensive this far north, but even they would be a limited resource. They'd have to watch their use of resonances—but on the other hand, being in the north meant not many opponents would have resonances to use either.

They stopped at a hoary stone-and-timber inn nestled in the swale of a grassy hill, buying oxtail and sour cheese and bread for lunch. There were no travelers there to work for information, but the innkeeper, a toothless woman in her seventh decade with a gaggle of idle daughters filling the common room, confirmed the road was emptier than usual, save for whitecoats.

They crossed a fourth checkpoint a few thousandpace beyond the inn, Ella's stomach tightening despite the previous encounters going well. She had no doubt they could deal with a few soldiers —shatters, she could deal with them on her own, if she wanted to burn life hours—but the risk of anyone seeing or surviving was too great. If word spread, trying to get through occupied Aran with authorities looking for them would be impossible.

Fortunately, this checkpoint did not look overly severe: a pair of youthful whitecoats sat on three-legged stools to one side of a minor crossroads, their platoon's tidy square of tents a few paces back from the road surrounded by a palisade of sharpened logs.

"Halt," one of the soldiers said, standing and adjusting the hang of his trousers.

"And state your business," said the other, a hand taller than the first.

This was standard procedure. "Pilgrims, good sirs," Ella said, "on our way to Aran."

"Awfully mixed company for a band of pilgrims," the first one said. He nodded at Tai. "You there, you a true believer?"

He didn't say *darkhair*, but it was implied. Few outside the Yershire followed Eschatology. "Can't say as I am," Tai said evenly, "but the woman pays well enough."

"Where you from?" the taller one asked, eyes lingering a little too long on Marea.

"Hafeluss," Ella said. She'd picked it for being one of the most racially diverse places in the Councilate.

"Long way," the shorter one said.

"Bags," said the taller.

A note of panic shot through her—bags? None of the other

checkpoints had searched them, not even the officer at Califf. But what could they find? They were carrying a lot of marks, but had sold all their yura, and otherwise carried very little, having abandoned almost everything in the flight from the Yati waystone.

They opened their bags then, Feynrick grumbling as the men pawed through his plugs of sageleaf. All except Eyadin, who kept his bag on his back.

Shatters—Eyadin, who was so secretive and protective about the message he carried. Who lied about it to Councilate soldiers even though the message was ostensibly *for* the Councilate legion. Of course he wasn't going to let them search his things. Find his message.

But Eyadin could get shattered. If she'd had her way he would already be out of the equation. "Eyadin," she said, nodding at him. "Open your bag for the men."

"I can't," he said quickly, eyes darting from her to the whitecoats. "House secrets."

"We represent all the Houses, square and equal," the taller one said, as he finished with Feynrick's pack. "Let's have a look."

"I can't," Eyadin said again, something more like panic coming into his voice. "The—House orders. Please!"

"Now we really *do* need to see what's in there," the shorter one said, looking up from Marea's things. "Open it up or you get no further."

This was it, then. The fight that would cost them the whole quest if they didn't do it right. Because Tai had to invite along shatting *Eyadin*.

She was going to have a serious talk with the man come nightfall.

"House rights," Eyadin squawked, as the taller one laid hands on him. "I have my rights to privacy as a representative of Mettelken! Ask your commanding officer!"

The shorter one looked uncertain at this, glancing to the taller one, but Ella's stomach sank. There was no version of asking the commanding officer that turned out well for them, but what else could they do?

With a start she realized she was feeling a whine in her bones —Marea's resonance. Was the girl trying to sabotage them? Or was this lucky, considering their other options?

Tai cleared his throat, nudging his yet-unexamined pack to reveal two rolls of marks. "It's unfortunate," he said, "that the lowest-paid members of a party often have to do the bulk of the work."

Shorter one glanced at the coins, then to taller one, who stared openly. The rolls were unbroken, which likely meant a thousand marks, more wages than an infantryman would make in six months' time.

"You trying to bribe us?"

"Only if you ask your commanding officer," Tai said. "Otherwise, I have just found your marks in my bag, and we'll be on our way."

Shorter one grunted something at taller one, who was still staring at the coins. Marea's resonance rolled on in the background, almost too high to feel, and Ella's heart raced. Counciliate soldiers were not supposed to be biddable. They regularly court-martialed men for taking House bribes in Worldsmouth. But they weren't in Worldsmouth, and these men were young.

Then again, if the soldiers didn't take the money they would all be under arrest. Ella felt inside for her resonance and made ready to strike.

"Check it," the taller one said at last, glancing back at the camp.

Shorter one bent down and broke a roll open, hundred-mark coins spilling out. He bit one, then cursed and nodded. "It's real."

"Then get out of here," taller one said, snatching the unbroken roll. "Pack your scat and disappear and we can all pretend this never happened."

"Of course," Tai said, bending to repack his bag, likely wanting to hide the rest of what they had. Bless the man for thinking of a bribe. She'd been about to strike resonance and cut the two men down.

"And don't go thinkin' to blow the whistle, once ye got your rolls pocketed," Feynrick said. "Awful hard to 'splain that kind of money, on your person or in yer tent or even buried in some patch of ground. Best to keep it all quiet. Soldier's bonus, we used to call those."

Eyadin was already down the road, and the rest of them followed in short order, Ella still tying up the last of her roll.

"Thank you," the man said, when they were around the next bend. "That—I don't know what to say."

"Say you're sorry," Marea said, "for almost getting us all mecked back there because of your big secret."

Eyadin reddened. "I'm sorry. And I will see what I can do to get my, ah, House to repay your expenses."

"We wanted the attention as little as you did," Tai said.

"Let's just pray we don't run into the same situation again," Ella said. "We do not have the funds for a second bribe that size. Eyadin, perhaps you can find a different way to store whatever it is you carry?"

"Yes," he said. "That is a great idea."

They stopped for the night at a single-story inn outside the hamlet of Galven, Eyadin insisting on paying for their rooms and meals. Supper was roast lamb in a turmeric broth with carrots and potatoes.

And then, finally, she got Tai alone. "What," she said again, closing the door to their room, "was that?"

"What was what?" he asked, dropping onto the creaking bed.

"Don't be daft," she said, keeping her voice down. The next

room over was Marea and Avery, their voices raised in some kind of spat, but there was no telling who could be listening at the door.

"He needed our help," Tai said, nodding at the wall as if to say *it isn't safe*. "I wasn't going to just turn him away."

Ella sighed. "Take me for a walk?"

Twilight was descending when they left via the common room, star's light more of a glow than a shine this far north. A path wound back through a stand of goldbark toward a low hill and they took it, Tai's hand in hers.

"I'm sorry," he said, when they had walked for a few breaths. "I know it must have seemed crazy—"

"Crazy? Crazy is not half-strong enough for what it seemed like when you invited a *Councilate representative* carrying a message that could get us all *killed* to come along on our little walk!"

He took a deep breath. "I know. I'm sorry. But I just—I can't swallow killing him for the message he's carrying."

"Then what are you planning to do?"

"What I *have* been doing all day is reading him," Tai said. "Watching his thoughts as we talk, and what he thinks about when we're not talking."

Ella stepped around a big stone, feet aching from the day's walk like she was sixty years old. Maybe she was, technically. "And?"

"And he is who he says he is, I think," Tai said. "He works for Mettelken as a messenger, and his thoughts keep coming back to getting this one to Aran as fast as he can."

Ella shook her head. "Why would Mettelken send a message to put Aran to the sword? That kind of order should take a full Council vote."

Tai shrugged. "I don't know how the Council works, but that's what he's carrying. They made him memorize it. And he's not just getting paid. They threatened him too, threatened his family. That's most of what he thinks about while we're walking. Wonders if he'll get back to see them or not. Hates feeling responsible for what's going to happen to Aran, but he can't not save his family."

Ella chewed on that for a moment, goldbarks opening up to reveal the first stars peeking through the blue night. "So he's in a hard situation. I get that. But how does that change what we have to do? We can't let his message get through."

"No," Tai said, "we can't. But he's an innocent man, Ella. Not even a soldier. Think about his family, if he doesn't come back."

"Yes," Ella said, "it will be awful. But not as awful as the thousands of families dying in Aran."

Tai shook his head. "That's how we thought during the rebellion. Whoever we killed, we would eventually be saving more lives. But what does that matter to Marea?"

"To Marea? What—" She made the connection: Marea's parents. Karhail had cut them down in their assault on the Newgen gates. Two innocent people who happened to be in the wrong place at the wrong time. Like Eyadin.

Ella turned to him, a warmth in her chest overcoming the frustration she felt. "You're too good, you know that? Nobody worries about this stuff. You're like a minister or something."

"Would a minister do this?" He leaned in for a kiss, adding a grab that a minister definitely would *not* do.

Ella sighed when they broke off. "I needed that. *Missed* that. But you *are* too good, Tai. We're not going to fix the world's problems, even with everything we're doing. People die."

Tai looked toward the hilltop. "I'm not too good, I'm tortured. I keep coming back to these same thoughts, to this impossible choice."

"Ydilwen again?"

"Yes. Or no. I don't even know whose thoughts are whose anymore."

Ella's belly twisted—she knew how hard revenants could be.

"Don't worry," Tai said, "I'm not believing in him or whatever. I'm still me. But he has a point. What are we doing, killing people every time they're in our way? What's the point, if we're no better than the people we're fighting?"

He started walking again. "Nauro used to talk about revolutions of the wheel, about how the Councilate was a noble revolution once. How all noble causes get corrupted. He was talking about politics, but I feel like it's true for shamans and revenants too."

"What do you mean?"

"I mean why should we take the spear? To protect ourselves and Ayugen from someone else taking it and killing us? That feels noble, yes. But we kill a bunch of people to do it, doom their spirits to become revenants to torture other people and feed more *uai* into the archrevenants? What's the point of saving Ayugen if Aran has to die? Or even someone like Eyadin, who's caught up in this just like us, even though he doesn't want to be?"

Ella sighed, skirts swishing in the grass. "When did you become the philosopher and me the street thug ready to kill whoever's causing a problem?"

He grinned. "Guess we rubbed off on each other."

She smiled back. "You're hard to stay mad at, you know that? But what if there *is* no greater point? Or what if you're right but it's impossible to do? I would rather live with a few hard choices than die chasing some impossible dream."

Especially when she had so little time left, but there was no need to say that. How much time did she even have left? How much less if she had to timeslip?

"You're still mad about the checkpoint."

"Shatters right I'm mad about the checkpoint! Eyadin almost got us all arrested because he wouldn't open his scatting bag!"

They walked under a solitary puceleaf rustling in the breeze. "He doesn't know who we are. Probably thought there was no harm in it."

"Did you read that in his thoughts?"

"No. But would you honestly kill him to avoid things like that?"

"If it saved you?" Ella snapped. "If it saved us? Yes. In a heartbeat."

Wouldn't he do that for her? He'd done it a million times already. What had changed?

"I don't judge you for that," Tai said slowly. "I wish I still felt that way. But Eyadin wishes us well, Ella. He's *grateful* to us. How can we just kill someone like that? No, not kill. How can we murder him?"

He was right. She knew he was right. But no one could actually live like that. "What other way is there? We wouldn't even be feeling this way if he was still a stranger."

"Not knowing wouldn't change the truth about him."

"It would have made it easier. Like LeTwi said, better to swim in a sea of unknowing than drown in truth." She shifted, realizing he had probably never read LeTwi. Or any Councilate scholarship. "Why did you ask him to join us? Wouldn't it have been best for everyone if they kept him in Califf?"

"He would have gotten through. He's too motivated not to. Too scared. I asked him because I want to believe there's a way to stop him without killing him."

Ella was out of breath from climbing the hill, but had enough left for a snort. "Like what?"

"Like *talking* to him. Treating him as a human being instead of an enemy."

"Talking to him. How far do you think we would have gotten

if we'd tried talking to Semeca? Or the shamans that attacked us in Yatiland?"

"But that's the thing," he said, taking on new passion. "I *did* talk to them. And I saw into their minds. That's how I beat Semeca, in the end. I saw that she was only fighting because she was afraid to die. I found the moment in her life when she'd stopped wanting to live. And then I talked to her about it."

He'd told her the story. "And that gave you the opening you needed to kill her."

He nodded. "Same thing with the second shaman that attacked us on the road, the one with the furs? I found the person in his past that had given him such a lust for power, and reminded him of it. Shocked him enough that he lost control for a second."

Ella cleared her throat. "I believe *I'm* the one who killed him?"

"With the help of some fatewalking. And yes, I know, it might not work. But isn't it worth trying, before we start killing and making revenants and all that?"

"It is. It probably is. But there isn't always time for that. If there are other shamans at the stone in Aran, are you going to try to convince them our cause is more just? Bribe them like you did the guards today? If they're anything like Credelen or Ollen, I don't think it's going to work."

They crested the hill and Tai sighed. "I don't know. I'm still figuring this out. If it comes down to it, I'm still going to kill them to protect you, to protect our friends. Of course I am. But I need a reason to do it, something better than just protecting my own people. That's what everyone's doing. That's all the Councilate is, all the shamans are doing, probably all the archrevenants see themselves as doing too. And it's always a justification to make more suffering for other people, to give them their own reasons to fight and kill and die."

Ella didn't know what to say to that. He wasn't wrong. He was just—too good.

The stone at the top was flat and mossy, and they took a seat looking eastward toward Aran, the scattered lights of Galven twinkling below. "So, what's your plan for Eyadin? To talk him out of it?"

Tai put an arm around her waist, and she could feel the tension in his stiff back. "If I can."

"And if you can't? You're not going to let him deliver the message, right?"

"No. I just need to try talking first, because I can, because he deserves a chance. Because in a different life any of us could have been him, or Marea's parents, and I would have defended them to the death."

She gave his leg a squeeze. "When did you get so noble, anyway?"

He shrugged. "I assumed it was all your Councilate morality civilizing me."

"Hardly. The most moral person I found in the Councilate was someone who denied morality existed at all."

He glanced at her. "Guess I'm not enough of a philosopher to get that one."

She leaned in close. "How about this one? It's an old debate among philosophers: two people madly in love finally get some time alone, after weeks aboard a ship pining for each other. Would the most pleasant way to spend their time be discussing ethics, or more… intimate pursuits?"

He grinned. "I just figured I'd try talking first."

"Well, it didn't work."

He put his other arm around her, drawing her in. "Then I'd better try again."

He did, and this time he got it right.

46

Theories on the origins of the waystone are as common in Aran as hanging gardens and back-alley teahouses. Of course the official version is that the Ascending God left it in her wake when she ascended, but you will find the Aranese surprisingly tolerant of alternate notions. A few of these: the stone is the weathered remains of an ancient feline statue; the stone was built of clay then fused using a technique lost to time; the stone is the last of a ring said to surround the true site of the god's ascension; and the stone is the offal of the old Ealan serpents. Take your pick.
—Arenia Melthesan, *A Walking History of Aran*

Marea woke in her lover's arms. And though they had fought most of the night, though they still hadn't really resolved what was wrong, it still felt like heaven. Like coming home, for the first time in too long. She snuggled in closer, Avery's chest wide and deep. In the end it had hurt too much to stay angry, and they had agreed they cared about each other too much to let it keep them apart.

And then they'd made love, actually done what they'd been easing towards the entire journey, and it had been... intense. Something beyond just pleasure and pain. She felt deeper this morning, more like a woman. A woman who had a man. Her worries about him leaving her were gone—he loved her, and he wasn't going to leave her even if they disagreed sometimes.

It sounded stupid, when she thought it so plainly, but living it was a lot different than reading it in books.

Oh, my pepper. I hate to have to say this to you, but what happened last night doesn't mean anything. Do you think you're the first woman he's bedded that way?

Marea shook her head, angry at the voice for intruding. She needed to get Ella to help her overcome the voice today, even if Eyadin saw. The sooner the better.

Avery stirred beside her and she pressed herself against him, not wanting to get dressed, not wanting to leave the mess they'd made of the bed, the warmth of their bodies intertwined. Not wanting to see Ella and Tai and get back on the road and face whatever waited for them in Aran. Now more than ever she hated the idea of any harm coming to Avery.

What would she do without him?

A knock sounded at the door. "Marea?" Ella's voice came. "Avery? We're headed out soon."

Avery opened his eyes, and Marea cursed the woman and her vainglorious quest. She could have laid here all day.

"Morning," Avery croaked. "Time to go, already?"

"Or we could stay," she whispered, running her hand down his stomach, feeling bold but also entitled. His body was hers.

It is no such thing.

He smiled, and kissed her like he was going to agree, then sat up. "Got a world to save first, I guess," he said, then rolled out.

One flash of pale, perfectly formed cheeks, and the intimacy they'd shared disappeared beneath linens and furs.

Well, there was still tonight. One more evening together before they faced Aran.

She rolled out too, and dressed, and found the rest of the party waiting for them. Most of their eyes looked elsewhere a little too obviously. Feynrick gave her a wide grin.

Marea blushed like a child caught with one hand in the candy jar. The walls of this inn were entirely too thin.

The road that day looked much like it had the last, but it *felt* a hundred times better with Avery beside her, Feynrick filling the empty hours walking with more exaggerated tales of his conquests in the Councilate army. He added winks in her direction, every time some unlikely romantic dalliance was part of the story, and she blushed anew each time.

Gods, all she had wanted was privacy. And now that she'd gotten a taste of it, all she wanted was *more*. No wonder it was traditional for newlyweds to sleep their first night alone in their new home. She would have that home with Avery someday, even if the sleeping would already feel familiar.

They passed a few more checkpoints that morning, with none of the drama of yesterday. What *did* change was the number of people on the road. What started as a few more patrons sitting in front of inns and bakeries swelled to overflowing taverns and tents pitched alongside guesthouses by midday. The road filled up too, pilgrims carrying bags and farmers pushing carts and even squadrons of whitecoats, advising people to turn back, to stay where they were, that the rebels were dangerous.

No one paid them heed, and everyone traveled the same direction: east, toward Aran.

"Pissing curs," Feynrick said, after they'd had to wait to cross a bridge so glutted with travelers others had taken to fording the stream. "What do they all hope to find?"

That was answered soon enough, as Ella worked her conversational magic with the travelers they passed. "Can't you feel it?" asked one woman, an infant tied to her back. "We were in close, almost to the city, but Henle was hungry. Soon as I find food, we're going back."

There was a light in her eyes, a shine like Marea had seen in marketpool preachers, proclaiming the next coming of the Prophet or the return of the Descending God.

Only this time, half the pilgrims weren't even talking of Eschatology or the kind of faithful nonsense they'd heard nearer Califf. They were talking about the stone.

"Got right to it, I did," one shoeless man confided, leaning in with breath that stank of decay. "Can't get there now, they got soldiers all around it, but I got there before, gods guiding. Put my hand up against it and," he shuddered like Avery would at the height of sensation. "Like I was young again. Could do anything. *Be* anything!"

"And are you headed back there now?" Ella asked. They were waiting in line for a peasant family selling loaves of seeded bread.

"Oh, no," he said. "Got me wife to think of. Things were getting rough in there when I left. Feeling young again's not worth dying for, you ask me. I got mine."

"Rough from rebels?" Tai asked, one hand firmly on the pack that held their money.

"Rebels they mighta been," the man said. "Weren't no friends of the whitecoats, that's for sure. Nor anyone like me taking my time with the stone." He shook his head. "I'll make it back someday."

The group exchanged glances then, Tai to Ella to Feynrick and Avery. Marea would have been annoyed she wasn't worth the troubled glances, except they ignored Eyadin too. At least she had company now.

The messenger cleared his throat. "What could these men be, if not rebels?"

Eyadin didn't know about shamans. Probably had no idea the one who'd sent him with such haste was an archrevenant. Marea was seized with an urge to tell him, to warn him. Much as he might think he was bringing death to Aran, the city might be his death just as easily, if the shamans discovered what message he carried.

They continued walking once they'd gotten their bread, at a whopping fifty marks per loaf, the pace slower with so many people on the road.

"It appears there may be opportunity for your House after all," Eyadin said to Ella, "if this situation extends all the way to the city."

"Aye," Ella said, "mayhap there is."

Did the woman feel as bad as Marea, about not being able to warn Eyadin? But the man was not warning them of his message either. More untrustworthy travel companions. She would be glad when they were out of this and it was just her and Avery.

If they made it out.

The crowd thickened on the road as the day wore on, with as many coming *from* Aran as heading to it. Some looked starved, and many spoke of food shortages, others of violence, of people dying if they approached too close to the stone.

"Rebels," one hirsute farmer confided in them. "But not like they have in the south. These are more like… Titans gone wrong. Whitecoats are going to have problems, they try taking back the Old City."

More significant glances were exchanged at this, including one from Avery to Marea, but of course they couldn't talk about anything with Eyadin there. Even with their lives in danger. It was so stupid.

They began walking to the side of the road, making better

time weaving through encampments and clumps of people sitting by the side of the road than actually walking on it. Most of them seemed torn between finding safety or food and the shine-eyed reverence with which they spoke of the stone.

No doubt they were going to the right place, then, curse it. Would that this was another dead end and she had more weeks on the road with Avery before any true danger faced them.

You do not have to follow this man into danger, my pepper. He is in league with your mother's murderer.

"Ella," Marea snapped, for once not giving a scat about all their secrecy, "any chance we can get a harmony going some time today? I'm really getting tired of this voice."

Ella's tone was sweet and her look was pure daggers. "Kidtalk again? Afraid I can't help with that one, love."

Eyadin did give her a strange look, but *damn* the woman. What was the good of knowing how to oust revenants if they didn't use it?

Ella continued fishing for information as the pastures and even fields to the sides of the road filled, hearing more of the same stories: no food to be found, dangerous rebels in the old city, whitecoats arresting people on trivial charges, and a stone so wondrous that it was all worth it.

"Pity no one can get in, though," a woman said to them, eying them from the far side of a smoldering fire. "They don't know the old ways."

"The old ways?" Ella asked, making a shushing motion with her free hand to slow them down.

The woman grinned, revealing a perfect set of white teeth. "The old emperor never died," she said. "The last *true* emperor, when Shatterbrook came and overran the city. Had his own ways in and out of the city. Few know of them now."

"Precious good it would do you," said the man next her, eyes bright but sunken. "Nothing but hunger and death in there now."

"Do you know these ways?" Ella asked, casually though Marea had traveled with her long enough to know the woman had piqued her interest.

The woman cleared her throat, glancing at the other travelers around the fire. "I have a camp, a few thousandpace off the road," she said. "Somewhere we can talk without being overheard."

"Lead on," Ella said, at a subtle nod from Tai.

The woman led them away from the fire, following a cart track back from the road past a bow-roofed farmhouse with a scattering of tents in the yard. As she did, Marea noticed Eyadin falling behind, one hand holding Tai's sleeve. Senses suddenly alert, Marea slowed too, wanting to hear.

"She's dangerous," Eyadin said, almost too low to hear.

Tai glanced at him sharply. "What?"

"She's like Avery," he said. "A… witch doctor."

Marea stared at the man, just as Tai was doing. Witch doctors? Avery?

"How do you know that?" Tai asked in a fierce whisper, keeping his eyes ahead. Ella glanced back at them, a question in her eyes.

Did the man mean shamans? But how would Eyadin know about shamans? Only shamans knew about shamans. Marea unfocused her eyes—there was no trace of revenants about him.

"I just do," Eyadin said. "We need to turn back."

Tai looked to the front again, and his resonance hit like a struck bell. Marea's stomach dropped: if the woman leading them was a shaman, they were in danger. A *lot* of danger.

"Very astute, Eyadin," the woman said, not slowing, "but you should have turned back long ago. Brayliegh?"

The ground erupted in fire.

Tai screamed, his clothes burning, his skin burning, hair in flames on his head. All thought of fighting vanished in pure pain.

No, came a voice inside, calm and steady. Avery's voice. *This is not real. It is a shamanic attack. Touch your body. You are not on fire.*

In the middle of the flames, Tai touched one hand to his other forearm. And instead of cracked and charred flesh, he touched the sleeve of his shirt, fabric rough under his fingers.

This is an attack of the mind. Don't believe in it. They will target me, to thrall my revenants. Help me. Fight back.

Flames still roaring, Tai ran his hands over his face, his jacket, his hair still bound behind his head. They all felt normal. This was not real. An attack of the mind.

It still hurt, his heart still beat like the heart of battle, but the more he checked himself the less pain he felt, real as it all seemed. *It's an attack of the mind*, he repeated to himself, pushing up from where he'd fallen. *Don't believe it.*

Through the flames he could see the pasture, see his friends rolling in the grass as two men approached from the far hillside,

Avery facing them alone. Ella lay a few paces ahead, hands clawing at her face, screaming.

No. Whatever this was it was not real, but the danger to Ella was. And all philosophy aside, anyone who threatened her deserved to die.

Tai struck resonance, flames growing less distinct with each moment. The resonance felt good, the power he'd had to hide the past few weeks flooding into him, the strength, the raw ability.

He shot forward, but flying wasn't fast enough, so he struck out with air too, sending wedges of wind at each of the three shamans' throats.

Then the resonance left his bones and he was falling, plummeting from the sky, even as a scream ripped through his mind. A revenant. Someone sicced a revenant on him like Ydilwen and Sablo but had.

But he'd practiced for this, prepared for it, and in the heat of battle all his training came back. *Not real*, he thought, striking resonance again, momentum carrying him over the attacking trio and toward the far hillside. *Just a revenant. My uai is mine.*

He struck again, the *uai* responded this time, buoying him up a few paces from slamming into the ground.

Tai grinned. "You won't get rid of me that easily."

He circled back, warier, dropping to the hillside and striking mindsight. It was a skill he'd been practicing, during the long days on the boat, refining his vision to focus on just one mind at a time, to get better at following the current of their thoughts forward to their plans, and backward to the motivations they might not even know drove them. To their fears.

But there was no time for that now—now he sought only which of them was attacking their minds. Sought only the barest outlines of their plan so that he could disrupt it—because these were clearly stronger shamans than they'd faced, and everyone else except Avery was still rolling on the ground screaming.

There—the man on the right, short and stout with a flowing fur cape. Delusions of grandeur. A giant stream of *uai*. Tai shot for him, summoning boulders of air to smash the man from either side, to disrupt him, to give Ella and the rest a chance to fight back.

Because he had no doubt, if they *did* fight back, it wouldn't matter how strong the shamans were. They would be destroyed.

The man stumbled, then spun for him and took to the air. *Blurred* in air, using his *uai* to act as a wafter and timeslip at once. Tai shot left, knowing he was unlikely to escape, but that every second was another second for his friends to wake up, then spun backwards, upside down, wafting like the cats of Riverbottom ran when they sensed danger. And as he did, he sought ever deeper with his mind, trying to find the man's goals, his fear, his *weakness*.

Something slammed into him, screaming, and his mindsight cut off. *Not real*, Tai thought, striking at his resonance, shoving at the revenant as he'd shoved at so many in his life. *You're not real.*

His resonance came back just as something hard and real connected with his back. He reacted with the momentum, throwing himself further that way, groundward, taking the worst of the blow in speed rather than his bones.

Mindsight came back with a vengeance: Brayleigh. The shaman's name was Brayleigh, eldest son of a minor Yersh house, desirous of power, studying shamanism to become immortal—

Another slam, a flying length of timber. Tai rolled with this one too, sent air billowing back at it, kept pushing deeper with his mind. Brayleigh's desire came from fear, a fear around women, an inferiority he'd always felt, Dleana the woman they'd met at the fire—

A third revenant slammed into him just as the timber did, and there was no disbelieving in it, no rolling with it. The roaring wind and green hills blinked out, and Tai fell from the sky.

48

Ella went from dying in flames to lying on her back on a cool stretch of grass, friends screaming all around her. Then back to dying, but the words she'd been hearing struck home: *not real. Shamanic attack. Not on fire.*

It was Avery's voice, calm in the midst of the screaming. *Touch your body. You are not on fire.*

Just as she did, the flames stuttered again, the pain disappearing like it was an illusion.

"Because it is," she cursed, pushing up, flames roaring back but without their heat somehow, now. Avery had said defense against revenant attacks was based on disbelieving in them. Whatever this was, disbelief must be the answer to it too.

Ella stood, flames still there but translucent, like fire viewed through hazy glass. Ahead of her Avery and the woman faced off, while in the sky above Tai and another man circled and fought, the other man moving almost too fast to see.

Stains—while she'd been rolling around delusional, Tai and Avery had been risking their lives for her. Time to return the favor—even if it meant shortening her own life to do it.

Ella struck resonance. Better short-lived than dead.

The world slowed, Tai going from a zip to a drift, his pursuer slowing down too, a portly man in some kind of cape circling around him, fast but not so fast as she was.

Ella ran. If Avery and the woman were facing off, then they were dueling in the traditional way of shamans, trying to thrall each other's *uai* away in a battle of wits. There was a wiry man walking down the hillside unopposed, arms at his side. But her illusions had stuttered, which must mean the man Tai was battling was causing them. Her man looked outclassed, but every hit he scored was a chance for the rest of them to see through it and wake up.

Trust Tai to think first of saving everyone else. As she ran a timber rose from the meadow grass and caught him in the middle of a dizzying loop. He drifted out of it as though without resonance, which didn't make sense—unless he'd been hit with a revenant too.

Ella unfocused her eyes and saw the trailing threads of something hooking to Tai's spine. *Prophets*. These were no ordinary shamans, if there was such a thing. But Tai's strategy was right: Avery appeared to have met his match, and Ella was unlikely to defeat the other two without help. So she had to kill the fat one first, to get Feynrick and Marea back into the fight.

Which meant stealth more than speed—the fat one was drifting toward the ground now, slowing as he apparently dropped the shaman's version of timeslip. Still the second she stopped or dropped resonance he would see her, and she didn't trust herself to battle his illusions.

So instead of running for the place he'd land she ran past that, under him getting to Tai just in time to break his fall. Then she laid him in the grass and laid down behind, using his much-bigger body as a hiding place. With any luck the fat man would not notice her gone from the three others rolling on the ground, and she could get in a surprise strike.

Ella watched over Tai's mass of black hair as the fat one touched down, moving slower now, likely trying to distract Avery with illusions as he kept Marea and the others down. Had he noticed she was gone?

It didn't matter. She had one trick and there was no time like now.

Ella got up and started running, fat one facing away from her as the others were. Mid-stride a thought occurred to her: she had more than one trick these days. Surreptitious practice over the last week had her reliably grasping revenants and moving them. How much harder could it be to sic one on somebody, like the fat man had on Tai?

She scanned the meadow as she ran, heart beating faster if that was possible. She wasn't good enough to see what resonance a revenant was, which meant she didn't know if they were safe to thrall, but that shouldn't matter right? She didn't expect the thing to actually *seat* in the shaman. Just distract him long enough for her to cut his throat.

She seized a nearby revenant even as she pulled her blade, the wiry third man in the shaman's party beginning to look her way.

Too bad he was moving at a glacial pace. She closed the gap, dragging the revenant close. At the last minute the fat man turned and the world went black. *Illusion*, she thought to herself, but more importantly she could still *see*, just not in the world of colors. In the world of revenants.

She slammed the revenant at the shaman, not sure what she was doing but sure harder was better. The blackness dropped and in the clarity of sight she chopped her knife into his neck.

His eyes opened wide in shock but she was already turning to the wiry man. Every second in slip was hours of her dwindling life. No time for gloating.

The wiry man was facing her, raising his arms in regular time. He could slip too. *Stains*.

"Impressive," the man said, voice clear among the rumbling screams of her friends. "I did not have you marked for a shaman. But Brayleigh was a friend of mine, even if he was an arrogant bastard. And for that you must pay dearly."

Ella ignored him, already halfway across the hillside to where he stood. Then a sudden weight pulled at her left arm, and she looked with horror to see the hand holding the knife encased in stone. *Growing* stone.

"What—"

A weight pulled at her right arm then too, and she stumbled under the weight.

"A pity we cannot kill you outright," the wiry man said over her curses. "But we need all the *uai* we can get, and you have a remarkable stream." He smiled. "So be quiet while I deal with your friends, hm?"

Cold stone wrenched her mouth wide, and she tripped over a foot turned suddenly leaden.

The wiry man smiled and turned back to the battle. "Good girl."

*M*area knew rationally, somewhere in the quieter recesses of her brain, that flames did not spring from thin air. Just as she knew they wouldn't go on for hours or days without fuel, impervious to her best attempts to roll and beat them out. She had even heard Avery's calm words as soon as they'd started, telling her it was an illusion.

But that knowledge was just one cool, rational voice. A voice drowned out by the panicked, screaming mob that was her mind.

Then suddenly the flames were gone, and the pain with them. The panic took a moment longer, but without the mob screaming the cool, rational voice was able to make some headway. Marea pushed out of the grass, heart still thudding, to see Avery locked in some kind of staring contest with the woman who'd led them there, a wiry man striding toward them and Ella laying in what looked like an odd collection of boulders, two bodies nearby.

Feynrick whistled beside her. "Burn ye to death and they're still not done, are they, lass?"

"We have to do something," Marea said. "Avery's in danger!"

Feynrick unlooped an axe from his belt. "I have to do something, ye mean," he said. "Battle like this is no place for a pretty little girl."

Irritation threatened to replace panic for a moment in her. "I am no little girl," she said, standing and striking resonance. "You know what I can do. Go, and I'll give you all the luck I can."

"Luck?" Feynrick grinned. "Always needed more 'o that."

"Avery first!" Marea called, but he was already running. Cursing, she focused her mind. Envisioned Feynrick slamming his axe into the shaman woman's throat, hearing the thud, seeing the shock on her face, tasting the iron—

Then boulders started rising from the earth in Feynrick's path. Marea added them to her vision, Feynrick dodging and weaving between them. The boulders grew thicker in front of him, walling him in. Feynrick leapt to the top of one with a brawler's grace, and she added *that* to her vision, the stout Yatiman leaping between boulders with shouts and yells, always finding one for his feet, leading him ever closer to the woman threatening Avery.

And then the boulders started throwing themselves at him.

Cursing and pulling hard at her resonance, Marea imagined his leaps dodging the oncoming boulders, imagined them slamming into each other, opening pathways for him, more islands to hop on, until—

With a shout she could hear two hundred paces away Feynrick slammed his axe into the woman's neck, *exactly* as she'd imagined it, and the blood sprayed and the shock showed and the revenants swirling around Avery suddenly sucked back into him.

Marea dropped resonance. "Oh, thank the Prophets." Then a boulder hurtled toward *her*, and she would have been crushed beneath it if Eyadin hadn't tackled her from the side.

Cursing, Marea struck resonance again. "Come on!" she yelled, imagining a lucky path for them through the sudden rain of boulders, willing them to collide and bounce off each other, hearing the thuds and crashes and feeling the debris in as much detail as she could imagine. Prophets send Avery or Feynrick could deal with the last man, the one raining the boulders, because he'd apparently figured out she was a fatewalker, and it was all she could do not to get crushed.

Through a gap in the stones she saw Avery now facing the man, hands raised like they had been against the woman. *Hurry, my love*, she thought inside, skipping between two boulders meant to sandwich her, then ducking under another hurtling sideways in air. *I don't know how much longer I can do this.*

She saw Feynrick too, good old trusty Feynrick, running for the wiry man like he'd run for the woman, bloody axe in hand. Eyadin pulled her back just before a boulder landed in front of them, and she split just the tiniest part of her mind off from imagining herself surviving this to imagining the Yatiman's axe finding a second bloody home in the wiry man's chest.

Then kept running and burning *uai* and dodging stones and holding to her visions like a drowning woman holds a ship's line.

Four boulders slammed down all around her and Eyadin, cutting off their escape but miraculously missing hurting them.

"We're trapped," Eyadin said, face pale, but she had no space to respond, concentrating as hard as she was on a fifth boulder *not* dropping directly down on top of them, trapping them even if it didn't kill them.

"He'll drop another one down on us," Eyadin whined. "Trap us in here till they can kill us."

"I know, you idiot," Marea snapped, though it already should have happened. She looked up despite knowing she should stick to her vision, to not worry about *reality*, sure she would see the fifth boulder descending, a whopper made to crush out her life.

There was nothing above but clear blue sky. No screams or shouts sounded in the distance.

Eyadin met her eyes. "Did they—"

Marea took a deep breath, letting herself believe it only

because that would work as well as whatever else she was trying to will into existence. "Climb up and check, will you? I need to concentrate."

And that's what she did, till Eyadin looked back down, a shocked grin on his lips. "They did it," he said. "Bless the Ascending and Descending Gods, they *did* it."

Marea dropped resonance, suddenly exhausted, but she couldn't help but respond, "No, they didn't. *We* did."

50

The worst thing about having a mouth stuffed with solid stone was you couldn't call for help. Ella watched, bent painfully over all four limbs encased in rock, while Feynrick first made a mad dash for the female shaman, then against all odds sank his axe into the chest of the wiry shaman while the man hurled boulders at both him and Marea. Tai hadn't stirred the entire time, but she couldn't think about that. They had won. He would be fine.

But then after Marea had come running from the boulder field and she and Avery had had a very public reunion and Feynrick had made suggestions and Eyadin had looked abashed, her thoughts started to gain a little urgency. She really *could* use some help getting out of these stone manacles, and Tai really *did* probably need some attention after taking a few logs to the back. The only problem was she had a mouthful of granite.

The party eventually remembered her and Tai. She was gratified to see Avery run, at least, and he had the sense to lay his hands on her cheeks first, *uai* buzzing.

The rock turned to grit in her mouth and she spit great mouthfuls of it, grateful despite the grating sensation on her teeth. "Thank the mecking prophets," she coughed. "Tai. Is he okay?"

"Fine!" Feynrick called from where Tai lay up the hill. "Breathing, anyway, and I don't see any bleeding. Takes more'n something like this to hurt our little milkweed!"

"Then if you don't mind?" Ella asked, nodding to her trapped limbs.

Avery got to work on them. "What happened, anyway?" Marea asked.

Ella told her as much as she knew, leading up to getting trapped in rock. "Shouldn't this have disappeared when he died?" she asked Avery, shaking a freed hand gratefully. "The other illusions stopped when I killed the first shaman."

Avery shook his head, still concentrated on her left foot. "These are not illusions. The first shaman was what we call an avisceror, using his *uai* stream to create illusions that distract or confuse opponents. The second one was a visceror, using his *uai* to alter physical reality."

Marea shook her head, staring at Ella's foot as the orb of rock grew a series of cracks then shattered into sand. "Why would anyone make illusions when you can change actual reality?"

"They're easier," Avery said briefly, concentrated on Ella's other foot. When it shattered he went on, "A visceror has to find the right materials for what he wants—in this case, soil in the earth he could use to make stone. An avisceror already has the thoughts and perceptions to work with, though they do have to be very precise."

"And they use revenants for that?" Ella asked, trying to imagine how it worked.

"They use *uai* streams for that," Avery said, standing from the last of her limbs. "And belief. *Uai* is... a basic force of the universe. Like sound or heat. But it needs shaping, like sound needs the shape of a lute or horn to make music. Winter plants shape the star's light into *uai*. Regular people shape *uai* with their resonances. But shamans—we're not limited by the shape of our revenants. Our *uai* doesn't come through their channel, it comes direct, and so we can use it for whatever we want. So long as we believe strongly enough that it's possible."

Ella motioned them toward Tai, concern warring with curiosity. "So that's why we need disbelief to fight a revenant attack, or to see through an avisceror's illusions?"

Avery nodded. "But you would not have been able to crack these stones without *uai* as well. Illusions are easily made and broken. Physical attacks," he nodded at the low valley, now littered with boulders, "they need more strength."

"What you're saying," Marea said, "is that the man was a powerful shaman."

"They all were," Avery said. "My guess is they've been here a while, luring shamans off the road into an ambush. Then they would control them with physical or mental attacks while the woman in the lead thralled their revenants. Then they shared the power between them."

"Making them harder and harder to defeat," Ella said. "The visceror, he mentioned something to me about getting strong enough to take the stone."

"If these three weren't strong enough to take the stone," Feynrick said as they approached, "how in piss are we supposed to do it?"

Someone answered, but Ella missed it in a wave of concern, running to Tai's side and kneeling, pressing fingers to his head and chest and back. She knew little of healing, but his breathing didn't sound good.

"Tai," she whispered, hand returning to his forehead, brushing away a stray length of hair. "My Tai, are you alright?"

There was no response.

Avery knelt next to her. "I'll see what I can do for him."

"You... can do something?"

"Belief," he said, voice distant. "Belief and *uai* is all I need. And there are a lot of revenants offering *uai* on this hillside. Healing is easier because brawlers who've overcome their second resonance have the ability to heal themselves, so it's easy to believe in me having that ability, and only a little stretch to be able to give it to him."

Gods. There seemed little limit to what shamans could do—or was Avery just a very powerful one? Or knowledgeable one? How had he gotten so in his brief years? As *uai* roared and Tai sucked in a deep breath, arching his back, she couldn't help feeling she'd wasted her years studying ethnography. Would that she had joined the ninespears instead.

Then all feelings were eclipsed in relief as Tai opened his eyes, and his hand reached out to grip hers. "Guess I didn't quite get them all, did I?"

"Don't worry," she said. "I did."

Marea cleared her throat. "And me."

"Thought *I* was the one actually killed 'em," Feynrick said, stumping his axe head-first into the ground.

"It all would have been a lot harder if they'd been at full strength," Avery said. "You have me to thank for that one."

Tai looked between them, a smile playing on his lips, until his gaze landed on Eyadin.

"I—honestly have no idea what's going on," the messenger said. "You are all—witch doctors?"

"That is not a name we prefer," Avery said, "and no. I am the only full shaman here."

"But you already knew that," Tai said, pushing up to a sitting position with a grunt. "You knew the woman was a shaman before she attacked. Which means you have some explaining to do."

"What?" Ella said, turning to the slender messenger with the rest of the group.

"He said she was a witch doctor," Marea said. "While she was still leading us out here."

Ella turned on him, a slow burn starting in her stomach. "Oh, that *does* need some explaining. Why wouldn't you warn us straight away?"

A bead of sweat appeared on Eyadin's forehead. "I—there have been many," he said. "On the road. And I *did* say something. I pulled Tai back to warn him. She just heard and attacked."

"But you can spot shamans?" Ella asked. "How is that even possible?" She glanced at Avery, but the youth's eyes were trained on Eyadin just as hard as everyone else's.

Eyadin hitched at his pack. "I—haven't been entirely honest with you. I am not working for my House as I originally said. Though I *am* a messenger."

"Who are you working for?" Ella asked, glad they were finally getting honest.

Eyadin face paled. "I don't know," he said. "Someone high up. They never—they don't appear to me in person, or if they do it's with a mask. I'm not even supposed to tell you that! It's just the one message. That's all I'm supposed to deliver, and then it's done. I never meant to get involved in all this—" He gestured his hands, apparently not able to come up with a word for what had just happened.

"Well, you are involved in it," Tai said, voice even, "and whether you get to *stay* involved in it will depend a lot on how you answer our questions. How can you see shamans?"

Was Tai threatening the man? What about all his talk of not making revenants? Or maybe it was a bluff.

Eyadin paled further, if that was possible. "She—it told me I would need something. On the road. Told me to hold out my hand, and… and when it was done I could just see this halo around some people. Around her. Like their hair is glowing."

"Why did she give that to you?" Tai asked, picking up on the pronoun gender.

"She said they would be a special danger to me. That I should report every one that I saw to the commander at Aran, once I got there. Make sure they were among those—"

"Among those killed," Tai said, when Eyadin broke off. "We know about your message."

His face went white as a sheet. "How—"

"Mindsight," Avery said. "You people from Worldsmouth are always forgetting about mindsight. Which makes me wonder how competent your master is, if they failed to even think of that."

Ella frowned. "But wouldn't it have to be—" she hesitated, but Eyadin had already heard much, and apparently understood little, "an archrevenant? Who else would have the power to command armies, and an interest in protecting the stone?"

"There are many cells in Worldsmouth," Avery said. "More likely one of them. A shaman high up in the system, calling in a favor."

Marea gave him a strange look at that. What did the girl know?

"But Eyadin's vision," Tai said. "How is that even possible?"

"Belief and *uai*," Avery repeated, though Tai hadn't heard most of their conversation. "A powerful enough shaman could do this. Could imbue Eyadin with that kind of sight. Almost like a charm, or an extra power they feed from their own *uai*. I have heard of such things being done."

"And now you're going to report Avery," Marea said, eyes hard. "Report all of us, maybe, when you get to Aran."

"No!" Eyadin cried. "I would never—no. You saved my life. Multiple times! I swear I never wanted any of this. But whatever they say, I couldn't betray friends. I will say nothing of you to the commander. Though you must—if you know of my message, why are you still intent on going to Aran?"

"Our reasons are our own," Tai said, "as are yours, friend. If you say you will not betray us, then we have to believe it." He turned a sharp gaze on Avery. "The revenants those shamans had thralled. You're taking them?"

The youth nodded, eyes still distant. "I am."

"We will need our share of them," Tai said. "You keep a fourth of a half. That's our deal."

"I—can't give them to you. Not until you learn to thrall on your own."

"Then teach us," Ella said, hungry for that *uai* and buoyed up by what she'd done. She'd *attacked* with a revenant back there! Even if it hadn't really worked. "How hard can it be?"

"It is hard," Avery said. "One of the last tests before becoming a full shaman. If we waited until you could thrall them, we might delay weeks. Months."

Tai cracked his neck, obviously weighing the delay against letting Avery take all that power. "You can keep it for now," he said after a moment. "When we get the spear those revenants will all flow back to the holder anyway."

Ella nodded. It was the right decision—the *only* one, given the situation they were in—but still it didn't sit well. Those shamans had been wildly powerful, and Avery had just absorbed *all* their *uai?*

"Now," Tai said, shouldering his pack. "I don't doubt these shamans have some sort of place they were hiding, and we could all use some food and a place to rest. I know I could, at least. We enter Aran in the morning."

51

Take the holiest minister you can find, and send a cat 'cross his path in the dark hours—he'll still kick 'em and curse 'em. Old ways die hard.
    —Eschatolist pilgrim in Fenschurch, Yiel 113

They found the shamans's hideout a few hills deeper into the countryside, an overgrown farmhouse with smoke curling from the stone-and-mortar chimney.

Ella sucked in a breath when she pushed in after Tai. The inside was like a thieves den from some broadsheet epic: glass lamps lit the interior, highlighting colored silks on the walls and plush rugs laid over a worn plank floor. Coins and books lay in careless stacks around a large velvet sofa and three gleaming beds.

Feynrick whistled. "This how all you witch doctors live?"

"It's shamans," Avery said. "And no. I would guess most of this was purchased after they decided to become apostates."

"Apostates?" Tai asked.

"Shamans who hunt other shamans," Avery said, disgust evident in his voice. "Seeking to thrall their thralls. It's the fastest way to increase your *uai*. It's also the only thing all cells agree on, and work together to enforce: all apostates must die."

"Sleeping like kings tonight!" Feynrick called from the far side of the single-room house, sprawling on one of the plush beds.

"As long as you don't mind sleeping with Eyadin," Ella said. "Tai and I take up one, and I imagine Marea and Avery would like to share another on their last night before Aran."

Marea blushed but nodded, giving her a look of gratitude.

"Nothing I'd like better," Feynrick said, tipping Eyadin an exaggerated wink.

Eyadin looked as petrified as he had when they'd cornered him about lying, if not worse, and Ella couldn't help laughing. The rest of them joined in, and for a moment they were not six people on an insane quest, having just survived one mortal battle and preparing to fight another. They were just six people having a laugh.

"Speaking of which," Avery said, still chuckling. "Marea, maybe you and I should see if we can hunt up something for supper."

Feynrick guffawed as though Avery had said something much more lecherous. "I'll perk up these coals, then," the Yatiman said. "'Spect ye back real soon."

The two left, and Ella gave Tai a speculative eye. "Maybe we should do some hunting of our own." Last night had been wonderful, but they had more catching up to do.

Tai's eyes slipped toward Eyadin. "Maybe just for a minute," he said.

Feynrick laughed loudest at that, and even Ella couldn't help blushing as she and Tai left out the creaking front door.

The sun was low in the western sky as they came out, bathing the rolling Yersh hills in a gentle violet glow. They walked for a minute in silence, Ella enjoying the peace after so much danger and death. She took a deep breath. "This wouldn't be such a bad place to live."

"Yeah," Tai said.

"Hey." Ella pulled him close. "You're worried about Eyadin, I get that, but just be with me here for a second. It's *beautiful*, Tai."

He looked around, the old farmyard grown over in amberhock and tinnelsthorn, hillside sprinkled with the delicate blue blossoms of hardenswort flowers. Tai took a deep breath, and Ella breathed with him, smelling old wood and puceleaf smoke, but moreso the green breath of flowers living and dying.

"It *is* beautiful," he said, then turned his eyes to her. "And so are you."

Any doubts she might have had over whether he really did still find her attractive, with all these new wrinkles and sags, were cut short in the passion of what followed.

She sighed when it was done, star's blue glow overtaking the sun's amber in the skies above. "Do you want to talk about Eyadin?"

He lay on his back next to her, shamelessly naked though the air was growing chill. "Not much to say. Tonight I convince him to not send the people of Aran to their death."

Ella ran her fingers down his chest. It was too scarred for his age, but she still loved it. "How?"

He shrugged. "With my usual wit and charm? And some mindsight. And some cold hard logic."

"And if that doesn't work?"

"It will work. It has to."

Ella looped her arm around him. "You're insane, and there's a lot at stake, but I trust you. I wouldn't if I hadn't seen you pull off a lot of other insane things, but I have. So, whatever you need, I'll help you with it."

And if it fails, she added silently, I'll help you with that too.

He nodded. "Thank you."

They put their clothes on then, Ella glad to cover her new spots and loose skin, and made their way back to the farmhouse. Her joints hurt from laying in the cold so long, but she ignored them. She would learn to thrall revenants, if she had to stay awake weeks to master it. She would take her share from Avery. Nauro had lived one hundred thirty years on his stream. How much would she need to buy back the years she'd lost?

She just had to get it done without using so much resonance she died first. Which was a real possibility tomorrow. Ella worried at a nail with her teeth.

They came in to find Marea and Avery already in bed, curtains drawn around their four poster and low whispers coming from within. Feynrick was sprawled on the farther bed, snoring, and Eyadin sat up watching the fire. Wondering what he should do? Or hating the fact that he had to do it?

"Mind if we sit?" Tai asked, then sat at the man's nod. Ella settled herself on a three-legged stool, far enough to not feel an immediate part of the conversation, but near enough to chime in if need be.

And she imagined there would be need.

"I don't blame you for not telling us everything," Tai said, after a few moments of silence. "I'm not exactly proud of having watched your thoughts, but I had to put the safety of my people first."

"That's the thing, isn't it?" Eyadin asked, not looking away from the flames. "You may think you're an upstanding man, that you've always done the best you could, but when it comes to your people, you will do anything for them. Anything."

His last word was bitter. This was a tormented man.

Tai nodded, and when he spoke his voice was gentle. "Like bring that message to the commander of Aran."

"Like bring that message to Aran," Eyadin repeated.

Ella watched Tai hesitate, looking for the best way forward. How did you convince a man to abandon his family for a city of strangers?

"She threatened their lives?" Tai asked.

"Worse," Eyadin said, one hand working at the leather strap of the satchel he wore even now. "She gave them bluefoot."

Ella sucked in a breath. Bluefoot fever was a disease that had ravaged the Yershire three centuries ago, leading to the downfall of Aran and the unification of the plains under Shatterbrook. It was slow and ugly and painful.

"I saw the marks on my daughter's neck," Eyadin went on, breath ragged. "She said she will cure them after I get back. I didn't know, but watching Avery today—I guess it is possible."

Tai pursed his lips. "We might be able to cure that disease too."

"You don't want me to deliver the message," Eyadin said, no hint of a question in his voice.

"It isn't a matter of what I want," Tai said. "Some of us think it would be easier if you did deliver the message, to do what we need to in the middle of the killing. But there are thousands of people in Aran. Maybe hundreds of thousands, from what we saw on the road. Whatever the stakes are, it can't be worth letting them all die."

Eyadin kept staring at the fire, but his chin jutted forward. "It's not my choice to make. I'm just a messenger."

"A messenger with the power to save thousands of lives," Tai said, seeking eye contact with the man.

Eyadin wouldn't give it. "At the expense of my wife and daughter. Would you do it, if it meant losing Ella?"

An uneasiness grew in her belly—she didn't want to hear the answer to that.

Tai ignored the question. "What would your wife think if she knew you knowingly delivered this message?" he asked. "What would your daughter think?"

"It doesn't matter what they think," Eyadin said, eyes glistening in the firelight. "As long as they live."

"We can help you with that too," Tai said, voice gentle again. "Find a way for your family *and* Aran to live."

The thin man shook his head. "You don't know her. Know what she's capable of."

"You might be surprised. You saw what we are capable of today."

"And if you die in whatever you're trying to do tomorrow?" Eyadin snapped, finally looking from the fire to Tai. "You're going to be battling witch doctors in there. More powerful than the ones today, Avery said. And you barely beat these three."

Ella watched Tai's shoulders knot, then relax. He was trying so hard. How much easier to stick a knife in the man's throat? "If we die, then you can deliver your message. Give us a day. Two days. I can't tell you everything, but I can promise if we come out of Aran alive, we will be stronger than all the witch doctors in Worldsmouth. We will be able to defeat whoever sent you on this mission. To cure your wife and daughter."

"And if you don't come out?"

Tai spread his hands. "Then deliver the message as planned."

"I'm supposed to bring it with all haste," Eyadin said, looking back to the fire. "She could be watching."

"If she was powerful enough to watch," Tai said, "she would be powerful enough to bring it herself. To stop me from having this conversation with you. I know her position in the Houses and the way she made your family sick is scary, but trust me, there is a *reason* she is trying to kill all of Aran. Because she's afraid of what's in there."

Descending Gods, he was going to do it. Tai was actually going to convince the man not to go.

"Give us two days," Tai said as Eyadin worked at his satchel strap. "Sunset the day after tomorrow."

Eyadin kept working at his bag, staring at the fire.

"I know you don't want to do this. And if we fail, your family is still safe. But this is a chance to save them *and* Aran."

"One day," he snapped. "Until sunset tomorrow. Then I go."

A weight went out of Tai's shoulders, and Ella smiled from her chair on the far side. "Until sunset tomorrow then," Tai said. "Thank you. Thank you for giving us this chance. We'll make sure your family stays safe."

"And save Aran," Eyadin said, closing his eyes. The man obviously cared deeply about it, and hated the choices he'd been given.

"And save Aran," Tai said.

They slept then, or soon enough, fire burnt down to coals as Ella snuggled against her man. She hated the danger they would be in tomorrow, hated the uncertainty of having to trust Eyadin, but she loved Tai all the more for caring about it, for doing what she would have dismissed as impossible.

"You're amazing, you know that?" she whispered in his ear.

He grunted, half asleep.

He was amazing, for so many reasons. Prophet send she lived to see them all.

52

Kill him? I doubt I could kill the boy if an archrevenant failed—but there are other ways to defeat a man. Or a woman. And the best of them is love.
        —Meyn Harides, *personal journals*

Tai woke to Feynrick cursing. Not the loud, exaggerated cursing the Yatiman usually did, but low, serious cursing.

He rolled out of bed. The sun was barely up, amber light shining through the hazy farmhouse windows. Ella blinked at him. "What—"

Tai pulled a shirt on and rushed outside. If Feynrick was serious, that meant trouble. Danger. Shamans had found them, maybe, or whitecoats. Tai struck resonance.

Feynrick was standing alone in an unassuming patch of grassy farmyard, staring down. Cursing.

"Feynrick, man," Tai said low, not wanting to wake the others. "What is it?"

Feynrick turned to him with a mournful expression. "See for yourself."

Tai looked. Eyadin lay face down in the grass, as though he'd passed out in the night.

Passed out with a knife in his throat.

Tai's stomach clenched. "What—" It couldn't be. "Who—"

"Found him like this when I came out to piss," Feynrick said.

"Who would attack him and not the rest of us?" It didn't make any sense. Tai rolled his shoulders, suddenly tight. All that work, the compromise they'd made last night, Eyadin's family in Worldsmouth—

Gone. Because you still think you're entitled to the spear.

Tai shook his head. Ydilwen was the last thing he needed right now.

"Look at the knife," Feynrick said, face still mournful. "It's same as the other stock in the kitchen."

Same as the other stock in the kitchen. Tai thought through the words, struggling like they were in some foreign tongue.

"It was one of us," Fenyrick said. "Avery, Marea, or Ella. Don't see how it coulda been otherwise."

Meckstains. One of *them* did it? "But who—"

"It wasn't me," Feynrick said quickly. "You know I had no dogs with the man. Was willing to let him come so long as you thought it was right."

"Then who—"

"Tai?" Ella leaned out the open door, still in her thin nightdress. "What's going on?"

He hated the new light he saw her in, hated the *suspicion*, but Feynrick was right. It had been one of them. "Eyadin's dead," Tai said, putting it bluntly, watching her reaction. Evaluating the sincerity of her shock, the look in her eyes, the strength of her grip as she held him and looked at the body.

"Oh, no," she said. "You had finally convinced him."

"And now his spirit is another revenant," Tai said. And now I repeat again the pattern I was trying to break.

What that his thought or Ydilwen's?

"Think of it this way," Feynrick said. "Least this way we can be sure he ain't bringing that message to Aran."

Which was what Ella had wanted initially, whatever she'd said last night. Tai struck resonance, hating himself for it even as he had to know. He looked her in the eyes. "Did you do this?"

"No, Tai," she said, disgust and more than a little hurt registering in her voice.

Her thoughts mirrored that exactly and he relaxed. "Okay. I'm sorry. I just—"

"You think one of us did it?" she asked, turning back to the body.

Feynrick told her about the knife.

"Gods," she said, looking toward the open door. "So, it had to be Marea or Avery?"

"Or it was the shaman that sent him," Avery said, stepping out into the yard. "Taking her revenge and trying to sow discord among us at the same time."

Tai didn't wait to peer into the man's thoughts, little good though it would likely do. "How did you know about this?" Tai asked.

Avery shrugged. "I heard you talking inside. Pretty hard to ignore half the room getting up and leaving at the crack of dawn."

Avery's current of thoughts showed the same thing, with plenty of other streams traveling back to his care for Marea, his worry about the coming day, even a trickle that was sorrow for a man killed unnecessarily.

"Are you masking your thoughts?" Tai asked, hating that he had no other way to find out, hoping the blunt approach would make something happen in the man's thoughts at least.

There was nothing. "No reason to mask them if I don't have anything to hide."

Marea came out then, and saw the body, and screamed, eyes going wide. And all he read in her thoughts was shock and horror. "Who would *do* this?" she asked, staring at the corpse.

"One of us, apparently," Tai said. "The knife came from inside the house."

She blanched at this, looking from face to face, but her thoughts showed no sign of guilt. Could Avery be right? Would a powerful shaman be able to do this? He hated that he didn't know.

"This wasn't you?" Tai asked, knowing it was poor timing and rude, but needing to at least try every angle. Watch her thoughts for anything strange.

He got nothing but the indignation that mirrored her reply. "Of course it wasn't me. I *agreed* with you for once, that we couldn't kill him, even with his message. Why would *I* kill him? How could I even? He's twice my size."

Eyadin hadn't been *twice* her size, but the girl had a point. She could also be lying and Avery could be using his masking technique to make her thoughts *appear* normal. Or he could be doing that for himself. Or Avery could be right, that the shaman that sent Eyadin had killed him somehow. With their knife. Maybe planted it deliberately. There was no way to know.

And no time to figure it out. The longer they waited, the better chance someone else had of beating them to the spear, and then it would all be for nothing. Including Eyadin's death.

Tai clenched his fists. "I made a promise to this man. And if we survive, I intend to keep it. Feynrick. Avery. Help me find something to dig with. We bury him before we go."

Ella and Marea came too, unearthing a pair of shovels and some worn hoes leaning in a far corner, and together they hacked a rectangular hole in the grassy farmyard. Tai flung shovelful after shovelful, wavering between disbelief and anger. One of *them* had done it? Just as he'd convinced the man not to deliver his message *without* having to threaten him? It was like the universe was plotting against him, to keep him from ever escaping the violence that brought them here.

Or you are unwilling to accept what escaping that violence will mean. Walk away, Tai. The costs are too high on this one, and if you take the spear you'll only continue the cycle.

When it was deep enough to keep the animals out Tai called a halt, and they laid Eyadin's body down. Words needed to be said, something to honor the passing of the man, but Tai's mind was a blank, his anger settling into a dull emptiness. Another one gone. How many revenants had they made on this trip? How many more would they make today?

"We didn't know him well," Ella said, "and it was only the purest of chances that brought us together, but Eyadin was a true traveling companion, and a man who cared deeply for his family, and for the people of Aran. May his spirit find rest."

His revenant, more like. What would the religions have to say about death, if they knew the reality of it?

"Saints take ye up, son," Feynrick said, and Marea and Avery added something for themselves. Tai wanted to say something, to feel something beyond the melancholy of a funeral attended by strangers, but he had nothing.

"Atumbarye," he said at last, the traditional Achuri word of farewell, and they filled in the hole. Left a pile of stones on top, to tell the next person who came here there was a body underneath. Tai unfocused his eyes to shamanic sight, wondering if he'd be able to see Eyadin's revenant somewhere. If he could take it on like he'd taken on Ydilwen's. That would feel right, somehow, to give them some version of life from his own *uai*, since he was the one who'd taken theirs.

There was nothing to see, however, and daylight was burning. "Pack up," Tai said. "We still have a stone to open."

"Once we figure out how to open it," Ella said.

"And get past whatever shamans are there," Avery said.

"And the Councilate soldiers," Marea said, looking frail in the morning light.

"And generally crack some skulls," Feynrick grinned, hands on his axes.

They struck out overland, Tai reasoning the road was so crowded they'd make better time just cutting through fields. He knew he should be thinking through what was coming ahead, but his mind kept circling back to Eyadin's body, to the knife stuck in his throat. Could it really be some shaman far away? Why would they bother to make it look like one of their party? And if they were that worried about Tai's chances of opening the stone, why not attack directly?

It didn't make sense, which meant that someone in their party murdering Eyadin did. But Ella was the only one who'd wanted him dead, and he trusted her when she said she hadn't done it. Avery could be masking his or Marea's thoughts, but neither of them had wanted the messenger to die. Avery especially had wanted the man to live. So *had* it been some far off shaman?

And on and on. The farms they passed were increasingly abandoned, fields stripped bare, frequently with pilgrims camping in the yards or even living in the houses. He knew the pilgrims because they all shared a look: sunken cheeks and bright eyes.

Was the stone really that powerful? If what Nauro had said was right, it was radiating the *uai* of all the people with a mindseye revenant back out into the world. The power of an archrevenant. The power of a *god*, in ninespear terms.

The power he'd failed to grasp, the first time he could have.

This time he would be ready, no matter what came. *They* would be ready—Ella was siccing revenants now in addition to her timeslip, Avery came off as a more powerful shaman every time they were attacked, and Marea's powers were like a secret weapon. She was the only reason they'd won the battle yesterday, and the one at Yatiport.

He glanced at her, trudging through a cut field of barley stalks with her hand in Avery's. Did she still hate him? Something Ella had said came back to him then: *if you can win her over, you can probably win over anyone in the Councilate.* She didn't seem as hostile as she had been, but had he won her over? Could he count on her to turn the fates in their favor, instead of against them, in the coming battles?

Probably as far as he could count on Avery to hold to their side, because the girl was besotted. For his part, the man seemed committed to opening the stone. A fourth of a half of Semeca's power, the terms of their agreement, surely seemed a vast wealth compared to the few revenants most shamans managed to thrall. A fifth of a half of the *world's* mindseyes—how many would that be? Fifty thousand? One hundred thousand?

Enough, apparently, to keep him loyally at their side despite the dangers they'd faced, and Marea's attempts to get him to quit.

Five people, against the smartest and strongest shamans on the continent. In the world, maybe. Ancestors send it was enough.

53

By the time the steeples of Aran appeared, hazy in the distance, even the fields were beginning to fill with people. Ella had never seen so many people, not on the docks of Worldsmouth or the people crowding the Councileum on a festival day. They clustered around meager fires, walked thin-limbed toward Califf, or sat gazing back toward Aran, eyes burning with religious fervor. The ones she talked to echoed that, speaking of the Ascending God's radiance and getting healed from old wounds and all sorts of miracles that seemed impossible.

But Avery had said shamanic powers were all about *uai* and belief. With the *uai* the stone was giving off and the belief of the pilgrims, who was to say what was possible?

A good lesson. She was no Eschatolist, but if she could summon enough belief, the stone's *uai* might be the edge she needed in whatever was coming.

To opening the stone, even? But surely someone had tried that by now.

As the crowds thickened so did the whitecoats. They began to pass regular camps, orderly rows of tents surrounded by orderly rows of stakes, smelling of toasted millet and roast meat, drawing hungry eyes. Bands of whitecoats five and ten strong pushed through the milling crowd, one of them inevitably reading off the proclamation about the punishment for treason and the city of Aran being under martial law.

They were less threatening, outnumbered as they were one hundred to one by fever-eyed pilgrims. Of course, they were well-fed and armed too, where most of the people leaving the city seemed to have been stripped of all wealth as well as flesh from their bones, and those heading toward the city were road-weary as well as eager.

What would have happened, had Eyadin's message gone through? Would the whitecoats really have cut all these people down? Or would the people have overwhelmed them, and Aran become the second city this year to fight its way free of Councilate rule?

Better they did not find out. Ella harbored no love for the Councilate, but living through the Ghost Rebellion in Ayugen had taught her war was a social disease with no victors. Better that they all live under an imperfect system than the bulk of them die trying to make something better.

When the going became slow through sheer numbers of people, Feynrick bulled his way to the front and began clearing a path. He grinned and kidded and joked with the people he was shoving aside, of course, but there was no sugar-coating the kind of force needed to actually move forward as they approached the city's outer walls, and Ella felt the low buzz of his resonance as he worked.

Histories said Aran was thousands of years old, predating the Prophet by at least a millennium, and in times past had been a center of military as well as cultural might. In the centuries since the new Yersh king conquered it, however, and his kingdom was in turn conquered by the Councilate, its once-mighty walls had traded any real protection for lush ivy and the convenience of wide gates. Still, a phalanx of white-coated soldiers blocked the entrance to the first gates they approached, letting a stream out and only a few in. The sun rose a hand in the sky before they finally got in through a combination of Ella's words and Marea's resonance.

"Stay alert," Tai said as they passed through the heavy walls, air cool and damp. The people were not nearly so thick on the inside, the whitecoats letting more out than in, but the street was still full of pilgrims in flowing kaftans, glass beads clacking in their hair. The air smelled of bodies and musty wood, houses hanging over the street three and even four stories high. There were no whitecoats in the immediate vicinity, but the street opened onto a small plaza with a dry fountain ahead, and the place looked to be full of soldiers.

Ella took a deep breath and raised her head, marching at their front. They had passed through an official gate—these men should have no reason to question them.

And they didn't, though they watched the people passing around the crumbling fountain with hands on weapons. They looked tense, even sorrowful. It would be a hard life, trying to keep control of a city flooded with pilgrims, and likely facing danger from the shamans in the old city. Would there be whitecoats in there too? The soldier had said the old city was closed off. Because the Councilate had occupied it, or because the shamans were keeping everyone out?

They passed through the square unmolested and Ella chose a street angling deeper into the city on the far side. Such cities were strange to her, though she had stopped in many ports along the Ein, and spent her time in Ayugen. In Worldsmouth most streets were waterways, and by necessity the city felt more open, even if the water was often stagnant and the sky overcast.

"Any idea where we're going?" Ella asked, once they were out of Councilate earshot.

"The waystone is at the center of the old city," Avery said. "That should be east of here."

"Follow the crowds," Tai said. "Seems like everyone here is a pilgrim, and they're all trying to get to the same place."

She did, though the streets were crooked and windy enough that they had to backtrack more than once. She started following the crowds—the closer they got, the thicker the people were, leaning from windows or sitting against buildings or milling in the statue-filled plazas at every intersection.

The number of whitecoats increased too, with soldiers fingering bows and sharpening swords at most of the intersections, archers occasionally looking down from rooftops. Many of them held the same expressions of sorrow or fear she'd seen on the soldier at the gate, and they all had weapons close to hand.

"Something isn't right here," Tai said, after passing over a bridge lined on both sides with Councilate soldiers in full battle gear. "Whitecoats in Ayugen didn't walk around this armed even at the height of the rebellion."

"Councilate's not taking any chances," Feynrick said.

"Or they're preparing for something," Ella said, giving voice to the concern that had been growing like a weight in her belly.

"You think they know about Eyadin's orders?" Tai asked. "Were expecting them?"

"Maybe," Ella said. "Maybe there were other messengers before him, getting them ready, preparing them for the possibility."

"They sure don't look excited about it, whatever it is," Feynrick said amicably, spitting green onto the worn stone pavement. He was chewing dreamleaf like he had during the final battle against Semeca two months ago. Not a good sign.

"Would *you* be excited to try and control a city full of religious zealots?" Marea asked. "Especially with whatever's probably happening with the—in the old city?"

Ella understood her hesitance to say *shamans*. Even with Avery's soundproofing, it felt insane to say it here. Who knew who was watching? And what powers they had?

"Me? Yapping right," Feynrick said. "But I get yer meaning. I'm not everybody."

He certainly wasn't. They pushed on, Ella finding herself agitated she couldn't slow and enjoy the city. Of all the places in Yershire, this was one of the few she had wanted to visit, and the glimpses she caught around the crowds and soldiers didn't disappoint: curling vines drooping from rooftop gardens, ancient houses built one atop another in the traditional Yersh style, ornate shrines and grottos worked into every street, and every intersection with a statue or fountain and a name, a history. There were entire books devoted to Aran, like Melthesan's *A Walking History of Aran*. She'd read it during a particularly dark period, when her brother stopped visiting her and her parents had reduced her to one meal a day, demanding that she accept a suitor.

It had seemed a paradise then, and it *was*, and it was frustrating that they were always in a hurry, always in danger, always running to or from something. Ella found herself clenching her fists as she walked, muttering about how annoying it was, how frustrating the whole situation was. As the crowds thickened the pilgrims seemed to grow more fervent around them, gazing in holy wonder or grinning like children or shouting at each other in fights that often devolved into fists, soldiers looking the other way. Then at the intersection of a long narrow alley and two wide streets a woman stood perfectly balanced atop an ancient statue of a walrus, arms over her head, her skin literally glowing.

"What in *stains*," Ella cursed, glaring at the dope-eyed zealots who packed the square. It was like the whole city was determined to get in her way.

"Prophet's mercy," Marea whispered, looking as awed as the zealots.

Feynrick whistled, but his gaze said he wasn't interested in the woman for her glowing skin. Not the parts that were showing, at least.

Avery cleared his throat. "The *uai*. I'm sure you're all feeling it by now. The stone's power is reaching this far into the city. She must believe she is blessed in some way, and the *uai* is making her imagination real."

Feynrick gave a lecherous grin. "Blessed is one way to put it."

"Fight that," Avery said. "Feynrick, that pull towards sex. Marea, that awe and wonder you're feeling. Tai, that overwhelming despondency. And Ella, whatever it is that has you clenching your fists."

She started, relaxing her hands, realizing how strange her reaction was. They were in danger and she was frustrated about not being able to *sightsee*?

Feynrick and Marea did likewise around her, and she realized Tai had been staring at the cobbles for the last half hour.

"Gods," she said. "The stone is having that much effect already?"

"Yes," Avery said. "We are close now, maybe halfway to the old city, and beginning to feel the waystone's power. It's only going to get stronger. Watch yourselves. Your internal feelings, your reactions. *Uai* in these amounts can be like dreamleaf or Seinjial lager, and what we need are clear minds. So stay vigilant."

Ella shook herself. "Right," she said. "Sorry." Her frustration melted away, replaced by a heightened awareness, like the rush that came at the beginning of battle.

Or when she struck resonance, she realized. The heightened awareness of *uai*.

It took hold of the others too, as they came out of whatever state they had fallen into. Tai cleared his throat, giving the barest nod toward the roofs. "Best to keep moving. I don't think the whitecoats like this lady much either."

"Least we know we're in the right city," Feynrick muttered, looking around like waking from a dream.

Ella glanced up to find archers lining the rooftops around the plaza, some of them with arrows nocked. Prophets, what would all this *uai* be doing to them, who were unused to its effects? No wonder everyone in the city seemed out of sorts. They were all dreamy on *uai*.

The scholarly side of her wanted to stop everyone and start running tests. Take people out of the city and see what their natural tendencies were, then pull them back into the *uai* and see what it was doing. Why had she gotten frustrated? Why would Tai get despondent, and Marea religious of all things?

They started walking, and she realized that her curiosity was the *uai* too, distracting her down a different mental pathway, amping up whatever small tendencies her mind had. Gods. Focus, Ella. Focus because few people in this city are, and no doubt those who can keep their concentration are the ones who make it to the old city. No doubt the shamans there know how to handle all this power.

They saw more strange sights as they wove through the city, statues that blinked and shrines that floated and withered old men dancing like children. In one plaza thirty people knelt with their heads submerged in the fountain's water, not breathing but apparently alive.

They saw more whitecoats too, increasingly edgy and heavily armed and watching the *uai*-drunk pilgrims with suspicious eyes. There was no rebellion here, not in the new city at least, but there was like to be a battle from the looks of it. And Ella did not want to see what these power-mad believers were capable of, if the whitecoats interrupted their reveries.

Avery, bless the man, continued to wake them out of theirs,

when they would fall into it. Thrice Ella lapsed back into scholarly curiosity, beginning to drift away from the group as some question or other caught her fancy and she started to examine it. She could see now why so many leaving the city had looked starved—they had likely stayed in one *uai*-obsessed state or another until their bodies gave out. Indeed, there were bodies in the alley she could not be sure were live or dead.

She did her best to nudge Tai when he would begin to look despondent, or angry, and Marea when her eyes grew fearful or awestruck. Feynrick seemed able to keep himself sober, as it were, but maybe that was no surprise given the amounts of dreamleaf the man could handle.

Tai had to nudge her awake out of the thoughts that followed, when her scholarly brain began comparing the effects of free-flowing *uai* with other known intoxicants, and how dependence might alter its expression.

"Stains," she said, trying not look at the hard-eyed men in whitecoats clumped on one side of a tree-filled plaza they crossed, doe-eyed pilgrims dancing intricate patterns on the other. This city was ready to explode.

"Not far now," Avery said. "Keep your head. There's enough *uai* here that anyone could be a threat."

"No shamans so far," Tai said, walking clear-eyed with his head up. The challenge of staying focused seemed to have drawn him out of the mood he'd been in since they found Eyadin's body. "Unless they've fallen spell to the stone too."

"Could have," Avery said. "Journeymen, maybe. I doubt any full shamans would be so easily distracted. No, I'm guessing they're closer in. In the old city."

"Battling for the stone?" Ella asked.

"Or waiting," he said. "Ready to strike at whoever manages to open it first."

A jolt of fear ran through her, and it was all she could do not to follow it down a tunnel into panic and despair. Had the shamans tried all the things she planned? Would she open the stone only to have some all-powerful shaman steal the spear from under them?

They wound through another crowded street, and a plaza of women singing Eschatolist dirges in complex harmonies. Their voices carried power, something like power of the resonance harmonies. Were they singing with *uai*?

The street beyond was blocked with a solid crush of people, the sound of their shouts and cries echoing from the overhanging buildings into a dull roar. Ella craned her neck, trying to see over the shoulders of the pilgrims ahead.

"Whitecoats," Tai said, tall enough he could see over most of the crowd. "It's solid whitecoats up there."

"The old city," Ella said. "The soldier at the gate said they had it blocked off."

"That's where the stone is, right?" Feynrick asked, striking resonance. "Nothing a little grin-and-shove won't get us through."

"Have a care," Tai said, laying a hand on the man's shoulder. "I'm not sure the whitecoats will take to shoving as kindly as these pilgrims."

"They look entirely too eager to use their swords as it is," Avery said, pulling Marea close.

Feynrick grinned. "I was one a'them sword-eager lads once upon a time. You leave them to me."

With that he began clearing a path, and as before they followed in his wake, Tai and Avery holding the crowd aside for her and Marea. It helped that many of the people they pressed through looked half-delirious, murmuring excitedly and pointing at the sky.

No—not the sky. The waystone. Through a brief gap in the crowd Ella saw the stone, rising like a giant shrine amidst the steep roofs and tiered towers of the old city. Only where the

Eschatolist shrines were carved wood and gilt paint, the waystone was unbroken stone, rising twice as high as any of the buildings and appearing almost to glitter in the sun.

Then her view was gone, and Ella was almost glad. The Yati waystone had had a special presence to it, but this—it was like the stone called to her. *Pulled* her. No wonder people were pressed cheek to jowl. How long could the whitecoats keep them back?

They emerged from the long street into open air, and the dull roar she had heard swelled into song. The melody tugged at her memory—the *aeschatol*! An Eschatolist hymn sung at birthings and funerals if she remembered right, the Yersh so ancient scholars argued about the meaning. She had heard it as a girl, walking past the birthing center near her family's mansion, and at the funerals of state her father had dragged her to.

But never like this: what had been a pretty song then became something beautiful here, haunting, roaring from the throats of ten thousand believers pressed against the pikes and spears of the Councilate army. Because their weapons were out—she saw that now as they approached the front, rank on rank of armored Councilate men holding out weapons like a sideways forest of blades.

And yet the believers pressed on, impelled by the crush of people behind, by the magnetism of the stone glittering above the old city. It was impossible to see what was happening at the front, impossible to hear anything but the loudest shouts over the roar of song, but she read Tai's gesture well enough, pointing to the cobblestones beneath their feet.

She looked and almost lost her stomach. They were red, as were her boots, as were the hems of skirts and pants around her. Red with blood.

Were the whitecoats killing anyone who came too near? But she heard no screams, only song, and the crowd pressed forward around them.

A woman stumbled back from the front then, dress stuck to

her chest with fresh blood, mouth open in song, life's blood pumping from a wound to her heart. But even as Ella stared the wound began to close, like someone in the first rush of overcoming a revenant.

Feynrick pushed closer and they saw a man with a mending gash in his neck, then a girl holding her own arm, and believers too wounded to walk crawling back from the front, all singing, all healing, eyes fervent. Ella stared, caught in the wonder of it despite the urgency of the situation. Belief and *uai*. That was all these people needed.

Then her foot caught on something soft, and her wonder soured. Belief had not been enough for the man sprawled on the flagstones. Ella stepped over him, but as the crowd crushed in and such bodies became more common there was nowhere else to step without losing her feet, so Ella stepped on them, hating the soft feeling beneath her feet, chest tightening.

She tried to shout to Tai, to Avery, to anyone about what was going on, but the hymn was too loud, the crowd's roar shaking even the slick flagstones beneath her feet. Or was that *uai*?

Then the man ahead of them fell to a spear thrust in his chest, and Feynrick's push forward became a push back, nothing ahead but a line of Councilate spears.

Ella struck resonance without thinking, needing a moment to breathe, to process. To plan.

The world froze around her—Feynrick's mouth open in a bellow, the speared man halfway to the ground, the crowd's roar shifted to unending thunder around her. Ahead, a youthful whitecoat grimaced at the far end of the spear, his face and uniform splattered red, his expression more animal than man. The soldiers next to him looked same, holding a tight rank with the line of men behind them, all jabbing spears toward the crowd.

Leaning into the killing space Ella saw that formation repeating all the way down the square, saw whitecoats frozen in the act of jabbing spears, saw peaceful pilgrims with mouths open in song, accepting the blades into their bodies. Did they know they would be healed? Was someone coordinating this, or was it the very words of the song, words denying birth and death in the power of the bi-God's grace?

She didn't know. Couldn't stay here in slip trying to figure it out, her life hours draining away. They needed a plan. Feynrick had said he could deal with the whitecoats, because he used to be one, but looking at the bloodthirsty expressions on the soldiers' faces she doubted it. They were caught in the waystone's *uai* as surely as the pilgrims, only their experience was colored by fear and military training instead of reverence and belief.

And as soon as she dropped slip, that *uai*-driven fear was going to be directed at Tai and Feynrick. They could fight a few soldiers, but an army?

Feynrick's bellow had changed as she stood, the grizzled Yatiman's hand drifting for his axe. That plan would not work. *Think, Ella, think.*

The problem was even if she made a plan there would be no time to communicate it, to act on it. Feynrick was seconds from attacking back, and then there would truly be no time.

If only there was a way to speak to their minds, like Avery had done. Or slow them all down, so they could discuss here together.

Ella sucked in a breath—there *was* a way to do that. Nauro had done it to her, back at the Yati waystone, when he first told her of the costs of her resonance. He'd frozen them both in slip using his *uai. You could do it too,* he'd said. *It's your higher resonance.*

It would no doubt age her even more rapidly, but what choice did she have? She wasn't going to let them all die here. Ella reached inside and struck resonance again, not sure how it worked, remembering the time she'd saved Tai inside the Councilate prison, the day he'd driven the whitecoats from Ayugen.

Something resonated, something higher—an octave higher, Marea had said—and she tried to focus on the group around her, not sure how to limit who she included in slip.

"—out!" Feynrick bellowed, ripping his axe free and spinning to sink it into the spear-holder in front of him, who was still frozen in time.

Her friends slipped into regular motion, stumbling against the frozen crowd. Marea looked around in wonder, and Tai turned to her in confusion.

"No time," Ella said. "You're all in slip, but this could be killing me so let's make a plan quick. There's no way we're fighting through these soldiers."

"And doubtful we'd survive the fight the way the pilgrims are," Avery said, alone of the group looking unsurprised at her ability.

Feynrick pulled his axe out with a confused expression, the wound just barely beginning to seep blood. "Don't seem fair to fight a man who can't fight back."

"And these are not our enemies," Tai said. "This is not our fight. We just need to get through them."

Marea looked to Ella. "Can you keep this up long enough for us to just walk through them? Or on them?"

"No," Ella panted. "My back already hurts, and this costs more than *uai*."

"Right," Tai said. "We waft, and whoever chases us chases us. Avery, you get Feynrick." He wrapped one arm around her and another around Marea.

It wasn't much of a plan, but it was better than nothing. Ella dropped slip.

Tai shot them up, resonance roaring, as the spearman Feynrick had hit crumpled and the roaring hymn of the crowd crashed back in around them. Ella clutched onto his right side, eyes squeezed shut. Avery rose to his left, Feynrick clinging to his shoulders.

The crowd spread out below them, rivers of multicolored pilgrims flowing from every street into the cleared square around the old city. They were a sea crashing into a wall of spears and white-coated men, the soldiers hard against a moat surrounding ancient stone walls. The crowd was pushing them back, then—the soldiers would not have started with nowhere to retreat.

Tai shoved forward. Even as he did soldiers rose from the ranks of the whitecoats. No, not just soldiers—Titans, the Councilate's elite warriors trained in resonances. They wore gleaming metal suits and bore long spiked halberds.

Tai swerved around the first of these, but Titans kept rising, and rising *fast*. A pair shot forward to block him off from the old city, faster than he'd ever seen Counciliate wafters fly. But no wonder—the stone's *uai* would be strengthening them as it did him, and they weren't carrying a person in each arm.

Cursing, Tai pushed higher, trying to evade them, but they mirrored his movements, faster. He circled back to find a pair closing on them from behind, halberds raised. With no time to think, Tai struck his higher resonance and pushed a wedge of air between them, shooting through the gap.

To his right Avery was similarly pushed back, Titans circling him. Could the man not use some shamanic power on them? Below the crowd still sang, but fingers that had been pointing toward the stone were pointing towards them now.

Little help that was against supercharged Titans.

"Marea!" Tai called over the wind, sweeping high then swooping low in an attempt to get around a fresh Titan attack. "A little luck?"

"Working on it!" she yelled back, slim body rigid in his left arm.

Titans shot up to block him again, and Tai circled back again, catching sight of Avery wafting south along the line between pilgrims and whitecoats, Titans rising to meet him in a wave along the way.

Tai tried again, failed again, no amount of height enough to lose them, no amount of speed fast enough to get past them, whatever luck Marea was summoning not enough to make a gap he could get through.

Tai circled back above the pilgrims, *uai* inside feeling endless but at the same time not enough. He needed to be faster, stronger, some other edge. Mindsight? But what good would that do in this kind of fight?

Then he noticed waves in the crowd of pilgrims below, like the plaza facing the old city was a still pond struck with a stone. Only some of the drops of water at the crest of each wave flew up instead of falling.

Tai realized what was happening just as Marea gasped beside him. The pilgrims were wafting, but they weren't doing it one at a time. They were wafting *en masse*, arms pointing to him in the sky, waves of power rolling through the crowd and pushing them into the air. They wanted to get through as badly as he did.

So when Tai turned to come at the wafting Titans again, he wasn't alone. Thirty or forty wide-eyed pilgrims wafted in the air all around him, and if they looked amazed and moved awkwardly, their eyes were determined. Below them more kept rising up.

"Forward!" Tai shouted, forgetting to use Yersh in his excitement, but when he shot forward the wafters nearest him followed, like ripples spreading in the wake of a fast boat. And still they were rebuffed, Marea's luck and their bigger numbers not enough to get through the swirling mass of Titans.

Tai circled back but the wafters around him pressed on, singing, their eyes locked on the waystone. Titans flew to meet them, weapons doing deadly work, but everywhere their blood rained the crowd rose up, a wave as thick as those still on the ground. Tai slowed for a moment, awestruck at the sight of hundreds or thousands of people rising into the air.

"They just needed you," Ella yelled in his ear. "Needed to see a way through!"

And to his left Marea yelled, "Go! I got this!"

He went, circling again and rushing for the floating line of Titans, which was now a swirling mass of silver soldiers chasing pilgrims of all colors, spears flashing and blood flying but sheer numbers of the faithful overwhelming the Titan's training, people breaking through on all sides and shooting over the old city's walls, toward the waystone that rose like a beacon in the distance.

Tai shot straight through them, trusting Marea, having seen what she could do, straight toward a pair of Titans skewering a raven-haired pilgrim. Their battle broke apart at the last second and Tai flew past, bodies and soldiers falling all around them, the air a mix of song and scream.

Then they were out of the storm, moat flashing by below

them, over the line of whitecoats and into the old city, part of a flying wave of pilgrims. For one glorious moment Tai felt like a wagull in a massive flock, eyes locked on the stone, flying toward the goal they had sought for so long.

Then lightning arced from the roof of a shrine in the old city. Blinding blue bolts branched upwards, and each one found a pilgrim. The struck bodies flew up in the air, only to plunge smoking toward the buildings below.

"Shamans!" Ella yelled, but Tai was already dropping them toward the steep-roofed shrines and winding streets of the old city, more bolts erupting from the roofs around them.

All the glory he'd felt collapsed in fear. They'd broken through a wall of the Councilate's best wafters, but the battle was far from over, and he had no idea how to fight the enemies waiting ahead.

55

It is said the last emperor knew of Shatterbrook's plans, and had a series of hidden gates and tunnels built offering quick escape from the city. A few of these are known, such as the Rose Gate in Easthampton, but residents are always willing to show you a few more if you pass them the right shade of coin. For those interested, ask around at the Selenry Fountain.

—Arenia Melthesan, *A Walking History of Aran*

It was a piss of a thing to whip around the sky clinging to another man's back like a helpless babe. Feynrick swung his axe where he could, managed to dent a few helms maybe, but mostly had to cling to Avery for dear life and try not to yelp like a lost puppy when the Titans got too close.

So it was a relief when lightning bolts started shooting from the ground, because the lad had to stop wafting. As much *uai* juice as was pumping through him, Feynrick felt like he could fight lightning bolts or ninespears or whatever they needed to—

just put his barking feet on the ground. Let the milkweed do the wafting if someone had to.

They came down in a moss-covered shrine, air a thunderstorm around them, ozone in his nose. "Good work, lad," he yelled over the noise, clapping Avery on the shoulder.

Boys his age, they needed to be told they'd done good. Craved it.

Avery gave him a funny look back. "You too, Feynrick."

Something hot and fiery roared over their heads and some people screamed. A body hit a roof next door and clay tiles exploded outward like a melon hitting a pile of rotting rinds. Tai and the girls were crouched in the lee of a carved-up thing ahead and they ran for it, Feynrick keeping an eye out for lightning bolts.

"Praise me, Marrey," he muttered as they ran, "if I get out of this I'm hanging up these axes. I swear it."

Tai and the girls looked as shook as he felt. He offered them all a grin—no reason to let spirits lag. Going to die, you die with a grin, his old man used to say.

"What do we do?" Ella yelled, poor lady looking a decade older than she had.

"Run for it," Feynrick yelled back, eyeing pilgrims streaming overhead. "These flyers ain't going to last for long, but figure we got a clear run at the stone while they do."

They all shared that glance he remembered from tight spots, the *piss-dogs-this-ain't-what-I-want-to-do-but-got-to-do-it-anyway-I-guess* and *if-we-all-get-out-of-this-I'm-buying-you-a-mug-of-dreamtea* kind of look.

Then they ran, leaping carts and dodging bodies and smashing axes into old statues just to see 'em burst apart. Least, that's what *he* did cause piss on it if they were all gonna die he might as well enjoy himself, right?

Or maybe that was the buzz—brawling always felt good, but

he hadn't felt this high since he almost died breaking through the Newgen gates and came back to life again. Like his *uai* was the world's strongest plug of dreamtea and he'd just swallowed the whole thing.

The girls hung back so Feynrick started clearing a path for 'em, shattering the sloppy barricades across the road and looking through the windows to make sure no lightning-throwers were waiting there for him.

He missed one though, and a flash of light bright enough to leave his eyes watering told him his mistake. The thunder that followed about left him deaf in one ear but he spun, following the blue trace-lines in his eyes back to a little rooftop where a middle-aged man stood with his arms up.

Turned out shamans died as easy as anybody else, if they weren't looking for you. Feynrick leapt the two stories and took the man's head off his shoulders with Egwen.

"Good work, girl," he said, jumping off the roof and jogging back to see what the damage was. That was another reason he'd have to hang up his axes, is they were named after his former mistresses, and if Marrem ever found out she'd have *his* head.

He was ready for some burning bodies instead of friends, but they were all standing there staring at Avery like he was some kinda Ascending God.

"Killed him," Feynrick called, just to make sure they realized he'd done the important part. "Should be good."

"How did you—" Ella was stammering.

"Temporary *uai* grounding," Avery was saying, or something like that, looking pretty proud of himself.

Rotting ninespear, stealing the show. "So we keep running then?" Feynrick said, nodding toward the waystone sticking up above the next line of fancy roofs and statues.

The milkweed eyed the sky. "Pilgrims are thinning out."

"Best make time while we can then," Feynrick said. "I'll keep a better watch."

They all shared another of those *well-boarscock-I-guess-so* looks and ran. He kept a better eye this time, and pulled 'em back a few seconds before another flash and thunder hit and Avery did something that made a hole in the road.

"I've got this one," the lad said, and shot something out of *his* hands that didn't really look like thunder or lightning, but made somebody scream a few stories up.

Feynrick whistled. "Whyn't you do that the first time?"

"It's not easy," the lad said, sounding winded. "And every time I do it makes it easier for the other shamans to find us."

Feynrick glanced at the sky again. Most all of the pilgrims were gone, but his blood was up and his *uai* felt like it would last for days. And at this rate, when he dropped it the breaks were like to kill him anyway. "Best to keep going then. We stop here and they'll come to us."

They kept going but slower, Avery waving them back at every intersection to do some shaman thing at the buildings around them.

Then *he* missed one, and it was only dumb luck they didn't get hit with the fireball that came in a little crooked and torched the eight-roofed shrine to their left. Or maybe *not* dumb luck, judging from the way Marea grinned at it. The girl was getting good. Dogs, but he could have used her ability back in his women-chasing days. Avery sent another one of his not-spears through a building and grunted, so it must have worked.

They went even slower then, creeping around the blasted remains of what looked like a lot of battles already fought. Feynrick's buzz screamed at him to just *run*, to go *kill* and *destroy*, but his common sense said the lad probably knew better.

And he did, because a couple of shattered fountains closer in he waved them all to stop, and started looking like he was thinking really hard about something. Feynrick glanced at the milkweed, who gave him a shrug, then Avery started coughing like someone was choking him but still staring real hard. Feynrick was about to give him a hard slap on the back when they heard a pop and thud from the building behind them, and Avery straightened up.

"Visceror," he panted, whatever that meant. "A nasty one."

"Is there a better way we should be doing this?" Tai asked. "Maybe one of us go ahead?"

"You're not scatting leaving me, Tai Kulga," Ella barked, sounding as old and sharp-tongued as she looked. Genitors, did her personality age along with her body?

"I can't protect everyone if we split up," Avery said. "If we just go slowly enough, we'll be okay."

The pilgrims were all out of the sky, blasted down or got to the stone most likely. Feynrick rubbed at his beard. "Siege of Elsrock we had to fight house to house in the end," he said. "My officer wanted us to clear the street, but I knew he was full of rot so me and Gondlen took the houses. Crept up on more than one straggler that way."

"Took the houses?" Ella asked. "But didn't you still have to use the streets to get in and out?"

She was a smart lady, but book smarts weren't everything. Feynrick showed her what he meant with Egwen and Nynae, bashing a hole in the side of a carved-up old shrine then waving her through.

"Ah," she said, eyeing the shattered wood like it was somebody's mother. But she went through and so did the others, and that worked for a while, chopping house to house and Avery doing his careful-looking thing every time they had to cross a street.

Meanwhile the stone kept getting bigger and closer behind the buildings, glittering like somebody'd dumped fish scales on it.

Feynrick stopped to whistle at it when they were crossing the next street, partially to keep the girls from looking at the scatter of bodies laying where they'd fallen in the street.

"Rotting boarscock," he said, looking up at the thing. "You think they—"

Big flash of light and a thunderclap and Avery was standing there over another smoking hole.

"Musta missed one," Feynrick tried to say, but his ears were ringing too loud, and then there was *another* flash and clap and he came to on his bottom and there was a new smoking hole by his feet and somebody was wafting towards them.

Feynrick leapt up pulling Nynae but something kicked him like a mad goat and after the flash there was only black.

56

Tai watched with gritted teeth as two shamans closed on them from above, sending bolt after bolt at them. Avery managed to deflect the bolts into the ground, but each time the smoking hole was closer, the stocky man paler, the fear in Tai's throat stronger. Feynrick was down, Marea wept, and Avery knelt with his hands held up almost as if to ward off a blow.

"What do we do?" Ella screamed, sound echoing like it came through a long tunnel.

"Grab onto me!" Tai yelled after the next roar, striking his resonance. He could save her at least, get them—

Two bolts struck simultaneously and Avery screamed, the hair on his head smoking, the red-hot holes just a pace away from him on either side.

This was not how it ended. Not like this. Ella grabbed and Tai pushed up, knowing the shamans would strike him down, knowing it was stupid but needing to do *some*thing.

He shot for the space under the nearer shaman, hoping it would take the man time to turn, to re-aim, and the shaman's back arched, then doubled over. He fell to the ground.

Tai turned, too surprised even in his haste not to look. The man lay where he'd fallen, dead. On the far side of the group the other shaman did the same, dropping two paces to the ground to flop like a beheaded blackfish. Dead.

And in their place, striding into the street like he owned it, was an unassuming Seinjialese man, black hair bound in a simple band. He crouched over the first body, pressing a finger to its wrist, then the second, then laid his hands on Feynrick.

Tai made a quick calculation. Try to fly out of here and they were almost certainly dead from one shaman or another. But this man had killed the shamans attacking them, and he didn't seem like he wanted them dead, no matter how powerful he was.

He wafted back, just as Feynrick jerked his head back and gasped, eyes wide. But alive, praise the ancestors. He was still alive.

The man looked up. "Get to shelter. There. Take Feynrick."

Tai stared, despite the tension of the moment. How did he know Feynrick's name? Ella gave a soft gasp too, as though in recognition, but there was no time. Not with other shamans around. Mindsight. It had to be.

Tai helped a struggling Feynrick to the fire-charred building the man had pointed to, Ella running to Marea as Avery dragged himself to his feet and followed.

The man came last, backing in and watching the skies.

"I know him," Ella whispered as he approached. "I remember his face—"

"One of the workers," Marea said. "From the Wanderer."

The Yati waystone? A worker? That made no sense.

The man finished backing in and closed the door behind him then turned, afternoon light filtering in through holes shattered in the wood ceiling above. "There. We should be safe here."

"Who are you?" Tai asked, not striking resonance, knowing it would do little against someone this powerful, but readying himself all the same.

The man gave a sardonic grin. "Do you not remember me?"

There *was* something familiar in his voice. Not the voice even, but the *tone* of voice. Tai squinted, trying to make out what it was.

"You were at the stone," Marea said. "The last stone. The brewer! You served me lager."

"Yes," the man said, looking displeased. "I suppose I did. Or this body did anyway. And you got too drunk and nearly gave us away."

"This body?" Tai asked. What did that even mean?

Ella sucked in a breath. "Nauro?"

He smiled, and Tai recognized it, that world-weary smile he'd seen so many times. It had just been on another man's face. "Nauro?" he repeated. "I saw you—"

"Die? Yes, in a sense. My body *did* die. But revenants are harder to kill."

"You're—a revenant?" Marea asked, gaping at the man.

"No, fool girl. I am a body and a spirit, same as you. This body just happened to have a different spirit once, and then I came and convinced him that *my* revenant should be in control. And now he's a voice in *my* head." Nauro grinned, looking pleased with himself.

Ella was frowning beside him. "You—overtook your host?"

"Like Naveinya tried to do to me," Tai said. "Like a hermit. But you actually did it?"

"I got lucky," Nauro said, "and it wasn't easy. But that's a story for another time. Marea, I see you've discovered your talent."

Her eyes widened. "Yes, I have. You knew?"

"It's why I was against you coming. Fatewalkers are too volatile for such a journey, but no matter now." Thunder boomed in the distance. "You boy, which cell are you from again?"

Avery's back straightened. "Yatiport, sir. Though originally south end of Worldsmouth."

Tai frowned—Avery looked at once abashed, like a beggar caught playing gang leader, and at the same time resentful or jealous. Because he knew Nauro was more powerful? Because the older shaman had saved them where Avery couldn't?

"And you're a journeyman?" Nauro asked, voice calm. Though that meant little with Nauro. At Avery's nod he leaned in. "Where did you learn that grounding technique?"

Avery's eyes squinted, and Tai got the sense there was a deeper exchange going on here. What weren't they saying? Or were they trying to read each other's minds? On impulse Tai struck mindsight, the resonance coming easy and strong this close to the stone, and tried to see into either one's mind. They were opaque as hard-packed clay.

"I did a lot of reading," Avery was saying. "And now I have the *uai* stream to test it."

"And you got it right on the first try?" Nauro's very absence of surprise underlined it all the more. "Lucky for Tai and his friends."

"He's been teaching us too," Ella broke in. "We can all see revenants now, and I can grasp them."

Nauro scowled. "Fool boy. You know the dangers in teaching the uninitiated."

"Are they worse than the dangers we face here?" Avery asked, setting his jaw.

"Yes," Nauro said. "These are shamans. Thrall the wrong revenant and you face the gods themselves."

More thunder shook the room, dust and debris raining down through the rents in the ceiling. Enough of this. Tai cleared his throat. "Speaking of those shamans, we still have some to face. Nauro, can you keep protecting us like you did back there?"

"From shamans like those, yes," Nauro said, casting a cool

glance at Avery. "Once we get into the garden around the stone, well, it's not just a matter of skill there. You may have noticed your *uai* increasing as you get closer to the stone."

Tai nodded, but Feynrick grinned. "If by increasing you mean taking twenty years off my back."

"It is an exponential rather than incremental increase," Nauro said. "We are strengthened out here. Those closest to the stone wield powers near to Semeca's herself."

The burly Yatiman shrugged. "Milkweed here killed her once. Hounds, *I* almost did! We can do it again."

Nauro pursed his lips. "Semeca was something of an odd case. We suspect other archrevenants are like her, but… there is a laziness that comes from having a wealth of *uai*. A certainty you can defeat anything or anyone. We in the ninespears have not had that luxury, so we've had to make the most of our limited *uai*. Innovated over the centuries, even if we as often hoard that knowledge as promulgate it."

Tai swallowed. "So you're saying I beat Semeca because she didn't know how to use her own power?"

"Not as these shamans do. They have the benefit of our innovation along with new strength."

Marea shook her head. "Then why aren't you with them? You killed those two out there like they were nothing."

Her face only paled slightly when she talked about it—the girl had hardened in the days since their first attack on Ninefingers Pass.

"Because they cannot open the stone," Nauro said. "And because I don't think I could either, even if I was willing to break our contract."

Ella raised an eyebrow. "So you've just been here, waiting for us to arrive?"

"Not long, but yes. Once I got a body I then had to thrall

enough revenants to have a stream, find where you were likely headed next, and waft. I have been here about a week."

Tai tried to keep his mind off how powerful Nauro was. If the man decided to hurt them, or betray them at the stone, there would be little they could do. "So, you can't open the stone, but you think we can?"

"I am a student of history, Tai, and if my studies have taught me anything it is to pay attention to the anomalies. The Prophet was one such. The merchant Eynas Mettelken was another, and you are a third. If anyone can open the stone, if anyone was *meant* to open the stone, it's you."

Tai didn't know what to say to that.

Marea did. "So you think he can open the stone because you *believe* in him?" Her tone made it clear how stupid she thought that was.

Nauro cleared his throat. "He killed a god, without any shamanic knowledge, after centuries of our best shamans trying and failing. The descendants of whom are here now, and once again failing. But no, I do not expect it to open from his touch alone. We also have the edge of knowledge."

"Knowledge?" Ella asked. "We know hardly more than we did—just Ollen's passage on an *unholy chorus*, and your line of *She who seeks uai from the stone must first give it.*"

"And all the things that have failed in the week since I got here," Nauro said. "And there have been many."

"Like what?" Tai asked.

"Physical attacks against the stone. I've seen shamans blast it with lightning, burn it, slam boulders into it, try to melt it, even a Seinjialese man with a massive iron wedge to break it apart. Nothing works."

"Okay," Ella said. "That makes sense. Those are all pretty literal solutions to opening the stone, and they fit giving *uai* to the stone to get it back, but not an unholy chorus. Do they not know of the other passage?"

Nauro glanced at Avery. "Ninespears are normally very secretive with our knowledge, especially with ancient texts. It may be that Ollen's cell was the only one in possession of that passage, or that read it in light of Semeca's defeat. That secrecy is part of the reason I have seen so many attempts on the stone in the past week."

Tai frowned. Talking to Nauro was like trying to read one of Ella's books. "What do you mean?"

"I mean the shamans closest to the stone, and there are four, are not lacking in power. They each wield essentially a quarter of Semeca's power. They could easily destroy anyone who enters the garden, no matter our skill. But they have all tried and failed to open the stone on their own. They have power but lack knowledge."

"They're letting people in, aren't they?" Ella asked. "Watching what they do before they kill them."

"Yes. Or they were until two days ago, when a pilgrim nearly opened it."

"A pilgrim?" Tai asked, surprised. "Not a shaman?"

"And she nearly opened it?" Ella said, looking just as surprised. "Why didn't they repeat what she did?"

Nauro shook his head. "They tried, but whatever got her that close did not work for them. Still, they're not taking chances anymore. Anyone who enters without their thoughts blocked is killed almost immediately, and anyone who can shield their thoughts is allowed to live only until the shamans break through and read what they're intending."

Ancestors. Their secrets were usually what put them in danger —now they'd be the only thing keeping them safe.

"And this pilgrim, she was trying to break the stone as the others did?"

"No," Nauro said. "I am not sure what she did, but since then the shamans have been trying to alter the chemy of the stone, or enter into it."

"And none of those attempts have worked?" Ella asked.

"None."

Something boomed outside. Shamans battling each other, or more pilgrims trying to get in?

"Doesn't sound like they're letting them live long," Feynrick said, glancing at the shreds of afternoon sky visible above.

"No," Nauro said. "The shamans out here are those who've failed to earn themselves a place in the garden, and their outlook is quite different. Most of them hope the shamans inside will eventually turn on each other, and make room for new ones. Until then, they are doing their best to keep anyone else from getting in."

"Including an entire whitecoat legion," Tai said, then filled Nauro in on the scene at the moat, and all the military they'd seen in the outer city.

"We'll deal with them once we have the spear," Nauro said. "As I recall, Tai, you have some experience defeating armies with *uai*?"

Marea looked at the slender man, open-mouthed. "Nauro. Was that a joke?"

The shaman looked embarrassed, of all things. "I—have been long without company. Excuse me."

Ella appeared to have missed the entire exchange, eyes distant in thought. "Most of the attempts you describe fit with the passage on giving *uai* to the stone to get it back, but not with Ollen's notion of an *unholy chorus*."

"Good," Tai said. "Hopefully they don't know about that. And we've seen lots of failed attempts on the unholy chorus too." He turned to Avery, who still cast troubled looks at Nauro. "Did any of the songs Ollen tried have any more effect than the others?"

"None," Avery said, licking his lips. "We tried every possible song by every possible faith, multiple times, with nothing."

"And the formations of revenants we saw?" Ella asked. "What was that?"

"A different way of thinking about *chorus*," Avery said. "Credelen thought maybe it meant chorus like in the old Yersh sense of the word, when their dramas had big groups of actors chanting together and dancing in unison. His theory was that the makers of the stones would be familiar with that, and revenants could be an unholy version of the old holy plays."

Ella twitched her lips, likely looking for a pen to bite. "But it didn't work?"

"No."

"But this time could be different!" Marea exclaimed. "This stone is active, and all this *uai*—"

"Unfortunately," Nauro said, "we will not have weeks to experiment, or even days. So long as we keep our thoughts firmly blocked I do not think the shamans will attack us. But with the amount of *uai* they're wielding, I suspect it will take all of Avery's and my skill to keep them from reading our thoughts. And I doubt we can do it for long."

Tai's shoulders knotted. "For what, like half a hand? Enough time to try a few things?"

Nauro adjusted his cuffs. "More like a finger. We need to have a plan."

"I do have a plan," Ella said. "I thought about this a lot, as we traveled north. The clues are about *uai* and a chorus. Musical. And we discovered the resonances are musical—they can be tuned with each other, and that harmony helps people overcome their revenants. So maybe the chorus they're speaking of is like that, too. We give the stone *uai* in the form of a resonant chorus."

For a moment they just stared at her. Then Marea broke into a grin and said, "Ella, you're a genius!"

Even Avery lightened up, and Feynrick slapped Ella on the back hard enough to almost knock her over. "There's them brains!"

"That... could work," Nauro said.

Ella finally smiled, and Tai felt his love for her get bigger yet. There were so many ways she impressed him, felt like someone miles beyond him, and this was just one more: she was a genius.

"It is also exactly the kind of thought we need to keep them from reading," Nauro said, glancing around as though he might see shamans peeking in. "That may be the best idea anyone's brought to the stone so far."

"And it's an idea no one else could even have," Marea said, "because they don't know about the resonances."

"They're the whole reason Semeca was attacking us!" Tai said, excitement and relief welling inside. *This* was a plan. This was something they might pull off. "It wasn't our rebellion, or the yura—she said we were discovering things better left hidden."

The smiles around the circle got even wider.

"Okay," Feynrick said. "Ye figured out the smart part. Now the stupid part: how do we get in?"

57

*W*hat they came up with *did* feel pretty stupid. At least that's what Marea thought as they walked the final streets to the garden of the waystone, boots scraping on loose debris. The old city was demolished this close in, ancient temples shattered, exotic gardens withered and burnt, air smelling of smoke and the bodies that littered the cobblestones. She tried not to look at them, or to think about the danger they were going into. But every few minutes lightning would strike or stones would start falling from the sky, and most of the time they were pointed at Avery.

Avery, who had been so close to dying before Nauro came. Avery, who was her reason for being here. Her only reason to be anywhere, anymore.

Avery, who'd pulled her close as they left the last shelter and whispered in her ear, "Stay close to me. We'll get through this. I love you."

Said the words as casually as Feynrick talking about dinner. Then walked out into this sea of death and danger with his back straight and his head up.

She loved and hated him for that confidence. Thunder clapped and she jumped, but there was already a smoking hole in the ground, and a man screaming somewhere in the leaning buildings above them. Nauro nodded at them to keep walking, and a body hit the street with a wet thump.

Marea took a deep breath. Ella had a plan and Nauro was strong and Avery had said they'd get through this. But she still screamed when one of the few multi-roofed temples still standing suddenly fell at them and wood and tile and gilt-inlaid stone shattered all around them and the structure blasted apart to reveal two shamans floating in the sky and Nauro did something with his right hand that killed them both.

Screamed not only from sheer terror, but because they were trying to kill Avery. And if she lost him she lost everything.

Marea walked on, shaking. She was relieved to see Ella looking the same. She wished she felt confident enough to strike resonance. They could all use a little luck right now, but without her mind in solid control, she was as likely to bring bad luck down on them as good.

And that was the last thing they needed, with temples falling from the sky.

"This is the last street," Nauro said when they'd climbed from the wreckage. "Remember the plan."

The plan was insane, but then so was the whole situation. They were to step into the garden around the stone, full of the world's most powerful shamans, and not do *any*thing but walk to the stone. Don't think, don't speak, don't strike resonance, don't do anything they might construe as a threat. Just walk. While the strongest shamans in the world looked for an excuse to kill them.

Insane. Stupid. But mostly because it meant she could do nothing to protect Avery.

Ahead of them the waystone rose like a giant glittering knife, like someone had stabbed Saicha itself and left the hilt sticking up to mark what they'd done. To her right a body lay face down in the street, blood dried in a black pool around it.

Marea looked away, almost wishing for another firestorm, an ambush, anything to take her mind off that body. Avery was worth it, was worth everything she'd done, but the thought kept coming back to her: what would it matter if they died today?

Or worse, if just he died, and she had to live with what she'd done?

She couldn't help the sick dread in her stomach as they reached the end of the street, as the cobblestones opened up into a circular plaza three hundred paces across, the land rising in terraced gardens to the base of the massive stone. The dread had nothing to do with the carrion birds circling overhead, crying, waiting for the next kill. Nor the looks of apprehension on her friends' faces, nor even the shamans circling the stone, cloaks rippling in an unseen wind.

It was dread because she could not protect Avery here, and if he died she would be worse than dead.

"Forward," Nauro muttered into the thick silence. "Quickly now."

They went, footsteps echoing in the stone-walled enclosure, climbing the long shallow stairs that led to the stone, passing concentric terrace gardens once filled with life, now blasted or bloodied or blooming in isolated patches. The air felt thick against her skin, like a thunderstorm in late summer, only instead of humidity this was pure *uai*. Her heart beat faster and all her senses hummed, drawn to the stone towering over them, glittering in the late afternoon sun.

Somewhere in its heart lay a spear with the power of a god—and the key to her future with Avery. All she had to do was keep him safe until they got it.

"Stop," a voice rang out from the heights.

Marea's head shot back. There was a fifth shaman, floating at the very top of the tower. She could only imagine the power he controlled, if the raw *uai* coursing through her veins was any indication, still two hundredpace from the stone.

"What is your purpose here?" the man called down.

"You know what it is, Aeyenor," Nauro said, not raising his voice or his head. His face bore a look of intense concentration.

"Nauro of Speyshore," the man said, voice booming against the multi-tiered temples ringing the garden. "And Harides of Seingard, if I am not mistaken. Do not waste your lives here. Give me your knowledge and I may spare you."

"Keep walking," Nauro said, even as Marea's mind spun. Harides of Seingard? He could only be talking about Avery, but Avery was from Worldsmouth. Avery was *Avery*. And why would he know of him, only a journeyman in their society?

"You cannot keep us out forever," Aeyenor called down. "This *uai* we have—" he spread his hands and laughed, and there was more than a little madness in it. Marea shuddered. She wanted to scream at Avery to do it, to throw herself down and beg the man to spare her lover's life, but Avery walked as grim-faced as the rest, eyes on the stone. He wouldn't give up. That wasn't his way.

So she walked on with him, feeling the *uai* build inside like a giant breath being drawn in, ever in, ready to blast out as song or horn or tempest wind. What fates could she walk with this much *uai*? Could she stop his death?

One hundred fifty paces. One hundred, late afternoon sun beating down on them, her bones humming with *uai*, the hairs on her arms beginning to stand, into the long shadow the stone cast across the old city. The four shamans at the base of the stone circled to face them, to stand between them and their goal.

At fifty paces Nauro said "Now. Strike them."

Feynrick struck first, as they'd discussed, the grizzled man grinning as brawler's resonance buzzed out of him, stronger than

Marea had ever felt it. "Yapping finally," he said. "When do we fight?"

Tai struck next, the wafter's resonance rattling from him even stronger than usual, a peace coming into his eyes as the power took him. He'd been troubled the whole trip, since before the first stone. Had he found some peace with his voice?

Tai and Feynrick were out of tune, jarring sensation in her bones, but she could feel the wafter flexing his resonance, trying to make it fit. They had never tried six resonances at once, not even five. It meant every resonance had to sync with the others. The higher resonances were easier to flex than the lower, so they'd decided to start lowest, with the higher ones fitting in to what the lower ones made. Ella would strike last of all, for obvious reasons.

There—the vibration in her bones settled into a harmony. Avery struck, using the mosstongue resonance he'd been born with, and quickly found a third note to complete the chord.

What is this? her voice said, suddenly waking up.

She smiled. This is most likely your undoing, revenant, she thought at it. If I die here, at least I can die without listening to you lie.

Nauro struck, representing the mindseye resonance, his tone already a perfect fit for Feynrick's, a full octave above. They were thirty paces from the stone now, the shamans raising their hands as if to strike. But they would not strike until they discovered Ella's plan.

If Nauro was right, that was.

"What is this?" Aeyenor's voice boomed down. "What are you doing?"

Marea struck resonance, and the power flooding her bones felt fuller than it ever had, richer, like the difference between a street bard's cheap instrument and the fine, deep-bodied sandalwood lutes of a Brinerider bard. She found her place in the harmony easily, an octave above Tai, and as her resonance settled in the power in her swelled again, like the chaos of the sea channeled into a single current, rushing from the stone through her.

She felt giddy on the strength of it, almost drunk. Ella had said they wouldn't need to use their resonances, just strike them, but what if she did? What luck could she cause, what fates could she change with this kind of strength?

"Stop," Aeyenor demanded, and the shaman nearest them raised his hands.

At ten paces Ella struck, lined face pale but determined. Despite her giddiness, despite her dread, Marea found a moment of compassion for the woman. Her man had dragged her here too, and the power they needed to open the stone was the same one that was killing her.

The timeslip resonance locked in like the keystone of an arch, an octave above Tai's, and Marea's whole body shook. It was like *she'd* been struck, like she was the fourth note of a lute now vibrating on all strings.

Looking at Avery she realized her mistake—his body shook the same way, as did Ella's, as did the shamans. She hadn't been struck, the *stone* had, like a massive bell. The power they felt rattling through them now was its power, a giant instrument laying silent for centuries suddenly come to life.

Marea stared. The shamans stared. Even Nauro looked about in wonder. And at the head of their group, Tai brushed past the shamans to place his hand directly against the vibrating stone.

It sank like water into sand.

58

Tai moved on pure instinct, pressing his hand to the stone, something deep within it calling to him. It sank in past the wrist, and he had the feeling if he reached deep enough he would touch the spear, could draw it out in his fist.

But thunder erupted in his right ear, a flash of light and heat so bright it blinded him. Tai felt the lightning strike him, directly in the chest. The shamans. This was how they'd killed Nauro.

Only the lightning passed through him into the stone. It was one wave in a mighty current, a current he floated in up to the elbow. He turned and found the shaman just behind him. Turned and extended one hand to touch the man.

Another thunderclap sounded and the man spun backwards in air, smoke trailing from Tai's fingertips.

It was effortless, but he had more important things to do. Tai pushed deeper into the stone, feeling the pull of the spear, like the center of a whirlpool where two rivers met, the current of power swirling around it.

Then something impossibly strong ripped him from the stone, sending him hurtling into space. Tai struck resonance while he was still tumbling in air, slowing himself enough to see a storm of fire and lightning descending on one small area at the base of the stone. The area where his friends were.

Where Ella was.

With a cry Tai shot back toward them, his *uai* a trickle compared to the stone's current but swelling as he got close. Distance from the stone—that was the key. These shamans were only strong so long as they were physically near the waystone. That was why they'd thrown him off it, because with a hand in the stone he'd been more powerful than they.

Time to use their own tricks against them.

He swooped in close, seizing the nearest shaman to sling him out of the garden. Instead thunder clapped and he found himself spinning away again, chest aching like he'd been struck with a giant hammer. He'd probably be dead if it wasn't for the strength of *uai* surging through him.

Tai pushed against the outward spin, slowing then shoving back toward the stone. Distance. So long as the shamans were closer they would be more powerful—but he could do better than close.

Tai wafted onto the stone ten paces and a quarter turn away from the fierce firestorm around his friends, praying Nauro's skill and the stone's *uai* would keep them safe a little longer. He stuck his hand into the stone.

Only to smash his fingers, like the stone was ordinary rock. He frowned, heart beating. What was wrong? Fire and thunder roared from the other side of the stone, where his friends held the other five notes of the harmony.

That was it! None of the shamans had entered the stone, though surely they'd tried—likely because they were not part of the harmony. His resonance had probably fallen out of tune too.

Tai focused, pressing himself against the stone, feeling for the group's resonance, for the way it reverberated through the stone. There. He flexed his power—and felt the rock give under him, like the soft mud under the docks of Riverbottom. Power rushed again into his bones, doubling the roaring current already there. Tai wafted himself around the stone, dragging hands and feet inside the stone, until he caught sight of the fight.

No need for lightning here—that was a shaman's trick. He was more familiar with air. Tai opened himself to the raging *uai* current, letting it flow through him, and directed it out in three giant fists of air, each aimed at a different shaman attacking his friends.

They exploded outward, tumbling in air, lightning bolts sparking out. Nauro spun as they did, clapping his hands together to send something light-eating and silent, like black lightning, streaking toward the nearest of them.

The shaman's body turned to ash.

Tai dropped down the face of the stone, trusting Nauro and Avery to do the rest, and rushed to Ella. "Are you okay?" he asked. The lines on her face stood out and her breath had a rattle.

"Fine," she panted. "Fine, I just need to—"

Her eyes went dull and she fell.

"Ella!" Tai cried, catching her limp form.

Feynrick spun at the cry, face deadly serious for a change, axes raised. "What is it—"

The axes fell from his hands to clatter on the stones. His body followed a moment later, flopping like scarecrow with the stick pulled out.

"Feynrick!" Tai called, but behind him Marea was falling too, slumping against the waystone. Avery followed her.

Some shamanic attack. It had to be. "Nauro!" he called. "What do we do?"

Nauro turned to him, face still calm despite it all, and held out a hand. Then he fell like the rest, body slumping over Marea's.

Tai stared, still holding Ella's limp form. He held two fingers to her neck. Nothing.

How was that even possible? "It can't be," he whispered, looking around, seeking some explanation. "It *can't* be."

One of the four shamans wafted toward him, arms spread, his face beatific. "They are gone, Sekaetai. As you should be. Give up, and join them."

"Never!" Tai yelled, summoning the *uai* still raging through him.

A harmonic *uai*.

Suddenly all the strange parts of the last few moments clicked: the too-easy deaths of his friends, the strange coincidence of him not dying, and the harmony still shaking his bones. A harmony impossible if his friends were dead.

"It's a trick!" he yelled. "Hallucinations!"

And as soon as he realized it, the scene snapped back to focus, Ella screaming and Marea cradling something in empty arms, Nauro and Avery still standing, trading black lightning and volleys of stone with the shamans in the sky. Their harmony was coming apart, and without it they had no chance.

Tai seized Ella by the shoulders. "I'm alive!" he yelled into her ears. "It's an illusion!"

Her eyes met his, dazed at first, then clear. Her resonance snapped back in place. "The spear," she said, voice deadly focused. "Get it. I'll wake Marea."

He spun for the stone, only to have her spin him back. "I love you," she said, eyes bright on his, the eyes he'd always known despite the newly lined face. She kissed him.

There was no kiss like one in the middle of a battle. It was over too soon, not soon enough, and Tai ran for the stone, praying their harmony held up long enough to get his hands in. Something slammed into his back as he ran, a pepper of stones, each one burning like a stab wound. The momentum flung him into the stone and his whole body sunk in, light blotting out as the pillar swallowed him.

Power flooded him and even as pain burst in a constellation along his back. *Power and belief,* Avery had said. *Shamanic magic is at its base just power and belief.*

He had power. So he just needed to disbelieve in his wounds?

No—believe in their healing. Like brawlers did. Like the way he'd healed, when he overcame his voices.

The moment he thought it the pain in his back stopped, like it had never been there, and in his heightened awareness he felt five stones push out of his back.

The spear still called to him. He could feel the current of *uai* pulling him toward it. If he took it they won—all the power animating the shamans would cut off. But who knew how long it would take him to find it, while those shamans sent hallucinations along with lightning bolts and stones? They'd killed one. They could kill the rest, then deal with the stone.

Tai turned, rolling in the stone like it was a forest pond in the heat of summer, stone melting cleanly off his face as he pressed it out. Two shamans were left, closing on them from either side, Avery and Nauro trading attacks with them in what looked like an even fight.

Time to change that. Tai let the stone's power flood into him, hardened it into two fists of air that struck each of the shamans, knocking them away from the stone, from the source of their power.

Nauro again reacted without pause, spinning to follow them and sending two arcs of black lightning after them. One shaman dodged it, sending a narrow bolt of lightning arcing back. The other puffed to ash.

A hail of pebbles shot from Avery's hands, streaking through the air with an audible whine, and spots of blood appeared on the last shaman's clothes. A moment later a second arc of Nauro's black lightning caught him, and the man ceased to exist.

"Yes!" Marea cried, face exultant.

"Go," Nauro barked, looking upwards. "All of you. Go now. Get the spear."

"Very clever," a voice boomed from above, as Tai was beginning to push into the stone. "Harmonizing the resonances. I never would have thought of that. Thank you."

Despite himself Tai looked up. Aeyenor was there, the one perched atop the stone, only now he was walking down its side as though gravity had shifted, feet ankle-deep in the stone.

"The resonance," Tai said. "He must have figured out how to tune to us."

"Very good, Sekaetai," Aeyenor said. "Or should I call you Savior of Ayugen? The Achuri Menace? Pity for you you didn't take all this power when you had it in your grasp the first time. Or did you have these pathetic notions of victory without violence even then?"

He knew Tai's inner thoughts—Aeyenor had broken through whatever screen Nauro and Avery had held then. He knew their secrets, their plan. All that would matter now was who got to the spear first.

"Go," Nauro said again, voice more urgent. "I will handle him."

Aeyenor laughed at that. "Will you, Nauro? Like you handled me last time we fought?"

"I have learned much since then," Nauro said, thrusting a hand into the stone. His whole body seemed to light up. "And we are on equal terms this time."

A black sword appeared in Aeyenor's hands, the blade drinking light as Nauro's black lightning did. "No," Aeyenor said, "we are not. I have centuries on you, old friend. And while you have chased your myths across three continents, I have been honing my skills."

He streaked downward, raising the blade behind him for a downward strike. Nauro met it with a black blade of his own, and where the two met there was neither clang nor thunder, but absolute silence, like the sound had been sucked from Tai's ears.

"Go!" Nauro shouted when it came back. "Go now!"

He was right. There was nothing Tai could do here, but he could still feel the spear inside, pulling him, like a current in the river. He pushed into the stone.

The stone turned to rock around him, most of an arm and a leg trapped inside. Tai looked back to see Feynrick staggering, clutching an arm spotted with blood as the shaman's had been. His resonance—he must have lost it when he got hit. And with only five resonances, the harmony was not enough to soften the stone.

Meaning he was trapped.

Tai growled helplessly as Aeyenor and Nauro once again exchanged blows, black blades stealing light, anything and everything they touched turning to ash. Avery shot more pebbles at the shaman, but they vanished almost as an afterthought. Tai summoned the power of the stone and sent that at Aeyenor, who Nauro had managed to separate from the stone, but the man cut through fists of thickened air like they were a light breeze, eyes intense and focused on his opponent.

Then Avery was at Feynrick's side, hands on his arms, and with a howl Feynrick stood bolt upright. The stone softened around Tai's limbs. Time to go. Aeyenor could likely end his friends while fighting Nauro, and Tai would not be able to help until he got the spear.

He pushed in, stone molding around him like churned butter. It was warm inside, almost hot. The sounds of battle came muted through the stone, punctuated by moments of silence when Nauro and Aeyenor's blades hit. Good. So long as they were fighting he had a chance.

Tai felt for that internal current—up. The *uai* was flowing up. He tried swimming with it, or pulling himself up, but couldn't get traction. For an awful moment he thought he might be falling, even, sinking deeper into the earth.

Then he remembered wafting, and pushed up. It seemed to work, stone flowing against his face and the spear's call getting closer. He reached out a hand, an arm, ready to grasp it and end this thing.

Then the stone went solid around him again, and he remembered he needed to breathe.

59

*E*lla watched Tai disappear into the stone, heart beating with fear and hope. She had just seen that stone turn to rock around him. What if it did again?

But she felt hope, too—hope that they had killed all but the last of the shamans. Hope that Nauro was holding Aeyenor off, however desperately.

Hope that Tai would walk out holding the spear, and everyone else's power would vanish.

Silence thundered as Nauro and Aeyenor traded blows in the sky, and a thought occurred to her: she didn't have to wait for Tai to get the spear. *She* could get it too. Prophets, she probably stood less chance of dying in there than out here.

What better time for a swim in some stone?

Ella took a deep breath and pushed inside, the stone flowing around her like the black sludge that would take unwary boots along the outer islands of the Worldsmouth delta. It was warm, which was surprising, and dark, which wasn't. She had the strange sensation she was floating, the solidity of the ground replaced with more softness beneath her feet.

Focus, Ella. You've got maybe sixty seconds of air, and a small spear to find in a big stone.

She could feel it, faintly, somewhere above her. Ella tried to pull her way up, then kick up, then sort of worm her way up, but all it seemed to do was get her out of breath. Which was bad, when you couldn't breathe.

She pushed out of the stone again to find Nauro and Aeyenor spinning around each other in air, black blades a blur. Avery and Marea watched the battle, similar looks of concentration on their faces.

They were fighting too, in their own ways—Marea trying to push luck in Nauro's favor, and Avery doing whatever clever shamanic tricks he could do.

"The stone," Ella said, panting. "Put your hands in the stone. More power."

Aeyenor blasted Nauro back in the sky, and spun to hurl a fistful of newly-formed boulders at them. Marea shouted and the boulders crashed all around them, each one miraculously missing. Ella shivered. She hated surviving on pure luck. But what could she do in this fight, or in Tai's?

Nauro attacked again, the narrow man surprisingly elegant in his motions, the blades leaving trails of darkness in their wake. Ella turned back to the stone. How long had Tai been in there? Was he taking air breaks?

Marea screamed and Ella spun back to see a cloud of daggers flying at them, jet black like Aeyenor's blade. She held her arms up instinctively, though it would do no good.

The daggers hissed all around her, making ash-filled holes in the ground, but she felt nothing. Marea's luck.

Then Avery shouted and fell clutching his leg. His resonance dropped out of the harmony, and Ella's stomach lurched as a significant portion of what had been his thigh drifted away as ash.

"Avery!" Marea cried, running to him, eyes full of fear. Then the full meaning of Avery's resonance dropping out hit her and Ella's stomach clenched: the stone would go solid. Trapping Tai inside.

"Your resonance!" she cried, crouching down next to them. "Avery, you have to strike resonance! Heal yourself!"

"Can't—heal—calignite," he whispered, eyes squeezed shut in pain. Two clashes of silence sounded above, then Avery's body went slack. He'd passed out from the pain.

Ella lost no time, dropping to one knee and slapping him. "Wake up!"

"What are you doing?" Marea screamed, grabbing her hand.

"Tai! He's trapped inside the stone!"

"And Avery's hurt! We have to *do* something!"

"If we don't get his resonance back," Ella said, clenching her jaw, "it won't matter *what* we do, because Nauro is not winning that fight up there, and once Aeyenor gets the spear we are all dead."

"But he's *hurt*!" Marea cried, voice carrying the full weight of terror.

The cold, calculating part of Ella's brain saw there would be no convincing the girl, and likely no waking Avery either. But the passionate, in-love part of her brain refused to accept that meant Tai was going to die. What could she do?

If Nauro was to die, Aeyenor would likely strike his own resonance again, and slip into the stone. She could harmonize with him and pull Tai out. But he'd be dead by then.

No.

She could use this *uai* to break the stone apart and pull Tai out, or at least give him room to breathe. But Nauro had said the shamans had all failed to break the stone, no matter how much *uai* they used.

No.

What she needed was Avery's resonance back—the mosstongue resonance to complete their harmony.

Ella started. That was Avery's resonance because he'd earned shamanic sight, the second level ability of any mosstongue. Which was why he'd given them all mosstongue revenants on the ship, so *they* could gain shamanic sight.

She had a mosstongue revenant in her. She could use it to complete the harmony and save Tai if she did it fast.

Ella stood, determination rising like a waystone in her heart. Good thing she knew about the harmonies. Good thing she'd overcome revenants before. Good thing she used to *teach* people how to overcome them. Because Tai had one lungful of air, or maybe a half now, for her to overcome hers and complete the harmony before he suffocated in there.

60

Someone would soften the stone. Tai told himself this as his lungs began to burn, as the warm darkness of the stone began to feel like a trap, as the current of *uai* leading to the spear changed from inviting to maddening. They would soften the stone. They had to.

His chest heaved, but solid rock surrounded him. It felt like he'd lost the strength in his limbs, like he was the one frozen, not the stone. Tai lashed out with air, shoved with wafting, kicked and clawed in an animal upwelling of fear, but nothing worked. He was trapped.

And dying. He knew that rationally even as the panicking animal mind in him took over, thrusting with his arms and legs, lungs hitching wildly against the stone.

Mindsight—Tai struck out with mindsight, the endless power of the stone rushing through him. The garden and the old city spread out for him in the strange not-vision of mindsight. He threw himself into it, desperate for an escape from his panic, for some shred of hope outside. He saw the wicked blur of Aeyenor and Nauro's thoughts, minds focused torrents of shamanic attacks and the stroke and counter-stroke of trained swordsmen. He felt

Feynrick's frustration, flush with strength and no one to fight, saw Marea's panic and the calm slumber of Avery's mind. So he was the one who'd fallen out—from Marea's rushing stream he could see most of Avery's leg was gone.

Closest in he saw Ella's thoughts, like the stormy confluence of two rivers, both flowing impossibly fast. His body convulsed again and he threw his mind deeper into mindsight, into the cool rationality it offered. She must be in slip, which meant she had good reason to do so, which meant she was probably trying to save him somehow.

It also meant she was dying to do it.

He could catch only bare glimpses of her thoughts rushing past, thoughts of old age and death and love and determination. The image of a woman looking like a scowling, thin-lipped Ella. Her mother.

His body convulsed again, a dark halo beginning to close in on his sight. *You can do it, Ella*, he thought at her, knowing practiced mindseyes could send their thoughts out. *And if you don't*, he thought, even the words beginning to grow hazy, *I love you, anyway. I love you.*

His body convulsed. His lungs filled with fire. Mindsight narrowed to a single point, but in it he saw one of Ella's two streams of thought suddenly end. And his next convulsion met not unyielding rock but buttery stone, limbs sloshing free.

Tai wafted out with the last of his strength. His head and shoulders thrust from the stone near its top and he sucked lungfuls of air. He had never breathed anything sweeter, never seen a sweeter sight than the battle-scarred tableau of the garden and the furious light-drinking battle of two elder shamans in the sky beyond him. As he looked Aeyenor turned his direction, their eyes locking across the distance.

"I heard you!" Ella screamed up at him, looking impossibly old. "Now go!"

The spear. Right. Neither Ella nor Marea could waft, Avery was unconscious, and Nauro was losing ground in his flying sword fight. The spear would end all this.

Tai took a last lungful of air and plunged in. The current spiralled downwards now. He wafted after it, letting it pull him along, spreading his arms out inside the stone to catch the spear if he passed nearby.

A boom reverberated through the stone, and Tai had the distinct impression of waves in the stone current lapping over him, like someone splashing into a pool where he floated. It had to be Nauro or Aeyenor.

A second boom sounded. Both of them, then. It changed nothing. Ancestors send Nauro could hold Aeyenor off long enough for Tai to take the spear.

He increased his pace, breath beginning to burn in his lungs, body not fully recovered from being trapped inside but no time to take a break. Instead he used the massive power of the stone to push air in towards him, creating a tube out to the surface, and gulped lungfuls through that. Then let it melt away, closing his eyes and following the swirl of the current in his bones, in and up inside the dark stone.

His hand brushed something solid, and he started. The spear! He twisted, wafted himself toward it, but found only stone.

Then a pair of hands seized him and slung him outwards. Tai wafted against it on instinct, but the throw was so powerful he flew out of the stone.

Aeyenor. It had to be. Tai flipped himself as he slowed, then shot feet-first for the place he'd come from, aiming to break something in Aeyenor's body.

And slipped through the stone like an arrow through ripe melon, coming out the far side.

"Stains," Tai cursed, and pushed himself back in. How had the shaman found him? Mindsight. He must be using mindsight.

Tai struck his own, slipping into the stone. The world opened up again, Ella and Marea outside and the further-off minds of shamans spreading out against the pitch black of the stone. There was no one inside the stone. No—Nauro and Aeyenor were here, they were just blocking their thoughts.

Of course. And here he was broadcasting his thoughts into the world. No wonder Aeyenor had found him. But if the shaman wasn't attacking now, that meant he had something more important to do.

Tai cursed internally, feeling for the current and wafting after. And he would be able to sense Tai coming just as easily, and Semeca had already shown him the hundred-mind defense they'd used on the streets wouldn't stop a real shaman. Tai had no idea how to block him out.

But he knew someone who did.

Nauro, he thought, as though speaking to a revenant. *Nauro, can you block my thoughts from him?*

I can try, came the man's dry voice, as though he were whispering right in his ear. *I...was wounded badly in the fight. I am trying to heal, but I may need to seek a new body.*

Just give me this, Tai thought, racing after the current as fast as he could follow it, bracing for the moment he felt something solid again, hoping it was the spear but ready for it to be Aeyenor. *I will take him down.*

There is little you can do to each other in this place, Nauro's voice came again. *We are all equals in power here. You have to find the spear.*

The current banked left and Tai followed, then swooped down a long decline, like a waterfall in the current, rock curiously smooth as it rushed across his face. Was this even the right way to find the spear? The stone was so large, he knew he was missing sections of it. What if the spear was back there?

Something solid again—a shred of cloth? Tai grasped it and pulled. A boot connected with his jaw.

Something cracked. Pain blossomed and Tai swirled backward in the stone, blood metallic on his tongue. His jaw was broken—but he had the power of a god flooding through him. Power and belief. So he believed himself healed and in a shock of ice the pain was gone.

Tai grinned. This changed everything.

He shoved himself back toward where he thought the kick had come from and connected with something. A fist, an arm, a shoulder, kicking and flailing. Movement was awkward in the stone, like fighting underwater, but Aeyenor was incredibly strong. Another kick connected and Tai tumbled backward. He healed himself even as he spun, catching himself with a waft.

In here we all share in the spear's power, Nauro had said. Tai imagined himself an incredible brawler, like Sigwil had been on the day he overcame his revenant during a Broken attack, and suddenly his limbs were suffused with power.

He shot himself back at Aeyenor, and for some unknown amount of time they grappled like gods, bodies twisting and gripping and punching and kicking, limbs breaking and reforming, the darkness a chaos of force and pain.

Tai's lungs burned. He tried believing himself full of air again, but apparently there were limits even to the stone's power. Then Aeyenor got an arm around his throat and it was all he could do with wafting and punching the man repeatedly in the eyes to get away.

As he did his hand touched something solid. Not fabric, not flesh, but smooth wood.

"Yes!" Tai roared, air bubbling from his lungs into the stone. He seized the spear.

It pulled against him.

Tai grabbed it with his other hand, adding the force of a waft to his pull. The spear pulled back harder, drawing him in.

A hand brushed his along the spear and he understood: Aeyenor. That was the brush of fabric he felt. Likely the reason he'd run into him the other times. The man had followed him to the spear, and now he was trying to take it.

Too bad for Aeyenor Tai grew up on the streets.

Aeyenor jerked on the spear again, and this time instead of fighting him Tai wafted *with* the momentum, shooting past him in the hopes of ripping the spear from his hand.

Instead Aeyenor mirrored the trick, doubling their momentum as he rushed past Tai. It was all Tai could do to hold on. He tried a chop then, risking a one-handed grip to slam his free hand down on the shaman's with all the strength of the stone's *uai* behind it.

He felt bones break in both hands and jerked on the spear, but still the man's grip held. "Give up," he growled, precious air escaping his mouth.

Air. It came down to air. Ice shot through Tai's broken fingers even as a vicious kick broke his right kneecap, and Tai retaliated with a boot to the crotch. They could fight like this all day and the stone's power would keep either from getting an advantage. But sooner or later, one of them would run out of air.

Even as he thought it, Tai felt Aeyenor waft backward on the spear, trying to drag it toward the surface. Tai wafted the other direction, strengthening his grip and pushing all the *uai* he could muster into stopping Aeyenor. He kicked out, kneecap mended, sending a boot to the gut meant to knock Aeyenor's wind out of him. Tai's own lungs burned, but the longer they waited, the more chance Aeyenor would find some shamanic trick he didn't know about and take the spear.

Aeyenor pulled back just as hard and they slowed inside the stone, current swirling around the spear, power balanced equally between them. It would come down to who passed out first from lack of air.

Then Tai had a thought. A mad, wild thought. He broke his mind into a hundred different voices, just in case Nauro's shielding wouldn't work.

And dropped resonance.

Instantly the soft stone around them turned to rock. A wave of panic rose in him, the animal memory of being trapped there. He shoved it down.

Tai, Nauro's voice came. *What are you doing? You'll die in there.*

Good, Tai thought back. *Better that than Aeyenor get the spear. You know what to do.*

Don't be stupid! the old shaman snapped. *There must be some other way.*

Trust me, Tai thought back, a calm coming over him. *I have a plan.*

A plan that might actually work.

Tai felt a new resonance hum through the stone, Aeyenor striking a second resonance. The stone went soft, and Tai struck his own, wafting and pulling back.

Nauro, he thought out. *Drop your resonance.*

I can't, the shaman thought back. *I'll be trapped in here.*

Then get out and do it. I can't resist Aeyenor forever. Just keep my mind shielded. I have a plan.

A moment later the stone hardened again. Tai's lungs hitched, begging for air, but Aeyenor's had to be even worse, with that kick to the stomach. How long before the man blacked out?

A *third* resonance rolled off Aeyenor, tuned to Ella, Marea, and Feynrick below. The stone softened again. Tai struck wafting, making sure it was out of harmony with the shaman's, and again resisted.

Nauro, he thought out. *Feynrick. Tell him to drop his resonance.*

Ancestors send Aeyenor couldn't hold all six resonances at once. Was that even possible? Tai had held two before, and even that had been a challenge.

The stone hardened. Tai's lungs ached, but he took comfort in the strength of the resonance shaking him through the stone. Aeyenor was just as desperate, and he didn't have a plan. Not one this good, anyway.

A fourth resonance rolled from Aeyenor, and the stone softened again. Aeyenor pulled at the spear with desperate strength and Tai pulled back just as strongly, keeping them in the stone.

Do it, he thought to the shaman on the other side of the spear. *Let go. Fly out. Would you rather live or have the spear?*

Aeyenor didn't let go. Tai's vision was beginning to sparkle.

Nauro, he said inside. *Ella. Tell her to drop her resonances.*

She won't do it, Nauro said after a pause. *Neither of them will.*

Tell her to trust me, Tai thought back. *I'm not dying in here.*

The stone began to harden. He struck his higher wafting and

slammed a column of air into the rock.

The stone hardened. Something like a scream sounded from a few feet away, where Aeyenor was trapped in the rock. And Tai took a deep breath of fresh air.

"You meckstain!" Ella's voice floated through the air channel he'd wafted in the rock. "You shattercocking, thrice-becursed *meck*stain!"

Tai smiled, still gasping, lungs only able to fill so far against the rock trapping him. A thought hit him, a wild animal punch of fear from Aeyenor, desperation driving his thoughts even through Nauro's shielding apparently. It didn't matter. The man would harmonize all six resonances, or he would die.

Tai took deep breaths, ready at any moment to strike and resist if Aeyenor managed it. Having no idea what he would do if it happened, but minute by minute his heart slowed, his breathing evened, and nothing came from the stone.

Strange to think a man was dying somewhere next to him in the stone. A man who'd lived hundreds of years, if he'd heard right. For once Ydilwen had nothing to say about Aeyenor dying. Apparently even *he* agreed Aeyenor had to go.

Ella says to ask if you are done being right yet, Nauro's voice came in his mind.

Tai grinned. *Just about*, he thought back. *Give me a few more minutes to gloat.*

How long could someone survive without air? No sense in taking chances. Especially if Aeyenor knew some shamanic trick.

The tube he'd punched through the soft stone was just wide enough that he could see a sliver of sky. The sun was sinking toward evening, light growing redder in the west.

"Enough already!" Ella's voice floated up from below, sounding desperate.

Tai smiled. *Okay*, he thought at Nauro. *Strike harmony once more, for old time's sake?*

62

You think they wasn't doing something in there, asking us for volunteers what didn't come back? You tell that to all the boys seen men fly up flamin' and screamin' from the tents. You tell that to ol Semeca and Tayo, what died when their little project went to shatters. Bad as the Achuri, if ye ask me.

—Councilate legionnaire, Yatiport tavern

Ella's lover flew like a god from the face of the stone, massive two-bladed spear streaming red ribbons in his right hand. Her breath caught. Something in the heavy evening light, in the whip of his long black hair in the breeze, in the knowledge that spear was last held by the Prophet himself—it choked her up.

He'd done it. No, *they*'d done it, together. She looked around her as Tai descended: Avery lay wounded but awake on the stones, Marea crouched concerned by his side, Nauro watched with an almost reverent expression, and Feynrick leaned on the haft of an axe, grinning proudly. Probably the world's most unlikely team, but they had made it against all odds. Solved the mystery not even the best shamans could crack, and defeated them all.

Tai touched down and she hobbled to him, circling her arms around his waist. Overcoming her revenant in slip had aged her even more, but she'd made peace with that. She knew why she did what she did. And she wouldn't let anxiety about an early death or gods forbid worries about how she *looked* get in the way of enjoying what time she had left. That was her mother, not her.

"Did you have to stay up there that long?" she asked, leaning in close. "Some of us are on a timeline here."

"My apologies," he said, and leaned in for a kiss. *Uai* thrummed through her at his touch, his body become like the stone was, a raging current of power. She reveled in it, reveled in the strength of his arms around her, in the knowledge that they were making history. She could die tomorrow, or today even. Better that than a long life without really living.

A slap sounded, and Tai's teeth hit painfully into hers. "You did it!" Feynrick cried. "Always knew ye had it in ye, milkweed. Though ye might have given me one good swing at him."

Tai cocked his head. "We could probably pull him out of there, if you really want to."

Feynrick blanched. "No need for that. We'll find more! Whole city of shamans out there, ain't there?"

"Shamans without power," Nauro said, limping up to them. "Now that Tai has the spear, all the power they gathered goes back to him. They'll be no threat."

Nauro's face still looked drawn, but nothing like it had when he tumbled from the stone. He'd given everything he had to the battle with Aeyenor. Just as he had in the battle against Ollen while she and the rest of them escaped. Shatters, he'd *died* in that battle.

Ella cleared her throat. "I owe you an apology, Nauro. You have always been a good man, and true, and my mistrust of you was unworthy. I apologize, and promise to do better."

Nauro's eyebrows raised. "Apology accepted, Ellumia. You had your reasons, I'm sure."

Avery cleared his throat. "Help me up," he said, reaching a hand to Tai. "I would stand and join you in this moment."

Tai unhooked his arm from her to reach down, his other hand holding the spear.

Avery reached up to grasp it, and Ella's stomach twinged. Harides, Aeyenor had called him. Of Seingard, not Worldsmouth.

"Tai," she said, pulling at his arm, dread suddenly rising in her chest.

Her words were lost in dead silence. A black blade appeared in Avery's free hand, slicing Tai's free hand off at the wrist.

The hand that held the spear.

Avery caught it and pushed up, smiling. "That's better," he said, taking a deep breath.

Pain hit her like a blacksmith's hammer.

63

Marea stared at her lover, uncomprehending. The rest of the party fell around her, screaming, clawing at their faces.

"Avery?" she asked

He gave her a smile. "Turns out I didn't need your luck after all, sweetheart. But, thank you."

His voice sounded different, his accent was different, even his face looked different. Older.

"Who are you?" she whispered.

He heard her over the cries of their companions. "You heard the man," Avery said, gesturing up to where the shaman had been. "Should have heard it from my friend back in Yatiport, too. My name is Meyn Harides, head seeker of the Yatiport cell."

She shook her head. It didn't make sense somehow. "You're not—"

"Avery, a sweet and simple young man from Worldsmouth who turns out to know a lot more about shamanism than a twenty-year-old should? No. But that's who you needed me to be, and you're who I needed to get in with Tai's party. So, thank you."

She took a step toward him, her world falling apart. "So you're not—you don't—"

"Love you?" Harides smiled. "Love is the excuse weak people make for staying weak. The sooner you learn that the better."

"You're not... Avery," she said, the words strange on her tongue. Wrong. And yet this man who looked and sounded so much like Avery was definitely not the man she'd spent the last few weeks with. Not the man who—

She choked up. A thread of black lightning cracked, stealing the sound from her ears. Avery waved it away like a fisherman waved at gnats. The tracery of missing light led back to Nauro, who had pushed up on hands and knees.

A bolt flew from the spear, three times as thick, and Nauro's body puffed to ash.

Marea's chest constricted. "Stop," she whispered. "You don't have to."

"Kill them? Let me ask you something," Harides said, as the rest of the party came to, screams dying away. "Have you ever heard of an archrevenant sharing power with underlings? Did Semeca bring the original members of her cell to the attack on Ayugen? No. They are always alone."

"You betrayed us," Tai said, clutching his arm where it ended in a clean-lined stump.

"Very perceptive," Harides said. "And you would have seen it coming if you weren't such a fool. It's the great fiction of the ninespears, that there will be some kind of power-sharing deal once they take down a god. That any seeker would be content with half the archrevenant's power, and the others will be fine with their fifth of a half, or tenth of a half, or whatever it might be. That the seeker would let those who knew their secrets live to oppose them."

Something zipped and her former lover waved a hand. Ella appeared in mid-stride, her withered face frozen in a snarl, a long dagger in her hand. Harides tsked. "You'd think she would learn by now. I was there in Yatiport when Credelen froze her, and stole half her life while she struggled in deep slip. I guess she needs the lesson again."

Tai yelled then and flew at Harides. Harides waved a black bolt at him, and the wafter just managed to avoid it.

"Just as well," Harides said, waving a hand at him. "You might still be useful. I'm the one who told Ollen who you were, you know. Made them attack you. How else was I going to get in your group?"

Tai froze in air, a look of outrage on his face.

"I *killed* for you," Marea whispered.

"Yes," Harides nodded. "That was... unexpected. I really don't think Eyadin would have been much of a threat."

But she had killed him anyway. On the slim chance he would be a danger to Avery. Who had been lying to her the whole time. Who had never loved her.

She was a murderer.

Feynrick woke up, roaring, and hurled an axe at Harides. It stopped mid-throw, frozen in air.

Harides raised a hand. Marea's heart clenched, as it had when Ella froze, as it had when Nauro died. "Not him, too," she said, her voice tiny.

Harides raised an eyebrow. "You care for him so much? Isn't he one of the rebels who murdered your parents? Or are you realizing how childish that all was?"

Marea looked at Feynrick, frozen mid-run. "He's a good man."

"What of this one?" Harides asked, bringing Tai down to earth with a gesture. "He is the one you blame, isn't he? Would you like to kill him finally? Cold revenge is not as good as hot, but it's better than nothing."

Marea gazed at Tai, leader of the rebellion, chief murderer of her parents. She'd hated him this entire trip, but all she felt for him now was compassion. He didn't deserve to die, and he had to stay there frozen while Ella aged to death in front of him. Yes, he had murdered her parents, or been there when they died. But he'd been fighting for something he believed in.

As she had, when she killed Eyadin.

Marea gasped, feeling like she was going to be sick. Like something was wrong inside. This entire time, she'd been wrong. Been loving the wrong person, and hating someone without really understanding who he was.

And now she understood, because she was that person too.

No, you were right, my pepper, her voice came inside, but it sounded strained, anxious. *He murdered us! They all did!*

She knew that anxious tone. Had heard it in her mother's voice, and in the voice before that, deep within the caves under Ayugen. It was the sound of a revenant in danger.

"Sweetheart?" Harides asked, the name vile from his mouth. "You're looking a little pale?"

This voice had glommed on to her hatred. Used it to control her. But all that had done was keep her from seeing who her true friends were. These people, who had risked their lives time and again for her. Who had taken her in then let her join their party when they had no reason to.

No. They killed me, pepper! We're your true family!

Family. She had never been excited about living with her cousins in the Mouth, she had just wanted to escape Ayugen. And that was why she'd fallen so easily and so hard for Avery. She saw that now, as the man toyed with Feynrick, battering him with his own axes. He was a monster. But she had needed somewhere to belong. Someone to belong to.

And the whole time they had been right here.

A scab ripped free from her heart. A revenant. And the wound it left bled pure *uai*.

Marea struck resonance, knowing what she had to do. She knew it was impossible, too—but that was what fatewalking was for.

She ran. She had no weapon, no knowledge, no shamanic tricks, not even Ella's speed to hide her coming. What she had was a single-minded desire, burning as clearly in her mind as anything she had ever seen or wanted: to save her friends. To kill Harides.

He turned to her, mild surprise registering in his eyes. "Decided you're not in love with me anymore, then?"

Marea crossed Nauro's ashes, plucked the dagger from Ella's frozen hand, and leapt at Harides.

"Oh, please," he said, waving a hand.

A hammer of air slammed into her, knocking her backwards, her resonance still roaring, vision still bright.

The knife tumbled from her grip, caught in her forward momentum, end over end. Marea watched it even as she fell, even as her back collided with the waystone.

It struck Harides right between the eyes, hilt first. He fell.

Tai shot into motion, Ella snapped out of slip, and Feynrick roared with anger, seizing an axe from the air and running at Harides.

"No!" Marea cried, pushing up though every bone in her body hurt. "I need to do this."

"Do away," Tai said, snatching the spear from Harides's fist and flying to Ella, who lay motionless on the ground.

Marea ran to him and snatched the dagger where it lay next to his head, tears streaming down her face. "For Nauro," she said, "and for Eyadin, and for my friends."

She rammed it home.

64

Tai landed next to Ella, pushing back the sick fear in his chest. Harides had trapped her in slip, like Credelen did in Yatiport. She'd aged decades that time. She didn't *have* decades this time.

"Ella!"

No response. He thrust his free hand—gods, his stump but it didn't matter—onto her body and sent healing energy into her like Avery had done with him, like he'd done to himself inside the stone.

Nothing. Her chest wasn't moving.

"No," he swore, somewhere between a curse and a sob. He tried again, gripping the spear and believing she was alive, believing she had years left to live.

It didn't work. He almost threw the spear in rage and frustration, *uai* raging through him. What good was the power of a god if it couldn't give her more life?

Then he remembered something. Tai opened her gnarled hand, wrapping fingers around the spear. Ancestors, they felt cold.

He let go. And prayed.

"Ancestors, if you're out there," he murmured, "Prophet, if

you can hear me, Ascending God, if this was really the place you left the earth, grant me this one prayer. I will do whatever you ask, destroy the spear, give my life, just please, please let her live."

You would never destroy the spear, a voice came in his head. Ydilwen's voice. *You killed so many to get it. What's one more?*

"No!" Tai yelled, seeing Feynrick approach, not caring. "I never meant to hurt any of them! Is that what you need? For me to destroy the spear?"

What I need doesn't matter anymore. I am dead.

The Yatiman leaned over. "What did you do?"

"The spear," Tai said, hope collapsing. "I thought—Nauro lived so long with his *uai* stream. Semeca lived forever, with *this* one. I don't know how it works but I thought, maybe, this would be enough. That whatever life she has left, it would stretch it out. Keep her alive."

He closed his eyes, pupils burning, something delicate and huge beginning to break inside. That wasn't how it worked. She'd done too much. To save *him*.

Feynrick cleared his throat. "Looking a little better, isn't she?"

Tai sucked in a breath, opening his eyes. Her focused on her face. There *was* more color in her cheeks. And was that—

Tai sucked in a breath. Her chest rose and fell, shallow at first, then deep and regular breaths.

He swept her up, stump burning, not caring, pressing her close to his chest, spear between them. She was alive. Praise the ancestors, she was *alive*.

Ella stirred against him. "Tai? I was having the strangest dream."

He laughed, or cried, something like that, pressing her even closer. "Of what? Tell me."

"That you—married me," she said, her voice dreamy. "That

we had a girl. Two girls." She shook her head. "Isn't that strange?"

"Not strange at all," he said, pulling back just enough to kiss her, keeping her hand firmly around the spear. "We can do that. We *should* do that. Will you marry me?"

She stared at him then started laughing, the wrinkles melting from her face.

"What?" he said, too relieved and happy to care. "What's so funny?"

"Of all the ways," she panted after a moment, "that I dreamed someone would propose to me." She shook her head, looking around. "This was definitely not it."

Feynrick rubbed his beard. "I thought it was pretty good, myself."

Ella met his eyes, grin falling off. "Are you serious?"

"Yes!" he said, realizing suddenly how serious he was. How much he needed her in his life. "Yes."

She eyed him a second longer. "I'll think about it."

Tai and Feynrick goggled.

"You'll think about it?" Tai asked.

"What kinda answer is that?" Feynrick said.

Ella frowned at them. "A lot has happened. I almost died just now. Not the greatest time to be making big decisions, okay? And I don't have the best history with marriage proposals. But if what you're asking is to be together, from now on? Then yes. A thousand times yes."

Feynrick cheered, and Tai thought the smile might break his face. He hugged her close, spear sandwiched between them.

Ella squirmed after a time, her face maybe that of a forty-year-old now. "Is this thing my engagement present? Most Worldsmouth men go for a tasteful necklace, you know."

"That," Tai said, "is yours forever if that's what you need to live. I don't know how this works. I just know that it is. Like the revenants worked for Nauro." His heart tightened a bit—Nauro. But time for that later.

"You're brilliant," she said. "Though I dearly hope I don't have to carry this thing around the rest of my life. It's huge. Besides, it's yours."

And so it begins again.

Tai shook his head, not sure who he was responding to. "It's not mine. We earned it together."

And together you will protect your people, right? Build another great civilization on the corpses of those who stood in your way?

Ella held it out. "I don't want it. I—this power is intoxicating. Here. Let's see if I croak when I let go of it."

She let go of it and Tai's heart leapt, but Ella seemed fine. The spear rattled to the flagstones.

"Go on," Feynrick said after a moment. "Take it. Somebody's got to."

Tai stared at the spear. How many people had died trying to get this?

Not nearly as many as will die if you take it up.

Ella and Feynrick were looking at him, even Marea where she sat near Avery's corpse. Still Tai hesitated.

"Can't leave it here," Feynrick said. "Bet some of those ratcockers out there got a much worse imagination than Avery or whatever his name was."

Go on. They're dying already anyway.

Tai stood. "I need some time. To think."

Ella looked concerned but nodded. Tai strode away, all his glory and relief gone in the weight that had followed him the last few weeks, settling back onto his shoulders. "Okay, Ydilwen. What are you talking about?"

I'm talking about your empire. About using your new power to defeat the Councilate and set up something new, and all the people you'll kill to do it.

"You're in my head," Tai said, frustrated that they even had to have this conversation. "You can see all my memories. You know killing people is the last thing I want to do."

What you want doesn't matter as much as what you do. And when push comes to shove, you always kill for your own. Just like the Councilate does. And so the wheel spins, and we get nowhere.

"Revolutions of the wheel—Nauro used to talk about that. And Sablo. But you *know* me. You know I don't want my own nation. I just want a place where people are safe from the kind of oppression the Councilate put on my people. And after talking to you, I want to find a way to stop making revenants."

Ydilwen gave a bitter laugh. *Then you'll have to stop people dying unfulfilled, and the world's already teeming with revenants like me trying to find someone to help them feel complete.*

"And what would it take for you to feel complete?" This was not how Ella talked about overcoming revenants, but he didn't care. He didn't even want Ydilwen gone necessarily, he just wanted to know. "Why did you attack us in the first place, back in Ayugen?"

To prevent *all this. I knew what would happen if a vulgar took the spear, and I knew you were the most likely one to do it. More wars, more revenants, more deaths for nothing. At least a ninespear would only kill a few. We all know. We're not looking for political power.*

"So you need a promise from me I won't do that? Start my own nation by killing our enemies?"

A promise. His voice was heavy with scorn. *I need action. What you've done today has already resulted in thousands of deaths. What are you going to do about that?*

Tai frowned. "Today? What do you mean?"

The battle, around the old city? Do you think it stopped when you flew past and got all those people to attack the Titans? You think all those angry soldiers and holy fools stopped hacking at each other just because you can't see them anymore?

Tai's stomach sank. He'd forgotten all about the pilgrims pushing against the whitecoats around the old city. "Ancestors. They're still fighting?"

And dying. You want to get rid of me, you want me to feel fulfilled? Do something about that.

Tai balled his fists. "But do what? I can't bring those people back."

You're a god now. Figure it out.

65

Tai strode back to where his friends stood, Ella holding a hollow-eyed Marea, Feynrick still staring at the spear. Ella didn't look to have aged much, thank the ancestors.

"Ye figure it out?" the grizzled Yatiman asked, leaning on his axe.

"I think so," Tai said. "I'll be back."

Ella slammed a foot down on the haft of the spear. "Oh, no, you don't. Where are you going, Sekaetai?"

"Back there," Tai said, waving toward the city. "The people are still fighting."

"And you're going into it without me? I don't think so."

"Ella," he said. "I'm going to need to waft for this one."

She blanched. Ella hated heights. "They're not actually our problem. You know that, right?"

Tai rolled his shoulders. "They might not be fighting if we hadn't convinced them all to try flying past the whitecoats."

She glared at him. "If you come back to me with *any* wounds. I mean any at all—"

Feynrick cleared his throat. "He's, ah, got the god spear now. I think he'll be good."

"I'll come back," Tai said. "I promise. You still haven't answered my question."

Marea looked confused at this.

"You were serious?" Ella asked.

"Dead serious," Tai said. "Now if you'll excuse me, I have a battle to stop."

She took her foot off the spear. He grabbed it in his good hand and struck a resonance that felt as deep as the ocean, shooting up into the air.

It didn't take long to see the battle, a roiling mass of whitecoats bleeding into motley pilgrims, pressing in on all four walls of the old city. But how to stop it?

Tai took a breath. Power and belief. Avery had said it just took power and belief, and it seemed like he'd told the truth about that, at least. Probably thought he had to, because he needed them to survive long enough to get the spear, so he could steal it.

The people, Tai. Remember? They're dying?

Right. Well he had power. Start with that.

Tai flew toward the nearest wall, a wispy crack of blue lightning rising from the old city, not strong enough to even hit him. At least the shamans wouldn't be a problem, now that he had their power.

The scene was awful closer up, whitecoats thrusting and slashing with a mad intensity, the pilgrims falling on them in sheer numbers. The battle lines swirled in every direction, bodies and blood littering the cobblestones.

Tai struck his higher resonance and started slamming down blankets of air, separating soldiers and pilgrims, swaddling them so they couldn't hit each other, his *uai* endless but not enough, only a small portion of one section of the wall stilled after minutes of intense work.

Power and belief. He needed both. Tai stopped, and imagined

the entire battle below him swaddled in that kind of blanket, an impenetrable wall of air working its way in between whitecoat and pilgrim. Then *believed* it, feeling the power roaring inside of him, knowing what it was capable of.

He waved the spear and a howl of wind like a midwinter blizzard rushed down the wall, parting soldier and pilgrim, driving an invisible wedge between the lines. Amazing, but he had no time for awe. Tai flew on, dropping another blanket over the north wall of the old city, then the east, then the south.

But this was no solution either—it was a temporary fix at best. How did you stop two sides from fighting?

Maybe you start by talking instead of using force.

Tai imagined himself talking to everyone in the square below, like mindseyes could send out their thoughts, then waved the spear and believed.

"I am Tai Kulga," he said, and a wave of gasps replaced the cries of surprise and pain below.

"I have taken the power of the stone," he went on, "and I am claiming this city in the name of the Ascending God. There can be no more bloodshed here. The old city and the waystone are open to any who wish to see it, soldier or pilgrim. I will strike down any who attempt violence in these walls."

As he said it he imagined it so, having no idea how it worked, but believing that it would.

There. That was enforcing peace. But they needed something more if this was going to work long term.

"You are not enemies," Tai said, sending his mindsight out into the crowd, seeing glimpses of the people down there, soldier and pilgrim alike. "You are citizens of the same nation and people of the same world. If you die here, your spirit will live on, unfulfilled. If you kill here, you will create those unfulfilled spirits, and maybe damn yourself to sleepless nights. I should know."

He pushed his mindsight further, seeing the hidden pains and hopes of the men in white coats and the people come seeking answers from a stone. "Your situation is not your enemy's fault, and it is not your god's to fix. It is yours. There is a lesson hidden in the voices you hear, whispering that you are not good enough, that no one loves you, that you don't belong. You'll have to talk to that voice to find it. But when you do, when you grow from it, no one can take that from you, not a political system that made you fight or an army of whitecoats or a man in the sky who speaks in your mind. It is yours."

Tai took a deep breath, coming back from the sea of pain and wonder that mindsight revealed in the crowd below. Something was shifting inside him, letting go. Ydilwen.

Thank you, Ydilwen said.

"I didn't do this for you," Tai answered, lifting the blanket of air and watching the crowd. Fights broke out in a few patches, but as he'd imagined, the aggressors fell over dead on the spot. More revenants on his head, but that was the price of power.

I know. But you have given me what I wanted. A little piece of it, at least. And I am tired. So tired.

Tai nodded. Below them the whitecoats and pilgrims began mingling, not fighting but flowing into the old city, like a stream of two waters.

"It's traditional for us to thank our spirit guides as they depart," Tai said, remembering Marrem's lessons on the old ways. "I do not think all revenants are guides, but I learned much from you, Ydilwen. Thank you."

There was no response, just that same sense of lightening Tai had felt with Hake and Naveinya. But where they had been painful, like scabs tearing off, Ydilwen felt like shedding clothes in the heat of the day, a lightening, a freeing.

Was this the better way to get rid of revenants? Were his people not totally wrong about the spirits being guides?

He didn't know. That was a question for Ella, or someone a lot smarter than him. And in the meantime, she had another one to answer.

People were already streaming into the gardens when Ella's lover dropped down from the sky. Some pointed and exclaimed when they spotted him and Ella saw Tai grimace. Was this how religion was born?

Power radiated from him like it had from the stone, but the smile he gave her was pure Tai. "You guys had enough sightseeing for one day?"

Marea tore her gaze away from Harides's body on the flagstones. "Yes," she said. "Let's go."

Tai waved the spear. A solid block of air rose under them, and suddenly the ground started getting farther away. Ella grabbed Tai and squeezed her eyes shut. She would *not* lose her stomach now, in front of all these people.

"Where to?" Feynrick yelled over the rushing wind. Just a nice breeze, she told herself. Solid ground under her feet.

"Anywhere else," Tai yelled back, "before these people start worshipping me too."

"Somewhere with a good lay-in of dreamleaf might be nice," Feynrick said. "Less you feel like flying us back to Ayugen tonight. I wouldn't mind seeing my Marrey."

Gods, with the power of the spear Tai could probably do it. It sounded exhausting—Ella wasn't as old as she'd been, but she still didn't feel up for an all-night wafting. "Maybe someplace a little closer!" she called over the not-from-wafting wind.

Marea raised her voice. "I know a place!"

The wind blew far too long. Ella kept her eyes squeezed shut. It stopped after an impossible downward lurch, and Ella opened her eyes to find the abandoned shaman's cottage, sun's rays lighting the rolling hills to either side. It felt surreal, after the crowds and grandeur and chaos of Aran. But peaceful too, crickets singing and the scent of fresh grass on the breeze.

She sighed, feeling a tightness leave her stomach. "Hard to believe we were just here this morning."

"Probably still coals in the hearth," Feynrick said. "And as I recall those shamans laid in a good stock of leaf. Who's up for tea?"

"Maybe later," Tai said, eyes on the patch of fresh dirt where they'd buried Eyadin. He looked somber, and Ella took his arm. Knowing Tai, he was probably feeling responsible for it somehow.

Marea walked to the dirt and knelt in it, her back slumped. She'd told Ella what she'd done, while Tai was away. Gods. She was too young to have to deal with this.

"Hey," Ella said, laying a hand on the girl's shoulder. "Harides was a twisted man. Whatever you did here, it was his fault."

"No," Marea said, sounding much older than her sixteen rains. "I chose it. He even said he was surprised I did it. Because I thought I loved him." She gave a humorless laugh. "What a pile of shit."

"We've all done things we're not proud of," Ella said. "You know my past. And Eyadin was already involved in this, in whatever shaman sent him from Worldsmouth. If you hadn't stopped him, the battle in Aran would have been much worse."

"He had a family," Marea said. "Children." Her fists clenched and her shoulders shook with silent sobs.

There was no need to say the rest: Marea had been that child once, not so long ago. Karhail had killed her father in the attack on Newgen. And now she'd done the same thing to Eyadin's family. What did you say to that?

"I know their names," Tai said. "I know where they live in the city. I promised him we would take care of them."

"I can do that," Marea said, head snapping up, eyes suddenly sharp. "I *will* do that. Tell me where they are."

Ella cleared her throat. "In good time. We've all been through a lot. Probably better to sleep on it tonight."

"Tell me," Marea insisted.

Tai nodded. "Edena Mettek is his wife's name. His daughter is Rena. They live in the West Cove district."

Marea stood. "Edena and Rena Mettek. West Cove. Okay."

She started walking.

"Marea!" Ella called out, running after her. "Wait! It isn't safe out there, even with your resonance. Stay with us. We can—"

Marea whirled on her, face contorted. "Don't tell me what I can't do. You don't—look, thank you, okay? You've been good to me, *too* good to me, but I have to do this. I have to go."

Ella started to say something, then Tai was there, good hand on her arm. "Let her go." He nodded to Marea. "You're welcome with us anytime. Ancestors guide you till then."

Marea's eyes flitted between then, mouth working, then she nodded and kept walking.

They stood watching her go, Ella's stomach a tangle of concern and worry and knowledge Tai was right. Marea had to go, just like Ella had had to go years ago. She hadn't even been as old as Marea when she'd run away.

"She'll be okay," Tai said, as if reading her thoughts. Maybe he was. He held a hand out to her. "Want to walk? I hear there's a lovely patch of grass around here somewhere."

She took a deep breath, then found a wicked smile. "And you have a considerably younger lady to lie with than you did last night."

He grinned. "Lucky me."

They walked for a minute, boots swishing the long grass. "Think Nauro's really gone?" she asked. His ashes were a weight in her pocket—she'd gathered them in a scrap of cloth before they left.

"No," Tai said. "He's too smart for that. He'll be back."

"Well, I won't be such a sow to him next time," Ella said.

"You were just looking out for us," Tai said. "Trust everyone and you end up traveling with a Harides."

"Hey, even *I* didn't see that one coming," Ella said. "And I used to—"

A zip sounded in front of them, and suddenly a richly dressed woman was standing in the knee-deep grass ahead of them. The cut of her dress was strange, high on one side with a separate color beneath, the fabric looking thin as spider silk.

"Tai of Ayugen," she said. "And the spear of second sight."

Tai tensed and separated from her, holding the spear flat behind him. Ella felt inside for her resonance.

"Who are you?" Tai called.

"A peer, now," the woman said. "Though an enemy, too, I suppose, because I was rather fond of Aymila."

Ella sucked in a breath. Aymila had been Semeca's true name. "You're an archrevenant."

The woman inclined her head. "That is one word for us, yes."

"If you're here for the spear," Tai said, "you won't get it without a fight."

"Oh, I don't want the spear, sweetness," the woman said, jutting one hip out. Ella couldn't help noticing the woman was curvy in all the right places. "What I want is for *you* to not bring hell and fire down on us because you don't know what you're doing."

Ella frowned, still ready to strike resonance at any second. She had life to burn again, now. "What danger could the spear pose to you?" Ella asked. "You have the same power."

The woman gave a lazy smile. "I have more power, actually. Aymila was lax in her tactics, but I find them sort of pleasant. A long-term game. No, I am not talking about the spear. I'm talking about your little trick around the stone."

"The harmony?" Tai asked.

"The harmony," she said. "I should have listened to Aymila when she said it was a threat. It's why she attacked you, you know. The rest of us thought, well, it doesn't matter what we thought. What matters is that you never do it again."

That set Ella's mind spinning. Why would an archrevenant care what they did? Unless the full harmony posed some sort of danger to them. Or was it the stones—did the woman fear they'd open the other stones and steal her power? But that wasn't how it worked.

"And if we do?" Tai asked.

"Do you think the fires in the moon burn on their own?" the woman hissed, suddenly angry. "Do you think the myths of the Descending God are just myths? You should be learning by now legends have their feet in fact. But never mind that. Let me tell you what will happen if you do. I will come for you, with Alenul and Teynsley and Hathrim and Gyelon, with all seven of the other archrevenants, and the spear you hold will be no protection against our combined might."

Ella stared at the woman, dread a cold weight in her stomach. She had no doubt the woman could do it. But what was so dangerous about a full harmony?

"But, pardon me," the woman said, voice sweet again. "I have been long off this continent, and am forgetting my manners. There's no need for threats. I'll give you some time to settle in, then come for a proper visit. But in the meantime, be a dear and don't strike a full chord again? You seem like such nice people."

She disappeared in a bang and a rush of air.

Ella stared at the waving grass where she'd stood, Yersh countryside once again surreal in the evening light. "Did I just see that?"

Tai rubbed his eyes. "Did you see a woman appear out of nowhere claiming to be an archrevenant and making strange threats? Cause that's what I saw."

"Well, good," Ella said. "I guess we're not crazy."

"No," Tai said. "It's the world that's crazy."

"At least she didn't try to kill us."

"Not yet anyway," he said, then took a deep breath. "Walk with me?"

She walked with him, sun slipping below the horizon in a show of scarlet and purple, lines of clouds illuminated in the sky. What did you do about an archrevenant suddenly appearing and threatening you? Especially at the end of a day in which you could have died many times?

You did nothing. You walked in the sweet grass with your lover and appreciated that for now, at least, you were alive and together.

"You never answered my question, you know," Tai said.

It actually took her a second to remember which one he meant. "Oh!" Ella said. "That one. Yes."

He stopped, a grin growing on his face. "Yes?"

"Yes!" she cried. "What did you think I'd say?"

"I wasn't sure, after you said you'd have to think about it."

"Well the answer is yes, Tai Kulga of Ayugen. Godslayer. Though you'll probably have to meet my parents to do it."

The words slipped out before she even realized what she was

saying. She hadn't seen her parents since she'd killed her brother and ran out the front door. But maybe it was time.

"I can do that," he said.

"Good," she said. "Now throw me down in this grass and have your way with me."

He grinned. "I can do that too."

She liked a capable man.

THANK YOU FOR READING APOSTATE'S PILGRIMAGE

We hope you enjoyed it as much as we enjoyed bringing it to you. We just wanted to take a moment to encourage you to review the book. Follow this link: Apostate's Pilgrimage to be directed to the book's Amazon product page to leave your review.

Every review helps further the author's reach and, ultimately, helps them continue writing fantastic books for us all to enjoy.

✷

You can also join our non-spam mailing list by visiting www.subscribepage.com/AethonReadersGroup and never miss out on future releases. You'll also receive three full books completely Free as our thanks to you.

Facebook

Instagram

Twitter

Website

Want to discuss our books with other readers and even the authors? Join our Discord server today and be a part of the Aethon community.

ALSO IN SERIES

BEGGAR'S REBELLION
PAUPER'S EMPIRE
APOSTATE'S PILGRAMAGE
ACOLYTE'S UNDERWORLD

Looking for more great Fantasy?

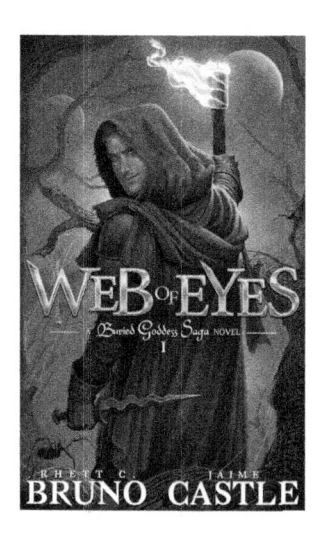

A rotten thief. A disgraced knight. Only together can they save the kingdom.

GET BOOK ONE OF THE BURIED GODDESS SAGA NOW!

Cursed from birth. Forced into slavery. It's time to fight back.

GET A TRIBUTE AT THE GATES TODAY!

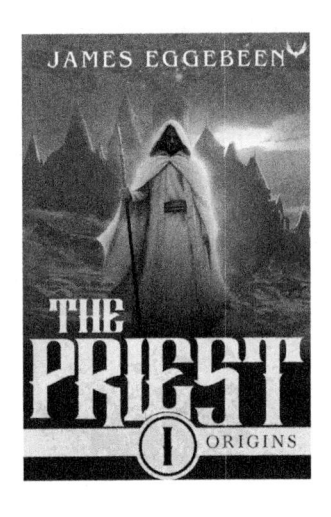

Everyone knows the gods are long dead. But what if one of them survived?

GET THE PRIEST NOW!

The barrier between worlds is broken. Only he knows the truth...

GET RANGER'S OATH NOW!

The thrilling start to a complete 11-book Epic Fantasy series!

When Citaria falls under the shadow of a demonic incursion, only a legendary hero can stop them.

GET SALVATION'S DAWN NOW!

For all our Fantasy books, visit our website.

ACKNOWLEDGMENTS

Thanks for reading! If you enjoyed this, consider leaving me a review or some stars on Amazon. Authors live or die by their reviews these days, and every one means a lot to me. For previews, deleted scenes, and a free novella not available anywhere else, click here for Beggars and Brawlers: the Resonant Saga Newsletter. Or if you prefer audio, check out the Beggars and Brawlers podcast!

The saga continues with book four, Acolyte's Underworld, *as Tai and Ella must learn to harness the spear's godlike power—or have it taken by the gods themselves.*

These books don't happen alone. Hell, even with a lot of help they rarely work out. So, some thanks to be passed around: to Nicki, Mike, and Debbie of HRFW for helping me cut 50% of my opening chapters, and to Debbie again for reading a whole draft. It's because of her that we get a few Feynrick chapters in here. To my editor Nathan for a speedy read in the height of summer, and reliably trenchant comments. You owe him a semi-understandable magic system. To my ever-patient wife Bri, who reads no fantasy (other than mine), but supports me 100% anyway. To the good people of North Dakota who buy enough fruit that I can sort-of write full-time without actually making money at it—I promise I'll keep getting you fruit even when the money gets better.

And to you, oh unknown reader, who has read and appreciated these words. As long as you're reading, I'll keep writing.

Levi Jacobs, Dickinson, North Dakota, September 2019

Printed in Great Britain
by Amazon